A Way of Forgiving

by the same author

Someday, Somewhere

EILEEN RAMSAY

A Way of Forgiving

Dear Bill
Best wishes for your own
writing
Love
Eileen

Eileen Ramsay

Hodder & Stoughton

Copyright © 2004 by Eileen Ramsay

First published in Great Britain in 2004 by Hodder and Stoughton
Published simultaneously in paperback by Hodder and Stoughton
A division of Hodder Headline

The right of Eileen Ramsay to be identified as the Author
of the Work has been asserted by her in accordance with the
Copyright, Designs and Patents Act 1988.

1 3 5 7 9 10 8 6 4 2

A CIP catalogue record for this title is available from the British Library

ISBN 0 340 82574 X Hardback
ISBN 0 340 83258 4 Paperback

Typeset in Plantin Light by Phoenix Typesetting, Burley-in-Wharfedale, West Yorkshire

Printed and bound in Great Britain by
Mackays of Chatham plc, Chatham, Kent

Hodder and Stoughton
A division of Hodder Headline
338 Euston Road
London NW1 3BH

For Helen and Tommie Allan with love

The poem on page 91 was written by Caroline E. S. Norton (Lady Sterling-Maxwell) 1808–1877 and is untitled.

ACKNOWLEDGEMENTS

For the joy of the piano I have to thank the teacher at the Benedictine Convent in Maxwelltown who had the vision to take some little girls to hear Eileen Joyce in recital. To all the great pianists I have had the privilege of hearing in all the years since – thank you.

A special thanks to my friend, Henny King, who gave me a CD of Mussorgsky's *Pictures at an Exhibition* played by Norman Beedie, Head of Piano Studies, Guildhall School of Music.

For the joy of Italy, very many thanks to all the Allans who first introduced us to Tuscany and encouraged us to love her.

Sylvie and Pascal Iovanovitch – thank you for having a beautiful wedding in such a lovely place. Every moment was a joy.

Emily, Rosie and Sophie, thank you for the duck race.

For help with the Italian language I thank Linda Strachan, *il signor* Gianni Donfrancesco, and Beverley Littlewood. Very special thanks to Lois Allan and Mauro Balestri – what would I do without you two?

Elizabeth and Dick Warfel, thank you for the use of your flat!

For details of 'trendy' Edinburgh, thank you to Sara Sheridan.

Members of the Romantic Novelists Association have been ready, as always, with advice, support and encouragement. Thank you all.

Teresa Chris, my agent, and Carolyn Caughey, my editor – thank you.

1

---❖◆❖---

'Brancaccio-Vallefreddas pay people to play the piano and to sing;
they do not become entertainers.'
'Papà, I love the sound, please, just for myself, for my pleasure.'
'I will pay for you to go to a fine school in England. English, with
an English accent, that is best for you, for your place in society. You
are so young, tesoro, *but you must surely know that the world is*
changing. Who knows what the future holds. Go to concerts when you
choose, but learn to speak English.'
But she had not gone to her fine English school because war had
come and her home was destroyed and the factories and vineyards that
had made her family's wealth. More importantly, however, her father
was gone, disappeared, and Ludovico dead. She could see his blood
on the square every time she was in the town. No one else could see it;
perhaps they saw the blood of their own dead.

She could not go to Italy.

Sophie Winter stood at the bedroom window of her flat,
looking out at Edinburgh's famous skyline but she was not seeing
the rain-washed front of the ancient building in the forefront, or
the roofs of the historic New Town in the grey-blue distance
because tears were streaming down her pale cheeks, and her mind
was full of colours so intense that even the memory caused her
to blink her eyes. She could feel the heat of the Italian summer
sun on her back and arched into its embrace, ah, so strong, so
hot. Sophie sighed and submitted herself to her memories.

She was sixteen and had just finished her first year at the Queen
Margaret School for Girls. She was, she felt, a child no longer.
With her first examinations safely passed she could give herself

up to the pleasures of Italy: bella Toscana, her favourite place in the whole world. In October she would be in the lower sixth, mature and serious, and ready to decide about the shape of the rest of her life. Until then, however, the summer months stretched invitingly before her. It would be a momentous summer. How could it not be? It would be the summer that marked that transition between the little girl she had been and the mature, sophisticated woman she would become. It would be her final farewell to childhood.

Every summer for several years now, ever since her father had gone to work as a government accountant at the naval base in La Spezia, her parents had rented a house high up in the hills above the town and today she had cycled all the way to the beach at Lerici; she was hot and dusty and sweating and dreaming only of ice-cold lemonade in a tall, misty glass. But instead of finding a table in the shade she stood transfixed, for there, on the wall, sat a vision. He was tall and slender in pristine white slacks and a blue shirt and he sat, quite still, as he stared out at the flotilla of boats lying at ease in the sheltered waters of the bay. She noticed his face first, for he was beautiful, and then his hands, and as she looked at his hands a shiver that she did not understand went through her. He resembled, she thought, one of those statues that surround the square in Florence, except that he was wearing far more clothes, and his hair was longer, just touching the collar of the shirt. An angel, that was it; in all the paintings, angels had long hair.

He laughed when he became conscious of her staring and thus proved that he was neither statue nor angel but a man, and she was enough of a woman not to take offence or to cower in embarrassment like a child.

'I know,' she said, assuming that he was laughing at her hot and grubby exterior, 'this is what vanity gets you. Can you believe I cycled down – on that road – to here.' Her arms, pale and still plump with the chubbiness of girlhood, had gestured to the hills.

'Vanity, signorina?' he asked, his dark eyes looking at her dirty face with a slight smile that was not unkind.

'I've had an absolutely ghastly year of stodgy Scottish food, and studying. Exams make you fat.' She obeyed the slight gesture of his hand and sat down on the wall beside him, although her father's voice in her head began to admonish her. Not for the first time she ignored that worried voice. 'I decided to work it off this summer by cycling everywhere I go in Tuscany.'

'I commend your dedication,' he said and gestured to a hovering waiter. 'Some lemonade, signorina or some of the excellent ice cream?'

She was furious; he thought she was a little girl. 'I am not a child, signore, and I can buy my own lemonade, or even beer if I want it,' she finished with bravado.

He bowed his head and his hair fell over his face and a fleeting memory stirred. '*Mi dispiace, signorina.* I had hoped that you would join me in some ice cream, but allow me to buy you a cool drink.'

For a moment she did not answer as her brain tried to find the recollection that was hovering just out of reach. No use. 'I really shouldn't do this,' she said a few minutes later as she sat with her cold lemonade, and, horrified, saw that her dusty shorts had deposited some of the red dust on his immaculate slacks. She prayed he would not notice. 'It's not done, you know, to accept hospitality from a stranger. My parents are always warning us: my sister Ann and me.'

'But then we will become not strangers.' He held out his hand. 'I am Raffaele. You?'

'Sophie.'

'Sophie. How do you do.' He took her hand and raised it, dusty as it was, to his lips. His beautiful eyes, not black Italian but deep blue like the waters far out in the bay, smiled at her over her hand, and she did not know it then but she fell head first into love.

He was easy to talk to and she felt completely safe with him. The time slipped by but, at last, listening to his slightly accented voice and watching the gestures of those beautiful hands, she knew that it was right to refuse the offer of a second glass. She stood up ready to go.

Her parents were apoplectically furious when later she confessed that a stranger had put her dusty bike in the back seat of his rather dashing sports car and driven her home.

'I'm not sure, but I think it just might have been a Ferrari, one of those fab red ones.'

Her parents ignored this. 'Who is he?'

But she did not know. She knew only that his name was Raffaele, and that she would remember for ever his face and the heat and the dazzling light on the sea.

Raffaele. Raffaele, the archangel.

In cold, rainy Edinburgh Sophie brushed the tears from her eyes, banishing the memory. Not once but twice today she had been reminded and not all the memories were sweet. Simon had been first. She had spent most of the afternoon in the debating chamber of the Scottish Parliament, shepherding a party of constituents whom Hamish Sterling MSP, her boss, had invited to listen to First Minister's Questions. As always she had returned to her office to find several messages, and far too many e-mails that all required answers that afternoon. One of the e-mails had been from Simon Beith.

'A drink at the Atrium – sevenish.'

Absolutely.

Simon was a curator at the Museum of Scotland and he was a good friend, although he wanted, he said, to be much more. Sophie liked him very much but, since she landed the job with Hamish, other men had taken second place. She smiled ruefully; working for an MSP meant that everything took second place. She rushed through her messages and managed to get to the trendy restaurant at a few minutes after seven.

Simon was already seated at a small table in the middle of the floor, almost under the peak of the cream-coloured tented fabric ceiling. The flame from the candle in the wrought-iron candlestick shone on his round face and lit up his scrupulously neat fair hair. Was Simon ever disorganised? Was his tie ever undone, his pants unpressed? 'I've ordered you a large glass of white wine,' he said.

Sophie looked at her friend and smiled. He was trying so hard to be calm and yet his thin frame almost quivered with suppressed excitement. 'Perfect. Come on, out with it.'

'You know me too well, Sophie, and not well enough.' He finished with a grin.

'Tell me.'

He leaned towards her, his pleasant, frank face full of enthusiasm, his pale blue eyes sparkling in the candlelight. 'I've got it, Sophie, three months at the Metropolitan in New York.'

'Wonderful; what a glorious opportunity for you.'

'Yes, three whole months in one of the world's finest museums. Sophie, you said you hadn't decided about a summer holiday. Why not come out with me for a few weeks? Galleries, museums, concert halls.'

She did not meet his eyes. 'Sounds like Edinburgh.'

'He frowned. 'It's New York.'

'I'm so happy for you, Simon. The Met is probably my favourite museum.' In her mind was a picture of porcelain angels suspended in the air around an enormous Christmas tree; trumpet-carrying angels of light lined Rockefeller Plaza and the air was full of music.

'I've taken you by surprise. Say you'll think about it. You have visited New York, haven't you?'

'Yes,' she said shortly. The Avery Fisher Hall. The Carnegie Hall. Music everywhere, and angels. 'Which is why I don't want to spend my precious two weeks there, Simon. You'll love it and the museum is, of course, air-conditioned but New York is hot, hot and muggy, not a place for a summer holiday. Different for you; you'll be working and New Yorkers are the world's friendliest people. You'll make friends in no time. I may still have some guidebooks.' She stood up. 'I'll look them out for you.'

Even though it had started to rain she decided to walk home because, at this time, that would be marginally quicker than going by bus, and because it was always a delight to walk in this beautiful city. She set off along Cambridge Street and on to Castle Terrace. At the end of the road she turned left on to King's

Bridge which hurried along crossing King's Stables Road in the valley. There were no stables these days but the name had stuck for centuries. The clip-clop of horses' hooves would be more musical than the steady hum of Edinburgh traffic. Above her in the soft, cool drizzle loomed the enormous bulk of Edinburgh's ancient castle, a sight, for some reason, she always found comforting. She followed the skirt of the castle, Johnston Terrace, all the way round to the Lawnmarket, that ancient area at the top of the Royal Mile. The street was busy as always although not nearly so frenetic or colourful as it would be in a few months' time during the International Arts Festival. Careful of her heels, Sophie hurried across the cobblestones and up on to the pavement. She laughed. She was exactly where she had been an hour or so ago, just outside the parliamentarians' entrance to the new Scottish parliament.

Her steps quickened as she reached her building, a renovated tenement in one of the most ancient and historic parts of the city. As always she looked up at her window to see the little pennants on the window blinds. She disappeared from sight into the close but did not continue to the Writers' Museum or the paving stones in the courtyard with their quotes from Scottish writers through the centuries. She turned right and there was the tower with its heavy oak door. It should have looked formidable, impregnable, but its bright red paint gave it a cheery air. She inserted the first key, opened the door, and closed the world and all its problems outside behind her. She took a deep breath, for ahead of her lay five flights of spiralling stone stairs. There were two flats on each floor and most of them were rented by people prepared to pay a little extra to live in such a historic part of the city.

Today, because of the rain, the stairs were wet but not dangerous. Whatever her mother said, the stairs were perfectly safe to climb. It was just that on rainy days they got wet. Two pigeons who had sneaked in when some tenant had left a stair door open cooed at her from a window and Sophie tried to banish her annoyance that they had left her their usual offering. She would not deal with it tonight.

By the time she reached the top floor she was holding on to the iron railing. Key number two opened the blue door with its funny little iron gargoyles grinning evilly down, and she was on her landing. From here she could gaze on a clear day across the city all the way to the great Firth of Forth and beyond to the Kingdom of Fife. On a drizzly night like this she could still stop to catch her breath before key number three opened the green door and she was in the little private landing shared by her flat and the mysterious occupants of the one next door.

The door to her flat was a warm dark brown.

Each and every time Sophie opened it she felt happy; she was home, safe and sound in a flat she was buying with her own hard-earned money. She was humming as she kicked off her shoes and began looking through the letters that were lying on the tiled floor of the little entrance hall, and still humming as she looked in the refrigerator for inspiration. Half a packet of Roquefort cheese, three or four sadly limp mangetout and a carton of orange juice told her that a visit to a late-opening supermarket was needed, but she was tired and she wanted a shower – or a bath; a bath, that was it, hot and deep and full of lovely smelling bubbles. She would have a bath and then eat oatcakes and cheese and fruit, a perfectly reasonable meal for the working girl who had had an adequate lunch. The food in the cafeteria at work was very good and because she had lunched with Hamish and his party of constituents, she had eaten more than she usually did at midday.

She was in the process of trying to decide whether or not to slide down under the bubbles, which would mean that she would have to wash her hair, when she heard her telephone ringing. She debated with herself over whether or not to answer it. She was too comfy and relaxed and decided to let the answerphone get it. She slipped under the bubbles, surfaced, and heard, 'So do ring me just as soon as you get in.'

She erupted from the water like Krakatoa from the waters of the Pacific and, *sans* towel, dashed across the floor. Too late. Zoë had hung up. Sophie pressed the button that dialled her young sister's Italian number and waited while long distance connected her. 'Hello, Zoë, I was having a bath, pleasantly poaching. Hold on a sec while I get my dressing-gown.' She put the receiver on the bed and hurried to wrap up. 'Sorry, here I am. Why did you call? Anything special?'

Zoë's voice was deliberately casual, so casual that Sophie could sense her excitement. 'Nothing much – just want you to come to my wedding.'

'Wedding! Zoë, how wonderful. Tell me everything.'

There was nothing flippant in the young voice now. 'Jim, do you remember hearing me speak of Jim, Jim who's at university with me? We find we just can't face the thought of parting so we're getting married right after graduation. Not much point in asking you to the graduation; I'm allowed only two guests to the ceremony, but you will come to my wedding, won't you?'

Zoë's wedding; a lovely little church in Surrey, of course she would be there.

'Of course I'll come to your wedding but what does Dad say, and Mum? Are they happy, surprised, furious?'

'All of the above. I think they thought we might be ready to discuss an engagement but that's not good enough; there's never been anyone else for me, Sophie, not since we first met. You understand.'

Sophie was crying softly now but tried to hide the tears. 'Of course I do. Point is, do Mum and Dad?'

Zoë sighed. 'You know them, rules laid out like driving instructions. You will meet a nice man at the proper time. You will fall in love and before you do anything hasty you will bring him home to meet us. At least he's English.' She stopped and then, since Sophie said nothing, she went on hurriedly. 'I didn't mean that; you know what I mean.'

'Of course.' She tried to laugh lightly but she was too cold, despite the thick robe, to laugh. 'Since that's good about him, what are all the bad things?'

'For a start he wants to marry me and then having a job in Australia isn't exactly endearing him to Mum. It's a two-year contract; Australia will be our honeymoon.'

'How fabulous.' Clever Jim: Zoë and Jim would be thousands of miles away from the help of their families but away from their influence too. 'I believe Australia is very exciting. What about Jim's family?'

'There's only his mother, who is so sweet even though my darling Jim is the light of her life, and his sister, Penny, who's seventeen and is so angelically pretty that she'll outshine the bride. Maude, that's Jim's mother, says it's probably a good idea to start married life well away from family. Mum, as you can imagine, is already making lists of all the things that can possibly go wrong. She was at S, scorpions and snakes, when I told her I just had to ring you.'

They laughed with exasperated affection as daughters do.

'She's happy making lists, Zoë, but tell me the date. July if it's just after graduation, and the whole family gathered together. Right?'

'Yes,' said Zoë quickly and Sophie felt a twinge of pain at the anxiety in the young voice.

'Brave girl. Even the dreaded David,' she added and was relieved to hear Zoë laugh.

'Of course. He is my godfather and he's very nice – deep down.'

'Deep, deep down,' said Sophie naughtily. 'Bridesmaids?'

'Lots. All my girlfriends who can make the trip – I don't want to leave anyone out – and maybe the twins. Ann wants them to be pageboys.'

Ann. So Ann had been told first. Well, why not. Zoë had no quarrel with her eldest sister. 'They're a little old for white satin.'

Zoë started to laugh. 'How did you know she'd say "white satin"?'

'Years of experience, my dear. Tell me the date and I'll make absolutely sure I have a day or two off.'

Zoë did not answer immediately and when she did her voice was shaky as if she were not far from tears. 'Sophie, Sophie don't be angry, and don't say you won't come. You promised. You said, "Of course I'll come".'

Oh, Zoë, beloved little sister. She was now ice cold. 'Where's the wedding, Zoë?'

'Tuscany,' said Zoë, and went on quickly. 'We have residence permits, Sophie, both of us, and so they say we can be married here and it's my favourite place in the world: all our holidays, our house, meeting Jim. You do understand?'

Yes, she understood, only too well. Tuscany: hills afire with red poppies, distant blue mountains capped with dazzling white snow, church bells that never rang the hours in synchronisation, one always a few minutes behind the other, wood smoke from the olive groves and the piercing tang of sun-warmed lemons.

'I understand, Zoë, but you know I can't come back to Tuscany, even for your wedding.'

'Please, Sophie.' Zoë was crying now and Sophie's heart was bleeding for the wound she had dealt her little sister. 'All the nastiness is over; no one remembers any more.'

I remember.

'I love you dearly, but I can't come to your wedding. There was too much ugliness there.' And so much beauty but that was over, for Rafael had not believed in her: he had not, in the end, loved her enough.

'The people who count miss you, Sophie: Stella and Giovanni. They ask about you every time I see them.'

'Forgive me, Zoë,' she whispered. 'If it were anywhere else in the world but I cannot go to Tuscany.'

Later she sat in the big chair at the window looking out and seeing nothing. It was just beginning to get dark and the streetlights were on. In a few weeks it would be light enough to read at the window. Was that her favourite time of the year, those long, soft evenings of spring or did she love it more later when Scottish evenings went on into the morning of the next day? It did not matter when the heart was heavy.

Twice today she had been reminded of what she wanted to forget: first by Simon and now by Zoë of all people. Sophie determined to pull herself together. New York reminded her of Rafael and Italy reminded her too. It was a common, rather dreary story. People met, loved, married, stopped loving, divorced. But why should she be so anxious to forget all those years? She was divorced but she was happy in her new life. How silly to try to cut five years out of her life as if they had never been. Rafael?

Sophie lay back in her chair and deliberately faced her demons, such small insignificant demons. What else, she asked herself, reminds you of Rafael?

Music, basil growing on a windowsill, snow falling in moonlight, angels flying on a great tree, white-hot sun and the smell of sun-warmed apricots, walking in the rain. Everything reminds me.

It was late, time to sleep if she was to be any use at all at her job tomorrow. She went into her bedroom, a postage stamp of a room. The bed had been specially built to stand higher than modern beds and was placed so that its occupant could sit in bed and look out of the windows, across the courtyard, across busy Princes Street and on to the roofs of the New Town and even further to the river and, on a fine day, the soft green landscape of Fife. Sophie pulled out her nightgown from the deep drawers beneath the bed, and when she was ready she climbed up the little painted steps and lay in the fairytale bed that she had never shared with Rafael and remembered the unbelievable joy of loving and being loved.

Zoë loved Jim and Jim loved Zoë, and Zoë wanted her sister there to share this happiest day of her life.

She heard four o'clock chime on the nearby St Giles Cathedral. She smiled. What, after all, is important? It was important that nothing should be allowed to spoil her sister's wedding day. Perhaps going to Tuscany where she had loved and been loved so much would hurt too much if she still loved Rafael; the memories would be more vivid, more painful.

'I have moved on,' said Sophie into the stillness of her room. 'I shall contact Zoë first thing in the morning.'

2

This could not be happening.

Sophie felt her heart beating in sheer panic. After a nightmare journey from Edinburgh she had finally reached Tuscany and was anxious to find her rented house. She had driven south from Milan to her parents' house in Comano many times but this time she knew not to carry straight on when she reached the little town of Licciana Nardi but to turn left on *strada statale* 63 and to meander up, up into the hills, towards tiny villages with lovely names: Gabbiagna, Bagnone. Somehow she had taken a wrong turning, for she was completely lost. It was the middle of the night and there were horses galloping straight towards her. What on earth was she to do? How was she to avoid them or they her? It was inevitable that they would hit the car and send it toppling over the edge to go spinning down to the foot of the precipice. She closed her eyes, waiting.

Without missing a beat the horses fanned round the car, which had stalled, while she crouched with her eyes closed until the sound of their hooves disappeared like their presence into the night.

'I hate horses,' she sobbed, which was untrue but perhaps more true than not so late at night or, to be accurate, so early in the morning. She had forgotten that occasionally an irresponsible farmer would allow his horses out to forage on someone else's land and should any householder wonder what had happened to his prize vegetables during the night he was met with innocent shrugs. Italy.

There was silence again; she lifted her head and breathed deeply. She turned in the driver's seat and tried to see them in the darkness. Nothing. It was as if they had never been there, as if the sound of their pounding hooves had never terrified her. Holding her breath, she turned the key. Something complained with a loud groan. She waited for a count of ten and tried again. Still that ghastly complaining noise.

An Italian in the same fix would, of course, invoke a saint. Sophie rejected the first name that came into her head. 'Any saint who's awake,' she hissed through her teeth, turned the key, and laughed with mingled relief and amusement as the engine caught. Then she drove on. The villa had to be there somewhere. It was. She reached it at just after two in the morning and reflected wryly that in Italy to be a mere eight hours late was perfectly under-standable. Not that it was Italy's fault or even that of the odd contraflow system which resulted in nerve-racking driving while she had tried to figure out where she was going.

It was her own fault that she was lost because had she made up her mind earlier to fly to Tuscany for Zoë's wedding she would probably have been able to get a flight to Pisa and would not have been on a plane to Brussels that was four hours late. The airline had, in turn, blamed Air Traffic Control for the logjam over Europe. The delay, however, had meant that she missed her connection to Milan which in turn resulted in this creeping around, looking for a house she did not know, in the dark. She neither knew nor cared who was being blamed for the loss of her luggage.

Tuscany, thought Sophie, must be one of God's favourite places, but not in the dark.

According to the instructions from the estate agents the key was under the flowerpot at the top of the flight of stairs. It was not. Bravely resisting the temptation to burst into hysterical tears, Sophie returned to the car, curled up in the small back seat and fell asleep.

In July Tuscany wakes up around five. Stiff, uncomfortable and hungry, Sophie woke with it. Despite her fatigue she took time to notice the incomparable beauty of the mountainside. Down there lay a village, its red pantiled roofs beginning to steam gently in the wakening sun. Row upon row of vines quivered in the slight breeze and the gentle tinkle of the clear, cold water from the well beside the house accompanied her walk to the rough stone stairs. Rugged men who needed only a secure home to keep out the elements had built the house. They had not thought of beauty, for the world around them was beautiful and in its original state the house would have said loudly: basic home of peasant farmers. On ground level the stones were large and uneven and a rotting door on a broken hinge revealed what was now a wood shed and had probably housed the family's cow. In the lovely morning light she could see easily what she had missed in the black Italian night: a second staircase that climbed up around the house. She followed it and found herself on a recently added terrace complete with a huge terracotta pot of the almost obligatory perfume-less red geraniums, and under it – a key.

She opened the front door and went in. The house was dark and cool because, of course, all the shutters were closed. She groped for a light switch; found the lavatory and its pristine Swiss plumbing, and next to it a large bedroom. She fell on the bed, and slept. The church bells woke her at eight and she sat up, for a moment wondering where she was.

Gabbiana, Tuscany, Italy. Home.

No, not home, not now. She would not remember previous arrivals in Italy, chauffeur-driven limousines, staff who whisked her through all the annoying little things that beset unluckier travellers. Never, while she had been married to Rafael, had her luggage been lost by an airline; that was not, however, a good enough reason to stay married.

Coffee first. Next, she would find an open *farmacia* and she would replace her toothbrush, soap, deodorant – and then she would make a phone call. She was here; she would have to let her family know that she had finally arrived. But first she would look around at what she had been too tired to appreciate before. The original house had been completely changed inside; only the old window frames remained. This floor consisted of a sparsely furnished living/dining room that went from the front of the house to the back. She threw open the shutters and stood at the back windows with a stream tumbling down the olive grove behind her and looked out of the front windows with their view of the distant Alps. There was the huge bedroom whose windows also looked out to the mountains, a small but very up-to-date kitchen and an equally tiny and efficient bathroom. She would shower.

The water in the bathroom was slightly brown and very hot. She stood under it until she was fully awake and then she dried herself on the clean towel that was hanging on the rack and dressed again in yesterday's tired, travel-weary clothes. Then she went round the house throwing open the remaining shutters. She had time to notice that the interior was attractive, just as the agent had said it was. She would explore later, after she had been to market, after she had telephoned. For a few minutes she stood on the balcony looking across the valley towards the mountains. Carrara was there somewhere among that beautiful misty blue. Perhaps she would have time to drive over there one day; her flat cried out for a small marble table.

She went downstairs to the car and then ran back up and locked the doors. This was not Rafael's Italy where no one would touch anything no matter if every door and window were left open. This was twenty-first century Tuscany where an open door was an invitation to steal. She sighed as she went back down the wide stone steps but whether she was sighing for a changed Italy or for something else, she was not sure.

Coffee and bread. Sophie realised on the way into the town that she had eaten nothing since Brussels yesterday. She had meant to eat at the airport and then had decided to stop on the way to her rented house but nothing had worked out properly.

She drove down a winding road where bougainvillaea spilled in purple abandon over white walls and soldier-straight irises held themselves upright behind them as if disapproving of such vulgarity; she turned into the square and parked near the gnarled old olive trees that spread their branches into arches over tables where, later in the day, milk-white tourists would congregate to escape from the heat of the sun. The square in Licciana Nardi was empty, except for the ubiquitous skinny dog who nervously watched her and then, realising that she posed no threat, lazily waved his tail as she passed on her way to the open *pasticceria*.

Cappuccino and a brioche had never tasted so good. Did they taste better because the smell of fresh coffee had assailed her nostrils as she had walked from the dusty square to the cool black and white tiled interior? Anticipation and now the bliss of actualisation. She knew that it was culturally permissible to drink cappuccino before ten thirty, maybe eleven and no later. No self-respecting Italian would drink it at lunch time. That was when one drank strong black coffee. 'Espresso is always *corretto*.' Once these cultural differences had mattered to her but not now. She toyed with the idea of having a second cup but she was merely avoiding the inevitable and it wasn't as if she did not long to see them – and the house, Villa Minerva.

'Vorrei fare una interurbana, per favore.'

She smiled and the barman smiled back; she was very pretty in that delicate fine-boned English rose way. He could not know that she was smiling because although she spoke Italian almost every day, it was the first time in five years that she had spoken it in Italy.

She took the *gettoni* he held out to her and made the call to Milan.

Her luggage was still inexplicably lost; in Brussels, or maybe it went to the wrong airport in Milan. *'Mi dispiace, signorina.* I'm sorry. We'll find it and drive it straight to your villa.'

With that she had to be content. No point in showing her annoyance. It wasn't the clerk's fault. She gave him her parent's address, assuming that it was easier to find than her rented villa, and went in search of toothpaste.

She was in the *farmacia* on the other side of the square, almost indistinguishable, she supposed, from a chemist's shop anywhere in the world, before she realised that there would have been everything she needed at . . . the house. She had almost said *at home* but Villa Minerva had not been home to her for a long time now. She shrugged, paid for her purchases and went back out to her car.

'Sophie, Sophie, how absolutely lovely.' It was Stephanie Wilcox, a neighbour of her parents. 'How lovely to see you, dear. You've lightened your hair; suits you, dear, but my, you're too thin.' Stephanie looked down at her own too generous roundness. 'I knew you would come. Of course, Sophie will come, I said. We've missed you, dear.'

That was so palpably untrue that Sophie almost turned away. She recovered just in time. No point in antagonising one of her mother's oldest friends. 'How nice to see you, Stephanie, but I must go. My parents are expecting me.'

Her parents had expected her yesterday; they had no idea when she would arrive. She felt, however, that she should talk to them before she talked to anyone.

Stephanie held on like a small dog with a tiny bone. 'You'll be at the luncheon Giovanni's giving? I'll see you there. I want to hear everything.' She smiled and looked, had she but known it, just like the worst kind of predator as it leans down to eat its hapless victim. '*Ciao.*'

Giovanni? Yes, it would be nice to see him again. 'To hear everything.' No, I don't think so, Stephanie.

The road to her parents' villa was as tortuous as she remembered and as beautiful. It hugged the mountainside and Sophie had to keep both hands on the wheel and both eyes on the road; so easy to be distracted by the flowers that rioted down the embankment, threatening to throw themselves into her path, or the incredible views that forced one to look and gasp in awe just around every bend. On every bend too there was a painted Madonna in a little shrine or a realistic picture of the Sacred Heart. Then there were the cars or, more usually, dilapidated trucks that raced down the mountain overtaking the old ladies on their bicycles.

Worse to meet them when they're going back up, remembered Sophie, for a least going down the mountainside they had no knobbly bags of bread and fruit balanced between their legs or hanging from the handlebars. The Madonna must work overtime in Italy. She stopped on the road just below the driveway to her parents' home. She had not been in Italy for five years, had not seen this house that she had loved so much. Of course she had seen her parents; they did not winter in Tuscany. Kathryn said she hated snow and would not be convinced that Surrey had more than Tuscany.

'With a name like Winter I should love it, shouldn't I?' she was compelled to say at least once a year. There was always someone asking why, when they owned such a beautiful house in such an incredibly lovely place, they chose to spend four months of the year in England.

'Obviously someone who has never seen the Alps in the winter,' said her father wryly.

Instinctively Sophie looked in the mirror and did not like what she saw. She was tired and she was clean but she needed, oh so badly, to clean her teeth. I'll feel able for anything once I've done that. Stupid little thing to worry about. She restarted the car and reluctantly drove the short distance to the house. There were three cars: she recognised her father's; the small Fiat must be her mother's; and the third, a very expensive recent model, belonged, no doubt to Ann. No escape. She would have to meet her and it might as well be now. She parked beside her father's Range Rover and sat looking down at the villa. A child's ball was caught up on the roof of the terrace – impossible, without circus skills, to retrieve it. It was all even lovelier than she remembered. Of course it was, time did not stand still and neither did gardens in Tuscany.

Once this hillside had been a flourishing chestnut grove. To make room for the house several fine specimens had been felled but, without rancour, the remaining trees stood stoically year after year, sheltering the house from the heat of the sun and the rigours of the winter storms. The sun was already high and a slight welcome breeze stirred the leaves of the ancient chestnut trees.

How stupid I was to let him spoil this for me too, thought

Sophie as she stood there quietly looking down on the low grey house with its red tiled roofs, now as much a part of the Tuscan landscape as the trees themselves. But apportioning blame was unfair. It was Sophie herself who had decided never to return to Tuscany after her divorce. Rafael had not said, 'Stay away,' and neither had the unseen, unknown enemies who had started the whispering campaign of hate. She shook her head, clearing it, for the moment, of all unpleasant thoughts.

The table, under its huge yellow umbrellas on the patio, was set for breakfast: blue glasses, blue plates, a bowl that was bound to contain her father's all-time best fresh fruit salad. Sophie got out of the car and waited.

'Archie, breakfast.' Her mother came out of the kitchen door, a heavily laden tray in her hands. How trim she looked and how very English: immaculately neat white blouse and well-cut navy trousers, every hair of her carefully permed hair in place, and sadly, surely that little bit more grey. She put the tray down on the table before, as if aware that she was being watched, she looked up, squinting, into the sun and Sophie's heart lifted and danced with joy. 'Sophie, sweetheart, you're here.' Her mother was almost running up the steps to meet her daughter who was running down. 'Archie.' Her voice was loud with excitement. 'Sophie's here.'

They met and hugged and kissed as they always did on both cheeks like good Continentals. 'Oh, darling, how lovely to have you here again. What a nuisance about the journey.' She put her hands one on each side of her daughter's face and looked into it as if she were memorising it. 'We've missed you so.' She made it sound as if they had not seen one another for years.

'I saw you last winter, Mum.'

Mrs Winter shrugged and swept the garden and the villa with her hands. 'Here, darling, we've missed you here.'

Sophie heard a shout and saw her father, hair and beard wilder and – sadly – like Kathryn's hair, greyer than ever, hurrying from the top garden where the pool was.

'Hello, angel,' he said, enveloping her in his arms.

Sophie relaxed against him, savouring the smell of Lifebuoy soap and . . . chlorine?

'You've been swimming,' she teased, because she did not want to notice that he had lost weight since Christmas. 'The father of the bride doesn't have time to swim.'

'Keeps me sane. Oh, you haven't met Harry. Harry, this is our middle daughter, Sophie. Harry Forsythe, darling.'

Sophie, in her turn, looked up into the sun to where Harry Forsythe was standing as if he did not wish to intrude. Who was he? Quite tall, especially when compared with Archie, medium build, carelessly dressed – or was it that he did not feel it important that his clothes fit well? – fair hair streaked with silver. Her mind refused to work. Zoë's fiancé? No, he was Jim something or other. She wished she could see him but the sun allowed her to see only vaguely. She smiled and held out her hand. 'Hello, Harry.'

'I teach at the university,' he explained as he took her hand and moved down the steps so that she no longer had to look into the sun, 'and I'm delighted to have been invited to the wedding.'

She recognised him now, from Zoë's description. ('He's fab, Sophie, tall, lovely smile, and the sexiest voice.') Harry had to be the 'dishy professor'. But Zoë had not said how incongruously her favourite teacher dressed. His jacket, in Tuscany in July, was lightweight tweed. Like its owner it was a little worse for wear, mellowed, more pleasing perhaps because of its age. She could see why even a girl as young as Zoë would describe him as 'dishy'.

'Sit down, everyone, and have some breakfast.' Kathryn Winter was nervous. Sophie recognised it, and was sure her father did too. 'Poor Sophie has had a nightmare journey, Harry. What time did you arrive, darling? We waited till twelve.'

The words, I asked you not to wait up, were forming on the tip of Sophie's tongue, but Kathryn was plunging on. 'Harry has an apartment in Florence.'

'Lucky Harry,' said Sophie and began to pour coffee. 'Where is . . . everyone?'

Her father answered. It was easier for him; he had simply refused to become involved in any of the arguments; a split in his family just did not exist. That was his way of handling the situation. 'They've found a marvellous new hairdresser in Aulla; name's Claudio. This is the trial day so everyone can decide they love it or hate it before the wedding.'

So she would not have to meet Ann just yet. She relaxed a little. 'By the way, to add to the general nightmare, my luggage got lost. I've asked the airline to send it here.' Airlines and their faults and failings. Wonderful topic of conversation. It kept them going through the first cup of coffee, the wonderful figs. Sophie excused herself and in the bathroom off her parents' bedroom she cleaned her teeth and applied deodorant. She did not want body odour to drive the 'dishy professor' away.

The conversation stopped when she emerged into the sunshine. Had they been rapidly filling him in? 'Our middle daughter, career girl, was married: what a disaster. He broke her heart but she's fine now.'

Harry Forsythe stood up until she was again seated at the table. 'Your parents tell me you've taken a villa near Gabbiana. There's a superb little *trattoria* on the main street; you must try it.'

She would not explain why there was no room for her at this huge villa. She smiled. 'I will.'

'Fantastic view of the Alpi Apuane. Even if the food were ghastly I would sit on that terrace and just wonder.'

'But it's not : . . ghastly, I mean.'

'No, superb. If you have time . . . well, perhaps we could go together.'

'Even the best food is better in the company of a beautiful girl.' She tensed but he did not, in fact, say it. He was British after all, not Italian. 'That would be nice, if I'm here long enough.'

'Sophie?' her mother began.

'Leave it, Kathryn.'

Sophie looked from her parents to Zoë's professor. He was looking uncomfortable. 'July isn't a good time for me to be away, Mum. There must be bad times to leave a university, Harry.'

'I try never to leave during term time but there are conferences one doesn't like to miss. During the vacation isn't much better because I want to do research.'

'We can't compare a professor and an office girl,' said Kathryn waspishly and inaccurately.

No one seemed to be able to find anything to say to that or to Sophie's look of astonishment.

Harry finished his fruit and his coffee, looked at his watch and stood up. 'I must go. I'm sorry that I missed the bride but I'll see her on Saturday or at one of the pre-do's.'

'He's not married,' whispered Kathryn as Archie walked their visitor back to his car, 'although Zoë says he has a . . . relationship.'

'With a woman?' Sophie asked naughtily and laughed as her mother blushed.

'Of course with a woman; the things you do say.'

'I get it from my mother.'

Kathryn put out her hand and caught Sophie's sleeve. 'I'm sorry, darling. It's just not the life I had planned for you.'

'Assistant in charge of European questions is hardly office girl, Mum, but leave it, please. I didn't come to fight.' She picked up another soft ripe fig and then, regretfully, returned it to the plate. 'I've had three already; probably one too many.'

Kathryn smiled as if relieved that Sophie had not 'come to fight'. 'Everything will be fine, dear,' and Sophie wondered down what tortured avenue her mother's thoughts were straying.

'Walk up to the pool with me,' suggested Kathryn. 'I want to see how my new shrubs are managing; it's been so hot.'

'Who is here already?' asked Sophie as they followed Harry up the broad white steps.

'Almost everyone,' said Kathryn. She hesitated before adding, 'Judith is coming, darling. You don't mind really, do you? She *is* Daddy's sister.'

'Step-sister.' Sophie spoke automatically. 'No, I don't mind, Mum, although I do sometimes wonder how this family manages to attract more than its fair share of spongers.'

Kathryn fluttered. 'She means well, dear. Things have been so hard for poor Judith.'

Sophie ignored that and stopped in admiration at the top of the steps. 'It's perfectly lovely. Rico didn't do all this.'

Kathryn nodded complacently. 'With all his sons and his cousins and his wife's sisters' sons. You know how it is. What do you think of Daddy's new toy?'

Sophie laughed. There was a tiny solar-powered fountain in the middle of a flowerbed.

'The hotter it gets, the more water shoots out, or at least that's how it's supposed to work,' explained her mother. 'That's what Professor Forsythe was dragged up here to look at. He brought a gift – wasn't that nice? Some absolutely lovely Venetian glass.'

'Is there a suit to fit me, Mum? I'd love a swim.'

Kathryn looked around wildly as if swimsuits might be growing on pool-side bushes. Two, in fact, were. Small, male suits.

'The twins. I'm longing to see them. Where are they?'

'They stayed at Giovanni's last night and they'll spend the day with him. They were torn: stay here and see Aunty or stay at Giovanni's and help in the kitchen.'

'Poor Giovanni.'

'He adores them. You know he still loves Ann.'

'You only think he does, Mum. Don't feel sorry for him.'

Kathryn looked round again. 'George is a good husband, and, well, maybe it's better to marry your own.' She stopped, embarrassed.

'I made a mistake, Mum. That's not to say marrying an Italian would have been wrong for Ann.'

'She didn't know he was going to own the most prestigious restaurant in La Spezia when she said no, did she?'

How shallow and how like her mother – or was it? 'Mum, Ann dated Giovanni but she fell in love with George.'

'George is so . . .'

'English.'

'So is Dad but he's not . . .'

'Dull.'

They laughed.

'I'd forgotten how good you are at finishing my sentences.'

'Only the ones you don't want to finish.'

Sophie turned to her mother. 'Dad's lost a lot of weight.'

Kathryn smiled with pleasure. 'Oh, good, you noticed. He's been slimming for the wedding. Now, if he could only straighten those shoulders he'd look much as he did when we first met – apart from his hair.'

'I think his hair is quite distinguished-looking.'

Her mother gripped her hand. 'I wish you were staying here, you should be. You do understand?'

'I'm too old to sleep on a sofa, Mum. The villa is lovely and I want everyone to come and see it. Now that suit.'

'Of course. In the pool house probably; I think there's a bluey-green one I haven't seen anyone wearing.'

The suit was a little too big but there was only her father to see if bits were revealed that shouldn't be. She could see him sitting there in his chair, reading yesterday's *Times*. He paid no attention to her at all as she dived in and swam vigorously up and down.

'Harry brought it,' he explained when she climbed reluctantly out of the pool. 'Saved me a run down to La Spezia. We've missed you, angel.'

Sophie understood what he meant. She wrapped the towel more securely around her. 'I just couldn't bring myself to return. Too much happiness was here. Do you understand? Not just Rafael but before, when we were girls and came for two weeks every summer.'

'You'll make up with Ann?'

She had no intention of 'making up' with Ann. She intended to be civility personified. 'Don't worry; I'll let nothing ruin Zoë's wedding. How was the graduation?'

'Fantastic. I was so proud; one of my beautiful girls a university graduate – and your mother. Come on, get some clothes on and I'll show you the pictures before anyone gets back. Your mum's face. "See me, the mother of the graduate." I look a little worn perhaps, rather wrinkly.'

'Yet distinguished.'

He laughed. 'If you say so. We had a meal here to save expense, you know, with a wedding coming so unexpectedly. Stella was wonderful.'

'Stella. Of course, that's what's missing. I was sure she would be working today. Where is she?'

'At the dressmaker's. I know having your cleaning lady at your daughter's wedding is not quite the done thing but she was the first person on Zoë's list. You know Zoë.'

'Stella's hardly the home help, Dad,' she chided. 'She's done everything for this family for nearly twenty years. She was there . . . for me.'

He turned away from her and started on the white stone path. 'We won't talk about that. Go on, get dressed. I'll lay out the photographs.'

She was just as happy as her father not to 'talk about that' and so she hurried back to put her clothes on for the third time.

Clothes. What are they after all but something to hide behind?

3

'Sophie, your cases are here.'

Sophie hurried after her father. She had heard the car and assumed that it was her sister. 'I'll have a shower and change, Dad; do my hair.'

He stopped and turned back to her. He was of average height but because she was above him on the path they looked into each other's eyes. 'You look just perfect to me.'

Holding her towel tightly she kissed him lightly on the bald part on top of his head and hurried to the house. Ann had to be there soon and she did not want her sister to see her, for the first time in years, falling out of an ill-fitting swimsuit.

She heard voices as she left the bathroom and saw Ann come down the hallway. Short of diving back into the bathroom she could not avoid her. Her first thought was that her sister had aged; she had certainly put on weight. Perhaps that was what made her appear older, for her hair, if anything, was darker than it had ever been, and short, too short. The women sized each other up as strangers might. This is my sister. Sophie was amazed at how quickly thoughts and memories and feelings flashed into her mind: fury, disillusionment, disappointment, regret . . . affection? 'Hello, Ann.'

Did Ann start forward spontaneously? If so, she stopped in mid step and stood awkwardly as if she too were remembering. Sophie thought she saw her hold her head up as if to say, 'It's over and I suffered too.' 'Sophie, you always were late,' said her sister flatly. Five years, five years since they had spoken to each other – no, screamed and sobbed at each other, and the first words were an aspersion and one that was untrue. 'You always were late.' Say nothing. Shrug. Airlines.

There must have been a time when she and Ann did not fight, when they had liked each other. She *had* loved her, hadn't she? She had worried when Ann had had pneumonia two years ago; that was because she loved her. When had she stopped liking her? 'I missed the plane in Brussels,' she offered brightly into the heavy atmosphere, 'and then spent hours trying to find my luggage at Linate.' She was not looking directly at her sister. She did not want to look into her eyes.

'Such a nuisance.' Polite. Strangers on a train.

The words meant nothing. She could have just as easily been saying 'Dead fish.'

Sophie tried to look directly at Ann. She is . . . how old? Stupid; only a few years older than I am. Am I as changed as she is? 'Is George with you – and Zoë?' Her voice had more animation. Zoë, beloved little sister.

The answer came in a shriek as Zoë catapulted herself around the corner. The almost indecently brief shorts certainly showed off her slim suntanned legs but did not quite suit the elaborate hairstyle. 'Sophie, how wonderful.' The younger woman hugged her sister and kissed her heartily on both cheeks. 'Isn't this marvellous? Another wedding in the most beautiful place in the world.'

'Let's hope it's more successful than the first one,' said Ann waspishly and walked off into her room. Ann, obviously, had decided to brazen it out.

Childishly Zoë stuck her tongue out at the closed door and so did not notice the spasm of pain that distorted Sophie's face. 'Don't mind her,' she said, putting her arm around Sophie. 'She's in a foul mood because Claudio says her posh London hairdresser ruined her hair and that he can't possibly repair the damage by Saturday.'

Sophie held her by the upper arms and looked at her, at the joyous vision. 'Where is my baby sister? Who is this gorgeous girl? Don't tell me those stumpy little pigtails turned into a

and how would they persuade them to race down the river? No doubt they would tell her. She was anxious to meet them again. She had made a point of visiting her parents once or twice over the years when the children were staying and so they were not strangers. Her rift had been with Ann.

She sat up cautiously and, to her intense pleasure, the headache was quite gone. She felt refreshed and rested, and once she had cleaned her teeth she would be ready for anything. A quick glance at her watch told her that it was nearly four. She had slept for at least five hours and she was starving. Clean teeth, make coffee, unpack, explore villa. No, explore villa, then unpack.

She had taken a house with two huge bedrooms. The larger one was on the second floor and that was also where the dining room, kitchen and bathroom were located. The other bedroom, that she had thought the twins might want to use at least once, was on the lower level and could be reached either by an outside door or, more interestingly for the twins, by a spiral staircase from the dining room. Downstairs too was an enormous sitting room, and had she been staying longer she would have had the entire family over for an *alfresco* lunch. She climbed down the staircase with a mug of coffee in her hand, opened the outside door and went out into the sunshine. There was another terrace here, not so large as the upstairs one but eight-year-old boys would love it, and again there was that fabulous view of the mountains. Sophie went down the outside staircase and then back up the other staircase to the door of the dining room and she was laughing. 'I can't see Mum or Ann on that spiral staircase – or the ghastly Judith.'

The dining room stretched from the front to the back of the house. From the back windows one could see beyond the garden, terraced hills where vines and fig trees were cultivated. From the front windows the vista stretched all the way to the Alps and it was stunningly lovely, a too-beautiful-to-be-real calendar picture that was right there before her awed eyes. Two hundred years ago this old stone house had belonged to a peasant farmer. He, his family, and his animals had sheltered inside its thick stone walls. Now it had been modernised by a Swiss industrialist and was a perfect blend of old and new. Only the views remained the same. That long dead peasant had stood here with a glass of his own wine looking in wonder at the Alps and Sophie Winter was standing in the same spot opening a bottle of local wine and feeling kinship with all the people who had gone before. 'You knew nothing of the wonders of that Swiss fridge-freezer,' she whispered to him, 'but I'm sure you appreciated this view as much as I do.'

She sat for a while watching the mountains and the lizards that ran up and down the walls, feeling the sun warm on her face; she ate some bread and cheese and drank a glass of wine and she almost said, 'I could stay here for ever,' but she did not. She washed and carefully made up her face. Then she pulled on a pair of capris and a striped cotton top, took a deep breath and closed the house. On the way to her parents' villa she took time to notice the *trattoria* on the main street of Gabbiana. The pleasant terrace shaded by huge vines heavy with ripe kiwi fruit was already busy and, as was usual in Italy, the customers were family groups of all ages. The grandfather of this family, gnarled and hard as the trunk of the vine, made his way slowly across the road, oblivious of Sophie's car. She slowed down to give him plenty of time. Out of the corner of her eye she saw one of the sad markers with which Tuscany is littered: on this exact spot in the dreadful days of the last world war someone from this village had been killed by the occupying German army. Or was an army occupying if the host country was their partner in the conflict? As the old man reached the safety of the *trattoria* Sophie shrugged and drove on down the hill.

There was another car parked at the villa but since it had Italian registration she assumed correctly that it belonged to Giovanni Piola. The house was deserted and so she went back outside and followed the sounds of voices to the swimming pool. For a few minutes she was able to study them as if she were examining a painting. Two sturdy, brown-haired boys, her nephews, appeared to be trying to drown each other in the pool. She reflected on how quickly little children grew; she would not have recognised in these boys, already tanned by the hot summer sun, the two pale children she had seen less than a year ago. Her parents, in shorts and T-shirts, were watering the roses they hoped would be at their perfect best on Saturday, and Ann and George and Giovanni were standing, sunglasses at the ready, studying lists. Of Zoë there was no sign.

The boys saw her first and yelled to her and to their parents and grandparents, and the tableau became animated.

'Darling, feeling better?' Her mother.

'*Carissima.*' Giovanni.

'Drink, Sophie?' George.

'Peter, Danny, don't hug your aunt. You'll ruin her clothes.' Ann.

Sophie tried to answer everyone – except Ann. There was no correct answer for her. She hugged the suntanned boys who graciously permitted themselves to be kissed, accepted a glass of wine from George and allowed Giovanni to hug her until she was sure her ribs had cracked. Success had gone to Giovanni's waistline and the slim boy she had known had grown into a rather rotund man. His face, which now sported a handlebar moustache, was, although fleshier, as friendly as ever.

'You need feeding up, *principessa*. Just you wait to see the banquet I prepare for the little Zoë. Puts your wedding into the cocked-up hat.'

'We did tell you Giovanni is catering the wedding, darling.'

'Of course, Mum; it will be the wedding feast of the year.'

'Of the century,' said the modest chef. 'I got to go, Sophie. I stay only to kiss you and tomorrow you all coming for lunch, Jim's mother too and his sister. She's pretty, that Penny.'

Arm in arm, she walked with him to his car.

'You happy, *principessa?*'

'Of course, Giovanni,' she answered lightly. 'Isn't the garden beautiful?'

He ignored that. 'Then why your eyes not sparkle like before?'

'I'm older, *amico.*'

'Me too, honeybun, but my eyes are sparkle. See.' He opened his dark brown eyes wide and gazed at her. 'The *castello* was open for a few weeks but it's close again.'

Her heart, that had begun to beat rapidly, slowed down again. 'I would expect the contessa to live in her own home.'

'Or her son, or his lady friend?'

'None of my business, I'm happy to say.'

'Then why your eyes not smile, *principessa?*' He looked at her, serious for once. 'I see you tomorrow. I make *cacciucco*. Zoë will think it's for her but we'll know better, honeybun?'

The Ligurian seafood stew was a particular favourite of Sophie and she appreciated that her old friend had remembered. 'I can't make up my mind whether you stayed too long in New York or not long enough, *amico*.'

He laughed, a sound that resembled a bark. 'Honeybun, sugar pie. I stayed long enough, baby.' He kissed her again and eased himself into his car. 'How you like the reins of success?'

'The trappings are just fine.'

'I take you for a drive one day.'

She waved him off vowing, as always, that nothing would persuade her into a car with Giovanni as the driver. For him and his passengers even the Madonna had to be reaching breaking point.

The family were wandering back from the pool towards the house and she joined them, pausing with her father as he pointed out all the new plantings. 'Watering's a nightmare. Mummy's English flowers are a bit silly but we spend so much time here she has to have a piece of home.'

'It's lovely,' said Sophie truthfully.

'Zoë and Jim have gone to Pisa to pick up their friends,' explained her mother. 'They'll wait for Judith who's on a slightly later plane – with David.' She stopped and looked nervously at Sophie. Would her daughter say anything about those two favourite relatives? Sophie said nothing. 'They'll drop David at his hotel; he's rather unhappy that there's no room here.' She shrugged her shoulders in a gesture that was almost Italian. 'Then they'll come on here, I hope in time for dinner. We can always have some *antipasti* with drinks while we try to get these arrangements right. We've spent hours on them. You look at them, darling, you're so good at sorting out who should sit where.'

Unwillingly Sophie took the lists of guests. They were in alphabetical order, thanks to her father, and she looked quickly for the name she did not want to see. It was, of course, not there and she risked smiling at her sister. 'Don't know why Mum thinks she had to involve me in this. You know these people better than I do.'

'But you're so much more experienced than I am, Sophie. What could a mere librarian possibly know about society.'

'Mummy, you always say librarians know everything,' put in Danny. 'Aunty Sophie, do you want to come down to the river and see the route for the duck race?'

'Later, darling. I promised Granny I'd look at this. But I am fascinated by the ducks. Where are you getting them from?'

The boys burst out laughing. 'We brought them in a suitcase,' they yelled and fell about again, laughing uproariously, at the sudden shock on her face. 'You're the second person. Giovanni thought they were real too. He said he'd barbecue them after the race.'

' 'Cept the winner,' yelled Peter. 'He wouldn't cook the winner.'

'Enough, boys,' said George. 'Had you forgotten how noisy kids are, Sophie? Go and fetch a duck and give it to Sophie. She can choose a number.'

'She's got to give us pots of money first,' said the boys almost together. 'Princesses have pots of money. It's for little kids with Aids.'

'The duck, now,' said George, and the boys recognised the implied threat and ran to their room.

'Wish my boys didn't know about horrible diseases. Awful world sometimes.'

'You can't wrap them up in cotton wool, dear,' said George.

'Watch me try,' said Ann, and got up and walked into the house.

Sophie pretended to study her lists and she and George sat quietly for a few minutes. Then Kathryn and Archie came out on to the terrace carrying trays and they were followed almost immediately by the sound of piano music. Kathryn almost dropped her tray. She looked fearfully at her daughter.

'It's not . . .'

'It's Lief Ove Andsnes,' said Sophie quietly. 'He's quite brilliant, isn't he? I heard him a year or so ago at the Wigmore Hall; his encores were longer than the recital.' Her hands were almost steady as they accepted a plate from her father.

George had gone inside at the first sound of the record and they could hear his voice, quiet, angry, and Ann's angrier and louder. 'So we can't even play CDs now. Is that what you're saying?'

'Oh dear, oh dear,' began Kathryn, her voice more tremulous than Sophie's hands.

'Mummy, it's all right. I don't mind. Why on earth should anyone think I mind? I'm glad Ann has developed some taste,' she finished waspishly and was immediately ashamed of herself.

The twins burst out of the door again, their sunburned arms full of yellow plastic ducks, and Sophie began to laugh. Just in time she managed to control the mounting hysteria. 'Boys, you clever things. I actually thought . . . Come on, let's go down to the river and you can show me the course. Is there a prize?'

The river that ran through the lowest part of the Winter property had always been a favourite place for Sophie and her sisters and she was delighted to find that it was just as special to Ann's boys. The ice-cold water from the Alps gushed down most of the year, running through gorges overhung with trees and jungle-like ferns, forming deep pools where some retreating ice field had gouged holes millions of years before. At the foot of the steep path that wound down from the terrace to the river were a beach and a narrow neck of furiously tumbling water that spilled out of one deep pool and into another.

'Perfect for the race, Aunty. We'll start above that pool, down through the narrows – we'll lose a lot there; no cheating, you're not allowed to help your duck if it gets beached – then into that pool, and then Daddy and Grampa can stand at the neck and catch the winner. Stella's son brought us some flags from the different nationalities and we can line the bank and cheer. Grampa's giving champagne to the winner unless it's a child. They get to go to La Speranza for the biggest ice cream they can eat and Daddy's paying so it doesn't come out of profits.'

'If I win, can I have the ice cream?'

They looked at her in horror. An adult asking for ice cream instead of champagne. 'No, that's not in the rules. You have to have the champagne.'

'Very well.' She tried to sound chastened. 'It's a super idea. I'm very proud of you both. We'd better go back up. There's so much to do.'

'It's so boring; all anybody talks about is this silly wedding and food, food, food.'

'But you like food,' Sophie tried to point out reasonably as they climbed back up the path.

'To eat,' they said in unison, 'not to talk about.'

'Sophie, what's society?' The boys had stopped halfway up the path and were looking at her. She had not seen which child had spoken.

'I'm not sure that I know what you mean.'

'Society, you know, the wedding. Mummy says you know about society.'

'It just means the people who are coming to the wedding.'

'No, it doesn't, else Mum would know about it because she knows everybody and you don't.'

Sophie took a deep breath and started on up the hill. 'Mummy was just being kind, boys, getting me involved.'

'Is it because you're a princess?'

How they did cling on with their strong little teeth. 'I am not a princess. Giovanni calls me that because he's Italian and he likes to exaggerate; it doesn't mean anything.'

'But Mummy says,' began Danny but his Aunt had gone ahead of him.

The family was on the terrace and again they were talking about food. Zoë, her fiancé Jim Thorpe, his mother, Maude, Penny Thorpe, quite lovely in a very short, sleeveless, pink dress, other friends of Zoë, and Judith Lantz, Archie's step-sister. Since Ann wore clothes that were too matronly for her she and Judith looked almost like sisters, although Judith was thin to the point of emaciation. There was, in fact, no actual relationship between them; perhaps it was the look in the eyes, alert, inquisitive, always searching.

'Hello, Sophie. How kind of you to come,' she said graciously as if she were the hostess at a party, and Sophie's good intentions began to buckle under the strain.

'To my sister's wedding, Judith?' she began.

'Sophie.' Zoë jumped up from the piano stool she was sharing with her fiancé. 'Come and meet Jim properly, and Maude and Penny. Don't let Judith rattle you,' she added sotto voce. 'Aren't I marrying into a handsome family?'

'You are indeed,' agreed Sophie as she held out her hand to the very young man hovering protectively beside her sister. Jim and Penny could well have been twins, since they were both tall and thin, with large brown eyes and short dark brown hair. If she had thought Jim rather shy she found he was not, since he ignored her hand and kissed her twice heartily.

'I've become very Italian,' he explained.

'Excuse to take liberties,' his mother said with a laugh.

Had there been fifty unknown women in the room Sophie would unerringly have picked out Maude as Jim's mother. Maude was shorter and, of course, older, but her son and daughter were almost carbon copies of their pretty, dark-haired mother; all three were smiling happily and obviously prepared to enjoy the wedding festivities to the full.

'Isn't this fun, Sophie?' said Maude. 'Do you know I never managed to visit Jim when he was studying in Italy but now that I'm here I'm enjoying every minute.'

'You look very Tuscan already, Maude,' said Sophie as she admired Maude's elegant palazzo pants.

'All the Italians will be running after that girl,' said Judith waspishly but Sophie merely laughed.

'Lucky girl,' she said.

Over dinner Kathryn and Archie gave everyone copies of the timetable for the wedding festivities.

'See,' whispered Peter to Sophie, 'food, food, food.'

She smiled. There were rather a lot of formal parties. 'Most people are coming an awful long way, sweetheart. Jim's cousin is coming from Japan. Grampa just wants to say thank you.'

Japan. How exciting. The boys were delighted to think they might have a Japanese relative in their extended family.

'Sorry, boys,' said Jim after listening to their excited questions. 'He's a boring old salesman from Somerset. Nothing exotic about him at all.'

'Exotic?' This time the twins did speak at the same time. 'Mummy says we don't want exotic. Rafael was exotic, she says. Was he, Aunty Sophie? Was your husband exotic?'

Later Sophie would think that the dining room must for an instant have resembled another tableau. There was a stunned silence as they spoke and every head turned towards her, except Ann who had the grace to flush and look away. 'Gosh no, darlings,' she said to them, trying to keep her voice steady. 'There was nothing exotic about him at all.'

4

'I just want everything to be perfect. Is that too much to ask? There was so much ugly talk and I want everyone to see that everything is . . . perfect.' Kathryn had stopped crying but her frame still shook with sobs.

'Come on, darling. That was years ago and what difference does it make? They got divorced; it happens all the time, even in Italy.'

'Not in my family it doesn't.'

They were in their bedroom, thankfully quite a long way from the guest bedrooms where Zoë and her young friends were doing whatever it is that girls do in the precious hours before a wedding. Next door in the tiny bedroom where Sophie would normally have slept, Judith was wrapping her thick hair on tubes of fat pink foam in the hopes that it would curl, even a little, in the heat, while in the bedroom downstairs Ann was being yelled at by George, if such a mild-mannered man ever yelled.

'Sophie has never got over Rafael,' moaned Kathryn. 'He broke her heart and she's never looked at another man.'

'She hasn't sworn off men, Kathryn, and she certainly looked at Harry this morning.'

Kathryn dabbed at her rather washed-out blue eyes. She decided to treat this remark with the contempt it deserved. 'Why has she never married again? If she's not in love with him still why hasn't she found someone else, someone steady and . . .'

'Not exotic.' Archie regretted his attempt at levity because Kathryn burst into tears again. He sat down on the bed beside her and held her, rocking her back and forth. 'Sweetheart, your youngest daughter is getting married in two days' time; there are hundreds of things to do and you must stop being upset about Sophie; she's perfectly happy.'

'It's Ann. Why did she tell the boys Rafael was exotic? They can't remember him; they weren't even three years old. Why was she speaking about him? She's jealous of Sophie; she's always been jealous. It has to be my fault, what Ann did. How did I go wrong as a mother, Archie?'

He looked at her in amazement. Surely all this weeping and wailing and handing out and receiving guilt was in the past where it belonged, with Rafael. 'Stop it, Kathryn. We're not going back there. Whatever Ann did, or Judith, or even Zoë, it's all in the past. You'll make yourself ill and you'll have swollen eyes in all the wedding photographs.'

She shrieked and jumped off the bed to rush to her dressing-table. She dabbed at her eyes with some cotton wool. 'I was supposed to ring him, the photographer.'

He laughed. 'I did, when you and Ann were arguing. He's coming tomorrow morning at ten.'

'Ten?' Kathryn snorted. It was a strange sound, something between a sniff to pull back unshed tears and a note of derision. 'He's Italian; we'll be lucky if we see him by noon and there's Giovanni's lunch for Zoë in La Spezia. We should never have given in to Zoë, Archie. You have always spoiled the girls. A lovely wedding at home . . .'

He ignored her remarks about his parenting skills, having had them hurled at his head too often before. 'Zoë thinks of Italy as her home: all the holidays and three years at the university. Jim loves it here too and Maude thinks having a wedding in Tuscany is romantic. Besides, Judith said it was raining at home, and set to rain all weekend.'

'Stella says the *castello* was open this week.'

Archie looked at his wife and sighed. 'For goodness sake: it's his home. Is he supposed to go somewhere else because they divorced?'

'What if they bump into each other?'

Archie stood up and walked over to the door leading to their private terrace. He opened it and looked out, listening. Below them the River Tavernelle jumped and poured itself over rocks in its headlong rush to the sea. A gentle breeze stirred the curtains carrying warm, lemon-scented air into the room. Archie relaxed. 'Do you enjoy finding things to worry about, Kathryn?' he asked as he turned back to his desolate wife. 'Sophie and Rafael have been divorced for five years. If they meet, and they won't,' he added as he saw her shudder, 'they'll be perfectly civilised. Besides it's probably his mother or his brother or – and here his voice began to rise – 'for God's sake, Kathryn, his second cousin twice removed. I don't give a damn who's there.' He stopped, having shocked himself by his own uncharacteristic outburst.

She tried to retrieve her dignity. 'There's no need to swear,' she said stiffly. 'I'm so pleased that Jim is such a nice responsible English boy. There were no worries meeting Maude, no undercurrents.'

'There were no undercurrents meeting Gabriella; she was perfectly delightful. You can't blame her because the marriage broke up. Now this wedding and this marriage deserve all our thought.'

'Jim's not like Rafael. He and Zoë were just meant for each other.'

'Let it go, Kathryn.'

Kathryn hung her flowered dressing-gown over a chair. It was her 'Italian' dressing-gown, too thin and, perhaps, exotic for Surrey. 'Did Sophie finish the table plans for Giovanni's lunch?'

'Why you bothered Sophie with something that's been done for weeks I do not know,' said Archie as he sat down on his side of the bed.

'She has to feel part of the family.'

He looked at her as if he would like to say something but obviously changed his mind. 'She took them back with her to her house though how she'll get anything done with the boys for company is quite another question.'

★

Sophie and her nephews were all engrossed. She had spread the guest lists together with the table plans on the large table in the dining room and she worked there quietly while the twins were outside trying to catch fireflies. Some of the guests she did not know but Zoë had written explanatory notes. Jim's cousin's wife. Lucy's (bridesmaid) uncle. Try to put him beside someone who can keep him away from the *vino*. How was she to manage that one? Carlo di Angelo. Of course, of course. Who else could diplomatically and skilfully keep an elderly alcoholic from drowning himself in fine Tuscan wines? Oh, how wonderful it would be to see him again. Sophie's hand was shaking as she scratched out one name and inserted Dr di Angelo. That was it, if she put Josefina di Angelo beside Lucy's uncle, then she could put Carlo across the table. The old man would be so enchanted by the beautiful Josefina that he would scarcely notice that Carlo was waving the wine waiters away.

Sophie sat back in her chair. Yes, that was one part of the past she would be happy to remember. She had met Carlo through his friendship with Rafael; the men had grown up together, but Carlo had soon become her friend too and he had been there in the darkest part of her life. It was not a question of reawakening the past; that was silly. It did not sleep, it was there every second and so seeing Carlo would not bring pain. The pain was there already. The family could be just as difficult. Judith? Sophie sighed. It hardly mattered where she put Aunt Judith. She would make a beeline for the person in the group that she decided was the richest, the most important.

'You're marrying Raffaele de Nardis. Well done, little girl; how very useful he will be.'

And Rafael had been useful, laughingly allowing his name, his family, his prestige to be exploited, until even he – or was it his mamma – had grown tired of being used. She got up and went to the window. By the light from the security lamps she could see the shapes of the boys as they darted around as fleet of foot as the fireflies. 'Caught any yet?'

Two voices came back. 'No, but almost.'

She returned to her lists. David! Did every family have their David? The family member who could not be left out but whom no one really liked because there was nothing to like. 'I'd better have him. That should put me in Ann's good books for five minutes. If he tells me what I've done wrong with my life and what I should do to change it, I'll tell him . . .' Sophie laughed at the appalling words that had almost slipped from her tongue. 'I shall tell him, quietly, of course, but firmly. I shall look forward to it. I'd much prefer the dishy professor.'

She went on with her place settings and then, aware that it was ominously quiet, she returned to the window and leaned out. The boys were sitting on the side of the well and their feet were in the ice-cold water. They were chatting quietly and watching the water as it tumbled out of the pipe that was bored into the mountain.

As if they sensed that she was there they looked up. 'You have never felt such cold water,' they said. 'We want to see how long it will take to freeze our feet.'

Sophie went down and sat with them and they were right, it was very cold. She insisted that they remove their feet while still unfrozen.

'Aunty, will you tell us something honest and truly.'

'That depends. I'll try. Is that good enough?'

'Daddy slapped us; he doesn't do that very often,' said Peter and he sounded very despondent. 'Because we repeated what Mummy said and she shouldn't have said it if we couldn't repeat it, should she? She didn't get slapped.'

'Bet Daddy's yelling though,' Danny contributed. 'Sometimes he yells.'

'Not very often.'

Sophie thought it was time to take their minds off their parents. 'What did you want to ask?'

'What does exotic mean?'

'Depends how you use it.' She saw the almost identical little faces take on that 'here comes another grown-up cop-out' and hurried on. 'Strictly speaking it means something foreign, different, and therefore a little bit exciting.'

'And Rafael is exotic because he's foreign?'

Rafael. They had scarcely known him. They were babies and he was quicksilver, here, there, everywhere. He was part of the past and she wanted to be free of him and she was, she was. 'No. Yes, he's foreign to us because he's Italian but your mother wasn't thinking about that. It was because he was . . . is so different. His way of life is . . .' What could she say, should she say? She took a deep breath and could laugh at herself enough to realise that authors were right: in moments of crisis a deep breath helped. 'Raffaele de Nardis is one of the world's greatest pianists. He travels all over the world and everywhere he goes thousands of people come to hear him play.' She had been among them once, sitting happily in concert halls and auditoriums, watching his hands and thinking of all the magic in those hands, pitying the others in the hall, waiting, waiting for the concert to be over so that they could be alone. She shivered and shook the memories away. 'He was born in that castle up there on the hill: that makes him different from us.'

They were impressed, their innocent eyes as round as saucers. To them a world-famous pianist was merely a piano player but a man who had been born in a castle, now that was something. 'So he is a prince,' they gasped.

She smiled. 'No, his father was a count, not a prince. Come on, boys, it's long past all our bedtimes.'

'A count; that's not as good as being a prince, sort of down a bit?'

'Sort of.'

'Is he coming to the wedding?'

'No. He has nothing to do with this family any more.'

They accepted that but not happily. 'My chum Brian's parents are divorced but his father is still in the family. If Rafael came we could ask him to show us the castle. It's for a project and grown-ups like helping with projects.'

When she had got them into their room Sophie went back to the seating plan. She finished it to the accompaniment of boys' voices and then suddenly then were quiet. She went down the spiral staircase and looked in. They had fallen asleep, probably in mid sentence. She stood for a moment looking down at them. With their eyes closed she could not tell them apart, two slim healthy boys, stretching towards maturity. She pulled the floral cotton sheets up over them and turned off the light. She went back upstairs and folded up the papers. They would have to do. In her bedroom she closed the dark green wooden shutters and when she was in bed she lay and looked at the light patterns on the walls. It was wonderful to have her nephews here in the house with her. Family ties were important. She had seen so little of them, her own fault mostly, but she would change all that, make more of an effort to be with the family in future, but not in Tuscany, not in Tuscany. She turned her face into the pillow to shut out the memories that came flooding in through the bars of the shutters but they were still there behind her closed lids.

'Face them, Sophie. Even the air of Tuscany is heavy with memories and most of them beautiful. Maybe if you lie here and drag them all out then they'll go away and leave you in peace.'

How surprised the world had been when they married. Both worlds, his and hers.

'Sophie, you're too young, ten years younger. Are you sure it's not his fame you're in love with?' Both mothers said that although the tone of voice was so different. Her mother anxious, loving, but excited in spite of herself, his mother cold, angry. 'You have nothing in common with my son, nothing.'

'Enough, Mother. That is enough. You will accept Sophie or you will lose me.'

The contessa could not bear to contemplate that he might be speaking seriously, that she might indeed lose touch with her mercurial brilliant son. For him she would tolerate anything, even a silly girl with no qualifications, no background, little Italian, a non-Catholic and, what was much worse (although that last defect was almost unsurpassable) only the most rudimentary knowledge of music.

'I'll teach her, Mamma, and besides, I'm glad she's not a musician. She talks to me about other things.'

'What? Art, literature, politics?'

But although Sophie loved the great Italian painters, she knew little about Italian literature and nothing at all about politics. Rafael laughed. The contessa did not as she did not like that Sophie used the English Rafael instead of the flowing Italian Raffaele; it was such a small thing, so that she could have something of him that the world did not. In truth they talked little of anything outside their own special world, but they loved much. When had the rot begun to sink in there too? Had she, deep down, believed his mother, that she was not good enough for him? She had had plenty of time to study, language first, although Rafael spoke perfect English. Music.

'It's enough that you appreciate me.'

Was it enough? She needed to be able to share his life, his interests. Carlo befriended her. Carlo and later the beautiful Josefina, both so very much part of Raffaele de Nardis's life. But they did not come on the exhausting world tours and there were days, weeks sometimes, when no one but hotel staff spoke to her. 'Coffee, madame?' in so many different languages. His schedule was not geared to real social intercourse. He was in most cities for a few days only: no time to make friends. She sat for hours in hotel rooms or in auditoriums listening and, of course, learning, learning. And then, after the performances . . . ah then. Still Rafael spoke little but his hands, his lips, his body spoke for him and only then, when they were making love, did she feel that she was giving her brilliant, demanding husband what he needed. Then only did she feel his equal.

She began to go alone to museums, art galleries; she began to learn to read in Italian, in German, in French. Gradually her worldwide circle of acquaintances, and then friends, grew. She would see that another artiste, someone known to Rafael, was singing or playing or dancing in the same city and she arranged a small dinner party. These were judged to be much more fun than the huge parties arranged by management.

'That was a lovely party, *amore*.'

'Thank you.'

He reached for her. 'What a blessing you are to me. Everyone adores you.'

His mother did not.

Sophie sat up. She could hear a piano. The music was there tantalising, teasing. It grew louder and louder, soaring into an orgasmic climax. Who was it? Where? She began to sob. There was no music, no pianist. The sound existed in her head. I should never have come back here. I knew I couldn't keep him at bay here. She scrambled out of bed, pulled off her nightgown. 'I'll leave. I'll drive back to Linate and get the first plane.'

She sat back down on the bed, exhausted. There were two little boys asleep downstairs. Her young sister was getting married and she had promised her father that she would do nothing to spoil it. 'I can survive for a few days. Nothing has been dredged up. So silly; no one remembers. No matter what anyone says I will leave on Sunday and then I will never come back to Tuscany. I made that vow once but this time I'll keep it.'

She lay down, pulled a sheet over her and eventually she slept. She had, she thought, barely closed her eyes when the twins erupted into her bedroom. Defensively she grabbed the slipping sheet.

'Can we go to Grandma's now, Aunty? We want to swim before this silly party.'

She shooed them out.

'We'll make you coffee,' they promised as they retreated. 'We're good at that. Mummy showed us. Sometimes she just can't get going in the mornings.'

For the first time in years Sophie felt some sympathy for her sister. She showered and dressed, drank some of the boys' too weak, lukewarm coffee, threatened them with a real lesson in coffee making – but that brought another memory of Rafael and her marriage so she stopped in mid sentence – and drove over to Villa Minerva to leave them with their devoted grandparents.

'Tell Grandma I'll be back in an hour or two. I have someone to see first.'

If she stopped she might change her mind so she drove immediately to Aulla, the big town at the junction of all the roads, and parked in front of the imposing office building. Carlo, naturally, had appointments all morning.

'But he will see you for a few minutes, signorina.'

'*Cara, è così bello,*' he said as he enfolded her in his arms. This man was married to Josefina but yet he could tell her she was lovely and sound as if he meant it. 'You are, you know,' he said as if he could read her thoughts. 'It is so good to see you here, Sophie. How are you?'

She looked at him and smiled because he was good to look at. He was tall and broad but not fat, and his head was as perfectly modelled as she remembered. His hair, now showing some grey flecks that made him look even more distinguished, still curled around his noble forehead. His suit, as usual, was expensive Italian couturier, and he wore it effortlessly.

'*Mi amico,* Carlo di Angelo; he has the head like an angel, no?'

'No, the boy David.'

'Fine.' She smiled brightly, maybe too brightly.

'Good. Let's have some coffee. I have a patient,' – he looked at his watch – 'in fifteen minutes. You are too thin.'

She laughed. 'This from the husband of the divine Josefina.'

'She is slim. Slim is good. Too thin is not. We shall feed you up in Italy.'

'That's what Giovanni is threatening.'

He laughed. 'Giovanni knows what is beautiful.'

How easy it was to be with him. Why she had worried . . . 'The lunch, Carlo. There is an uncle of one of the bridesmaids.' She stopped.

He put his elbows on his desk, his fingertips together. Consultant in consulting mode. He looked at her over the beautifully manicured hands. 'And you want me . . .?'

'To make sure he doesn't drink too much.'

'*D'accordo.*' He dismissed the uncle and his problem. 'Now, is there a possibility we can see you? Katia we will bring to the wedding but we do not stay for the dancing. Our little one will stay with his nurse.'

'I don't know, Carlo. I'm leaving on Sunday.'

He stood up. 'Sunday? Your career is so important – no time for old friends? No time for Tuscany? Your parents can maybe spare you to us for a few days. Then you can admire our babies, and we, you and I, we can talk.'

He thought, naturally enough, that she was staying with her parents. 'I've taken a little house near Gabbiana.'

He looked surprised and she spoke quickly, maybe too quickly. 'You know how it is at weddings. The house is bursting at the seams. Zoë, her bridesmaids, Ann and George, their twins. What great fun they are, Carlo, eight years old.' She would not let her voice slow down. 'They stayed with me last night. We sat in the well.'

Once he had been a boy who sat with another little boy in the water of an icy well. 'Yes, I have seen them several times.' He struck his beautiful forehead with his hand. 'And the human tank? She is here?'

Sophie laughed. The tank. Poor Judith. If only she knew how others saw her and her scheming.

On the desk in front of Carlo a light began to glow. 'My patient is ready, Sophie. We will talk again, at lunch maybe – I will try to be on time. Think about it, *cara*, visiting with us.'

She kissed him, Italian fashion, on both cheeks. 'I promised the boys they could come again, but thank you.'

'I talk at lunch.' He walked her to the door with his usual courtesy.

Sophie left and went out to her rented Fiat. She felt better. She had not wanted her reunion with Carlo to be staged before thirty interested people. He had been, no doubt still was, Rafael's oldest and closest friend. Everyone would be watching.

Heart lighter, she drove back to the villa. Another crisis.

'Your mother can't find her hat.'

'Don't worry, Dad. The greatest list maker in the entire world never forgets anything.' Sophie patted him on the shoulder as she passed and went into the villa. The doors leading to the terrace were open and a refreshing breeze blew through the rooms. The house was a cool sanctuary after the heat of the town.

Her parents' bedroom looked as if the nastiest type of burglar had ransacked it. Clothes, hats, shoes, open cases and boxes were everywhere. Kathryn was standing in the middle of the chaos and she was, Sophie realised unbelievingly, wringing her hands. She saw her daughter and burst into tears. Sophie put her arms around her, pushed a daffodil-yellow suit off the bed, and sat down with her mother in its place. 'Stop crying, Mum. Save them for Saturday.'

'Oh, Sophie, Ann says she doesn't want to come to Giovanni's party and I've left my wedding hat at home.'

Sophie ignored the reference to Ann. This 'I won't come' nonsense was quite typical. Ann wanted coaxing and, as usual, she would get it – but not from her sister. 'I'll tidy these up, shall I? Then you'll see better.'

'It's no use. It has to be at home. I just know it is.'

Sophie ignored her and began hanging the clothes in the ornate Italian wardrobe. 'This is pretty,' she complimented as she hung the yellow suit in the wardrobe. 'Are you wearing it at the wedding?'

As she had hoped her mother lost her mood of despondency.

'Oh, don't be silly, Sophie. I was going to wear it at lunch.'

'Lovely.' Today was a day for speaking brightly. 'Why don't you wash your face while I hang these up. Then when you've got it on I'll do you up: glam mother-of-the-bride. I have an eye-shadow, very discreet, that will look wonderful with this.'

Reluctantly Kathryn left the bedroom. Sophie stopped to pick up another dress, and a suit belonging to her father.

'No thank you, Ann; you have caused enough problems. Sophie is helping me.'

Sophie winced as she heard the exchange between her mother

and her elder sister who had met – by chance? – in the bookcase-lined hallway.

'Sophie. Oh, of course, the wonderful Sophie. She ruins her own life, embarrasses the family and half the Italian aristocracy and goes off for years, five years, Mother, and back she comes for Zoë's wedding – the contessa herself, without the count let us not forget, and what do I get? Oh, Sophie will do it, Sophie knows about table arrangements, Sophie knows this, that and everything except how to keep her husband.'

'Good gracious, Ann. You sound more in need of a smacking than any ten-year old. You're not totally innocent here.' That was Aunt Judith, roused from her nap or a rest by the pool. Certainly she had not been working anywhere. 'If I remember rightly there—'

'Don't say it, don't say it,' shrieked Kathryn.

'Mind your own business, Aunt Judith.'

A wail from Kathryn and a pained cry from Judith. 'Am I to stay here and be insulted. Archie? What your father would say if—'

A door slammed and Sophie realised that she was on the floor kneading the fabric of a dress between her fingers and that she was crying. She dropped the dress as if it were red-hot and sniffed loudly. Whether or no she could find the matching hat, her mother would not throw the dress she intended to wear to her daughter's wedding on the floor. Sophie stood up, shook out the dress and hung it in the wardrobe. Then she pushed coat hanger after coat hanger aside and, sure enough, a plastic-wrapped dress hanger with the name of a top London shop was hanging in the recesses. Through her tears Sophie noticed a bulge. It was, of course, the hat.

'What was all that stuff about *for the want of a nail the shoe was lost etc. etc.?*'

This last little family contretemps just did not need to happen. Sophie blew her nose and went on with tidying the mess, paying as little attention as possible to the weeping, wailing and gnashing of teeth going on outside the door. She heard her father's calm voice and George's, and her mother, Judith and Ann all sobbing. She closed the wardrobe doors. 'I don't need this. I'm going home now.'

When the last pair of shoes was tidily on the shoe rack she took a deep breath and opened the door. It seemed that everyone except, thank God, Zoë had joined in the fracas. They stopped yelling and sobbing and turned to look at her. 'Your dress with hat is in the wardrobe, Mum. I'm going to Giovanni's, but if there is one more outburst like that one I am taking the first plane back to Edinburgh. *Caio.*'

5

Tuscany 1941

'Our home? These gross, illiterate Germans are going to live in our home? You must forbid it, Papà.'

'They are our allies, Gabi. And, dear child, they are not all fat. The general is a very cultured man; he does not like his job any more than we like it.'

'Then he can sleep in the stable where he belongs.'

'I cannot talk to you, my darling child, when your mind is so closed. Talk to your sister, Ludo, see if you can make her see sense. The general is a decent man; he will keep his men in order. Help your sister to pack some of her favourite things; the general assures me that everything here will be as we leave it when this is all over.'

'And you believe him? You look at what these wolves are doing in the rest of Europe and you believe him?'

'You try my patience, Ludo.'

'I agree with Gabi. The English are our friends; so it was in the last war. You cannot like either the Germans or the fascists. Italy is governed by greed and corruption, that is what I have heard you say, time and time again, and now you are handing the keys of our home to a friend of Mussolini.'

'E che diamine! Where did these baby firebrands come from? Pack, Gabriella, and you too Ludovico. We leave in one hour.'

Why do I do it, why do I do it? Ann stood beside the river watching her sons swimming like demented little ducks in the icy cold waters of the Tavernelle and stopped wishing that she were dead or that the ground would open up and swallow her whole.

She had once seen an amateur production of Mozart's *Don Giovanni* and the last act where the ground had seemed to open showing hell and all its furies spewing forth had affected her very deeply. Don Giovanni, when you thought about it, hadn't really done anything too bad in the course of the opera. Goodness knows, he had tried to seduce everything in sight but when you actually sat down and analysed what he was supposed to have done, there was a powerful amount of hearsay.

Should the ground open before her now – it would incidentally swallow up the Tavernelle and her two darlings – definitely the devils who came out to grab her would be green, not red or black but green, green for envy.

'Ann, boys, it's time to leave.'

George, old, dependable, dull George. Ann threw a stone viciously into the water for the joy of hearing it splash. I should have married Giovanni when I had the chance and I would be giving this bloody lunch. I would have been up all night finalising the table arrangements and making everyone proud of me. I don't mean that. I don't. 'We're coming, darling,' she said as she turned to look up the hill towards her husband. 'I thought if I could tire this pair out they might behave better this afternoon.' She smiled brightly at George who looked back at her sourly.'

'Did you try exhausting yourself?'

Ann looked up at her husband. The sun was shining down on his head and she saw glints of silver in the thick hair. Dear God, he's getting old. I am too. How stupid, I'm not forty yet. He's going to say it, he has had enough and I'm no good at keeping husbands either? What a bitchy thing to say. I didn't mean it, I didn't, but every time I see her, every hair in place, no extra pounds . . . but she's never done anything like I did. Stupid, stupid. Why did I do it? Ann cringed at the memory she usually kept well fastened down. How humiliating that had been. Sophie has never been embarrassed like that, rejected.

'Why are you smiling?'

George looked hot. Dear George, he hated heat; he came to Italy only to please her.

'Smiling? The children, dear.' She could not tell him of her feeling of delight that Sophie had indeed finally been rejected.

She saw the words she feared hovering on the tip of his tongue but he choked them back. I'll make it up to him; not one more gripe about Sophie this entire holiday. She swallowed. 'Danny, Peter. Come now. Did you hear Daddy?'

Reluctantly the boys came out of the river. They were blue with cold and their parents automatically wrapped them in huge fluffy towels.

How often have we done this? I love it; I love pulling them out and warming up their little bodies. I want to go on doing it and my stupid jealousy is endangering everything that really matters. I will be mature. I will.

'Grandma is talking to the photographer,' said George to the boys. 'Thank God he was late,' he added sotto voce to his wife.

An Italian could handle it, thought Ann and started to laugh. Her husband looked at her questioningly. 'Sorry, George, but I was thinking about opera down at the river and . . . oh, never mind. It's not so funny trying to explain it.'

'Living in an opera, soap or Italian, gets wearing, Ann.'

She was quiet, chastened again. She took his hand and felt anxiety clutch at her insides as for a second he let his hand lie there but then he squeezed her fingers. Thank God, thank God. Over this hurdle. I will never be bitchy again. They reached the terrace and she smiled at her parents, allowing them to observe, in case they were in doubt, that she and George were fine. No problems with this marriage.

'Has he gone?' She pushed the children towards the bedrooms. 'Go and get dressed; the clothes on your beds – exactly as laid out,' she yelled after their retreating backs. She sat down on one of the green wicker chairs and put her sandalled feet up on a cane stool. She smiled. Overweight or not, at least she had nice ankles. 'Is he nice, Mum?'

'He's up at the pool with Judith. Stephanie Wilcox recommended him,' Kathryn said, as if that should be enough. She sensed that her oldest daughter was bottling something inside and added defensively, 'I know she's rather bossy, Ann, but she is artistic.'

'The photographs are none of her business, Mum. It's not as if she's paying for them and if she gets this Pietro's back up you'll be without a photographer.'

'Don't worry, Kathryn,' said George. 'He's extremely good at pretending he doesn't speak English. I reminded him that Zoë wants some shots down at the river and he'll look down there later but now we had better go. Giovanni will be tearing his hair out.'

'What about Zoë?' asked Archie.

'She's driving with Jim and Maude, and I think Penny is with them. Ann?'

'Leave it, Kathryn. Everyone's nerves are too taut at the moment.'

It seemed to Ann that her father, like her husband, had had about enough of hysterical women. That thought made her angry. That was men all over. Women, women, women and their hysteria. Who caused the hysteria? Men. She wanted to shout. 'If you, Daddy, had appreciated me more and Sophie less, none of these problems would have happened.' But Sophie was his pride and joy, his bright daughter, the one who would do wonders. Five years younger than her sister, Sophie was the one who was going to shine academically while Ann had no real ambition. She wanted to do something pleasant until she married, working in a library perhaps. With all her promise Sophie had not graduated. But you still love her best and you blame me for some of that awful misery. But I didn't do anything too awful. I didn't steal anything. I made some mistakes, that's all. Anyone can make mistakes, except the mighty Saint Rafael and his ex, ex, ex wife. The mutinous thoughts refused to be beaten down and kept going around and around in her head.

The boys, hair sticking up all over, rushed in, and in having to fuss over their hair Ann managed to keep quiet.

'Where did Sophie find your hat?' she asked as they finally left the villa and walked up through the flowering shrubs to the parking area.

'In the bag with the dress. I feel so stupid, Ann, but I put the whole outfit together for convenience, and I don't know why I panicked.'

'Remembering the last wedding probably.'

Her mother stopped and the twins almost collided with her. 'The last wedding? But, Ann, what do you mean? Sophie's wedding? Surely not. That was just perfect.'

'You spilled wine on your coat and Rafael's mother let you borrow one.'

'That was so kind of her, wasn't it?'

Ann said nothing and got into her car. 'Kind?' she said to George. 'Do you remember Sophie's wedding? All those ghastly Italians looking down their aristocratic Roman noses. The old countess gave Mum a coat, do you remember. "Keep it, Kathryn. It goes so much better with your dress." Ghastly woman. It hid Mum's dress.'

'Only in the chapel, Ann. She took it off at the reception. Lovely coat. Your mother's nice in tailored things. She wore it at the twins' prize-giving.'

'I remember,' said Danny and, once again, to their chagrin, the parents understood that small children hear everything. 'Grandma said, "Watch your ice cream you two; this is an Armani." I forget what she said an Armani was. I thought it was a creepy-crawly with lots of spikes.'

'That's an armadillo,' shrieked his twin and the parents had to stop the car to separate them.

'This is going to be the holiday for spankings,' said George. 'You two behave like gentlemen or I'll wallop the pair of you.'

This quietened them for a minute as they digested and analysed the threat. Minimal? 'Aunty says Rafael is a gentleman but Mum says he dumped her so he can't be, can he?'

'Not another word from anyone until lunch,' said George through tightly gritted teeth.

Ann stared straight ahead and saw nothing of the dusty road.

Marriage was a minefield. When did I say, 'dumped her' in front of the boys? Damn it. Being a mother is so hard. They remember nothing you want them to remember and everything you don't. Now George is angry again and that means he'll get indigestion and be as grumpy as an old toad all day. Damn you, Sophie. You said you would never come back to Italy. Why the sudden devotion to Zoë? I must stop going over and over this, justifying myself. It's like a sore tooth and I can't resist putting my tongue in it even though it hurts me.

George's temper and digestion were not helped by having to look for a parking place. Outside the restaurant the attendant happily pocketed a bill and promised to guard the car with his life. 'I'm never sure if that guy's a crook or if Giovanni does employ him.'

'Both,' said Ann tersely. Seeing her sister Sophie talking animatedly with Dr Carlo di Angelo did not cheer her. Too good-looking for his own good, thought Ann, who had always been afraid of Carlo. Professor of gynaecology at a huge Italian teaching hospital, he was as well known for his gentleness and charm as he was for his very Italian good looks but to Ann he was first and foremost a close friend of Rafaelle de Nardis. Try as she might, she could not relax in his company.

'Ann,' said Sophie too brightly. 'You remember Carlo? He has time only for *antipasti* and then he must go.'

'Signora,' said Carlo and took Ann's hand. For a horrible moment Ann thought he was about to raise it to his lips but he merely bowed over it and released it. To the overwrought Ann it looked as if his eyes were twinkling with suppressed amusement.

How dare he laugh at me? Ann was not having a good day. He knew, of course. He had to know; those two had no secrets from each other. She would be civilised. 'Is your wife here, Doctor? Everyone tells me how very beautiful she is.'

'Thank you and no. Josefina is at home with our children.'

'They have two, Ann, like you, and Josefina just gets more beautiful, or is that just a doting husband talking, Carlo?'

'You'll excuse me, I'm sure,' said Ann stiffly. 'I think Mother needs help.'

'What did I say this time?' asked Sophie, watching her sister's departing back in its too tight, unflattering teal crêpe dress. Why so old maidy? Even Judith is trendier.

Carlo laughed gently and took her hand. 'You haven't changed a bit, Sophie. *Carissima,* you told a lady who is becoming, shall we say, nicely rounded, that other women can have babies and stay slim.'

She looked at him and laughed. Then she sobered. 'I hope I have changed, *amico.*'

'Ah, don't *cara.* You are you and . . . we wouldn't want it any other way.'

We. Who was we? She looked up into his gentle eyes. 'I have stopped trying to please everybody all the time.'

'Good, because to do so is impossible. Have some wine.' He handed her a glass from a tray on the table and signalled to a waiter. '*Acqua minerale, per favore.* Sophie, Raffaele is playing at the Verona Festival.'

She looked up at him quickly. 'What's that to me, Carlo? Do you remember when all four of us went to the opera there? How grumpy Rafael was. "I prefer music without singing." Do you remember?'

'He was teasing, *cara.*'

'I thought he meant it.' They had been married two years and she had thought she knew him but she had known nothing about him at all, nothing that was important.

'He is living some of the summer in the *castello.* His mother and Paolo and his family are there too, for the vacation.'

'I hope they all have a lovely time,' said Sophie lightly. 'We must mingle, Carlo. There's Lucy, the bridesmaid, and her dippy old uncle. Blast, I've put him beside Josefina and she's not here. Why did I think she was coming? Now the entire table is out and Mother can't take much more trauma.'

'Trauma. Can I help?'

'It's not medical, *amico*.' How much should she tell him? 'She lost her hat.'

'Ah, I understand, but Josefina has a hundred hats. I say, "*Carissima*, how many heads do you have?" but she laughs and buys yet another hat and surely at least one of them must be perfect for your mother.'

'You are the world's nicest man, Carlo di Angelo, but I found it.'

'Sophie . . .'

'I must mingle, Carlo.'

He bowed, a gesture only an Italian could get away with. It was more an inclination of the head than a bow but it managed to convey respect, understanding.

Stephanie waylaid her. 'Sophie, we must have lunch.' She gripped Sophie's forearms and held her as if she were examining a painting she was thinking of buying. 'Darling, that dress is fabulous. Italian, I'm sure.'

Sophie said nothing and Stephanie let go and stepped back, a slight flush staining her cheeks. 'I'm dying to hear everything. You're the same but different and pale green is great with your eyes. Pity dear Ann decided on such a strong colour and what on earth did she do to her hair?'

'Best find your place, Stephanie. Will you excuse me, I must see Zoë.'

Stephanie, who lived on the same mountain road, was of her mother's generation and Sophie saw no reason for a private tête-à-tête with her; girls together, I don't think. No doubt Kathryn had told her as much of Sophie's life history as she wanted her to know. Neither did she need to know that a dressmaker in Edinburgh had made the simple cotton dress. No designer labels. Those days were gone and not at all missed.

The restaurant was beautiful and very un-Italian. The lighting was subdued although every good Italian prefers to be able to see what he is eating. The décor was minimalist. No paintings adorned the white walls, but in recesses pinpoint lighting showed artwork that could best be described as abstract. There was nary a piece of statuary in sight, no trailing vines nor Chianti bottles in straw flasks. It was clean and bold and airy and could have been in London or New York. Sophie loved it. She told Giovanni so.

'But of course,' he agreed smugly. 'Obtrusive décor detracts from the food. My cooking is everything.'

She winced 'His music is everything, stupid child.' She managed to smile. 'You geniuses are all the same, Giovanni. Colossal ego.'

He kissed her loudly. 'But of course. Without it we cannot survive. Now the flowers? You like the flowers? I talk your mother and father and the little Zoë and then I must return in kitchen or everything will be shit, you understand.' He took her hand and she was pulled with him to the group that included most of her family. Zoë, stunning in a pale blue trouser suit, was ecstatically happy and Sophie relaxed and gave herself up to sharing her sister's joy.

No one paid the slightest attention to her carefully worked out place cards.

'Ann said it didn't really matter except for the head table,' said Harry Forsythe, 'and so I waited for you.'

Did she indeed? 'That will be nice, Harry.' Sophie tried to smile and then managed easily, for Harry had made an effort and was wearing a lightweight summer suit that hung well on his rangy physique. She was pleased that he had waited for her but stung by Ann's careless dismissal of her efforts.

'Your family is very Italian in their love of being together.'

If he only knew. 'It's a wedding, an excuse to party.'

He smiled and he really had a very warm smile. 'You needed such an excuse, Sophie, to come back.' He saw her withdraw herself. 'I'm sorry, none of my business but I couldn't help wondering about this mysterious big sister who never appeared at family gatherings.'

'An exaggeration,' said Sophie calmly. 'I see my family several times a year' – and that was her exaggeration – 'just not in Tuscany. Now we should find places.'

They had, in fact, to sit at different tables, but Carlo had remembered his promise and was sitting beside Lucy's uncle. He smiled and raised his glass of water as she passed. Cousin David, already a little parboiled by the Italian sun, was sitting in solitary state. He looked as if he had mistaken the lunch for a bankers' boardroom, and she sighed, glued a smile from ear to ear, and sat down beside his immaculately creased double-breasted suit. She decided not to see whether or not he was wearing a vest. 'Cousin David, how lovely to see you.'

He believed her: that was one of his greatest faults. 'According to the table plans I'm supposed to be sitting over there.'

'Never mind. Look, we're closest to the kitchens; we'll be served first.'

'I'm not fond of Italian food. I'm only here because it's family. Why couldn't Zoë get herself married in a nice little English church? You would think one Italian disaster in the family would be enough but would she listen to me.'

'She's not marrying an Italian.'

'Exactly,' he said triumphantly. 'So why is she not getting married at home?' He pointed towards the head table. 'His poor mother obviously can't take the heat.'

Sophie looked over at Maude who was indeed as rosy as her cotton jacket. 'That's happiness together with wine at lunch; she's having a wonderful time.'

The waiter showed them a tray of *antipasti*. Sophie helped herself lavishly. 'You ought to try some, David.'

He sniffed and liked none of the enticing smells that came his way. 'I shall drive back with your mother and have a sandwich.'

Sophie counted to ten and then on to twelve. 'Try the cheese. Did you and Judith have a pleasant flight?'

'Doing anything with that woman is a penance.' He sipped his glass of wine and then washed that down with some water. 'Look at that boy.' He gestured with his wine glass towards the beaming Jim who saw him and waved back. 'What a way to start a marriage. He should have put his foot down.'

Sophie waved back to Jim. She saw his eyes shining with love for Zoë. She glanced at her sister and looked away quickly, almost embarrassed by the love in the girl's eyes. Next to Jim was Kathryn, recovered from the trauma of misplacing her hat, and next to Zoë was Maude. 'Jim's coming over, David. Don't say a word.'

'Hello, Mr Walker. It's lovely to meet you. Zoë's told me so much about you.'

'Has she told you I hate Italian food?'

'No, sir.' The smile went out of Jim's eyes and, for a moment, he looked ill at ease and embarrassed.

Sophie stood up and took his arm. 'Cousin David is such an old tease, Jim. Come and meet Carlo.'

True to his commitment to stay only for an *antipasto*, Carlo was leaving the restaurant; she hurried after him. 'I didn't want to disturb your tête-à-tête, *cara*,' he said, but he was laughing.

Sophie introduced the two men and explained why Carlo was leaving. 'Thank you for taking on Lucy's uncle, Carlo. I promise you will have neither the lush nor my charming cousin David at the wedding.'

'But of course I will; they will flock to Josefina. Shall I bring a sword?'

'A sharp scalpel might be nice.'

'They're unhappy, *cara*.' He bent down and kissed her cheek. 'Don't become hard, *carissima*.' He shook Jim's hand. 'You're a lucky man. *A domani*. See you tomorrow.'

They stood at the entrance watching as Carlo hurried effortlessly across the parking lot, took time to press a note into the hand of the attendant, said a few words, opened his car and slid gracefully behind the wheel. They waited while he drove out of the car park. He did not acknowledge them there in the doorway. Was his mind already busy with his next patient or was he thinking of his wife, his children? Had he told Rafael that he had seen Sophie? Did it matter?

She sighed.

'Hey, Sophie. Why the big sigh? He's nice; great suit. Is he a close friend?'

'He was – a long time ago. Don't worry about David, Jim.'

Jim laughed. 'I said Zoë had told me all about him. I was telling the truth.'

'He's a miserable old so-and-so, but you'll only have to tolerate him once or twice a year.'

'Not in Australia, I won't.'

'*Cara*. I thought you left without say goodbye.' Giovanni was there. He leaned closer to her. 'Your cousin, David, is not a happy bunny.'

Sophie waited till Jim was out of earshot. 'He's a selfish old bore, actually. This is absolutely fabulous, Giovanni.'

He shrugged. *Davvero*, of course: he did not need to be told. 'I go for the cake.'

Wondering what her welcome would be, Sophie walked over to the head table where Cousin David was now sitting since Archie had moved to sit with his grandsons.

As she approached, David stood up. 'Excuse me. I feel a little stronger now, Kathryn and would be pleased if someone felt able to drive me back to my hotel.'

Kathryn looked wildly around.

'You can't leave yet unless you take a taxi,' said Sophie. 'Giovanni has gone to a great deal of trouble though and will be hurt if half the guests leave before dessert.'

'I can't eat cake; it's too rich.'

'Well, I'm sorry about that but, frankly, if you hate Italian food so much, why did you bother to come?'

'I'll take you back, David.' Archie was there. David, after all, was his cousin. 'Stop worrying, Kathryn, this is all pre-wedding nerves.'

'Sophie isn't getting married, or David.'

Archie totally ignored his daughter. 'Save me some cake and I'll have it with my coffee.'

'Where on earth are Archie and David going?'

Kathryn sat down shakily. 'It's nothing, Judith. Sophie annoyed poor David, and he's going back to his hotel.'

Judith sat down. 'Silly man; he's far too hot and he will not dress for the temperature but it was stupid to cross him, Sophie. He's very wealthy, you know.'

'And that gives him carte blanche to be hateful to everyone? He'll come to the wedding and if he doesn't find a way to take it with him he'll leave Zoë a fortune and everyone will be blissfully happy. Oh, look.' She stood up and began to applaud, and hearing her the other guests stopped chattering and looked up. Giovanni had returned to the dining room carrying a huge tray with a beautifully decorated cake on it. It was the most exquisite creation of fresh fruit and cream with little figures to represent the bride and groom. Everything was forgotten as cameras were whipped into action.

'Pretty nice, huh, Zoë honey,' said Giovanni. 'Come and cut it, baby doll.'

'I'm so glad you came to Italy, Sophie,' Zoë said much later as the family was leaving the restaurant. 'And I hope you really enjoy my wedding day.'

'Of course I will. I shall be cheering more loudly than anyone – well, except the boys,' she added as the twins shot exuberantly past them and were caught by their father and their grandmother.

'Sophie . . .' She stopped.

'What?'

'Oh, it's nothing, except sometimes I think of that ghastly year and wonder . . .' Her blue eyes were troubled. 'I wish . . .' If she had intended to say more she changed her mind. 'Please enjoy the wedding, no bad vibes.'

'Bad vibes? Oh, silly girl, because it's in Italy. I'm glad you forced me to come back,' she said and she almost meant it. 'I was always happy here and then there's Carlo, and Giovanni. I've missed them.'

'I remember every minute of your wedding day. You were so beautiful and Rafael gave me this ring.' She pointed to the gold ring that hung on a slender chain around her slim neck. 'He said he really loved me best but just couldn't wait any longer for a wife. He was so sweet, wasn't he?' She saw her sister's stricken face. 'Oh, Sophie, I'm sorry.'

'Don't be silly, little goose. I would never have married him if he wasn't sweet, now, would I? Go, Maude and Penny are waiting, and, more importantly, Jim. He is as nice as you said he was. I'll see you at home.'

She walked to the car park with Harry, chatting lightly about the food and the restaurant and the guests – most of them. At last, with a promise to see each other later, he drove away and she sat for a few minutes in her own car. Her wedding day? Zoë remembered it. Oh, so do I. She remembered her fear and excitement and anticipation as she woke up and prepared for the happiest day of her life. She remembered her gown, designed by one of Italy's leading fashion houses but paid for by her father.

'If I can't pay for the reception, sweetheart, I can at least pay for your dress.'

She remembered the heaviness of the lace de Nardis veil which had made it difficult to see Rafael at the altar rails and she remembered her feeling of blind panic. He hadn't come. It was all a dream. But no, through the lace and her tears she had seen him and he had taken her hand and nothing had mattered. Rafael loved her. Nothing else mattered. But he had not loved her enough and she, had she loved him too much?

'Something wrong, signorina?' It was the car park attendant.

'*Zanzare*,' she said. 'These blasted mosquitoes,' and gave him a tip.

'*Troppo gentile, troppo gentile*, too kind, too kind.' He bobbed up and down outside her window. She started the engine and drove away.

She cleared her mind of memory and filled it with the views, the valleys, the foothills, the peaks and the majesty of the mountains. How could anything unpleasant happen here, this perfection asked, but just outside the *trattoria* in Gabbiana was the memorial plaque and this time she wound down the window to read that it commemorated the lives and deaths of students caught up in the senseless tit-for-tat killings of the Second World War. Almost every town and village had such a plaque.

This was real. This was more important than solipsistic relatives and her relatively small unhappiness. Had David fought in the last war? It was probable; he had not always been a bad-tempered, fussy, old man. She would try again to be kinder and more understanding. It was Zoë's great day and nothing should spoil it for her.

6

They waited all day. What else could they do; they were children. At five o'clock Gabriella put on her best coat, her hat and her gloves and walked into Aulla. She went to her own home and demanded to see the general.

'Go home, little girl, before you find yourself in trouble.'

She was fourteen years old. She lifted her head proudly and looked straight into the eyes of the insolent soldier. 'I am not a little girl. I am Gabriella Brancaccio-Vallefredda. This is my father's house and I demand to see the general.'

It took twenty minutes and three different soldiers, each one more senior than the last, and including one who tried to manhandle her from the steps, but at last she was shown into her own father's study. The German general was seated at her father's desk, and through the windows behind his head Gabriella could see the gardens. They had not changed; surely they should look different, unloved, neglected, but they were beautiful, as if her father still walked there every day.

The general stood up. 'Signorina, I am sorry if you were subjected to any . . . unpleasantness, but I wish you had not come. I would have sent a message when I had news.'

'My father? Your host, General. I want to know why he was taken away and when he will return.'

'A matter of a few questions, signorina, that is all. Please don't be concerned. There are . . . adjustments to be made, and it is regretted that perhaps your father does not co-operate, as he should. We are on the same side,' he finished almost despairingly.

'Is he being held here, in his own house?'

'He is being questioned, signorina. That is all I am at liberty to say.'

She refused to sit down; she refused his offer of refreshment. She *refused to be driven back to their little house in one of his cars. She walked there through the dust with her head held high and only when she was outside the town did she allow the tears to fall.*

Her brother was waiting.

'He says it is nothing; we must wait.'

They waited for years. Their father died in a camp in Poland in 1944.

Gabriella lay still for a moment and mentally examined her body. 'Good, I am in charge today.'

Slowing down was to be expected of course. To everything there is a season and unfortunately for her it was the season for stiffness and little aches and pains. But today, there was nothing. She smiled slowly and stretched in the great carved oak bed like a girl expecting her lover. But there was no lover. Mario had been dead for thirty years and she had never looked at another man. She dismissed all the other men she had known as mere shadows of her husband; it was wrong to adore anyone but God and so she sinned, for she had adored Mario and since his death she had adored Raffaele, her beautiful baby with the face and the talent of an angel. She loved Paolo, her older son, too; such a thing does not need to be said. He was her son, Mario's heir, and sometimes, by candlelight at the dinner table, she could swear it was Mario himself sitting there, the same classic profile, the same quiet smile. Paolo had done nothing in his entire life to displease her. He had married the correct woman, had fathered two perfect children, daughters, but, in this age of enlightenment when no one had to use his sword to defend his acres, what did that matter?

Gabriella smiled again thinking of the picture-postcard perfect family. She loved them, but she did not commit sin. She did not adore. Adoration was reserved for Raffaele. And he, her angel, was coming today. Every summer she opened the *castello*. Yes, legally, it belonged to Paolo, but he would not presume to make decisions until she had gone to join his father. The contessa decided when the *castello* was to open and she opened it because, and only because, it was Raffaele's favourite home, the sanctuary to which he could escape when the pressure of his insane lifestyle threatened to smother him, or, to be prosaically boring and honest, and she was always honest with herself, these days it was when he was playing in Verona or Milan. The medieval count who had commissioned the building of this great impregnable edifice had not dreamed that one day a descendant, the greatest pianist of the twentieth century – mothers are never modest, and who is to say that history would not agree with her – would love to relax there, safe from the claims of the world.

Every summer, therefore, the contessa opened the *castello* and every summer for the past five years Raffaele had smiled his singularly sweet smile – and stayed in his apartment in Milan. But this year her prayers had been answered, proving that the Virgin was not furious that the contessa adored her son but, being a mother, sympathised. Raffaele was coming home while he played three concerts at the Verona Festival. Today he was arriving with his entourage but she could handle them. The only danger ever had been that girl and again she had been proved right. Sophie had not been the woman for her son. He needed someone cultured, sophisticated, from his own class, someone who appreciated and understood the demands that the world and his own genius made on him. Someone, for example, like Ileana.

She tugged the ornate bell pull beside her bed and when her maid came ordered breakfast. 'Orange juice, freshly squeezed, two figs, toast with honey and coffee.' She did not need to say what kind of coffee. The genius in the kitchen had been making it the same way for over fifty years.

Paolo will have to shoot us both soon, like old horses; put us out of our misery.

But today there was no misery, none of those funny little pains that proved, despite what the mirror said, that she was getting old. She rose from her bed, wrapped herself in the froth of lace and silk that its own creator had wept did not do justice to her beauty, and went to the window. To give her credit she did not dwell on her appearance, she merely accepted it as she accepted

– eventually – that Mario had been taken from her. Some things, though, she did not, could not, would not accept. Her childhood home. That villa with her father's beautiful gardens, gone, bombed into nothingness by the English. Ludovico's death, his murder; there, say it, his murder. The shadows drifted in to darken the room and she fought with them but there they were, some German, some English. She saw them, heard their voices, heard their laughter. Gabriella took a deep breath. She had promised Mario that she would not dwell on Ludovico's death.

Mario, Mario. Had she had more children, and no doubt, since Mario was lusty and she adored him, she could well have had several, she might not have had time to recognise Raffaele's genius. At the thought her heart skipped a beat. *Che disastro.* What a disaster. You see, God gives and he takes away. He gave her Mario and took him away so that she could devote her time to Raffaele.

She opened the window, tore up her toast and threw it outside on to the mountainside. Perhaps there were still some little birds there that might enjoy it and Portofino would be happy believing that she had eaten the toast. Portofino, what a name for a man. No doubt his parents had been happy there. Gabriella sighed. As Mario and I were here with our two beautiful babies. As I will be again, for Raffaele comes today.

She pulled the bell again. 'Marisa, Marisa, quickly. The maestro comes today. I must make sure that everything is perfect.'

All day she worked on menus, on flowers, on invitations. A dinner party the day after each concert, a reception in Verona on the night of each performance.

'Has Cesare moved the maestro into his old rooms?'

'Of course, Contessa. We have had his old rooms ready for years.' Marisa was as old as her mistress and almost as slender, but her face was the rounder, heavier face that betrayed her peasant origins. She had trained herself to think almost as the countess thought and to dress and sit so unobtrusively that she could remain in a room unobserved. Useful skills for a trusted servant.

'Remember, Marisa. He spent his honeymoon here. *Che disastro.* There must be nothing to remind him.'

There was nothing physical. She had never framed any photographs of her so unsuitable daughter-in-law, had never had her portrait painted to hang in the gallery with all the other wives. He had not noticed, so involved was he in his music, or he simply had not cared.

I was right, so right. Some faults could be borne. Are we not all with faults of one kind or another? Her lack of breeding, her paucity of education – thus she dismissed St Andrews University – superficial knowledge of music, literature, art. But her blood? 'She's English, Mamma.' I can hear his beautiful voice still in my heart. How could he, how could he bring one of the despised English into our home? Is it not enough that they buy up our villages and stagger around drunk and half naked in the streets? No, Gabriella, you exaggerate. Did Mario not scold you for this failing? She is gone and he comes today.

His favourite food. So difficult but no, she would not permit herself to believe that Raffaele was not easy. He was so involved with his music that he never said that he could not survive without Mamma's *fagioli all'uccelletto*, her special bean stew, or her *verzolini della vigilia*, the stuffed cabbage leaves that were served every Christmas Eve in the *castello* whether the family were there or not. It was not that Gabriella cooked for her sons but, like all good Italian housewives, she was there, ordering and supervising. Of course Raffaele loved these dishes and many others. He just did not say so. And why should he? Raffaele was a musician. His head was full of nothing but music. But he would still appreciate *soffiato di gamberi*, or would he?'

'Marisa, does the maestro prefer shrimps? Or should we have scallops rather than shrimps? *Capesante alla Veneziana*, yes.'

'Whatever you say, Contessa,' said Marisa with a smile. She had known the maestro since he was a baby, had spent more hours with him than his mamma, although she would die before she told anyone this, and knew that unless the scallop served in the Venetian style, very simply with best quality olive oil or the shrimp, souffléd perfectly with the freshest of fresh eggs, were to jump out of the plate and bite his beautiful aristocratic nose, Raffaele de Nardis would not notice. He ate to live; he did not live to eat. If all his senses had been heightened when the little English miss had been sharing his bed so that he had spoken seriously and knowledgeably in the kitchens about the delights he wanted to share with his wife, Marisa would not say. She loved Raffaele; he had her heart, but *la contessa* had her loyalty.

'I saw the little English miss in Licciana Nardi today, Contessa.'

Gabriella's heart flip-flopped painfully in her chest and she put up a thin hand to steady it. Had Marisa, as was possible, been reading her mind? 'What English miss, Marisa?' she asked lightly so that anyone who had known her less well than her maid would have been fooled by her insouciance. 'Tuscany sinks under the weight of them in the summer months.'

'The little Zoë. She is to marry in the square.'

'These heathens,' answered the contessa and would not allow herself to think for a second that Zoë whatever her name was's wedding could have anything to do with her son's return to the home of his birth. It was coincidence, coincidence that Raffaele should agree to return to the arena in Verona in the same month that the English girl was to marry in the square.

At least Sophie had had the decency to marry in the church, here in the chapel of Raffaele's ancestral home. She could not be made to accept his religion as she accepted everything else but at least she had acquiesced and the wedding had been . . . tolerable. The divorce, despite the fact that nothing so humiliating or disgraceful had ever happened in this family, had also been – almost – satisfactory although Raffaele sometimes used his Catholicism as a stick with which to beat his mother.

'I am a Catholic, Mamma. The church acknowledges Sophie as my wife.'

'She was your wife.'

'In the eyes of God, she still is.'

She ached to say that God would welcome a suitable wife and that it could be arranged, given time and words in the right place but she hesitated. She took consolation in the awareness that Raffaele did not live like a monk. One day one of these women would attract more than his sexual appetite and then, oh then, of course she would welcome the right wife. Raffaele was like his father. He needed a wife and it was his mother's duty not to stand in his way. The right wife would find her mother-in-law the most amenable of women.

Ileana Raisa. Such a pity that she was Hungarian but the blood was right. Her aristocratic bloodline went further back than the de Nardis line and, too, she was a musician, a singer. She understood the life. She would never sit sulking in a hotel room while her husband rehearsed for hours before a concert or stayed afterwards practising because he had seen a flaw in his performance. (An imaginary flaw, of course.)

'Where has Cesare put Miss Raisa?'

'The yellow rooms, Contessa,' said Marisa, mentioning the best suite of guest rooms usually reserved for visiting dignitaries and once used by a royal princess.

'I've changed my mind. Too obvious, don't you agree?' The contessa sank down on to her chaise-longue. 'This is all so exhausting, Marisa. Ask Portofino to make me some tea and ask Cesare to put flowers in the blue room. Contessa Beatrice should be in the yellow rooms.'

But at last, at last she could do no more and she stood in a deceptively simple lilac evening dress at the windows that looked down on the driveway. From this window countless wives and possibly several mistresses had watched for the return of husbands and lovers.

'Domenico has opened the gates, Contessa.' Marisa was as excited as her mistress and being only a maid was allowed to show her emotion.

Gabriella said nothing although she was praying. Raffaele had to be first. She had to have a day, even an hour, with her baby before the world pushed in. She saw two cars. Raffaele? The Hungarian girl perhaps? Oh, God, the blue rooms were miles from Raffaele's rooms but too late to change that now. Think positively. See, my son, I am not throwing a girl at your head.

'Mamma.' Paolo kissed her. 'How well you look. Raffaele will follow in an hour or so. He had some business in . . . Aulla.'

Gabriella decided to ignore the slight hesitation. So, he had not gone to Aulla. Where was he? She summoned up a smile and greeted her other guests, her daughter-in-law Beatrice, so elegant in deceptively simple peach silk, her grand-daughters Gabi and Mari'Angela (she would not mention how pretty they were, for they resembled her). Raffaele's German manager, Oliver Sachs, and his secretary Valentina Hewlett who was Italian but had been married to an American. The Hungarian singer was with him; that at least was positive. 'You see how it will be for you too, my darling,' she teased, linking her arm with Beatrice. 'Always the old friend is more important than the mamma. No need to wait for the naughty boy. He is so used to the world waiting, but here, he is at home. We are his family and to us he is simply our Raffaele. We will have drinks on the terrace. I will wait for you there. Girls, Portofino has made some wonderful lemonade.'

'We're going swimming, with your permission, Nonna.'

Family life. This was how it should be. With iron spine Gabriella walked to the terrace and sat down on a comfortable chair. She sat looking out over the mountains, watching smoke curling up from the valley, leaning back in her chair to see the *pecorelle*, the puffy white clouds like fat little sheep drifting towards the Alps.

'Tired, Mamma?'

She opened her eyes and sat up. The count was standing beside her chair. Thus Mario had stood, anxious, loving. 'No, dearest boy. Just preparing for your daughters. How tall and slim they are; no more little girls to sit on my lap and play with my pearls. Now they want to wear them.' She laughed and he laughed with her.

'How wonderful for us all to be here together, Mamma. It has been so long.'

'Too long, *caro*. But I have a feeling in my bones about this summer.' She leaned forward and took his hand. 'This girl, this singer; tell me about her.'

'What can I tell you, Mamma, that Raffaele or the papers have not told you already? He met her in Rio de Janeiro at a concert. She is a mezzo, one of the best of the new singers.'

'I know all this,' she said impatiently. 'Is he in love with her?'

'He's sleeping with her, Mamma. Is that what you want to know? Love, I don't know. When has Raffaele ever loved anyone . . .' He stopped, trying to interpret the expression on her face.

'Don't mention her name, Paolo.'

The count shrugged. 'I was going to say as much as he loves music.' He stood up and smiled as the terrace doors opened. 'Here is Beatrice. Are the girls in the pool, *cara*?'

'No, they have gone to the kitchens to see Portofino. Cupboard love. They are hoping he will make *suspirus*.'

'He has probably prepared all their favourites, Beatrice. Come and sit down beside me and tell me everything that is happening in Rome. Who made that divine dress, Valentino?'

The family members were left diplomatically alone on the terrace or perhaps the pianist's staff had things to do to prepare for the maestro's summer in Verona. The children had invaded the kitchens and found that indeed the cake tins were full of 'little sighs' and they had then gone to work off the calories by swimming in the pool on the top terrace. And still Raffaele did not arrive.

'We will have dinner,' announced the contessa at nine o'clock. 'The children cannot be expected to wait any longer.'

She led the way from the terrace to the great dining room on the second floor of the castle but they had just been seated when the very dignified Cesare announced that Signor Raffaele and the Signorina Raisa were in their rooms changing.

'For Miss Raisa we will wait, children,' said the contessa,

'because she is our guest and because she is not responsible for Uncle Raffaele's bad manners.'

They sat silently and the contessa sat at the head of the table where by right Beatrice should have been sitting and she bowed her head as if in prayer. And she was praying – that Raffaele would not see the pleasure in her eyes that the sight and smell and feel of him, her beloved boy, would bring. He is very selfish and I will not forgive him at once. Carlo di Angelo should have been made to wait, not his mother.

A few minutes later she began to laugh as not Raffaele but the passionate full-bodied sound of a genius playing Brahms' 'Hungarian Dance' swept into the room. 'What a bad boy he is,' she said as she rose to go to the music room. 'This, I suppose, is the concert pianist's equivalent of throwing his hat in first to see if he is welcome.'

Raffaele looked up from the keyboard as the family party, led by his mother, swept into the room. He allowed his nieces to throw themselves into his arms and he held them between his body and his mother as he smiled wickedly at her. 'Are we allowed to eat, Mamma, or must I ask Portofino for bread and milk in my room?'

The contessa ignored him and went, with outstretched hands, to Ileana. 'My dear, you are very welcome in our home.' She linked her arm into Ileana's and led her back into the dining room. 'You must not encourage my wicked son to forget his manners. Beatrice, my dear, sit in my place. I do not forgive Raffaele and will sit beside Paolo. There, my dear – she took Ileana to the bottom of the table and gestured to the chair on the count's right hand – 'now he is too far away to see how very pretty you are.'

'But I have two beautiful women here, Mamma,' said Raffaele as he waited behind each chair for his nieces to seat themselves. 'And so I am very content.'

7

On the morning of Zoë's wedding Sophie woke long before the church bells began to ring. If she had time, if this were a lazy, I'm on-holiday morning, she would make some coffee, open the shutters, get back in bed and listen to Italy waking up. But it was her sister's wedding day and she had promised to drive over to her parents' house to help, whatever that meant. Still, it was so early that a few minutes watching the mountains push their craggy tops out of the pink clouds would not hurt. Instant coffee, still better than that made by the twins . . . not nearly so good as . . .

Fine, Sophie. Say, instant coffee is good but not nearly so good as the coffee made by Raffaele de Nardis. There, that didn't hurt a bit. Rafael made wonderful coffee. It was the only thing he could make. He never made it in Tuscany, of course. That funny old man, or, that old man with the funny name, Portofino, made it and carried it to their beautiful bedroom in the west tower. They would wait till he had stalked majestically away and then they would hurry out on to the little terrace where medieval de Nardises had watched for the enemy, had fired arrows at the enemy, had poured oil on the enemy, the little terrace that Rafael had had turned into a tiny little garden where in the mornings they drank coffee while they watched the world wake and where at night they lay in each other's arms. Rafael made coffee for her in their apartment in New York, in their little house in London, or in the apartments they rented in Los Angeles, in Paris. He hated hotels whereas Sophie had found them exciting.

'You will get bored too,' he said. 'Much better an apartment where you can walk in your bare feet to the kitchen to make coffee.'

He began every day with the salute to the sun, a yoga exercise. 'It keeps me supple,' he explained, 'and it makes my mind and body ready for the day ahead.' He tried to teach her but she preferred to watch him. He did not behave as if he knew that he was beautiful. Of course he knew. It did not matter to him; he looked as the men in his family had looked since they had fought the Etruscans over this fertile piece of land.

She did not believe that she had fallen in love with his face. Had she fallen in love with him the first time they met or was it when she had first heard him play, or had it just grown until one day she had known with primeval wisdom that she loved Rafael and would love him till the day she died? He hoped it was not when she heard him first, when she sat in the balcony at the Usher Hall in Edinburgh and heard Raffaele de Nardis play Mozart's Piano Concerto Number 24 in C Minor, whatever that meant. Later she learned why it was important to him.

'Too many women think they are in love with me. They are in love with an illusion, with the feelings that this beautiful music gives them, not with a man who is selfish and self-centred and so bad-tempered when he doesn't get enough sleep. I do not help little old ladies across busy streets. I doubt that I would even see one – unless it was my mother, and she is not an old lady. She is the Contessa de Nardis. I spend most of my time inside my head, listening for my mistakes.'

Sophie remembered the year her parents decided to buy a house in Lunigiana.

'The area is really part of Tuscany,' her father wrote to her at school. 'It's the bit that sticks up like a naughty finger and it's full of Etruscan remains, and stones carved by the Luni, an Etruscan people.'

She remembered the excitement when they had been digging out a pool and a stele, a stone, had been unearthed. The curator in the nearby town of Pontremoli had decided it was one of the oldest in existence, dating from about 2000 BC, and that it resembled the goddess of wisdom, Minerva. The family had gone in triumph to see their stone taking its place beside its sisters in the museum and had named their villa Minerva.

Too much time wasted. Sophie showered and dressed in a suit she had bought in Edinburgh for the wedding: nothing remotely Italian about it, or was there, in the subtlety of the cut, the draping of the pale lemon silk, the elegance of the little jacket she could slip on over the sleeveless top if the evening were cold? She hurried out. Even on a day as important as this her father would have gone to the baker for bread, and the coffee and bread would be on the terrace. So were the twins. Sophie managed to persuade them not to jump into the pool and ruin their suits.

'If I look as sad as he looks,' lamented Peter, 'it's very bad.'

'You look like boys dressed by their mother for a family wedding,' said Sophie diplomatically. 'Everyone will understand and sympathise and then, after the wedding, you need never wear them again,' she finished hopefully. The satin sailor suits had obviously been made to measure and were extremely expensive and – to give Ann credit – the boys looked great if slightly archaic.

'I like your suit,' said Peter. 'Mum looks like a birthday cake.'

'With cream oozing out all over,' giggled Danny.

Sophie looked at them. What horrors they were. 'Sit down and stay clean or you will never come to my villa or' – she fixed them with a threatening gaze – 'my house in Edinburgh.'

That did it. They subsided on chairs and pretended to be asleep. Maybe they would stay like that till the cars arrived. Zoë, looking adorable and very, very young, sat at the table in the living room while Claudio and his sister fitted the tiny coronet into her hair.

'*Salve, signora,*' said Claudio. 'We have finish the mamma and she looks great. I can't do nothing with Ann; the hair has to grow out.'

'Jim would fall in love all over again if he could see you now,' said Sophie to her young sister as she edged past them.

Zoë opened her eyes and looked up. 'I'm wearing a sheet.'

'Stunning.'

'Oh, Sophie, you look lovely, sweetheart. I always like you in yellow. Can you take some pictures of the twins against my arch while I make some more coffee?' Her father, still in old shorts, had come out of the main bedroom with a camera.

'Yellow? Daddy, yellow is egg yolk. Sophie's suit is lemon and look at her perfectly wonderful hat.'

Sophie looked at her father. 'Daddy?' He would never be ready.

He shrugged. 'I can't go without the bride. Your mother's ready. Your sister's having a tantrum and I spent a fortune on that arch and I can't depend on that damned Italian to take a picture of it.'

Avoiding Claudio's eyes Sophie took the camera and went outside again and there she saw the arch she had been too occupied to see before. It was well worth a photograph. Over the stone archway of the imposing front entrance were generous garlands of fresh greenery. Nestling among the greens were perfect white rosebuds tied on with white silk ribbon.

'Photo call, you two.' She gestured to the twins and reluctantly they came.

'We hate having our picture taken,' they complained as she tried to get them and the arch into the right perspective.

'Can't think why when you're so gorgeous.'

'Are we gorgeous? Mummy says Rafael was gorgeous. Men can't be gorgeous, can they?'

'Why not? Dr di Angelo is gorgeous.'

'Yuck, he's old.'

Sophie smiled, glad that they were out of their bad humour. Old? Was Carlo old? Forty or forty-one probably: the same age as Rafael. She took pictures, drank coffee with her father – still in his shorts – helped her mother arrange her hat, and tried to avoid Ann. Since her sister was refusing to come out of her bedroom this was simple.

Still glorious in her sheet, Zoë begged everyone but her parents to leave and Sophie was delighted to escape and drive to the square where the wedding was being celebrated. There was to be a civil ceremony inside the Town Hall and then another exchange of vows outside to be witnessed by the hundreds of people who seemed intent on cramming into the town square. Townspeople, too, hung death defyingly out of their windows, anxious to see what was going on, to comment loudly on the clothes, the stupidity of these foreigners crowding into the square in the hot sun, to sigh over the bridesmaids, the for-once-adorable twins, and later the bride, who elicited sighs of happiness and envy of her slim-fitting gown and her lace parasol, and most of all to send her blessings for her happiness.

Sophie hid under the huge brim of her hat and lost herself in the crowd of butterflies. No, do some of us look more like ice cream cones? She heard snatches of conversation in English, French, German and Italian.

Ma che bella, signorina. How beautiful.

'Has anyone seen Sophie? We must look after her. Must be difficult for her after all these years.'

That was Stephanie Wilcox. God, what a gossip that woman was. Sophie wondered how her mother could bear her. And it's not difficult, why should it be? She stood unnoticed and alone well away from family and friends and watched the arrival of her baby sister, looking as beautiful as any bride has ever done. Many of the cries of admiration came from elderly ladies in shapeless black dresses; they applauded the lemon or lilac silks, commiserated over linens that were already badly creased. How sweet. Zoë had chosen to wear her chain and the gold ring that Rafael had given her almost ten years before. 'That must be the something old.'

The crowds parted to let the bride and her father through and then everyone stood in the blistering Tuscan sun and listened to a young girl sing from the balcony. Sophie sheltered under her hat and caught a glimpse of Ann, oh poor Ann. Why had she chosen to wear pink? Ann had poured herself into a perfectly simple, well-cut linen dress. Unfortunately it was a size too small – or was Ann now a size too large – and it was already wrinkled.

Her round face was even pinker than the dress and her hair was damp and curling in the heat.

Five years ago I could have said, 'Ann, everyone thinks your blue is so perfect on you,' and she might have changed her dress. She likes to be coaxed. Has George stopped cajoling?

Judith and Stephanie Wilcox and her husband, Charles the Insignificant, were standing together, handkerchiefs at the ready. Judith tried to catch Sophie's eye but she was thankful that she was still wearing dark glasses and so could ignore them without appearing rude. There was polite but not enthusiastic clapping for the singer on the balcony and then, at last, the bride and groom appeared with the bridal party and took their place of honour in the centre of the square.

There was complete silence as the official ceremony began and was translated into English for the benefit of those who did not speak Italian. The whole square strained to hear, to see the beauty of the young lovers. What was that stir? The bride was there, young, beautiful, so much in love. Why should there now be a stir? Whispering. Who was whispering? Why? So someone was late. This was Italy. Someone was always late. Big deal. Judith was making frantic hand motions that Sophie could not understand and chose to ignore. I'm perfectly fine over here. Why should I join family members I don't really like?

At last the whispering stopped. There was silence. Then Sophie heard a gasp, and then . . . music. Glorious music was pouring out of the piano that was up on the balcony. Bach: Jesu, Joy of Man's Desiring, played as it should be played. How did they get that piano up there, she thought, because she did not want to think about the quality of the sound. Oh, God, no. They wouldn't do that to me. Sophie refused to look up to confirm her suspicions but she knew. She refused to look across the square at Judith and Stephanie. It could only be Rafael. You're being stupid, Sophie. There are hundreds of good pianists and Daddy has hired one to play at his daughter's wedding. She bowed her head but quickly lifted it again. No one should know of her shock. Just as no one except Carlo knew of her greatest sorrow, no one should know what her family's treachery was costing her now.

'The entertainer.' That was what he called himself disparagingly. 'Put some money in his hat and the entertainer will entertain.' How he had loathed it when hostesses had expected him to play after a dinner or a lunch. 'They invite an author; they ask him to write them a book? They ask a painter. Does he paint a picture before he can go home? No, but a musician!' Sophie recalled one ghastly dinner when the hostess had asked if 'you'll give us a little tune.' A little tune. Raffaele de Nardis.

'You cannot possibly afford me.'

She shuddered standing there in the hot sun in the middle of the square as the piano and Rafael's coldly furious voice played duets in her head. For those he loved, of course, he played at any time. That was why he was here. He loved Zoë, had even given her some lessons but she had no talent and less willingness to practise. But why did no one tell me? And why is his name not on the lists? I'll never forgive my mother for this, never.

She wanted to turn and leave the square, turn and run and hide. But she had been running and hiding for five years and it was time to stand. She felt a bubble of hysterical laughter swelling up inside her. She had almost said, stand and face the music. Grimly she looked straight ahead at Zoë's glowing face as she promised to love, honour and obey the, for once, so serious young Jim. She would not let her eyes stray to the right where her mother was standing, tears streaming happily down her cheeks. Sophie could not see the tears but she knew they would be there. Kathryn always cried at weddings and this was the wedding of her baby. She had cried ten years before as they had stood in the chapel at the *castello* when Sophie had promised to love, honour and obey Rafael.

'And I did, I did,' her heart sobbed. 'I loved him, I honoured him and I obeyed him, but it was not enough. There was his mother and his brother and his family tradition and more than any of them, his mistress.' Oh, yes, he had been unfaithful to her, although he denied it, but that had never really mattered. It was music; music was everything to him. Sophie Winter could not possibly compete.

The music stopped and from various parts of the square came quickly stifled spontaneous bursts of applause. She could almost hear the smothered conversation. 'Don't. It's like a church; you don't clap in church.'

'But it's Raffaele de Nardis. *The* Raffaele de Nardis.'

Sophie stared grimly ahead. If she kept her eyes on the sweet little rosebuds that Zoë was carrying or concentrated on how very delicate the work in the coronet was, then she would not burst into tears.

I always cry at weddings; it's a family trait. But who would believe her? They would say, 'Oh, poor Sophie, she has never got over him.' And she had. She had. She lifted her head, if possible, even higher. She would look at him, acknowledge his genius, she would even smile. The formal part of the ceremony was over. She had been unaware of the voices translating into English, into French, into German.

'Sophie, how nice of you; that was just the sweetest gesture.' Stephanie Wilcox was in front of her, standing so close.

She looks like a horse, great wide-open mouth and big teeth. Why did I never see that before? Gesture? She thinks I brought Rafael. 'Lovely wedding, wasn't it? Zoë is absolutely stunning and so's Mum.' The voice sounded like her own. It was perfectly normal.

Stephanie looked over at Kathryn in the flowing aquamarine dress and the matching hat. 'I could kill for your mother's shape, Sophie. Does this mean . . .' She gestured to the balcony.

Sophie looked across at her mother. 'Family photographs, Stephanie. Excuse us. Aren't you coming, Aunt Judith?' She walked quickly across the square and was lost in the crowd, one bright flower in a meadow of others. The family photographs would be taken at the house. They had already decided that. Here in the ancient square there would only be photographs of the bridal party but she could make herself useful if Ann would allow it. Was Ann the traitor? No. First it would never occur to her to contact Rafael, and second she had never been at ease with him even when she was his sister-in-law. For her he was not quite human. He was a musician and they were made of different stuff.

Oh, God, suppressed laughter does sound like a snort. How awful. I hope no one heard me.

Her mother was fussing with Zoë's veil, her flowers and her pearls: anything to avoid looking at her middle daughter.

Was it you, Mother? What does it matter? I was his wife. I loved him and we fell out of love. That other ghastly business was a smokescreen. Big deal. I no longer love him and so, if he chooses to play at my sister's wedding – 'the entertainer' – what does it matter? If I still loved him, it might hurt to see him again, to be so close and not be able to touch him. But I do not love him.

> *I do not love thee, no, I do not love thee.*
> *And yet when thou are absent I am sad,*
> *And envy even the bright blue sky above thee,*
> *Whose quiet stars may see thee and be glad.*

'Sophie.' She turned. It was her father. 'Sweetheart.'

She smiled at him blindingly, reassuringly. 'What a lovely surprise, Dad.'

He looked stunned and his face, that had been so drawn when it should have been so happy, relaxed. 'You mean it wasn't . . . yes, I'm coming. I must go but if you didn't invite Rafael? I must go.'

The relief. He was not the one who had dealt her such an unkind blow. No, let's get this straight. We are divorced and I do not care where he plays. It's just that it would have been nice to have been told. Surely they didn't think I would avoid him. But I have avoided him for five years. Of course I have. We are nothing to each other.

'Sophie.' The voice behind her, the strong but gentle hand on her shoulder. Five years. If it were a hundred she would be just as aware. How to act for the audience? How to behave?

She turned and smiled into the so unusual but, oh yes, so

Italian blue eyes. 'Rafael. You surprised me. Everyone surprised me. "I don't do weddings and bar mitzvahs." ' She tried to imitate his slight accent.

He understood at once and he lifted his hand and touched her cheek, so gently, so sweetly. He would not want to hurt her. He had not loved her for a very long time but he would not wish to hurt. '*Perdona, cara. Mi dispiace.* Forgive me, dear one; I'm sorry. She said she had asked you. I am in Verona, so for her – for the child I knew.'

Such a flooding of unadulterated joy. Now she understood the odd remarks. 'Zoë asked you to play?' Oh, the relief, but of course he would do it for no one else.

'Come, I want you to meet a friend. Come, Sophie, everyone is watching us. We have given enough show, yes?'

'Of course.' She let him take her hand and tried to stop its trembling. The square seemed a mile wide. He walked as he had always walked, so close that she could feel his thigh; they were like children in a three-legged race as he automatically adjusted his long stride to match hers. Long long gone were the days when she had stumbled along trying to keep up.

'Look at Sophie and Raffaele de Nardis; they are so close. How civilised.'

A tall, blonde, elegant woman was standing in the doorway of a fourteenth-century building across the square from the Town Hall.

'Sophie, this is Ileana Raisa. Ileana, this is Sophie.'

Sophie took the hand that was held out to her. 'Miss Raisa, I heard you sing Herodias last summer. How very nice to meet you.' She was bigger than Rafael's usual women, almost statuesque. He had always liked them smaller. None of my business and I feel nothing.

'Sophie, hello. I've heard so much about you. I'm going to try Carmen, can you imagine? Raffaele says I am too much a Valkyrie.'

'But then what does he know about opera, Miss Raisa?'

'Oh please, Ileana.'

'Ileana.' Sophie turned to move away. 'It's been lovely to meet you. I shall look forward to your Carmen but now I must go. Perhaps I'll see you at the reception.'

Ileana looked questioningly at Rafael. 'I thought . . .'

'I came only to play, Sophie. Ileana and I are expected by my mother.'

And of course, what Mamma expects . . .

'How is the contessa?'

'Thank you. She is well.' He kissed her, oh, such a civilised divorce, on both cheeks.

'*Ciao, cara.*'

Ciao: till we meet again. 'Goodbye Rafael. Miss Raisa.'

She turned. She wanted to run but the square was full of people who should all have been looking at the bride but who seemed to be looking at her, analysing her feelings, her emotions.

'Sophie, beautiful wedding, wasn't it?' Who was this? She did not recognise the man, the voice. How stupid. It was Zoë's 'dishy professor'.

Had she expected his tweed jacket? Without it, in a lightweight summer suit, he still looked like a British academic. 'Harry, sorry, my mind was elsewhere. Yes, it was absolutely perfect and the loveliest bride, don't you agree?'

'Lovely. Listen, your father said that you were driving on your own.' He was removing his jacket and then his tie. 'That's better. Can I beg a lift? I left my car at the villa since parking in the town is so difficult.'

Did he know he was a lifeline? 'Of course. You may have to tolerate my nephews,' Conversation, or rather idle chatter, was easy. They walked together back across the square, stopping to greet old friends, family members.

'Sophie, Zoë is leaving. You must be in the line to see her off.' Ann managed to make everything sound an unpleasant duty but Sophie managed to smile.

'Come along, Harry. You can send them on their way too. After all, you have seen a great deal more of Zoë in the last few years than I have.'

'And young Jim. He did a year with us as part of his degree course.'

'There we are then,' said Sophie and led the way to where both families were standing watching as the newly weds climbed into their vintage car, Jim, now too without his jacket, desperately trying to bundle up yards of exquisite silk and stuff it in behind his bride. They threw confetti and in the general bustle Sophie was able to avoid too many questions. For a second she thought that her younger sister looked rather nervously at her. So she smiled and threw a kiss. Naughty girl to invite Rafael. He was standing waving too. Raffaele de Nardis, friend of the family.

Harry chatted again as they walked back to the town car park. 'That pianist was rather fine, didn't you think? The church organist, is he?'

She looked at him quickly but his face was innocent and she laughed. 'You're not a music lover then, Harry. You really didn't recognise the pianist?'

'Recognise? Should I have?'

'Raffaele de Nardis.'

'You're joking. How on earth did your parents—' he stopped, embarrassed. 'I beg your pardon.'

'You're right; they couldn't afford him but I was married to him for nearly five years, oh, a long time ago. He was very fond of Zoë. He did it for her.'

He said nothing and they drove in rather an uneasy silence. It was a perfect day. Italy is primarily a grey-blue-country, but in high summer on irrigated terraces away from the olive-blurred slopes, colours riot in voluptuous abandon. Bougainvillaea, acacias, even the strong lemon and orange colours of the fruit trees are everywhere. On the way to the villa they drove through a circus parade of colours, yellow houses with blue shutters and pink roofs side by side with pink houses or white houses with green shutters and everywhere the terracotta of churches. Sophie loved it. 'Damn it, I forgot the twins,' she said at last and that broke the ice.

Harry looked round in surprise. 'They're not abandoned are they? Should we go back?'

As if to answer him a blue Ferrari swept past them and they saw the excited faces of the twins as they waved madly to their forgetful aunt.

'Bless you, Carlo, and bless you, Josefina, for giving up your seat.'

'Ferrari or Fiat, which would you choose?' Harry asked and answered himself gallantly. 'Depends on who is doing the driving.'

Sophie laughed and suddenly the air seemed clearer, the day brighter. She had met Rafael for the first time in at least five years; no, don't lie to yourself, Sophie, the first time in five years two months and twenty days. No, I don't know how many minutes. Of course I don't count the minutes but I'll start to count them now. I'll count from the minute I said goodbye and walked away and discovered that nothing hurt at all.

'Sophie, before we go in and you get involved a sister of the bride, could you let me know about dinner, at Gabbiana. I mean.'

She gave him a brilliant smile. He was a very nice man and very pleasant indeed to look at. 'I'd love to have dinner with you, Harry. I was going back to Edinburgh tomorrow but I actually have next week off too, so why not. I mean why not stay for a while, till Friday maybe. I couldn't possibly miss the duck race, now could I?' She almost danced down the path to the terrace where the first of the family pictures were being taken. 'Champagne on the pool lawn, Harry,' she called back to him over her shoulder.

8

Giovanni surpassed himself with the wedding feast.

After the official photographs and the toasts beside the pool the guests were transported to his restaurant where an enormous marquee had been erected in the gardens. At the top was a semi-circular table for the bridal party and then marching down the centre of the marquee were three enormous tables, one English, one Italian and one loosely termed 'for foreigners'. Menus on each table were illustrated with reproductions of that country's most illustrious paintings: the English had Constable and Turner, the Italians had Titian and Veronese, and the 'foreigners', a motley crew, found their menus printed on a copy of a painting by Grandma Moses.

'Grandma Moses,' questioned a Dutch friend of Zoë. 'What about Van Gogh, or Rembrandt?'

'Too many nationalities to represent,' soothed George. 'Giovanni decided to please himself. It could have been another Italian.'

Sophie went off to chat with Carlo and Josefina before the girl could moan that an Italian might have been preferable.

'It is impossible to please everyone,' agreed Josefina. '*Cara*, enough of the small chattering. When will you visit us?'

'Not this time, Josefina. I really would like to, – and when she said the words, Sophie realised that indeed she meant them, for the friendship was one of the many things she had sacrificed when she had divorced Rafael – 'but I must get back to Edinburgh. I'm a working girl now.' They were too intimate with Rafael. He spent hours there. She did not want to be so close.

Josefina smiled. 'Kathryn says you are an office girl. What does your politician think of that?'

'He doesn't know my mother but if he did he would understand that she says "office girl" disparagingly so that Ann will not be upset.'

'Sit, Sophie, for a moment. Now tell me what the formidable Aunt Judith thinks of your, how you say, boss?'

Sophie and Carlo looked at each other and said together, 'She thinks he could be very useful.'

All three laughed with the ease of old and close friendship.

'Does she visit often?'

'Never. I have a very, very small flat. I hadn't realised that I must have bought it deliberately.' They laughed. 'She would, of course, prefer that Hamish was an MP instead of an MSP.'

'Not nearly so useful?' asked Carlo.

'Exactly. I must go, but there is just enough room in my flat for friends and you would love Edinburgh. You must visit me there.'

She saw very little of them during the banquet since they were at different tables and when she had worked her way through *antipasti misti,* and *crespelle con punte di asparagi* and *coniglio disossoto ripieno* and *ravioli* and *insalata* and all the other delicious courses that Giovanni had decided were necessary, Carlo was there to kiss her goodbye.

'But the torta nuziale, Carlo. You can't go before the wedding cake is cut.'

'Katia is tired and Josefina is anxious to see her baby.'

'I understand.'

'We should have asked you to be his godmother but—'

'The de Nardises,' she interrupted and he looked surprised and shook his head.

'The religion, my friend. We will come to Edinburgh, maybe later when Raffaele plays there.'

'You're still his biggest fan then?'

He held her at arm's length and looked at her. 'I was never that, *cara*: his loving friend, yes, but never the fan. I don't care for that word.' He pulled her forward as if to kiss her goodbye and then changed his mind. 'Ask yourself why he played on an upright piano in a town square, Sophie.'

She looked at him. She had never once asked herself that. 'Zoë,' she began.

'I saw that you had a chat. Maybe now you will see that it is easy to return to Italy; nothing bites.'

She leaned forward and kissed him on both cheeks. 'Everything bites, *caro*,' she said. And then Josefina was there with their pretty little girl and there was no time left. 'I'll try,' she said, but she was not quite sure what it was that she would try to do.

For the rest of the day she was very obviously sister of the bride and that kept her busy. She danced into the night, with her father, with George, with Giovanni, with the twins, with old friends, with strangers and with Harry who was neither an old friend nor a stranger. She sat with her mother, and with Maude, Jim's mother, and with Ann, all the matriarchs, except that she was not a matriarch, but she was talking easily to Ann although the conversation was uncontroversial.

'The twins are overtired.'

'Daddy's had too much to drink.'

'Haven't we all?'

'Was there ever a prettier bride?'

Rafael's name was never mentioned. That was unnatural; the appearance of a world-famous pianist at a small wedding should surely have caused comment, but Sophie decided not to bring it up herself. Tomorrow, tomorrow there would be time to say lightly, 'Wasn't it sweet of Rafael to play for Zoë; he always was so fond of her.'

Sophie kept well away from Judith and refused to catch her eye. She could feel her aunt bursting with pent-up frustration. Perhaps Archie had, for once, been firm. 'Not one word to Sophie, Judith. We want everything perfect for Zoë's wedding.'

Harry, too, had had a little too much wine although like all good Europeans he drank wine glass for glass with water, and he had eaten a large meal. He was happy and Sophie was happy but with a slight ache, for she knew not what but she knew that it would not be a good idea to drive back to Gabbiana with Harry, and so when the bride and groom had been sent off with firecrackers and laughter and much kissing and hugging, she promised her parents to see them at first light and then slipped away and drove herself back to her little villa.

She undressed and stood on her terrace looking at the night. Bats flitted from the roof of a nearby derelict barn and fireflies danced in the light from her windows. She could hear nothing but the soft trickle of water from the well and the occasional sigh as a piece of over-ripe fruit gave up the struggle to hold on to life and fell from its parent branch. It split open, releasing its warm aroma into the clear night air. There were little lights all over the mountainside. The cemetery lights twinkled away far down the valley, all those little electric candles reminding the living of the dear – and not so dear – departed, lights in lonely farmhouses, in expensive hillside restaurants; faint music drifted across the trees. She would not listen for thunderous chords from a Steinway. Stupid; from here you couldn't hear him anyway.

It was the wine, she told herself, but she found herself thinking about Rafael and the singer and wondering about their relationship. He never pretended that he didn't need regular sex; he never pretended about anything. Although she had vowed that she would not do it again she went over and over the days and weeks and months leading up to their divorce and wondering why they had allowed it to happen. Irreversible breakdown. Those ugly, ugly stories that started here in this beautiful valley – untrue, all of them. He must have known they were lies, should have known. That elegant woman in New York. They had dinner, that was all. It meant nothing, he said. It was her fault for not being with him, he said. But she had wanted to be with him but hadn't been well. Was he as confused as she was? She sat on a sun lounger in her silly nightshirt and realised that never once had Rafael said, 'I no longer love you, Sophie.'

Had she said, I don't love you? Certainly she had screamed, I hate you, but what did that mean? She must have yelled it a hundred, a thousand times, at one or other parent as she was growing up and even more often at Ann. The journey to divorce had been as much a helter-skelter ride as her journey to the altar in the chapel at the *castello*, inescapable, at break-neck speed. Too late now to say, wait, let me speak, hear me out. Ann. Ann and Judith and her father who refused to listen because he had never wanted the marriage in the first place.

'An Italian? You can't marry an Italian.'

At least Rafael's mother hadn't minded that she was English. The contessa never shouted; she was much too refined and perhaps her barbs had cut deeper because of that. 'You know nothing of Italian politics, Sophie; you embarrass Raffaele when you express an ill-founded opinion.'

'Mussorgsky's *Pictures at an Exhibition*? It was written for piano, you silly girl.'

Then the worst, the awful, the accusations she could not even bear to remember. 'I shudder to tell you, Raffaele, but your wife, she is . . .'

She was cold although the night was warm and she returned to the house and her big wide empty bed. She cried and then she slept. The alarm woke her at seven and she hurried to take a shower. The water was scaldingly hot; it cleaned but did nothing to repair the damage done by troubled sleep. Clothes for a plastic duck race? A one-piece swimsuit under some cropped pants; a cotton jacket to pull on if it was chilly in the evening. She did not like what she saw in the mirror. Instant coffee helped but it would be better to drive into the bar in the village for delicious Italian coffee. She drove to the villa.

'You're wearing far too much make-up,' Ann greeted her. 'I suppose that's to hide the evidence; thought you were having too much to drink. As long as you're not still taking pills.'

Enough, enough. She grabbed her sister by the shoulders and swung her round. 'Ann, shut up. I have never taken pills, as you so euphemistically say, in my life. You know that; you knew it then and you know it now. Haven't you caused me enough pain? Shall I bring out your list of sins? No, you don't like that.'

Ann pulled away. Her face was flushed with anger and, yes, with dislike. 'I made a mistake, a little mistake. It wasn't stealing; you said you didn't want them. Don't compare me with you.'

The sisters stared at each other. Sophie recovered first although she was trembling and her stomach was churning. 'You can't believe those stories, you can't,' she gasped. 'No matter how much you hate me you can't believe I ever stole anything.'

Ann had the grace to look shamefaced. 'Of course we know you didn't and you said you understood about . . . my little mistake. But you're going to keep bringing it up, aren't you?'

Sophie wondered if the contempt she felt for her older sister showed in her eyes. She was answered when Ann attacked again.

'I know for a fact that your precious Carlo gave you pills the summer Rafael dumped you. Some doctor.'

There was no chance to reply, even had she wanted to do so, and she did not. That grief she had borne alone.

'Sophie, oh, what a pretty top. Isn't it pretty, Ann?' Had their mother heard or was she playing her usual role of happy mother of three happy daughters? Least said soonest mended; the saying had been invented for Kathryn. 'I really didn't expect anyone awake so early. Wasn't it just the most beautiful wedding? Sophie, everyone loved your suit but I said you could wear anything since you're so slim. Judith's dress was nice too but Professor Forsythe always looks as if he's taken a wrong turning on the M6 – meant to reach London and somehow found himself in Pisa, but he's so nice. The twins are still asleep, aren't they, Ann dear? Let sleeping dogs lie. It was miserable not having you with us last night, Sophie darling. Help me with the tablecloths. If you do that I'll make some tea. Daddy went for bread; he'll be back in a minute. Ann, could you water the garden? It's bound to be a bit limp this morning, like all of us, too much food and wine and not enough sleep, but wasn't it worth it, and oh, Sophie, I wish Rafael had stayed; I did ask him, and that nice woman, Ileana something. It was so wonderful of him to play. Some people refused to believe it was him but I said we were all perfectly civilised.' She turned to Sophie and for a moment she looked wounded, frightened, old. 'That was the right thing to say, wasn't it, dear, and you're not angry with Zoë? We didn't know a thing about it, because he hadn't really promised you see, only if he could easily manage.'

'Of course, we're civilised, Mum, most of us. I'll put the cloths on the tables.' She picked up a pile of blindingly white tablecloths and went out of the cool house to the early morning heat. It would be unbearable by lunch time when all the English guests and assorted foreigners and, yes, some Italians who should know better but who were always so polite, would come to stand in the midday sun to eat salads and then race plastic ducks down the clear, cold waters of the Tavernelle. She could hear Ann clattering along behind her on the stone steps but she did not stop to let her sister catch up. They would not stand together under the shade of the chestnut tree to chatter about their younger sister's wedding and the guests, and their hats and their sunburn and their ease or difficulty with Italian food and wine, as normal sisters would have done. We have moved too far apart, Ann and I; Rafael and I. We have all said unforgivable things: Rafael, *la contessa*, Ann, me. How did it happen? Why did I let it happen?

Ann had come up beside her. 'Sophie, we can't avoid each other while you're here; what would everyone think? I'm sorry. I shouldn't have said that but we thought you were on drugs. You were so strange that summer and one night after dinner, I opened your purse and the pills were there and I couldn't really understand the Italian. I hadn't meant to open your purse,' she added quickly. 'I thought it was mine.'

Too cruel now to tell her what they were. 'I can forgive your thoughts about me, Ann, but Carlo.'

'I didn't mean it.'

'Don't ever make remarks like that to anyone. Reputations have been destroyed on a lot less. You should know that.' She put up her hand as Ann looked as if she were about to speak. 'It's over, Ann, there's nothing to say except you of all people should know how easily reputations can be destroyed; some might say it's a national sport here, like football.'

'It was all a misunderstanding; we decided, Mum, Dad, and I, that it was all a dreadful misunderstanding and it's over, forgotten, but the pills? Were you ill? You said nothing.'

'Forget it. This was a mistake – my coming. I'm going home and the rest, it really doesn't matter any more anyway.'

She sensed, rather than saw Ann take a deep breath. 'But it does. I told . . . Judith.'

Sophie stood still, noticing that slight hesitation before the name; what had she been about to say? Not Rafael. Please, God, not Rafael. She tried to turn to confront her sister but the ground under her feet seemed suddenly to have turned to wet concrete. She was incapable of moving. She wanted to turn and shout, what did you tell him and when did you see him and what did he say but nothing functioned, nothing.

Danny released this very unhappy fairy princess from her spell. 'Sophie, Mum, Grampa says come. Why are you drowning the lawn, Mummy? The tea's ready.'

Sophie walked past Ann, past the new flower garden, past the swing with the wonderfully seductive cushions and down on to the terrace. The rest of the family were there and they took one look at her face and, each in his or her own way, trembled.

'Sophie dear.' Mother.

'This is a new bread, Sophie, Try it.' Father.

'Where's Ann?' George.

'I'm going down to the river,' said Sophie through lips that seemed as heavy with cement as her feet had done. 'I need some fresh air.'

'Mum's crying,' yelled Peter, who was believed to be in bed but was here in his underpants leaping down the steps two at a time. 'She didn't mean to drown your grass, Grampa.'

'Oh, God,' said George and went up to see his wife.

'Fresh air,' whispered Kathryn, looking around at the trees and above them the sky. 'I don't understand fresh air.'

'It's cooler by the river,' said Archie desperately. 'That's what she means. Why don't you go with her, dear.'

'And who will arrange the feeding of the five thousand?'

'Stella's here, Gran, and Mrs Wilcox.'

That's all we need. 'Stephanie, dear, how very kind,' oozed Kathryn as, smiled fixed to her upper lip, she surged forward to meet their next-door neighbour.

'I thought you might need a hand this morning, Kathryn. Hello, Archie, and I wanted to see Sophie. How wonderful of the maestro to play at the wedding.'

'Is that today's paper, Steph?' asked Judith. 'Is it in? Were we right?' She turned to Archie. 'We were so sure that there were reporters there, Archie.'

Stephanie sat down and accepted a mug of tea. 'And just a sliver of that focaccia, Archie; I can't resist the smell of fresh bread.' She unfolded her newspaper. 'It's in all the papers this morning. They've written you up as frightfully county – isn't that funny – "Maestro adorns society wedding", and one paper speaks about reconciliation. Such a quiet girl, Sophie, and all this time . . .'

Sophie heard little of this since she had speeded up her progress down to the river. It was uncivil of her, and her parents would need everyone's help with the luncheon but she had to take some deep breaths by herself. She had run to the river for comfort countless times and it had never failed. She clambered over the rocks until she was in the middle alone on her own little island. The trees and the luxuriant ferns bent down over her from the bank and the water splashed and gurgled past: most musical of sounds, water in a stream. She let the sound wrap itself around her; she eased herself into the warmth of the sun through the thin stuff of her bathing suit. What did she tell you, Rafael? What did you believe?

'Sophie, dearest girl, *amore*, how many times I have to tell you that yoga is the answer. Come, exercise with me.'

'I prefer to watch. I know where exercising with you gets me.'

He turned and looked at her with his beautiful devil/angel smile. 'This is a problem?'

'No, never, and maybe this time . . .'

'This time, next time, some time, never time. This is not important. Come.'

But it was important. She knew he wanted a child. His mother wanted a child, his child, a boy, an heir. And she, Sophie, wanted it so badly that she began to avoid making love. Stupid, stupid, but she was so afraid that it would not be this time, or next time or ever, and her love for Rafael, her need for him, was being buried under this need for a child. In the last days of the marriage she found that she was not thinking of pleasure, hers or Rafael's, or fulfilment or anything but 'is it happening this time?'

'What do I have to say to you, Sophie? See, I am big enough a baby for you. I need all of you every minute, day and night.'

But she saw his face sometimes when he did not know that she was watching and she saw the hunger, the envy, the doubt.

'Sophie, there you are. I told Kathryn I'd find you. All hands to the wheel. Mind you, after all we ate and drank yesterday I can't believe that anyone will turn up – sleep until three if they're sensible. Come along and we'll help Stella with the salads. You know I cannot understand how that woman has managed to practically live with your family and not learn a word of English. The Japanese are like that too, I believe. They live for years in Los Angeles or wherever and still speak only Japanese. Sophie, I can't tell you how glad I am that that ghastly business is buried. How ridiculous to accuse you of stealing family treasures and was there a ridiculous rumour about' – she lowered her head and her voice as if they were in a crowd and not alone by a river – 'another man? Seeing dear Rafael yesterday just showed everyone—'

'We Brits are not awfully good at languages, Stephanie,' said Sophie, determined that she would not indulge this ghastly woman in her nosiness.

'You are, darling. I was amazed at how your Italian improved when you were with Rafael; just shows the value of total immersion in a language – or a man, for that matter. So glad—'

'Go on, if you're here to help.'

Sophie slowly picked her way back across the little river and followed Stephanie up the woodland walk to the terrace. Stephanie's behind was tightly encased in pink cotton shorts. Why? Sophie wanted to ask. Why shorts and why pink? Would she wear them in leafy Suffolk? Unlikely.

The pink shorts stopped and Sophie saw them turn round. 'Did you see Rafael's picture in the paper today, dear? You are naughty not to tell but we saw you talking to him. I couldn't see the balcony; the sun was in my eyes, but I told Charles – it has to be Rafael. He thought I was out of my mind but I was right. I'm so glad, Sophie, and your parents must be thrilled. Of course I don't need to tell you what Aunt Judith is thinking.'

Sophie felt herself grow cold and almost faint. She looked at the woman and tried to keep the distaste out of her voice. 'You must excuse me, Stephanie; I promised Mother I'd do the tables by the pool. Stella will be so grateful for your help. Or perhaps you can persuade Judith to help. The family gave up trying years ago.' She hurried up the pathway, leaving the older and plumper Stephanie to puff up the hill behind her.

Her father brought her a mug of coffee. 'Sit down, angel; you look fraught. Is it Steph: Don't let her get to you. She means well.'

'What did the paper say, Daddy?'

'Called us top-drawer people; that pleased your mum. Something too about remarriage, I think. Sophie, I don't read Italian too well but it was mainly about his playing.'

'I'll read it myself later.'

They turned as the first of their visitors drove into the driveway.

'Leave this now, sweetheart; looks great. Sophie, for my sake, for your mother, enjoy the afternoon. Help the twins make it a big success. Everyone gets to eat but if they want a duck or to play any of the games – they pay. Any currency acceptable.'

She smiled at her father and, arm in arm, they went to greet the first of the guests to arrive, and then the afternoon became a blur of eating and drinking and laughing. After the meal those who could manage the walk clambered down to the river, national flag and ticket in hand. Sophie and Giovanni were the marshals. They ran madly up and down the banks of the river yelling in English, in Italian, in bad German and worse French at the racers who were cheating joyously.

'You can't hit your duck; not allowed.'

'I'm hitting the water beside it.'

There was much laughter and great good spirits and Sophie was perched on a rock waving a flag like a modern-day Boadicea when a breathless Stella slid down the bank.

'Sophie, Sophie, *il signor; il maestro,*' and that was as much as she could manage.

Conscious of all the interest, Sophie asked no questions but slowly and carefully handed her flags over to the twins and walked calmly up the path. *Il maestro* could be no one but Rafael; Stella had adored him and had always treated him with the grovelling respect Italians usually reserve for tenors. Walking slowly was giving her time to slow her heart rate; she would not rush to see him. He was not there but the receiver of the telephone was lying on the hall table. She felt flat, like a deflated balloon, cheated. '*Pronto,*' she managed calmly.

'Sophie. I'm sorry to disturb the festivities but I am leaving tonight for London.'

'Yes.' Why on earth would he tell her; they had had little correspondence in the past five years.

'It was the newspaper, that silly article.'

'Oh, I haven't bothered to read that,' she managed – she hoped – airily.

'My office did not sanction it, *cara,* and I hope your parents are not annoyed.'

She tried to laugh. 'Oh, the top-drawer English family, *primo piano.* I'm sure if Mother can read that Italian, Rafael, she'll be delighted to be elevated. Actually we have so many guests that there's no time for trivia.'

'Reconciliation is not trivia.'

'No, it's fantasy.'

She thought she heard him wince. '*D'accordo,*' he said slowly.

'Of course, but I thought . . . I have accepted to play in the Usher Hall in November; perhaps we can have dinner, you can tell me how you are.'

'Miss Raisa might object to your ex-wife taking up your time, Rafael. There is nothing for us to talk about. I told your lawyers I want nothing; I have not changed my mind.' She hung up without saying goodbye and then immediately picked up the receiver and held it against her ear, hoping, hoping what? But he had disconnected and she sat down feeling suddenly foolish and bereft. Where was that damned newspaper?

Stella had left it open at the picture of Rafael. It looked more like a family snapshot than a publicity photograph. How beautiful he was, more film star than pianist, his priceless hands tucked well away out of sight in his trouser pockets. Sophie stared for a long time.

So, he's good-looking. She looked at the article. In highly emotive prose it recorded the singular honour accorded this English family; the great, the world-famous, the finest pianist, Raffaele de Nardis, had stunned the denizens of this small country town by playing the piano in the piazza and not only the splendid guests from all over the world but the humble people of the surrounding area had flocked to participate in this once-in-a-lifetime experience.

Those of us privileged to hear him play will never forget this sunny July afternoon. In the future we will tell our grand-children: I was there when Raffaele de Nardis played in the square. The exquisite bride is the sister of the maestro's former wife, the elegantly charming Sophie de Nardis, and this writer was thrilled to witness the tête-à-tête between the two. Will wedding bells ring again?

How utterly nauseating, shrieked the elegantly uncharming Sophie Winter. Do Italians ever think of anything but food and sex? She walked back down to the river, having first stuffed the newspaper in the wastepaper basket, and her face was so stormy that no one dared ask her about the call although it was obvious that Stella had announced to the world that *il maestro* was on the telephone.

'Hi,' yelled Peter. 'Daddy won but he cheated so we threw him in. It was great fun. What's a maestro?'

'An absolute . . .' she began but remembered his age and was able to stop. 'A teacher, sweetheart, a sort of expert.'

'Is Rafael an expert?'

'Course he is, stupid. Come on, Aunt Sophie, Grampa says we have to collect all the ducks in case they're a nuisance.'

She was quite happy to strip down to her swimsuit and walk down the river with her nephews and a few of the younger people, rounding up little plastic ducks; by the time they returned to the terrace many families were gathering their belongings together.

'Great party. See you in London.'

'Fabulous afternoon; we'll see you tomorrow.'

'Let's have lunch.'

'Ring when you get back to England.'

At last they were alone and as Sophie quietly helped Ann rinse plates and stack them in the dishwasher she had time to realise that what she had experienced when she walked up from the river to find not Rafael, but his disembodied voice on the telephone, was disappointment.

Sophie was not the only person who crumpled a newspaper in fury and threw it away. Marisa, the Contessa de Nardis's faithful maid, stamped on a copy several times with her exquisite high-heeled shoes – given to her, scarcely worn, by the countess – then tore the article furiously into shreds and burned them in her wastepaper basket. Portofino, who also read the article, sighed, wrapped the fish heads in it and put them deep into the waste bin so that foraging cats, or worse, would not reach them.

'*Primo piano.*' Civil servants, librarians, nothing 'top drawer' about them. All they had in their favour was the fact that they loved Italy enough to live there and that was a matter of chance, wasn't it?

Raffaele? Unforgivable. How could he play in the street, a de Nardis with the blood of the Brancaccio-Vallefreddas in his veins? The disgrace. Thank God his father was not alive to see it or his grandfather, Rodolfo Brancaccio-Vallefredda. She could almost hear his long-silenced voice. 'A piano player? *Il trovatore*, the troubadour, the musician who plays for pennies thrown in the dust? Over my dead body.'

Dead body. So many dead bodies. Who remembered them? Only what was left of their families. Names on a marker fixed to a wall in the piazza. One name for her would never die. Brancaccio-Vallefredda, Ludovico, sixteen years. *Italia consacra questi suoi martiri I loro nomi la Gloria ed il loro sacrificio . . .*

'Are you mad, Ludo? The Germans watch you every minute.'

'The general sees me as a child, Gabi. I am the same age as his own son who, no doubt, is studying like a good little boy. How to conquer the world is what he learns in school.'

'You should be in school. Papà will be furious with you when he returns.'

He looked at her sadly. 'If he returns. You are a child, Gabriella, but you have to face the facts. Papà did not co-operate with our allies and so he is rotting somewhere – if he is not already dead.'

She hit him then, she would not say it, think it, and she would not allow Ludovico to say it either.

He held her while she cried. 'Gabi, I have to help the Englishman; his ability with Italian is farcical; he won't last a minute on his own. Should the Germans ask, and I do not think that they will, you can tell them I have gone shooting in the countryside, to fill the pot. Maybe I will find a rabbit; won't that be nice, Gabi, rabbit stew.'

'I can't cook.'

'You must learn.'

She pushed those memories away and returned to the present. Why, why? Only one answer. That woman still had him in thrall. She had been cast out once and so, now, seeing that she is even more dangerous than we knew, we will have to get rid of her again, and this time she can take that dreadful family with her. But how? It must be done with subtlety, not like last time when Raffaele began to doubt, to worry, to take his mind from his destiny.

He was playing now. How music wraps the tired body in soft covers and carries it to serenity. What is he playing; Chopin, Liszt, the divine Beethoven?

Mussorgsky. For her, for her.

Sta calma.

9

There was a postcard from Simon, a picture of Broadway, the Great White Way. Sophie found that amusing; had she been asked to bet on what type of cards Simon would send she would have said immediately, 'A picture of the Metropolitan Museum, or probably something from inside the museum.' Discovering that she was so wrong cheered her up somehow.

Returning to the serenity of her little flat after Italy had also cheered her. The days there were slipping back into the 'bad dream' world. She was glad that she had seen Zoë married, and it had been lovely to talk to Carlo and Giovanni again but she would forget everything else, everything.

She got back to the sanity of work. Parliament was in official recess during most of July and August but Sophie, like almost every other staff member, had only twenty-five days' holiday each year and so the offices were still busy. Hamish, with a 'we really must have dinner when I get back', was off to the remote fastness of his Highland home but Sophie knew he would be in touch either by telephone or e-mail. Problems did not go on holiday. Constituents still queried everything from shellfish poisoning or pension rights after divorce to who pays for repairs to storm-damaged access to historic caves. It was obvious to many that asylum seekers and illegal immigrants were going to become bigger issues. Almost nightly desperate men and women tried to cross the English Channel. As yet Scotland's problems were not nearly so large as England's but they were growing. Filling the days with work buried the memories of Tuscany. Hurrying across the Royal Mile in the rain made her wonder whether she ever had felt the sun hot on her back, if sunlight on silver water had ever blinded her eyes.

She took a few days off to enjoy the Edinburgh Festival. She had tried to avoid performances that she feared would remind her of her life with Rafael but this was a new start. She would jump right in and so she went to a piano recital in the Usher Hall. It was one of those ghastly nights when almost everyone in the hall seemed to have a cold. Coughs, sneezes and rustling of cough sweets jarred the atmosphere. One or two misguided souls held in their explosions until the break between move-ments and then, thinking that they were being thoughtful, destroyed the peace of the moment by releasing their pent-up coughs. Eventually the pianist got up, told the audience very politely that he was going off to give everyone a chance to clear their throats, and walked off the stage. He did return and even played an exquisite little encore to show that all was forgiven, but next day the papers were full of his fury. There was no fury, no pianist angst, but that doesn't read so well as 'Angry pianist stalks off stage.'

Harry flew over to 'do some Book Festival' events and Sophie went with him to two of them. She had never regretted cutting short her holiday in Tuscany but she had regretted not having dinner with Harry; there was something there, something that, given a chance, could grow, and he certainly was the 'dishiest' professor she had ever met. She dressed with care to meet him in the beautiful private garden in the middle of Charlotte Square, one of Edinburgh's most prestigious addresses, given over for almost three weeks each summer to a carnival of the written word. Harry believed in 'doing the festival'. On his first day in Edinburgh he had been to an art show and then a play performed by university students in an old church: 'I didn't understand it at all but they're so alive, I loved it.' On the second day he had bought a sandwich and a bottle of water and had sat on the grass in Princes Street Gardens listening to pop music from the band-stand and had then gone to a talk by one of his favourite authors. That evening he and Sophie had tickets for an event with several eminent philosophers. Afterwards they walked in that soft lilac light that is known as twilight, or, by the Scots, as 'the gloaming', to a restaurant.

'You remind me of me when I was in my first year at university, Harry. I fitted so much into the days that I was exhausted but, oh, was I proud of myself. Dreadful plays full of suffering, talks about the meaning of life by angry young men and angrier young women and, if I was lucky, Wagner in the evening. I equated education with suffering, I suppose.'

Harry looked at her and laughed. 'Bad teaching: learning is fun. I tell my students to relax now and again, have a few beers. Life's too short for all that angst.'

'So you've spent the day listening to philosophy and ethics,' teased Sophie.

'Yes, but when I was a student I stole some time off to get pissed. Were you always so serious?'

She sipped her wine. Could she answer? Could she say, 'I had already met Rafael and life was deadly serious?' She tried to smile naturally. 'I never graduated, Harry, so I think I didn't take university seriously enough.'

He laughed. 'Sophie Winter, a hell raiser. I can't believe it. But Zoë tells me you have this fabulous job, that you're multilingual.'

'She's exaggerating. I learned Italian and German living with Rafael, and bits of other languages through constant travel; it can be said that life gave me an education.'

She would not tell him she could not concentrate on her studies because her mind was full of Rafael. If he was curious he was too polite to ask. Instead he asked about the name. 'Why Rafael instead of Raffaele?'

'My personal name for him; his family and friends called him Raffaele.' She changed the subject. 'Have you ever been married?'

'No, came close once and I lived with an Italian colleague for years, and then she went to Australia with the physics professor. Took me a long time to realise we'd been merely room-mates for too long. I won't make that mistake again.'

Too dangerous. Too intimate. 'So, it's V.S. Naipaul tomorrow, Harry.'

He took the hint. 'Yes, I'm quite excited about that talk and then it's a play at the Lyceum. Pity there were no seats left.'

The evening ended with polite continental kisses but Sophie invited Harry to supper after his final book event. They sat at the open window and Harry put his arm round Sophie protectively and she did not move away as they looked out on to the Royal Mile and watched people. Street-sellers lined the pavements with their handmade jewellery, or their mass-produced prints of famous sketches of Edinburgh's historic buildings. Friendly young people gave away countless samples of their latest drink and hundreds of broken plastic cups littered the street. Dogs of indiscriminate breed ran around and between people's legs, occasionally finding a morsel of discarded sandwich.

'Almost medieval,' said Harry, who was leaning so far out of the window that once Sophie feared that he might fall out to join the rest of the debris.

'No plastic in the Middle Ages, Harry,' she said as, thankfully, she saw him haul himself back inside. 'Nor is Edinburgh's street cleaning department medieval. It will be round tonight to tidy up before the Tattoo and at the crack of dawn tomorrow.'

They ate their salads and eventually the sellers wrapped up their goods. Their places on the pavement were taken by crowds lining up to wait for permission to climb the esplanade of the castle to watch the annual Military Tattoo.

'Bird's-eye view of everything up here, Sophie. How on earth did you find such a fabulous little eyrie?'

Now they were watching a few unarmed policemen control hundreds of people from all over the world with nothing but humour. 'It belonged to an American who gave me a job after the divorce. When she returned to the States she offered me the flat.' She turned back into the living room. 'I may own it outright if I work until I'm about ninety-three. Now, look, see that policeman in the middle there. He's going to yell stop and every single person will stop.'

The rest of the evening passed comfortably and she did not object when this time Harry kissed her mouth as he left.

'I want to see you again, Sophie.'

'London at Christmas?'

'Come to Florence for a weekend.'

No, not Italy. 'London, Harry. I'll look forward to that.'

The festival, or festivals, for there are several running at the same time, ended. Edinburgh emptied itself of thousands of tourists: rich tourists who stayed at the Balmoral or the Howard, poor tourists who slept occasionally on benches in public gardens, and all the tourists in between.

In October, Simon, still pale after three months in New York, returned wearing a T-shirt that said, 'I may not be perfect but parts of me are excellent' and Sophie laughed at what his sojourn in America had done to him. He was certainly not the same man.

'But better, Soph.' That was a change too; he had never shortened her name before. ' "All work and no play etc. etc." I learned so much; the museum collections are mind-blowing. I haven't even begun to know them. When I go back . . .' He stopped as he saw the confusion on her face. 'I'm going back, Soph. I met someone, a girl.' He smiled an idiotic smile.

Sophie smiled. 'Good thing I didn't go with you.'

He looked at her gratefully. 'She's coming to visit in November; she's a teacher and they have a week off at the end of November, the week with the fourth Thursday or something like that.'

'Thanksgiving.'

'You don't mind?'

'I'm delighted for you.'

She took a bus home and sat at the window looking out at lights shining through the rain and feeling glad that Simon's news disturbed her not at all. He had been, she reflected cruelly, a useful evening accessory, but just as easy to replace. As she climbed the winding stairs to her turret she could hear her telephone ringing and she raced up and caught it on its last ring.

'I was about to leave a message.'

Her heart could not possibly pound any harder than it was doing after her mad sprint in high-heeled shoes. 'Rafael, this is a surprise.'

'I'm at the Usher Hall next Friday. Can you come?'

Of course she could but would she? That was a different thing altogether. 'Why?'

'You like music. I want to see you. You have nothing better to do. Any one of those would suit?'

'There's a drinks party I have to go to – business.' She waited but he said nothing and all she could her was air humming along the line. 'Where are you, Rafael?'

'Berlin.'

'What are you playing?'

'This makes a difference? In Berlin or in Edinburgh? Rachmaninov 2 and maybe a Beethoven variation if they want.'

They would want; they always did. 'I could come straight from the party.'

'That would be nice. We could have supper afterwards?'

He ate very little on days when he was performing and so was always very hungry afterwards. She almost said, 'Come here,' but caught herself in time. 'Aren't you leaving immediately?'

'No, I am in Glasgow the next day. How is Zoë – and your parents?'

'Fine.' He did not ask about Ann.

'Valentina will send the ticket. *Ciao.*'

'*Ciao.*'

I'm out of my mind. Why am I seeing my ex-husband? I certainly don't feel jilted because Simon met someone in New York. And why on earth does Rafael want to see me? It can't be about our divorce. He can't want to rake over that ghastly business. He knows I stole nothing from his home; he said so at the time. It wasn't Ann either. She took some things from the house but only after the divorce and they belonged to me anyway – silly, avaricious Ann. Had she asked I would have given them to her, thrown them at her probably – except the angel; I would never have given away the angel. Her hands were still on the telephone and before she could change her mind, she picked it up and dialled her parents' number.

'Sophie.' Her father sounded delighted. 'Your mum's in bed and I'm on the way to clean my teeth.'

'Sorry, I forgot time zone. How are you?'

'We're fine. We're having everyone over tomorrow; last big party until next spring. This is a nice surprise. Just a chat, is it?'

'Yes. I was just thinking of you so I pushed the little button. How's everything?'

'We're looking forward to Christmas at home.' He hesitated and then started again. 'Some kids pulled up all your mother's English flowers the other day; such mindless vandalism, didn't think to see it here. Not a nice note to end the summer on.'

She remembered the gardens lovingly planted for Zoë's wedding and grew cold at the thought of someone running through them, pulling up her mother's tenderly tended roses. 'I suppose kids are getting out of hand everywhere, Dad.'

'Doesn't seem very Italian but – not to worry. It's only plants after all and they can be replaced.'

They chatted on for a few minutes and before she hung up Sophie told him that she would see them some time over the Christmas break.

A few days later a ticket for Rafael's concert at the Usher Hall was delivered. Sophie looked at it. What am I doing? I'm going to a concert. The pianist is your ex. So, he's superb and I like music. This is the twenty-first century; we're civilised.

She managed not to think of him at all on the day of the concert. Hamish had been in town for several days and she was busy, not invented business to keep her mind occupied but real work, the kind that had made her apply for the job in the first place. Eventually office hours were over although work went on at dinners and receptions all over town. Sophie changed from her business suit into a lightweight knit dress that hugged her figure and then flared at the embroidered hem, and went along to the reception in the whisky bar of the Scotsman Hotel; she didn't

drink whisky but was able to relax for a while in a really comfortable seat and chat to Hamish. Almost a date.

'Wow.' He admired the picture she presented in her green
dress. 'I hope that dress is for me; if you dressed like that in the
office I would never get anything done.'

'Thank you, kind sir, but the dress is for me, not you or . . .'
She stopped; she could not tell him about Rafael.

'I can enjoy the picture,' he said as colleagues joined them.

In no time at all it was almost seven. Sophie stood up. 'I can't
be late, Hamish. They don't let latecomers into concerts until "a
suitable break".'

'I was going to ask you to have supper with me.'

She was angry. How many times had she waited, hoping, that
he would ask her out as a woman, not as his executive assistant?
Perfect timing to choose the evening that she had a date with her
former husband. 'I'm off, Hamish. See you Monday morning.'

He walked with her to the door and waved down a passing taxi.
'Monday. You'll bone up on asylum laws.'

'Naturally.' She jumped into the taxi and had the satis-
faction of seeing him standing looking almost dejected outside
the hotel.

'You'll just make it, miss,' said the boy who looked at her ticket
and he was right. She slid into her seat just as the conductor was
clapped on to his podium and then she gave herself up to trying
to relax. It was a concert, just a concert, and that she would watch
Raffaele de Nardis play for the first time in five years was im-
material. The stage was dominated by a beautiful Steinway,
remote, silent. She did not open the programme; she thought the
first piece was Shostakovich, and she tried to breathe slowly and
let the music absorb her but she was too keyed up.

Polite Edinburgh applause.

The conductor left and returned with the soloist. For a
moment he stood dwarfing the conductor and then he turned to
the piano; it had been tuned to his exact specifications and the
stool was placed exactly where he wanted it and adjusted for his
height. He pushed his coat tails back and sat down, bent his head

for a moment, his dark hair falling over his eyes, looked up unsmilingly at the conductor to show that he was ready and began to play. The chords came one after the other, eight of them and each one louder than the one before. They echoed in Sophie's head and her heart. The pain was intense but then the strings picked up the melody and swept over her and she forgot everything but the sound.

When the concerto finished there was an intense silence that lasted for four perhaps five seconds and then the audience erupted. People clapped, they cheered, they stamped their feet and most of them stood. The pianist, looking a little surprised, bowed. He always looked like that after playing and it was because while he was playing he was aware of nothing but the music. Now once more back in Edinburgh on a rainy Friday, he shook hands with the conductor, with the leader of the orchestra, and bowed again. Still the cheers went on rolling round and round the newly painted dome. Rafael gestured for the orchestra to stand to share the applause and then he walked off. He came back, he bowed, he left and by the fourth time Sophie was both crying and laughing in her seat.

'The Italian community must be out in force,' said the woman beside her frostily.

What could you say to a remark like that? Sophie clapped more loudly than ever. Her hands were sore; she was on her feet but had no memory of standing up. Rafael returned to the stage and she sat down quickly just in case he could see her. He bowed again and returned to the piano, and the audience, having been given what they wanted, began to quieten down.

The pianist waited until there was silence, his hands resting on his knees. Then he began to play.

A Beethoven variation? No. Why, Rafael? Why?

When it was over he left the stage with the conductor and Sophie knew that he would not return no matter how they clapped.

'What was that?' asked the woman on her left. 'I feel I should know it but I didn't quite recognise it.'

'Mussorgsky,' said Sophie. 'It's from the original scoring of *Pictures at an Exhibition.*'

During the interval she remained in her seat reading the programme from cover to cover as if the programme notes were completely new. There was a photograph of de Nardis, the pianist, and Sophie scarcely looked at it. The orchestra returned too quickly; surely they had not been gone for fifteen minutes. The evening would be over soon and then she would find herself face to face with Rafael.

When the concert was finished she stood in the always-busy Ladies' room waiting to wash her face. She could not let Rafael see her with tears on her cheeks. He was used to seeing people cry when he played, but not her, never her. When they met she did not ask why the encore he had chosen to play was 'Ballet of the Unhatched Chicks', the piece he had always played as an encore when they were married, his personal message to her.

'Beethoven's variations on "God save the King" are too obvious, *tesoro.* Mussorgsky will be our secret.'

He said nothing either about the music when they finally had supper. After concerts there were always people waiting to see him, old friends, fans, journalists and critics, but at last they were alone and Sophie was acutely aware that she had not been alone with him in a long, long time.

'A receptive audience,' she said, because she did not know what else to say.

'I like that old hall; it's full of ghosts,' he said seriously.

They walked to a nearby restaurant and chatted easily about Zoë and her new life in Australia. 'I must see her when I play there,' he said as he helped himself to pasta and then he laughed as she sat back as she had always done to watch him eat.

'*Mi dispiace*; the meal after a good concert is always the best meal ever. You're picking at your food, Sophie. You're too thin.'

'So Giovanni said.'

Unconsciously he echoed Carlo. 'Giovanni knows what is beautiful.'

He said it unconsciously, merely stating a fact. It was not meant as a compliment and why should he compliment her? The last time they had talked, before the divorce, before she had left for ever, no compliments then, just thinly veiled acceptances of what his mother had said. He was her husband and he had not said, as a good husband should, 'Don't be ridiculous. Sophie didn't steal the manuscript, or the Vezzi teapot or anything else.'

Sophie looked away from him, across the almost deserted dining room. 'How is the contessa?'

He put down his fork, his plate empty. 'She didn't go back to Rome, said it was still too hot. That's not like her.' He played with a piece of bread, slowly and methodically tearing it apart.

Had they still been married, she would have taken it from him. 'Tell me, *tesoro*, what's worrying you?' But they were not married.

'I heard about the flowers.' Did he colour a little under his permanent tan? 'Paolo told me; he is told everything that happens.'

'How feudal,' she said coldly.

'Perhaps. But he takes his position seriously, as our father did, and his.'

'It's a long time since your family owned the valley, Rafael.'

'It doesn't stop us caring. My mother is passionate about Italy; she doesn't like to hear that Italian vandals have destroyed a garden.'

'Who says they were Italian? Just as easily they could have been lager louts.'

He shrugged. '*D'accordo*. They would have had to drive a long way, *cara*. Nothing else was disturbed that night. It wasn't random vandalism. Why Villa Minerva?'

She shivered. 'It's just an incident, Rafael. A final act of drunken stupidity at the end of summer.'

He looked at her and she looked into his eyes and then down at his hands and then, because there was no danger there, she looked into her coffee cup. 'It was just a silly incident, Rafael.'

'*Davvero*. Sophie, I still care about you; you do know that, don't you?'

'Please,' she began but he interrupted her by taking her hands in his. Almost absent-mindedly his long fingers caressed the place where her wedding ring had been.

'Sometimes I think that maybe I was wrong or maybe I didn't do things correctly, five years ago, that ghastly summer.'

She said nothing and eased her hands away and he let them go.

'I was stunned, Sophie, in shock. To see my mother in tears; never when we were growing up did she show fear or stress and all that time she carried this huge burden. I never saw the Battista manuscript, I never heard of it, or the porcelain teapot, or that cross. I should have been thinking, How did it get there? I was not there. Sophie was not there, but this beautiful and historic jewel was there. But you had been so strange and you did not deny like I thought maybe a woman would. An Italian woman would throw the Vezzi teapot at my head and scream and shout but you withdrew further and further. Was I so wrapped up in myself that you could not see me. Sophie, you could not reach me, you who are closer and more precious than the fingers on my hands?'

Still she said nothing and he did not know that it was because she could not, for she was full of anger and despair and hurt and they were sitting in a restaurant and if she were to lose control she would teach every Italian woman the real meaning of anger.

He tried again, gesturing to the waiter for more wine that she refused. 'I took my place in the world for granted, Sophie. I was the son of Count Mario de Nardis; everything I wanted I was given, by my mother, my brother, Marisa. I did not say, Mamma, you can afford this wonderful piano, this most famous teacher in Europe? I took it completely for granted that I should be given all these things. Never did I think that maybe my dear mother had to strive to provide this lifestyle while she struggled alone to rebuild two great estates; the devastation of Italy in the war was great, Sophie.'

'It was a world war,' she said coldly.

'*D'accordo.*' He stood up and so she did too. As always he towered above her but somehow she knew that she was in control, not Rafael, 'I am here if you ever need me, Sophie.'

'I needed you once.'

He insisted on taking her home in a taxi and leaving the taxi with its meter running while he climbed the spiral stairs with her. 'Sophie, why are you living in an area like this? You can easily afford a better place.'

'This is a better place,' she said lightly as she fitted the key in the door.

'Why are you so damned proud? The London place is in your name. Sell it.'

'Goodnight, Rafael.' She looked up at his tired face and he looked down into her eyes. His eyes were sad. She did not want to question any expression that might lurk in her own. 'I like my apartment; this is a very good part of—'

'There is a shop on the street floor,' he interrupted her.

'It's a very expensive shop. I'm fine. I'm buying this flat with my own money, not yours, not my father's; it's a wonderful feeling.'

He reached for her gloved hand. 'Promise you will call me if you ever need anything.'

'I won't,' she began.

He gripped her shoulders; his fingers were strong. 'Promise.'

'I promise,' she said and went in, closing the heavy brown door behind her.

10

Jenner's Department Store on Princes Street had transformed itself overnight. An enormous fresh Christmas tree seemed to be growing out of the floor and its branches stretched out and up towards the roof. The miles of lights and the colourful decorations were gazed at in awe from every gallery. On the mezzanine a group of carol singers from a local high school collected for charity as they sang out the old favourite Christmas carols; 'Deck the Halls,' 'Jingle Bells,' 'Rudolph the Red-Nosed Reindeer'.

Sophie stood in the china department where she had gone to look for something for Ann and George and watched them. She saw one girl singing at the top of her voice, belting them out in fact.

'Isn't she lovely,' said one Edinburgh matron complacently to another as they listened.

Sophie watched 'isn't she lovely' pinch the boy in front of her while the teacher's attention was distracted. 'Looks a right little madam to me,' she said and walked on, blissfully conscious of the glares behind her. Probably a doting granny, she decided, refusing to feel sorry at her lack of seasonal joy.

In spite of the magnificence of the tree she did not feel Christmassy; no feelings of warmth towards her fellow man, no feelings of awe at the miracle for which the world waited. I'm trying, I'm trying, she told herself. I just need to get some of the things on my list done and then when I feel less panicky I'll be able to look forward to the holiday.

It would be the first time she had seen Ann, and George of course, since the summer. Every Wednesday she rang her parents and they telephoned her on Sundays. She had not seen them either since the wedding, but a reunion with them did not assume gigantic importance. It was the way things had been for twelve years since her father had taken early retirement and her parents had gone to spend eight months of the year at their house in Tuscany.

'Why don't you and Ann make up?' her mother asked but there was no answer to that.

She did not fully understand what she had done to make Ann so antagonistic so that everything she said or did was misinterpreted. She did know what Ann had done and that could never be forgiven.

Ann was five when Sophie was born and they had grown up like loving sisters everywhere, sometimes fighting, mostly loving. They had both fallen in love with Tuscany, its breathtakingly narrow roads, its sweeping vistas like paintings come to life, medieval towns clinging to hillsides, huge fortesses dominating those hillsides and the countryside around, snow sparkling almost all year round on the tips of the distant Apuan Alps, ice-cold water rushing down through valleys cut by glaciers, wide beaches with space to walk, to play, to picnic, *castagneto*, the chestnut trees glorious every spring with carpets of orchids carelessly strewn around their venerable roots. They loved the people, whose initial shyness deepened into friendship that was received in wonder at their amazing generosity of time and skill. Most of the time they even forgave them for their idiosyncratic behaviour, learning to shrug like everyone else.

They had Italian boyfriends and had ridden around on the frighteningly inadequate *motorinos*. Ann had fallen in love with Giovanni, a waiter in the *trattoria* in the nearest village and then Sophie had fallen in love with Rafael.

'He's a pianist, Mummy. Can you believe I actually heard him play when I was at school? He has a lock of hair that . . .' She had stopped. Mothers cared nothing for shining hair that hid beautiful blue eyes. 'He's quite famous now, and this is the most amazing thing – he lives up there.' She had pointed a slim, sun-bronzed arm up, up to the suddenly threatening pile that was the *castello*, home of the de Nardis family for hundreds of years.

Her parents had been singularly unimpressed. 'Sophie, he's an aristocrat, an Italian; they're worse than ours. What age is he?'

She had flushed and looked down and finally admitted that he was already thirty, ten years older than she was.

Her parents had looked at each other. They knew what he wanted, of course; an Italian and a musician at that. 'And he's damned well not getting it from my daughter,' said Archie.

Like everyone else they had come under his spell when they met him. He did not try to please; he was just himself, aware of his looks, his education, his background – how could he not be? He could read about them constantly in the papers if he wanted but he did not trade on them, seemed unaware of them. He would shrug when Sophie mentioned his appearance, the first thing that she had noticed about him as he sat on the wall at La Speranza in Lerici.

At the time of that first meeting, four years before, her parents, could not find words for their terror. 'Thank goodness he was a decent bloke but for goodness sake, Sophie, you don't even speak the language properly.' My God, the snares that lay in wait for daughters, especially friendly ever-trusting ones like Sophie. 'Never, ever, get in a car with anyone I do not know, especially an Italian.'

'An Italian. How can you think of buying property here if you don't even respect the people.'

'I know Italian men,' said her mother who was, as far as Sophie knew, on nodding acquaintance with one or two local businessmen.

She had spent the rest of the holiday looking for the archangel but he had gone. He had gone from her sight but not from her mind and even in the heady excitement of her final year at school and her first year at St Andrews University she had never quite forgotten him. 'Maybe he was an angel, just sent to give me a lift home,' she had said.

Two years later when they were in Italy, living now at the beautiful villa they had built, she had met him again. He was with another man, another beautiful man with the classic Italian face, not so tall and heavier. She had been walking with Ann in Florence and there they were just in front of them. 'Quick, Ann, that's Raffaele.'

The two men had gone into a shoe shop and before Ann could protest Sophie had hauled her in after them. He had looked at her, looked away – the pain, the pain; he does not know me – and then looked back and smiled.

'Sophie signorina, the cycling worked.'

For a second she had been nonplussed and then she smiled through her blushes. He stood waiting to be introduced to Ann. 'Oh, Ann this is Raffaele . . . oh.'

'De Nardis, signorina. How do you do,' he had said easily, taking Ann's hand and bowing over it.

He did not kiss her hand, exulted Sophie, just a bow. 'May I introduce my friend, Carlo, Dr di Angelo.'

'Oh, an Italian doctor,' Sophie had rushed in before anyone else could speak. 'How very useful. Our parents have just built a house in Lunigiana, near Aulla. Are you near there, Dr di Angelo?'

'Indeed, signorina.' His voice was deep, calm and musical, a comforting, accentless voice. 'But for you, not yet very useful.'

She had smiled at him artlessly, innocently. 'But doctors are terribly useful.'

He had smiled at her. 'I will recommend, signorina. I am an obstetrician.'

'Come away at once, Sophie,' begged Ann, who was ill at ease in the company of two men she could see were sophisticated, wealthy. The cut of their suits alone . . . 'I think these gentlemen find you amusing.'

'Amusing?' began Sophie.

'No, *cara*, we think you are enchanting.'

Ann was coldly furious. 'Now, Sophie.' And she pulled the younger girl from the shop and walked her back to the train station talking, talking. 'How could you, how could you? The doctor one was all right I suppose, although you made an absolute fool of yourself, but the other one, too handsome for his own good. He was sneering down that well-bred Italian nose. "*Cara.*" How dare he call you dear. What they must think of us, chasing them into a shop. They probably think we're loose women.'

Sophie burst out laughing. 'Oh, Ann, Carlo is a doctor and Raffaele is . . . my friend.'

'How can he be?' Suddenly Ann stopped stock still in the middle of the crowded pavement. Her eyes narrowed and she glared at her sister. 'I don't believe it. I suppose he's the knight in shining armour who brought you back from Lerici, showing off his flashy car. He didn't even remember you, you stupid girl.'

But Sophie knew that he had remembered and she knew too that he was her friend. She met him a week later at La Speranza – he did not tell her that he had driven there every day and sat on the wall for hours, wondering if she would come and why he should even care. He had sent her a ticket for his next concert in Edinburgh and had invited her to a reception – a treat, as he thought, for a nice young girl. A few days later, at a concert in New York, he was surprised to find himself playing Beethoven's variations on 'God Save the King', and had laughed aloud with the joy of his amazing discovery; he had waited a year to tell Sophie that he loved her.

She was suddenly aware of Christmas carols.

'Are you all right, lassie?' A woman was offering her a Kleenex because she was weeping.

'Oh, how stupid. You're very kind but it's Christmas carols. "White Christmas", Bing Crosby, it always gets to me somehow.'

'Me too. You should maybe have a wee cup of tea, afore you do more shopping.'

'Good idea. Thank you again.' And she had fled out of the china department and down the stairs. Lingerie, she would look at lingerie. A slip for Ann, perhaps – she could not go without gifts – and then she would go into the men's department and get a hat, yes, a nice fur hat for poor old George. She did buy a fur hat.

Dear Harry, I saw this and thought of you in the freezing cold
of northern Italy.
Santo Natale, Sophie.

Before she could change her mind and think how sending a gift
to man she had met only a few times could be misinterpreted, she
wrapped it in cheerful Christmas paper and went back out to
stand in line at the post office. Then she struggled back through
the crowds to her flat. The telephone was ringing but she ignored
it until her cold hands had managed to light the gas fire.

'Sophie, it's Zoë. I have the most amazing, stupendous . . .'
The answering service had switched on.

Zoë. Dear God, it was early morning in Australia. She dashed
to the phone and picked up the receiver. 'Zoë, I'm here. How
lovely. What news? What is it?'

'Can't you guess?'

How could she not know; the tone of voice told everything.
'Amazing? Stupendous?' she teased. 'That has got to be that your
dustbin man didn't leave the gate open and the neighbour's
horrid dog didn't do his business in your pocket handkerchief
garden.'

'I'm pregnant.' Sophie heard a voice and a squeal of laughter.
'We're pregnant, Jim says it takes two. Can you imagine, Sophie,
me with a baby.' The squeals again. 'Okay, me and Jim, Jim and
me with a baby. We want you to be godmother, will you?'

Godmother.

'Sophie, are you there?'

'Of course, dear. I'm just so happy and so honoured that
you've asked me. What does Mum say?'

'You can guess. First she was ecstatic, then she remembered
that we haven't even been married a year yet and so we're too
young.'

'And Dad?'

'Don't do too much. Eat for one and breathe for two; Ann
always said she was eating for two.'

'Fashions change.'

'Are you well?'

'What a funny question. I should ask you. Are you well?'

'Of course. All my friends are jealous; no morning sickness, no nothing.'

'That's great but big question – when?'

'June, and we'll wait until we come home for a christening. Now, tell me. What about you and my dishy professor?'

'Cheeky minx. He came for the festival; I saw him once or twice.' Four times actually. 'Grown-ups do that sort of thing. He's coming home for Christmas – his father lives in London – and so I'll take a run up to see him. Satisfied?'

They chatted for a little longer and then, conscious not only of the time difference but that her clothes were drying on her, Sophie said goodbye and went to run a hot bath. Zoë a mother, and she was to be the godmother. And I'm pleased, I'm thrilled, all of the above, but would things have been different if I'd found out earlier or if I had told him? No. He had fallen out of love with me. It would never have worked. Will I call Mother and listen to her excitement over this new grandchild or will I wait till the weekend? Selfish, selfish Sophie. Ring your parents and share their joy.

Just as she slipped into her lovely hot bubble-filled bath she heard the telephone again. The answering service caught it eventually and she heard the low tones of a man's voice. Business probably.

The message, however, was from her father. 'Just heard Rafael's new release on Radio 3, *bella*. It's a one-off, they said. He's accompanying that Hungarian singer: some *lieder*. Wonderful news about Zoë.'

She had to ring them but first she made herself something to eat. I'm avoiding them, she admitted to herself as she tore basil leaves and added them to her blender. Absolutely no need to make fresh pesto sauce. No, no, just because I live alone and don't have to think about feeding anyone else, no need to get sloppy. Pine nuts? Pine nuts? Dash it all, I have none and now all this out-of-season basil is wasted and it's so expensive.

She smelled the strong, heady scent of the crushed herb and memories of Italy filled the little kitchen. Fat pots of basil sitting all along a wall at the villa, fighting for space between the rioting geraniums, a window opening, and . . . Rafael, who had decided to learn to cook, calling, '*Cara*, bring it now, right now or it's ruined.'

Apricots, oh, the smell of a sun-warmed apricot as it was picked from the tree, the colour like no other colour – and the taste. 'Bring them, *cara*, as many as you can carry; it will be the world's best ice-cream.'

'Oh, Rafael, what a waste. We must eat them like this. Pity the poor people in the world who have never tasted an apricot like this.'

He had joined her on the terrace and they had eaten apricots until their stomachs hurt and then had gone inside to their cool white room with its big carved bed.

With shaking hands she began to dial. 'Hello, Mum, wonderful news, isn't it.'

Her mother chatted for a long time and she was glad that she had at least some hot tea to drink. 'Your father wants to talk to you.' Sophie could hear Kathryn scolding her father. 'Now, don't keep her too long; she hasn't eaten yet and the weather's ghastly in Edinburgh.'

'Hello, sweetheart. Are you snowed in that you haven't eaten?'

'No, it's raining and I had a bath first, that's all. Dad, I have to go. I just wanted to say how pleased I am about Zoë.'

He sounded gloomy. 'So was I, but your mother . . . You'd think no one ever had a baby before and of course, Ann's been here. "You didn't make this much fuss when I was pregnant." We just can't get it right with her.'

'Well, let's pray Zoë doesn't have triplets.'

He laughed. 'I won't tell anyone you said that but that really would be game set and match, wouldn't it.'

He hung up but she felt better having talked to him. She threw the basil mixture out and toasted some cheese, consoling herself that it was nourishing.

★

On the Thursday before Christmas she took the night train to London. She splashed out on a first-class berth and stuffed her weekend case and her parcels down beside the bed. She had not been in a sleeper since she had divorced Rafael or, to be truthful, they had divorced each other. She tried to sleep but memories kept whirling around in her head: those ghastly months when she had struggled with ill health, when she had decided to keep her worries from Rafael instead of sharing them. Stupid, stupid.

'Something is wrong, *diletta*. I thought in the fairy tale it was the little boy who refused to grow up but I get older and older and you remain the same.'

'Of course I've changed. It's you; no, it's your mother who won't let me take my proper place.'

'Little Sophie, little Sophie. She's just a child, *caro*. I'll do it as I've always done it. Her job is to be pretty for you.'

Sophie sat up and looked in the mirror. Did I stay pretty for you, Rafael? Was that all you wanted, a pretty, adoring little wife? You said I had not developed but I had. I could speak about anything easily – except when we were with your mother. That was your mother's fault, *caro*, and now I see that she did it remorselessly, coldly, determinedly. I should have fought her. She punched the pillows and lay down again. I should have fought about those accusations too, Rafael.

She closed her eyes so as not to see her memories but there they were in her brain, as loud and colourful and as horrifying as ever.

The countess, looking her age, haggard, the elegance and sophistication, even her incomparable beauty, gone, destroyed by what had happened. 'Why, Sophie? I would have given you anything you wanted. You are Raffaele's wife.'

She saw herself, as distraught as her mother-in-law but for other reasons. This is insane; it's ridiculous. Rafael, you can't believe this?'

'Raffaele; my son's name is Raffaele.'

'Rafael. Tell her. Tell her I know nothing about manuscripts and porcelains.'

Rafael's mother had looked up at her son as he stood, transfixed, like a dazed animal caught in a strong light by a hunter's rifle, between the two women he loved. 'I never wanted you to know. Maybe she did not think to remove from her husband's home is to steal.' The relief in her voice, on her careworn face. 'That was it, Sophie. You have Ludovico's manuscript to give back to Paolo.'

Unable to bear any more of her own memories Sophie turned over on the rough blue blanket and cried herself into an exhausted sleep.

Her father was at the station; she could see him hurrying along the platform, scrutinising the passengers, worrying that she had changed her mind yet again.

'Dad, here I am,' she called and was vaguely unhappy when she saw his relief. Had he been afraid that she would not come, that he had finally lost his second daughter?

The huge Victorian house was just as she remembered it: the paint on the door and the fences was fresh but the colour was the same dark green that it had always been. The bushes and flowerbeds, the little lawn, as neat as ever. And, as always in the winter, lights streamed from every window. 'So much more welcoming than heavy curtains showing not a chink of light.'

How strange to be back in her childhood bedroom. Who was the girl who had slept and dreamed in here? How sentimental her mother was. Nothing was changed. The same teddy bears sat on the pink bedspread; the same posters of horses and film stars graced the walls; the same over-hyped Renoir reproduction. Wait a minute here. Is the painting a bad painting because millions of people hang a print on their living room wall?

'What snobs we become about music and art, *carissima*. Millions of people can hum the melody of the "Moonlight Sonata". Does that make it a poor piece of music or does it make it even greater because it is accessible?'

Sophie shook the voice out of her head. Renoir is accessible.

He is still a great painter. She would leave the print on the wall even though her older more sophisticated self would not have chosen it.

A knock on the door and there was her mother with a tray.

'Mum, I was coming down.'

'I thought you might want to rest first, that long journey. Was the train cold?'

'Overheated. It will soon be the year 2001; trains, even in Scotland, have heating, running water.'

'I know but somehow, no matter how much travelling I do, London to Edinburgh just seems such a long way.' She was pouring tea for both of them. 'Your father says I can have you to myself for a little since he got to pick you up.'

They had always done that: each parent trying to have a few minutes alone with each daughter. No doubt Kathryn had read in some magazine that it was important for children to have a parent's undivided attention. Sophie prepared herself.

'Judith's driving down later. I did tell you she was coming, didn't I?'

'No, Mum, but you didn't have to. She always spends Christmas with you.'

Kathryn sipped her tea and then looked down into the liquid as if she might find something there, an answer to a question perhaps. 'Poor Judith. I do wish she could have found someone but now that she's nearly sixty . . .' She sighed.

'No mere man would measure up, Mum.'

'Her standards are so high, dear.'

'Mother, face it, Judith sees everyone she meets, man or woman, only in terms of how useful they will be to her.'

Kathryn squirmed a little on the bed as if the conversation made her uneasy. 'Nothing wrong in being ambitious, dear. You're ambitious: Judith pointed that out. After all you did marry the son of a nobleman and now you have a lovely flat and a job working for a member of parliament.'

I won't lose my temper, not with Mum, maybe with Judith, not with Mum. 'I was in love with Rafael before I knew who or what he was and as for Hamish, he wanted an assistant who was familiar with Europe and who spoke German and Italian. I was in the right place at the right time.'

'Judith says your connection with the de Nardis family opens doors for you. There is nothing wrong in poor Judith wishing you might introduce her to a few people.'

Sophie stood up. 'I did. We did. Now, Mum, no more of Judith. I think I'll have a shower before lunch.'

Kathryn ignored the hint. 'We had a lovely card from Harry Forsythe. It was such a shame that you changed your mind about having dinner with him in Gabbiana.'

Gabbiana . . . the *trattoria*. No, she had had to get away, away from the shadow of the fortress on the hill, the fear that she might walk into a bar and find him . . . no, find her past life waiting for her.

Today is the first day of the rest of your life. Leave everything else behind. 'I had dinner with him in Edinburgh, Mother.'

'How lovely. University lecturers do spend a lot of time visiting one another.' Kathryn swelled with pleasure. 'You didn't tell us, but never mind.' She finished her tea and stood up, picking up the tray as she did so. 'Come down when you're ready, dear.' She smiled at her daughter. 'What a wonderful Christmas this is going to be.'

The tree was in the window of the drawing room and was already decorated except for three old and tattered toys, one belonging to each girl, and two newer ones, a little cardboard piano and a bell with George written on it. Sophie ignored the piano and hung her little elf. 'You haven't got the twins, Mum, or Jim, and next year you'll need yet another special one.'

Kathryn glowed. 'Wonderful. Mind you, she's far too young. Maybe you should hang Zoë's bear, dear; how I miss her.' She sighed. 'She used to hang Rafael's piano every year, didn't she, Archie?'

'The twins did it last year.'

Kathryn, who was kneeling on the rug sorting through a box

of decorations, sat back on her heels. 'So they did. Danny hung your elf and Peter hung . . .' She stopped.

'Rafael's piano,' said Sophie easily. 'Hang it if you want, Mum.' She looked at her mother steadily, forcing Kathryn to look at her. 'But he doesn't belong to this family any more. He played at the wedding because he loved Zoë when she was a little girl and for no other reason. We are civilised people, Mum, but we are no longer married.'

Kathryn looked away. 'Silly, isn't it, but I can't bear to throw things away.'

Archie jumped in. 'Ann is keeping up some of the family traditions with the boys, Sophie. Isn't that lovely, and now maybe Zoë and Jim.' He stopped talking, remembering perhaps that only this one daughter had no one with whom to carry on tradition.

Family traditions. Sophie remembered her first Christmas in Tuscany, a lightning visit between cities on Rafael's world tour. The countess celebrated traditions that had been handed down for generations but on Christmas morning Rafael had surprised his new wife with Christmas stockings embroidered with their names. Hers had flying angels. His, flying reindeer. 'Our own English tradition, courtesy of F.A.O. Schwarz,' he had teased. 'Look at all your little guardian angels.'

Wrapped up inside the stocking Sophie had found an exquisite porcelain angel.

'See him, *carissima*, the archangel. You know that his name means God heals but did I tell you that he is one of the three most important angels. He controls greed in man and even the mighty all-powerful sun, but also he watches over medical personnel and scientists. Maybe, you never know, that is why Carlo and I are so close. Do you see that this Rafael has the six wings of a seraph but he belongs also to the Cherubim, Dominions and Powers. It is said that he is the friendliest of all angels and also the funniest, like me, no? I think he would speak to lovely young ladies with dirty faces before they had been introduced. He is known as the healer; in Hebrew Rapha meant doctor or surgeon. Do you think that is why my mother called me Raffaele so that I might be a healer, a bringer of peace? That's what a musician does, is it not so? He is so important, the archangel, not the pianist. He is a prince of heaven. Are you impressed, *cara mia*, by my namesake? Poor old Paolo; he is not an angel, merely a repentant sinner.'

She looked at him archly. 'Perhaps it's easier to be a repentant sinner than to be such a wonderful angel.'

He had made love to her then and that became their second Christmas tradition.

'Good, here's Judith.' Archie went to the door. 'I was beginning to worry. Bit of a night out there but your aunt does like to drive.'

Cold kisses, then hot mulled wine, the mingled scents of cloves and cooked apples. Dinner was simple and then Judith and her brother sat drinking coffee by the fire while Sophie and Kathryn tidied up.

'Sophie, will you come to the watch-night service?'

Watch night. She was in England, not in Tuscany, and she was repairing bridges.

The exuberance of the twins made things easier; they were blissfully unaware of undercurrents and were excited that it was Christmas and that their aunt was visiting. 'You're exotic too, Sophie,' they agreed. 'You were married to a prince.'

Here we go again. 'A pianist, not a prince, and that was a long time ago. I'm not at all exotic.'

But they would not be persuaded.

Ann, George, and the boys came for Christmas lunch and they talked about everything except why Sophie had avoided being with her family for nearly five years. There were some near disasters.

'Did you have dinner with us last Christmas, Aunty?'

'Ann, did you know this sly sister of yours has been seeing the professor who was at Zoë's wedding?'

'Have we ever had Christmas at your house?'

'Where is your house?'

'Why have we never been there?'

'Aunty Judith says Aunty Sophie is rich, Daddy. Are you rich, Aunty Sophie? Aunty Judith says you used to fly all over the world on private planes. What does private plane mean, Daddy?'

'Sly puss. Are you trying to make someone jealous?' Wine made Judith too familiar.

'Aunty Zoë says Rafael is her most favourite person. He came to her wedding. Are you going to get married to him again?'

'They don't have to get married again because they're still married.'

'No, they're not.'

'Yes, they are. Sophie, Mummy said Rafael's a Catholic. Jim says that means you're not divorced. Catholics have to stay married for ever and ever.'

'Time out.' Sophie had had enough. I will not lose my temper. I will not lose my temper. 'Boys, do you want to visit me in Edinburgh?'

'Yes.'

'Then I never want to hear the name Rafael again. Understand?'

George helped Sophie prepare coffee. He was embarrassed, ill at ease. 'Sophie, we don't talk about you all the time. You do understand that, don't you?'

She looked at him dispassionately. 'From the boys' conversation, and dear Aunt Judith's, it seems I am all you ever talk about.'

'Judith was so sure – at the wedding – but we don't encourage her.'

'She has never needed encouragement.'

George carefully wiped the insides of six perfectly clean porcelain coffee cups. 'It's your own fault,' he said ruefully. 'Don't get angry. I don't know exactly what happened between you and Ann – maybe I'm too like Archie – and I should know everything and the real truth of those little porcelain—'

'She's welcome to them,' she said, but she would not look at him.

'Christmas isn't the time for truth. Damn it, I mean great

truths, laying everything out to be looked at. One day I'll ask for the truth, Sophie, although I really don't want to know. I was suggesting that if the boys were accustomed to you, if they had grown up seeing you around, then your divorce from Rafael would be like yesterday's pie-crust, soggy and uninteresting.'

'That is a new way of looking at it. For heaven's sake, George, you're going to rub the finish clean off those cups. I understand what you're saying but it is so wearing to labour over all these past histories. How do the boys even know the name Raffaele de Nardis? To them I have always been Sophie Winter.'

He finished putting the cups and saucers on the heavy oak tray. 'Interest in the castle, I think; maybe Judith and Stephanie. They're thick as thieves when they're together. I don't really remember.'

'You bring the tray, please.' Sophie picked up the coffee pot and carried it into the drawing room.

What a lovely family picture was presented to her as she entered. The children were on the floor near the floor-to-ceiling tree that, although denuded of most packages and brightly wrapped sweets, was still breathtakingly beautiful. Ann, her needlepoint on her knees, was sitting in a low chair near the log fire; Judith appeared to be dozing in the armchair on the other side of the hearth and Archie and Kathryn were playing snakes and ladders on a card table near the window. At four thirty it was already quite dark but since the heavy curtains had not been pulled the streetlights showed the garden thick with frost. To the twins' disgust there had been no snow.

Frost is white, was always George's answer to their complaints. Where does it say white means snow? They were not convinced and with the assurance of childhood answered, 'Of course it means snow.' Sophie agreed.

'We'll break off our game for coffee,' said Kathryn.

'That's because I'm winning.' Archie smiled at his middle daughter as he took a cup and saucer.

Judith seemed to have understood Sophie's unspoken message and they chatted easily while they drank their coffee and then, at the boys' request, the lights were turned off so that only the Christmas lights, the streetlights and the glow from the fire lighted the room. One by one, full of good food and wine, the family members napped, the twins on the floor like two puppies, their father, their grandparents and their great-aunt in their seats by the fire. Only the sisters stayed awake.

'At Christmas you think of the things that really matter, Sophie. Family,' said Ann. 'I'm glad you came.'

Sophie deliberated for a few minutes. 'So am I,' she agreed at last. 'It's been almost perfect, but nothing in life is, especially as you get older.'

Ann looked at her husband, his mouth hanging open, and at her children. 'Oh, it gets better as you get older, Sophie. I'm happier than I have ever been.'

'Are you happier now than you were when you first married?'

Ann took advantage of the semi-darkness to answer honestly. 'That stuff doesn't last. I think I'm content and I like being content. Love's young dream didn't last with you either, Sophie, but you're neither content nor happy. It's right what they say: "Life's a bitch." '

'Life is what we make of it.'

'You didn't make much of yours, did you? You were handed all the cards, Sophie, looks, brains. You were Dad's favourite and you went straight from him to Rafael. A home in a castle, world travel, designer clothes, fabulous jewellery, all the money you could spend, a world-famous husband who adored you, and you blew it.'

Sophie stood up; she was trembling. 'You were jealous of Rafael? But you never liked him.'

'Maybe I liked him too much.' Ann leaned over and refilled her glass. 'Not him,' she added hastily, 'but everything he repre-sented. George and I were struggling to find a down payment on a three-bedroomed house and you wrote about buying an apart-ment in New York. Everything dear Sophie wanted was just given to her because she was so pretty and so sweet. Do you remember at Zoë's wedding we had a fight and I said I told Judith

I found pills? I lied to you. I told Rafael too, Sophie, and it's been on my conscience ever since.' She stared open-mouthed at her sister as if she could not believe that she had actually made such a confession.

Sophie stared back. Ann, her own sister, had told a downright lie. Mischief, malice, wickedness.

'I didn't really mean to say it,' Ann babbled, 'but it came out and I knew I wanted you to struggle a bit, have to fight for him if you wanted him enough, but you didn't. You just gave in.'

There was a loud buzzing in her ears and Sophie felt her Christmas dinner rebel against the confines of her stomach. She turned and fled upstairs and after she had been violently ill, she went into the little girl Sophie's bedroom, locked the door and lay down fully dressed on the bed.

Merry Christmas to all, and to all a goodnight.

11

Harry phoned on Boxing Day.

'Did you have a good Christmas?'

'Lovely,' lied Sophie and wondered fleetingly how many similar lies were at that same moment being uttered all over Britain. Christmas did seem to bring out the best and worst in people. 'You?'

Harry told her that he and his father had enjoyed a delicious Christmas lunch in a very good restaurant. 'The works, even chipolata sausages and Christmas crackers. I miss crackers when I'm in Italy, isn't that silly?'

'No.'

'I also miss pantomime. You wouldn't like to go with us? *Puss in Boots?* Great fun.'

I'm living in a pantomime. 'More into *The Nutcracker* as Christmas entertainment, Harry, but we could meet for a drink. I really ought to brave the Christmas sales.'

'Great; we could meet at the Royal Society; convenient for all the good shops.'

How wonderful it would be to get away from the gloomy atmosphere and her mother's frantic pleadings. That morning had been ghastly.

'Sophie, you can't go back to Edinburgh and spend New Year's Eve alone.'

'I wouldn't be alone: I am not a hermit. Besides, Edinburgh is the "in" place in Britain to celebrate the New Year.'

'Please, darling. Ann wants us to spend New Year's Eve with them and maybe you two could have a long chat.'

Sophie stood up abruptly and moved to stand behind her chair.

She held on to the wooden back and glared at her mother. 'What is this with having long chats with Ann? We spoke yesterday – at great length.'

'No, you didn't. You said nothing of any importance. I think, your father and I think, that you need really to talk about all the dreadful things that you said to each other. You're sisters; you really have to work out these problems.'

What untapped depths there were to her mother? 'Mum, believe me, we talked.'

'And then you drank too much, got sick and locked yourself in your room.' Tears trembled in her mother's eyes but Sophie was harder now and the tears failed to move her.

'Is that Ann's story? Christmas Day was a nightmare, Mum, and I won't go through it again on New Year's Eve.'

'Chatting isn't the same as having a good deep conversation,' sniffed Kathryn. 'All the dreadful times, the rumours that you were a thief and worse, the whispers all around. People we had known for years turning the other way. Sophie, I don't know how I survived the misery, the shame; and your abandoning us didn't help. Now it looks as if we can be a loving, caring family again; so get it all out in the open and then bury it.'

I should have stayed in Edinburgh and I wish, I wish I had never gone to Tuscany. Do I? Rafael, my angel, heal me. She stood up and turned away from her mother's anxious eyes. 'I can hardly bury it, whatever it is, and bring it out into the open at the same time, Mum. The rumours in Italy were just that, rumours. Some people seem to prefer shadows, not brave enough to come out into the open and speak or denounce. As for Ann – we grew up and apart, I suppose. We never really got along that well as children; you and Daddy just didn't want to accept that.'

'Should she have married Giovanni?' asked Kathryn, following some convoluted trail in her own mind and thus completely surprising her daughter.

'For heaven's sake, Mother, when did I become the expert on holy matrimony? Had she married Giovanni she'd be fat and she'd be rich. Would she be happier? I do not know. Would Giovanni be happier? Most assuredly not.'

Kathryn ignored Giovanni and his state of mind. 'I don't think she's happy now. You're not happy. Where did I go wrong? It must be my fault.'

Sophie wanted with all her might to catch the first train north but instead she succumbed to the insidious pressure, as she always did, and put her arms around the bowed, seemingly fragile figure. 'Don't cry. I am perfectly happy and Ann is as happy, I would say, as any married woman. George is a decent man and she has the boys.'

'She wouldn't have any more, you know. George wanted to try for a little girl.'

Sophie said nothing. The joy, the responsibility, the power of being able to choose whether or not to have a child . . . Did Ann appreciate her position? She drew away, mentally and physically. 'I'm surprised she talked about it, Mum. Seems a bit between man and wife to me?'

'Like you and Rafael?'

Sophie stood up and moved towards the door. 'I've had it; I'm going to pack, Mum.'

Her mother ran after her and followed her into her bedroom, 'Sophie, please, I'm sorry, dear. I didn't mean to pry but I worry about you so much.'

Sophie turned and reached for her mother's arms and then she pushed her firmly down on to the bed. 'Please, if you want me to stay here, cut out all this claptrap. New Year's Resolution for you: I will stop looking for things to worry about.'

'You're not a mother,' cried Kathryn, unconsciously turning a knife in a wound she did not know was there. 'You think it will be easier when they're walking, then it's bound to get easier when they're at school, and you just know once they're married you won't have to even think about them any more, but it doesn't work like that, Sophie. When they're at school you're afraid they're being bullied, and when they start going out with young men you're terrified that'll they'll become pregnant and have to marry the first man they meet. And when they marry you worry that they'll get divorced and be unhappy.'

'Sounds a bit like wish fulfilment, Mum,' said Sophie coldly. 'Look, I'm a grown woman; I have a career, my own flat, which I am slowly buying, by the way; no one gave it to me; lots of friends, and there are men among them.' She thought fleetingly of Hamish and his 'One of these days we must have dinner.' 'Maybe you and Dad were right, I was too young when I married Rafael; I wasn't prepared, how could I be, for his lifestyle? There, I've said it. You were right, Mum. Does that make you feel better, or vindicated, or something?'

Her mother stood up stiffly. 'You never used to be hard and cruel.'

Sophie looked coldly at her mother. 'Carlo said something like that last summer. I don't mean to be cruel, Mum, but you must let me go my own way.'

'We did and look where that got all of us – almost hounded out of Italy. Have you any idea how that ghastly whispering campaign affected us, how many of Daddy's colleagues believed you were a thief or an adulterer or a drug addict or all of them? It was a waking nightmare, Sophie. Judith and Stephanie were so wonderfully supportive, trying to find out who started it; they thought it was Stella; poor Stella. And you just ran away, leaving us with all that. You only came back when someone accused Ann of stealing things from your London house.'

Sophie felt her legs begin to shake. 'That's ancient history.'

But her mother, now worked up, was not about to let go. She sat down again as if she could no longer stand up on her own. 'The rumours started and then you left and soon the whispers stopped. Who denounced you, Sophie?'

'There wasn't a formal *denunzia*,' whispered Sophie. 'It didn't get that far. Gossip starts like that in Italy: insidious. No one knows how it starts and no one knows how it stops. The countess probably – stopped it, I mean, or Paolo, he was always my friend. Starting the rumours, telling the lies? Marisa, maybe: she always adored Rafael. I don't know and I don't care. And to blame

Stella! Was that Judith? If she dared say one thing about Stella—'

'No, she didn't. She was wonderful. You never did appreciate her and all she did for you.'

'Please.' Judith, the most selfish, self-seeking of people. Sophie would never believe good about her.

'That de Nardis treasure or whatever it was, was found in your house. I know you didn't take it. Who put it there, Sophie?' Kathryn looked beseechingly up at her daughter but Sophie was looking away from her and said nothing. 'So many unanswered questions, so much evil and hatred.' She stood up. 'I'll tell your sister you don't care to bring in the New Year with us.'

She left the room, grief and ill usage wafting round her like a chiffon scarf on a windy day. Sophie sat down on the bed and swore fluently. Families. Impossible to live with; impossible to live without. What would she do for New Year if she decided to go home, home to her lovely little flat? All her friends had already made plans, plans that included family or significant relationships, if that was the latest descriptive phrase. She was neither one nor the other and would probably sit with some smoked salmon, half a bottle of champagne and ghastly television broadcasting. A book; curl up in bed with a book, or just wrap up warmly and look at the city out of the windows in her little eagle's nest? It sounded so tempting.

No, she would not do that. She would stay and soothe her mother's ruffled plumage and make meaningless small talk with Ann if she could even bring herself to speak to her without slapping her hard across her plump, pink face. But for now she would let her mother stew a little because what had just taken place was another example of her possessiveness, her bullying. My mother, the blackmailer. 'If you don't stay, Sophie, I'll be unhappy,' the words always unsaid but hanging there, almost tangible.

Suddenly Sophie laughed. Kathryn Winter and Contessa Gabriella de Nardis, two mothers cut from the same cloth. The sweet irony of that thought.

'But of course you must take an apartment in Verona, Raffaele. Here in the *castello* your home, everything would be done for

Sophie: no stress, no worries. She can devote herself to her husband but . . . if dear Sophie is happier in an apartment . . .'

I don't want my mother to be unhappy, for God's sake. Sophie tried to laugh. That was almost exactly what Rafael had said. She lay back on the bed and thoughts of other New Year's Eve parties flitted, into her consciousness. Vienna, city of romance, and Rafael there to play at the annual concert on New Year's morning. Her gown, her first from the house of Valentino, and round her neck emeralds, a Christmas gift from Rafael. They had danced alone in the middle of a crowded ballroom.

'Happy New Year, my darling girl.'

'Rafael, I'm not a girl; I'm a woman.' For a second the precious moment was sullied because it was his mother who kept reminding him of the difference in their ages.

'A woman? You must come back to our suite and prove it to me, *mio tesoro*.' And he had waltzed her towards the door.

'Maestro, Maestro, you can't leave; the party is just beginning.'

Duty, responsibility, and she did not mind; well, not very much because the hour would come when they would be alone and he would open the clasp of the glittering emeralds with his strong pianist's fingers and . . .

Sophie stood up. That life was over and the emeralds lay untouched with other jewels in a bank vault. She went out and stood at the top of the stairs and watched her mother, aware that her middle daughter had just left her room, go to the telephone table and begin to dial.

'George,' said Kathryn in a voice of unmitigated doom, 'is Ann there?'

'I'll see if there's a train north on the second, Mother,' said Sophie as she walked down the stairs and into the living room. She did not look at her mother but was aware of the look of satis-faction. She did not need to see it. Had she not seen it often enough before?

Her father was doing a crossword at the table near the window. 'Hello,' he said without looking up. 'Am I to take you to the station?'

'I suppose trains won't run much before Wednesday. Otherwise I would leave tomorrow.'

'So much haste to leave us. You won't mind too much, sweetheart. Your mother misses Zoë.'

'You'll take it in turns when they come back, Dad.' She leaned over his shoulder, took the pencil from him and filled in some squares. 'I get so tired of being manipulated.'

As usual he ignored the main point. 'Dash it, I had that word.'

'I know. I was merely saving you time.'

He turned the paper so that she could see it better. 'You know, this is one of the things that gets up Ann's nose.'

She looked at him in astonishment. So he did know that *something is rotten in the State of Denmark*. 'What? Doing crosswords together? We've always done them. That's how I learned my first big words.'

'And now you put them in for me.' He smiled sadly. 'Ann was no good at crosswords.'

'You know, Dad, that life is too short for nonsense like this. I'm going for a walk.'

He folded the paper, crossword page out. 'I'll come with you.'

'It's cold outside.'

'It's your mother who doesn't like snow, Sophie, or would you like to be alone?'

'Not if my favourite man in all the world wants to be with me.' She turned away to hide the sudden tears and ran back upstairs calling out that she was going for her coat.

Her father, wearing the funny old fur hat he had bought years ago in an outdoor market in Lucca, hometown of the composer Puccini, was waiting for her at the door when she came downstairs. He said nothing but merely opened the door and they stepped out into a really cold wind that made her gasp.

'You live in Edinburgh, and this healthy breeze has you shivering?'

She laughed. 'I shiver more in Edinburgh.'

Wrong thing to say. He looked at her. 'You opened like a flower in Tuscany, *bella*.'

He very seldom spoke Italian even though he loved the country, had worked there, even owned a property, and had spent countless holidays clambering over Etruscan tombs. But he had called her *bella*, beautiful one, in the year that she had married Rafael.

'Am I your favourite man, Sophie? I don't want to be. I am content to be your father, with all my failings . . .'

'And your strengths.'

'Strengths? I saw that your marriage was disintegrating and I had no strengths then to help you.'

She turned to him and stopped and they stood on the path while the cold wind blew around them. 'A marriage is between a man and a woman, Dad, and if the love between them is strong enough, then any . . . weaknesses anyone else shows shouldn't matter. Don't feel unhappy, and never ever guilty. We just didn't love each other enough.'

'I thought you adored him.'

Pain knifed through her. 'Adoration, don't they say, should be reserved for God who is perfect? Rafael was only a man.'

'I could have sworn he loved you.'

Sophie turned and bent into the wind. 'What is this, almost New Year, so everyone drags out the past, warts and all, and tries to make sense of it? Dad, it's over, has been over for five years. I saw him at the wedding and silly, sweet little Zoë thought she ought to try to bring us together but we're not the same people. I don't want to be married to him any more. Too many people were in bed with us. I'm perfectly happy. I love my job, my flat. Did I tell you I sent Harry a fur hat for Christmas? Yours is so tacky; I wish I had bought you one too.'

He did not ask about Harry as her mother would have done. 'I love this hat,' was all he said.

They walked on in silence but it was not a comradely peace. Questions were hovering on her father's tongue. She knew how he hated confrontation, always putting things aside. If he did not discuss them, they were not there. But he had not been permitted to ignore the chilling fact of her divorce. For five years, after the initial anguish and soul searching, what did I do, what did I not do that I could have done, the unasked questions had remained unanswered, the pathways had remained firmly untravelled and Sophie had stayed away from everyone, preferring to suffer alone. Now, the visit *en famille*, to Tuscany, had reopened all the old sores, and all the unanswered questions were hovering around like gnats in the Scottish Highlands.

'Sophie, you don't love Rafael any more? I don't think I could bear it if you still loved him.'

'Good heavens, Dad. I don't even remember the girl who loved Rafael.'

'What about the Rafael who loved Sophie? Do you remember him?'

'He never existed; I made him up.' She stopped again on the path and turned to look at him. 'Dad, I was afraid to go back to Tuscany, afraid, but I got there and exorcised all my ghosts. I met Rafael and he's charming and so is Miss Raisa. They're right for each other; they understand the same things. I honestly hope they will be very happy together and if you and Mother were hoping that romance would be rekindled, it's time you both grew up.'

'Your mother thinks sometimes that maybe if she had been able to see him as an ordinary person, not the son of the castle on the hill, or the world-famous pianist, if she had been able to be at ease with him . . .' He trailed off.

'I won't accept that burden too, Daddy. Tell Mother to stop torturing herself; the marriage didn't work. It had nothing to do with anyone but me and Rafael. Now, enough, or I will go home.'

She sensed him wince. 'Edinburgh is my home now, as Surrey and Tuscany were. I've moved on. Let me go.'

He tucked his arm into hers and slowed his stride to match hers, as Rafael had always done, but he did not know that. They walked back to the house, this time in companionable silence.

'I love to see smoke coming from a chimney.'

'Part of Christmas. The sitting room will be much too hot and your mother will grumble all morning about the mess coal fires make but every time I say we should block up the fireplace she finds a dozen reasons to keep it the way it is.'

' "The girls love it." ' Sophie quoted.

'Exactly.'

'She's right, of course. We all do but you'll note that we have all gone for clean, efficient heating systems.'

The house smelled of baking sponges and roasting potatoes. Kathryn, still elegant and only slightly flushed from her efforts, was in the kitchen. 'I'm doing a few things for the party.'

'I'll give you a hand,' said Sophie, but just then the telephone rang and it was Harry.

Harry to the rescue. Would he like to be seen as a knight in shining armour come to rescue the princess? She was not ready to ask him but she was so glad to have an excuse to get away for a day. In the evening he rang back to say he had tickets for a performance of the *Nutcracker Suite* and had he been in the room she would have kissed him.

Because they were almost giving it away, she bought an absolutely beautiful simple little black Escada dress that she didn't need at the Selfridge's sale and, although he had sworn that he loved the one he had been wearing, she bought a fur hat for her father.

Instead of meeting Harry at the RSA she took the Underground to Earl's Court Road where Harry's father had a large, untidy, book-filled flat. Old Mr Forsythe was delighted to meet her and they chatted over delicious mugs of hot mulled wine. The conversation ranged from the bargains to be had at Christmas sales to the new Scottish Parliament. Mr Forsythe had met no one connected with the parliament and was fascinated by it.

At last Sophie managed to change the subject and they talked about Italy, a country the Forsythes knew well, and seemed to understand and love in equal measure.

'I shall show you my most treasured possession, Sophie,' Said Mr Forsythe when Harry had gone to get his coat. 'Harry gave it to me for Christmas . . . why, it must be all of six or seven years ago.' He stopped in front of the bookcase and scratched his chin. She heard the rasp as if his beard were coming through. 'No, it may even be more than that; old age, my dear. One year is just like another.' He unlocked the glass-fronted bookcase and took down something wrapped in soft cloth. 'I ration myself, Sophie, because it's so fragile, but look.'

He put the package down on the cluttered tabletop, making space for it by brushing books and papers aside with his heavily veined old hands. 'Look, Sophie, seventeenth century and still completely legible.'

Sophie looked down at the particle of fragile manuscript with its spidery writing. She felt ill, cold and clammy; her mouth was dry and she tried desperately to pull herself together. She knew what it was, but still she had to ask, to assume a friendly interest she did not feel. 'What is it, Mr Forsythe?'

'Giovanni Battista, Count of Morone, seventeenth century. Only a fragment, of course, but there are several complete manuscripts in museums.'

Sophie swallowed the bile that was rising in her throat. 'It must be worth a fortune.' Was it the same? Who had sold it? Harry had bought it: Harry who lived in Florence and was an acknowledged authority.

'Now it is: what the complete manuscript would cost I cannot begin to think. Harry could never afford it; he bought this for me but it is, of course, an investment.'

'Never afford what?' Harry, complete with coat and the fur hat from Jenner's was in the doorway. He came forward. 'Oh, the family jewels,' he said. 'Have you any interest in old manuscripts, Sophie? I picked this piece up in Venice years ago; cost me a fortune but it was too good an opportunity to miss. I believe it was sold at least once before in Florence.' He watched as the old man reverently rewrapped the package and locked it away again. 'We find the arts of Italy allow us to forgive her all her other faults.'

Sophie managed to pull herself together sufficiently to wish the old man a happy New Year. Giovanni Battista, Giovanni

Battista: the name went round and round in her head, for a manuscript in the hand of the seventeenth-century Italian count was one of the treasures that La Contessa de Nardis had assured her son had gone missing from Il Castello de Nardis during his marriage.

She was too quiet on the way to the theatre.

'Are you all right, Sophie?' Harry swayed towards her with the movement of the train and she tried to smile.

'Yes, of course. I hate the Underground; one of the reasons I work in Edinburgh.'

Immediately he was contrite. 'Damn, I should have ordered a taxi; I didn't think. It's just so much faster this way.'

She smiled up at his honest, concerned face. 'No, no. What is it, ten miles an hour if you're lucky in the rush hour? Edinburgh's impossible too. Most of the time I walk. *Plus ça change*. Rome has been grumbling about traffic jams for centuries.'

They chatted easily until they reached the theatre, found their seats, and sat down. Sophie vowed to relax and give herself up to the moment but, for once, the lovely music failed to soothe or to delight. Try as she might, her attention refused to stay in the delightful hall and flew instead to the *castello*; again she saw the countess, usually so rigidly controlled, bowed under the weight of the burden she had been carrying alone for so long.

'I have tried, Raffaele,' she whispered. 'I encouraged Sophie's interest in the family history. Then one day after we had walked in the gallery I noticed that a glass was missing. I assumed that I had moved it myself, absent-mindedly, when Portofino came to fuss at me about his flowers or my appetite. Then, a brooch disappeared, and later . . . never mind. But the Battista manuscripts, so rare, so precious, such a part of our history, our culture; I could keep quiet no longer.'

And Rafael chose to comfort his mother and not his wife. 'It makes no sense,' he said much later when his lawyers were there to discuss the settlements. 'I would have given you anything.'

She wanted to scream: I didn't take them. You know I didn't, Rafael. But she was afraid of losing control. Carlo had said, The next few weeks are so crucial, Sophie. Take care. She refused the settlement, the lovely house in London and the jewels that he had given her, and her decision was misinterpreted. She wanted nothing to remind her of a dream that had turned into a nightmare and he thought she had to be expiating her guilt. With her mother and her sisters she went one last time to her London home, to remove the clothes that she would wear; she wanted nothing else. Ann wrapped up several of the small treasures that had been gifts from Rafael: 'You'll think differently in a year or two, Sophie.' She remembered howling, 'Do what you like with them,' and so could not complain when Ann eventually did just that and sold her unwanted gifts, including the exquisite archangel Raffaele.

Tchaikovsky's Christmas fantasy drew to its exquisite satisfying close and Sophie and Harry joined the hundreds of other theatre-goers on the rain-washed streets looking for a taxi. Impossible to talk, to ask him about the manuscript. Harry was an authority on medieval Italian manuscripts. The manuscript fragment he had bought for his father was genuine but where had he bought it and from whom? She would wait until she had had time to think and then she would ask him. Someone had stolen the manuscript from the *castello*, divided it into pieces, and had sold it. Just possibly, Harry knew who.

At last it was New Year's Eve and it was time to go to Ann's house. It was a cold, clear night and so Sophie threw a warm multicoloured shawl over her 'bargain' dress on the short drive to the modern development where Ann and George had bought their home. As a grudging concession to the festive season Ann had not pulled her sitting room curtains and the huge Christmas tree with its co-ordinated silver decorations could be seen from the road.

'The boys have a little tree in the dining room with all their handmade decorations,' said Kathryn as if she had known exactly what Sophie was thinking. 'What do you think of the new door?'

New door? The main door was in a slight recess in the centre of the house front. On either side were the identical and rather imposing bow-fronted windows of the sitting room and the dining room. Sophie stared; it was a new door but it was exactly like . . . no, at last she had seen it. Above the door a mock Regency fanlight window had been installed and a burnished brass lamp hung from the ceiling of the recess. Real holly and ivy was twined around the lamp.

'It's lovely; very Ann,' said Sophie as the door opened and the twins, in their pyjamas, hurtled out to greet their aunt and their grandparents. 'We get to stay up till midnight but not a minute after.'

'Seconds after,' added Peter or was it Danny. 'We've had dinner; you're getting fancy stuff but we had fish fingers. We never get fish fingers at Granny's house.'

George came and chased his sons into the family room. 'Go watch television. The grown-ups are having drinks in the lounge, then dinner, and if you two fall asleep then too bad.'

Ann, her hair newly done by the same hairdresser who, according to Claudio, had ruined it in the summer, came to greet them. The colourist had managed to restrain himself.

But why are her clothes always so frumpish? She looks older than Mum, thought Sophie and then mentally chastised herself for meanness.

'Black's not a good colour, Sophie,' said Ann, unknowingly getting her own back. 'You're too thin and it makes you look scrawny. Zoë, now, is putting on a little weight. She looks wonderful in their Christmas pictures, doesn't she?'

'Isn't she just glowing happily because of all those breathing exercises they do in pre-natal classes these days, Sophie?' said Kathryn.

Ann threw open the door of the drawing room. 'Mum, what would Sophie know about that? George has made Buck's Fizz. Pour us all a drink, George.'

Sophie stood looking at the tree and she could hear and see nothing, but she was aware of a humming of voices like the mosquitoes in Tuscany, *Zan, Zan, Zanare,* and the colours of the room, the tree with its lights and its lopsided decorations, the scarlet of the poinsettias on either side of the beswagged fireplace, whirled around and around like a kaleidoscope.

'Happy, happy,' said George and handed her a tall, cool glass full of orange juice and champagne. 'You okay?'

'I'm admiring the mantelpiece.'

George, ill at ease, relaxed a little. 'I think the pineapples are an American idea but I like them; I've forgotten what they're supposed to represent.'

'Does it matter? It's beautiful.'

'The boys and I collected all the greenery either from our garden, Archie's, or the wood.'

'You'll have to come to Edinburgh next year, George, and decorate me.'

Ann, who had been handing round great platters of smoked salmon, paused. 'Oh, he can't do that, Sophie,' she said, quite seriously. 'We're planning to take the house in Tuscany over every Christmas. Christmas in Tuscany, so good for the boys. The skiing is getting better at Zum. Aunt Judith always goes to Stephanie for New Year so if you and Dad would come, Mum, it would be perfect.'

'I've told you, Ann. It's too cold for me.'

'Nonsense. It's no colder than the south of England and the house is warm. Isn't it, Sophie? You're the expert on Italian winters.'

Sophie tried successfully to reach unconcernedly for another slice of salmon. She would not let Ann know that she hated her goading – and why was Ann doing it? What vicarious pleasure was she getting from this? 'I know nothing about Italian winters, Ann. Rafael goes to New York or London or South America every winter. But you know that, every year somewhere different.' She turned away from her sister. 'We went to Vienna, Dad. Do you remember I rang you? So beautiful.'

Was that where . . . ? No, she would not think about it. She laughed. 'Too cold for you, Mum. Snow up to your knees – and higher. That's as close as I ever got to an Italian winter. You tell us about winter, Dad. You spent several in Tuscany, all alone.'

'And blue,' said Archie. 'But not from cold. There was an unbelievable snowstorm the first year I went to work in Italy and your mother is convinced that it's always like that.'

'It is,' said Kathryn crossly.

'In the mountains, dear.'

'We'd best have dinner so that I can clear before my other guests arrive.' Ann turned as her pyjama-clad sons hurtled themselves through the door and on to the trays as if they had been starved for a week.

'Yuck. Salmon,' they said together. 'Sophie, we saw him, Rafael; that's why we came in, so boring.'

George – God bless George – questioned the boys so that Sophie was able nonchalantly to spear a lemon slice and suck on it; a disgusting habit, Rafael had scolded her. 'No food, that's it. What do you mean? When did you see Rafael?'

'He's on TV. He's in Prague, in a castle. I wish he would show us the *castello*.'

Sophie refused to move, to listen, to hear, to think, to feel. She sucked her slice of lemon.

'Sophie?'

'Yes, Mum?'

George had gone to the family room to see what it was that was exciting the twins. 'Too late,' he said as he returned. 'I think it was a news item but they may have shown a piece. Rafael is playing in the St Vitus Cathedral in Prague; something silly he said, something personal.'

The children laughed. 'It was twiddly stuff, unhatched chicks or something silly. Chickens can't dance inside their shells, can they?'

Sophie felt as if she had stopped breathing. 'I like that, Rafael; it's fun. I feel like dancing.'

'It is dancing, *cara*. "The Ballet of the Unhatched Chicks." Mussorgsky, *Pictures at an Exhibition*. Listen, I play it for you. Every time I play it you will know I am thinking only of you.'

'Silly piece to play in a cathedral,' was all she said.

I am thinking only of you.

'That's not what he's playing at midnight,' said George crossly. 'Peace, reconciliation etc, etc. for the New Year. God, I hope he's wearing woollen underwear.'

'Silk' said Sophie lightly. 'He believes in silk, George. Come on, Ann. I'll help you.'

'I can manage.'

'I know,' said Sophie brightly but fiercely. 'And then, dear sister, you will moan for weeks about having had to do everything while Sophie swanned around.'

'That's not true.'

Sophie had had enough. Rafael was playing her piece in Prague. He had played it in Edinburgh too. Had he forgotten or did it mean anything? A habit, that's all. A habit that starts with a lovely idea and carries on long after the idea is lost. No, of course he had forgotten; it was five years. She had forgotten her vow never to see her sister. 'It can't be that bad,' she had thought but it was that bad and worse. If possible she would return to Edinburgh and she would never ever ever see Ann again and she would thus live very happily ever after. She slammed the door of the oven and confronted her sister. They would have it out, New Year's Eve, cards on the table. 'Ann, tell me, what did I ever do to make you hate me so?'

'You were born, I suppose.'

In spite of her bravado Sophie had not expected such an answer and Ann had obviously not expected to say the words either. She was stunned by her own vitriol and began to flutter like a dying moth from place to place in the kitchen, achieving nothing useful while Sophie stood stunned, watching her as she fluttered waiting for her to alight. 'I don't mean that, I don't mean that,' Ann wailed. 'Oh, Sophie, you're my little sister and I've made a mess of everything.'

Sophie looked dispassionately at her and suddenly realised that she didn't give a damn. Maybe tomorrow when the Buck's Fizz wore off, she had never been able to drink champagne, except with Rafael. Why was that? 'Don't add your lovely dinner to the list, Ann,' she said coldly. 'It will be perfect. You can cook. Now let's serve dinner and then I am going into your drawing room and I am going to be very, very merry until one minute past midnight and then I am going and you need never see me again.'

Sophie counted the minutes from then until the blissful moment a few days later when her train left for the north, and as she counted she cursed British Rail and British Airways and anyone else she could think of who might be responsible for the paucity of reliable transportation north. Did the powers that be not realise that some people hated being with their families at Christmas and New Year and were anxious to escape? She went through the New Year's festivities like an automaton and congratulated herself that no one had any idea of how badly she wanted to escape. She had drunk, it seemed, gallons of wine, champagne, no matter, if it was poured she drank it and the more she drank the more sober she became. Funny old thing, alcohol.

12

Archie Winter noticed how merry his daughter was and he relaxed, congratulating himself. All in Kathryn's mind, this split. Look at them – sisters. Everything is perfect, except this divorce, and we've all got over that unpleasantness. Must invite Harry to dinner when we get back to Tuscany. Just right for Sophie. Sensible, solid.

Kathryn agreed when, the holidays over, he discussed his plans with her. Kathryn had tidily disposed of any residual worries the holidays had thrown up and was still as euphoric as her grandsons. As always she saw what she wanted to see. 'What a wonderful Christmas and New Year, Archie. Have we ever had a better one? Well, it would have been better with Zoë too.'

She answered her own question and, out of habit, Archie let her sail on happily in her little boat. 'I was in shock five years ago, Archie; I can tell you now. The countess, one minute all sweetness, giving me her unwanted Armanis, and the next moment saying such horrible things about our girls.'

'Ann did remove things from Sophie's house, Rafael's house.'

'Everything belonged to Sophie, even Rafael said that, and Sophie did say, "Do what you want with them." I was there; I heard her. But spreading rumours that our Sophie was stealing from her husband's family . . . that was unforgivable.'

'The countess wouldn't stoop to gossip, Kathryn,' ventured Archie. 'She was heartbroken when she had to tell Rafael; even Sophie agrees about that. Damn it all,' he said, standing up and striding around the room, 'it's all been neatly pushed under the carpets. Some treasures disappeared over a period of several years. My daughter,' he almost choked, 'my daughter was accused of stealing them. Nasty rumours slide around Tuscany like snakes in the ruins and then Sophie agrees to a divorce and, poof, rumours subside – we're just left with a nasty tint that has taken years to fade.'

'You are waxing poetic this morning, Archie love. Might as well say St Patrick got rid of the snakes and . . .'

'What on earth are you talking about? St Patrick? What's he got to do with it? For God's sake, Kathryn, you don't seem to realise that no one has ever been accused of stealing that stuff.'

He turned around and Kathryn, not the most observant of women, saw that her husband had turned an alarming colour. 'Archie,' she said and started up from her armchair.

'I've avoided this too often. I told Sophie I saw trouble and did nothing to help her.'

'It's over now. Sit down, Archie, you've gone all funny.'

He sat down but went on as his colour gradually got back to normal, 'We let them bully us. We should have demanded an apology, demanded to be shown proof that anything valuable went missing. Oh, God . . .' He had just remembered.

Kathryn looked at him, her lips trembling. 'They did; the count found the jewelled crucifix, the most precious thing belonging to the de Nardis family, in Sophie's dressing-table. She didn't take it, Archie.'

'Damn it, Kathryn, I know that, but who put it there? Rafael said he'd never seen it before in his life.'

Kathryn folded away her knitting, tidily and methodically, and stood up. 'It's all over, Archie. Let's not even think of it any more. What a good idea to invite Harry. He's quite charming. Zoë likes him, and Jim.'

She walked out of the room, still talking, and left Archie alone. He picked up the day's newspaper and turned the pages till he found the crossword. Better to let sleeping dogs lie. Sophie was happy; she was getting along with Ann, wasn't she, and she doted on the twins. They would help keep her with the family where she belonged. No point in stirring things up again. New Year. Time to move on, let things go.

Archie lost himself in four across.

On her way back to Edinburgh Sophie sat on the train and, behind her closed eyes, relived the entire Christmas holiday. She dismissed the time with her sister and her Aunt Judith as the price she had to pay to keep the family together; it mattered to her parents and she loved them. But the viewing of the fragment of Battista manuscript in Harry's father's home had been a tremendous shock. Not for a moment did she think that Harry had stolen it; apart from anything else he had no *entrée* to the de Nardis home, but the sight of the precious fragment lying there on the table before her, and the old man's childlike joy in ownership, had proved irrevocably that artefacts had been taken from the *castello*. That led to more questions: by whom and when? Nothing makes any sense, nothing.

Happy New Year, Sophie.

Christmas and New Year had always been perfect with Rafael.

'Home for Christmas? But I am home, *carissima*. Wherever you are is home.'

She would not think of Rafael. She no longer loved him. Why did she have to keep proving that point? He was in love – finally – with a singer. She would not think of him any more; she would not think, for these few hours, of stolen treasures or broken marriages. She would think instead of how refreshing it was to be away from her mother and her cloying blackmail. Mothers of the world. Would I have been a better mother than my mother or Rafael's? Don't think, Sophie.

But almost as if the rhythm of the train was sending her into a hypnotic trance, her mind refused to obey her commands. *La contessa.* Did she deliberately set out to ruin my marriage, or did she just make life hell, and then wonder helplessly at the result?

It had never occurred to her that Rafael's mother would not like her. All her life she had smiled at the world and it had smiled back. 'A countess? Your mother is a countess?'

'Retired,' he said immediately and then frowned. 'Not really. My older brother has a very nice wife and she is the Contessa de Nardis but everyone *thinks* of Mamma as the contessa and she is, of course, the dowager.'

'Horrid word, dowager.'

'*Precisamente*. It has no music, but my mother is lovely and you will like her very much. She has been a widow for a long time but Paolo and I hardly realised we had no father because Mamma did everything, hunting and shooting, sailing, skiing.'

'I have done none of those things.'

He looked at her in astonishment and she thought at first that it was because he could not conceive of anyone who had not grown up with this silver spoon, but it was because he was surprised that she thought it mattered. 'I think you are the most perfect person I have ever known, Sophie,' he said seriously.

She blushed; she was still very young. 'Perfect? Me? But I'm so ordinary, Rafael.'

He laughed and hugged her. 'You are extraordinary, Sophie Winter. You fill my heart, my senses, my dreams; you make de Nardis forget his music because he sees your lovely face on every page of manuscript.'

'I see your face all the time too – and I can't study, Rafael.'

'You know everything you need to know – but if you want to learn to shoot,' he said with a smile, 'I will teach you.'

'Of course I don't want to learn to shoot. You Italians are dreadful, killing all the little birds, and you, a musician?'

He laughed at her logic and kissed her. 'I swear to you that I have never shot anything smaller than a deer and then we ate it all winter. Does that make it all right?'

'You do laugh at me, Rafael. Ann said you did, and she is right.'

'I laugh for joy in your presence, Sophie.' But immediately he was contrite. He kissed her fingers, inside her wrist and he laughed as she shivered. Then he kissed her lips, but very gently.

'Oh, I want so much to be your husband, my Sophie. But for now I will be good. Come, we will go to see my mamma and she will tell you how perfect I am.'

The countess was in her drawing room, a vast room on the third floor of one of the towers. She was seated at a window and beyond the outline of her head, Sophie, had she wanted, could have seen the Apennines and the Alps spreading blue and lilac and green and purple and grey in the distance, but her eyes saw nothing but Rafael's mother. Her head was shaped as if by a sculptor's knife, high cheekbones, a straight nose like her son's, and slim dark brows arched over deep-set eyes. She rested her head on her right hand as if her delicate long neck was too fragile for the weight of the de Nardis worries, and diamonds on her fourth finger glittered in the afternoon sun. She was wearing a deceptively simple white satin jacket and camisole above black satin pants and round her neck hung a slender gold chain with a locket and a string of fabulous blister pearls, not one of which was the same shape or size as its neighbour.

How long, thought Sophie in panic, had it taken the divers to find enough of these pearls to make that necklace?

'Mamma.' Rafael broke the silence and hurried forward and the countess turned. For a second, no more, she looked at Sophie and instinctively Sophie knew that in all ways she had been found wanting, and then the countess's sad, dark eyes looked on her son and blazed with light.

Raffaele, my darling boy.' She spoke in slightly accented English. 'And your little friend.'

She kissed her son and then held out a slim hand to Sophie. 'Dear child, welcome to Il Castello dei Nardis, our home.'

Sophie looked at Rafael and he was smiling, happy and unaware that his mother had just, with a few words, destroyed Sophie's belief in a wonderful future. She hates me, and he so dotes on her that he cannot see it. Little friend, indeed. The most patronising . . . She wanted to cry, to run from the room down the flights of great stone stairs, out into the gardens with their miles of roses, their lemon trees, their fields of lavender.

'Come, we will have lunch on the terrace.' The contessa slipped her arm inside Sophie's and smiled at her. 'Raffaele tells me you love our Tuscan food and that you are learning Italian.

Too many of your compatriots assimilate nothing of our culture; they are happy with wine and pasta.'

They were out on the terrace that seemed to be suspended miles up in the air. All of Italy, it seemed to Sophie, was spread out around them. 'How beautiful,' she whispered instinctively.

'Look down there, Sophie. I may call you Sophie? Do you see those stones down there in the olive grove? That is an Etruscan temple. The Etruscans had a civilisation here before the Italians. You must visit that place but watch out for vipers, snakes.'

'I have visited several with my father, Contessa,' she would not be bullied.

'I will protect her if she chooses to go, Mamma.' Rafael's voice sounded troubled and then he dismissed whatever was troubling him and smiled. 'Come, we do not sightsee today. I'm ravenous.'

As if he had been heard, two immaculate waiters appeared on the terrace. One carried a tray with glasses so delicate that Sophie feared her nervous fingers would snap the stem. The other brought the first tray of *antipasti, bruschette* with Pecorino cheese, with prosciutto, with pesto, fat olives, cubes of cheese marinated in oil. Sophie glanced at Rafael and he smiled and she knew that he too was remembering her first dinner with him when she had attempted to sample everything, believing that the array of *antipasti* comprised the entire meal instead of just the first course.

'It is not necessary to eat everything. You choose only what really appeals.'

'It all does.'

'You will blow up and burst and I want you to be around for the *dolci*, the sweets. Oh, yes, my Sophie, I want you around.'

Now she accepted a glass of cold white wine and took a small *bruschette* from one of the trays. She would have liked an olive but how did the contessa get rid of the stones? She would not fall into that trap. Other courses followed and after two glasses of wine, Sophie changed to *acqua minerale* which Italians seemed to drink glass for glass with their wine. Maybe that was why she never seemed to have encountered an inebriated Italian, but to be quite sure these Italians were not seeing an inebriated Brit she decided to pass on what were probably fine vintages.

During lunch, in the sweetest possible way, the contessa questioned her. That her parents owned their home in Lunigiana was good, as was her university study. 'Paolo went to the University of Cambridge, after Padua, and my Raffaele – we wanted him to continue at the University of Oxford after Verona but no, naughty boy, all that was in his head was music. He had to go to New York, to this Juilliard, and it was very fine. St Andrews is good too, no? And what will you do with your life when you graduate, Sophie?'

She looked quickly at Rafael and he nodded and stood up. 'Mamma, Sophie has decided to spend her life with me, making me happy.' He looked at Sophie as he said it and she could sense his unspoken promise to make her happy too. 'She will not finish at the university. We want to marry this year before I go to Japan. There is no point in waiting; we know what we want.'

The contessa looked almost grey, certainly much whiter than her exquisite blouse. Against the sudden pallor of her skin her lips looked blue. 'Marriage? But you hardly know each other. She is a child, Raffaele. How can you think of marriage to someone you have only just met. I can't allow it. I forbid it.'

To Sophie's embarrassment Rafael knelt down on the terrace by his mother's chair. 'Mamma, I'm a grown man, more than old enough for marriage. Smile, *cara*. You know you have been telling me for years to find a nice wife. Here she is and I love her.'

The contessa stood up and turned to where Sophie was standing frozen into stone against the wall that prevented the diners on the terrace from tumbling down the mountainside to join the vipers in the ancient Etruscan temple. She shrugged, that all-encompassing gesture with which the true Italian can say everything – or nothing. She held out her hands. 'Come, child, you will have to forgive my first reaction. I don't think my wicked son has told you of his ghastly schedule, of how he locks himself upstairs for eight, ten, even fifteen hours and practises. Has he told you how he lives like a gypsy for most of the year, in and out of airports and concert halls so that he has to look in his diary to learn where he is? Your father, too, this so responsible civil servant from England, he is prepared for you to live this life? Perhaps your mother is excited, naturally, that Raffaele de Nardis has fallen so madly in love with their daughter.'

'They don't know, Contessa. I think they will like the idea even less than you do.'

That idea had simply not occurred to the countess and she dismissed it. That a middle-class family of no distinction should not wish that their daughter ally herself with a de Nardis was ridiculous. 'Nonsense. They will be thrilled and flattered; they see only wealth and position. Have you any idea what it is like to be Raffaele de Nardis, to enter a hotel through the kitchens to avoid the screaming ladies, and men too, who wish to throw themselves on his neck, offering him anything. They won't stop for the slight inconvenience of a wife, you know. I would not wish this life on the child of my closest friend, but' – she turned around and again the sun caught the great diamonds that seemed too heavy for her slim hand – 'Raffaele is correct. He is a man and I am merely his mother who wants both of you to be very happy in life.'

The unspoken 'but not with each other' was loud in the air. 'You should have told me before, Raffaele, and we would have had champagne. We will have it now.' She clapped her hands and a waiter appeared.

'No, Mamma. We must talk now with Sophie's parents.'

Sophie preferred not to remember that first discussion. Her parents were as angry as the contessa but not nearly so restrained. It was not his social position or even his career that they hated. It was his age.

'He is ten years older than you.'

'It won't matter in ten years because then I'll be where he is now.'

'I will not give my consent.'

Rafael would not marry her without it and so he went to Japan, and then South America and on to Russia and he telephoned from everywhere while she sat in her room at the university, played his records, and waited for his calls. She failed her exams, of course. But he was still in love with her when she became twenty-one and on her birthday he presented her with an enormous square emerald surrounded by diamonds.

'I bought it in Rio and have had it in my pocket to keep me company,' he said. They were married later that summer at the castello in Tuscany and they did not live happily ever after.

Stories abounded.

The police had provided buses to carry escaped prisoners of war into the mountains where priests hid them in their monasteries. What a stupid story; this could not be true, could it?

The death penalty was in force for any Italian found helping the allies but the partisans carried messages through the German lines; peasant farmers hid downed pilots, escaped prisoners.

Fathers of sons killed in action took up their dead sons' cudgels and joined the partisans.

Were sons of dead fathers doing the same?

Not Ludovico Brancaccio-Vallefredda?

They say he was caught by a patrol as he led an escaped prisoner through the mountains. They say he has done it several times, thumbing his nose at the Germans who took away his father.

Poor kid. He will be shot.

'Dear God, no; he is only a child.'

13

She should have flown back to Edinburgh. She could not think why she had not done so except that air travel had been one of the things she had put aside after her divorce. It was not that she never travelled by air, just that she ceased to take private jets for granted. Private planes had been a way of life for Sophie de Nardis but Sophie Winter did not miss them. She missed nothing, and she would not miss the constant friction with Ann.

Blood relationships were only, after all, accidents of birth. There were friends she had chosen that she liked much better than she had ever liked her sister. She would miss the twins though. The strength of her love for them had surprised her but losing them was another price she had to pay . . . for what? For being born? For marrying Rafael? Imagine her own sister saying that she was angry with her for being born. She hoped she could take her own advice to Ann and forget everything, including, if necessary, her nephews.

The boys, however, had no intention of allowing an obviously doting aunt to escape.

Life is too short for the working aunt of eight-year-old boys who have just discovered the wonders of the Internet. Every morning for weeks Sophie woke up to find a message from one or other of the twins clogging up her disk space. I love them; I really do and I am glad I am being allowed to know them. I really am, she found herself saying day after day as she deleted the most appalling jokes which the twins found riotously amusing. Sometimes they just said 'hello' or asked her when she was coming to see them, or worse, asked when they could come to see her. She must get them up for a long weekend. Ann would allow that, surely. She and George could have a weekend away while the boys discovered Edinburgh.

'We are doing a project on castles. Ask Rafael to let us see his castle when we go to Tuscany with Granny at Easter. Love Danny and Peter.'

She e-mailed back. 'Sorry, it's not Rafael's castle. Come and see Edinburgh Castle. It's bigger. Sophie.'

Next morning. 'Mum says we are to say Aunty Sophie.'

She replied. 'Always best to do what your mother says.'

Hamish was back in Edinburgh and the day-to-day business of government, perhaps to chastise itself for being on holiday, seemed to expand to fill every minute of the working day and beyond. On some miserable winter nights – dreich, the doorman called them – she reached home, usually wet and cold, and sank into a chair almost too tired to think of anything except a bath and bed. The problem of housing for asylum seekers was consuming a great deal of Hamish's time and so Sophie was kept busy making sure he knew everything that was going on or being discussed not only in Scotland but all over the world. Economic migrants, victims fleeing from persecution: it was a global problem.

As well as his membership of two committees, Hamish was a member of eight cross-party groups: usually there were several meetings each week that he had to attend. One day there might be a meeting of the Standards Committee and on other days he could be expected to attend meetings called by the Cross-Party Group on Asthma or on the Scots Language or any one of the other eight. Sophie made sure he knew about any news item relating to his committees, his cross-party groups, or his constituency. To do this she had to read every single newspaper; oh, for the time to relish the joys of a good old-fashioned murder mystery. Whenever Hamish made a speech and, since he was not only intelligent and totally committed but also young and personable, he was asked to make many, Sophie had to register any fee in the official register of Members' Interests; time-consuming, but necessary: £222 received from the BBC for participation in

Any Questions, Radio 4, Forms, forms, forms. Most days she agreed with the receptionist: 'You know, Sophie, you're meeting yourself coming in as you're going out!'

But she enjoyed her work and liked and respected her colleagues.

One February night she hurried back to her flat through a light snowfall that was threatening to turn itself into a raging blizzard. For once the heavy smell of distilling hops that seemed to hang always over Edinburgh had been defeated by the snow, and childishly Sophie held her face up to feel the cold softness of the tiny flakes; she looked up at the streetlamps and revelled in the haziness of light through snowflakes that made the Royal Mile look like an old print of itself. She locked herself into her eyrie and was congratulating herself that she would just have time to shower and change before she rushed out again to accompany Hamish to a new exhibition of modern art when her telephone rang.

She pulled off her boots and hurried over to the telephone table, peeling off her wet coat as she did so.

'Oh, Sophie, it has been just the most awful day,' began her mother.

Her heart that had been dancing so lightly seemed to plummet to the foot of her stomach. 'Mum, what's wrong?' she tried to toss her dripping coat back across the carpet to the uncomplaining tiles near the door, failed, said, Give me a second, Mum,' into the mouthpiece, and ran over to her coat which was now ruining her settee. She picked it up, looked wildly round and threw it again, this time managing to hit the tiles, and ran back to the telephone. 'Sorry, but I was dripping all over my new carpet. You've had a beastly day. Tell me.'

'Stella phoned. Someone has emptied the pool.'

Sophie knew very little about filling or emptying swimming pools. Such tasks were done automatically in the de Nardis households and she had never paid any attention to pool maintenance before her marriage. 'Wait, Mum, don't you just empty the pool in the winter?'

'Would I be ringing you in hysterics if we did it annually? It's starting again, Sophie. Your father says I wasn't to tell you but it has to be something to do with you.'

The icy knot in the pit of her stomach got bigger but she forced herself to stay calm: very difficult since Kathryn's hysteria was catching. 'Mum, I suppose you have considered a leak?'

Her mother was now angry which was marginally easier to deal with than her panic. 'Thank you very much, Sophie, but we are not entirely stupid. Stella says the pool has been deliberately emptied and she says too that the maintenance people say they are too busy to fill it.'

'But . . .' began Sophie who already knew that she was determined to believe that the emptying of the pool was no more than an accident; a nuisance, no more.

Kathryn would have none of it. 'Don't but me. We're talking about Tuscany; no one uses an outdoor pool in winter. Pool men are desperately looking for work and this firm is too busy, too busy to look at our pool.' Her voice had risen higher and higher until she was almost shrieking.

Sophie sat down on the floor by the telephone. 'What are you going to do?'

'Rafael's family knows everything about the valley. Ring him and tell him to find out who did this and why.'

'I think he's in South America; I can't bother him with something like this.'

'It's all your fault, Sophie. You caused all the trouble five years ago and then it was fine and now it's starting again, the vandals and now the pool, and it has to be because you went back and your father is getting very upset – he's not sleeping again'

Sophie crouched on the floor with the receiver clenched to her ear. She could hear her mother's hysterical voice and her father's angry one and then he spoke. 'Sophie, dear, are you still there?'

She nodded, unable to speak but, as if he could see her, he went on. 'Your mother's upset, Sophie. She didn't mean any of that; she never does mean half she says, and I'm fine – as usual she's exaggerating. The pool was emptied; perhaps there's a leak. Unfortunately, the pool men we use are very busy. There's been a lot of snow and freezing temperatures; of course that's going to cause problems but I think I'll fly out for a few days and have a look. What's the weather like with you?' he went on in a chatty voice and gradually Sophie relaxed.

'I walked home through the snow; it's beautiful.'

'But now you're cold and wet and hungry. Send out for pizza, *bella*, and light the fire. I'll ring you when I get back. Want me to bring you anything?'

'Yes, *focaccia* from the baker down the lane at the side of Galletti's in Crespiano.'

He laughed and hung up and Sophie, suddenly remembering that she had another of her almost-a-date events with Hamish, lit the gas fire in her high-ceilinged living room and rushed to change her clothes. She was going to be late but it was one of those events where punctuality is not of the utmost importance.

Hamish was there, catalogue in hand, when she arrived. His eyes lit up with pleasure when he saw her. 'What a star,' he said, as he took two glasses of chilled white wine from a passing waiter. 'You look stunning. The place is half empty; I almost expected you to call off.'

Sophie did take a moment to look around the gallery; it was exactly as Hamish had said. Many guests had failed to turn up, and, without people talking, looking, admiring, deriding, the room was cold and almost austere.

'Here, Sophie, grab a shrimp. There are some cracking pieces in the exhibition.'

'I'll believe you,' said Sophie as she did indeed grab, not one, but two shrimp from a tray. Modern art was not a compelling force with her as it obviously was with Hamish. She could mumble a few stock phrases about Picasso's blue period – which she found almost bearable – but knew nothing whatsoever about Georges Braque, or Hamish's particular favourite, William Littlejohn. She did know that he painted a fish into almost every painting and so Hamish was happily unaware that he harboured a philistine.

'Had enough?' he asked after almost two hours during which

he had gazed in unassumed awe at canvas after canvas and Sophie had run the list of fish and chip shops in her area through her mind. She could almost taste the paper-wrapped treat, so hungry was she. 'If you haven't eaten we could find a bite somewhere.'

That was certainly a date, wasn't it?

'I'll call ahead to make sure but I think I might be able to get us a table at Fishers Bistro.'

Less than thirty minutes later Sophie was tucking into spicy sweet potato and pumpkin soup in the bar of the crowded restaurant.

Hamish watched Sophie eat and laughed aloud. 'Either that is wonderful – and I know it is – or you haven't eaten all day.'

'Correct to both.' Sophie smiled as she put down her spoon. 'Two shrimp since this morning.'

He said nothing while the waiter removed their soup plates. 'You work too hard, Sophie, or I work you too hard.'

'I work me too hard, Hamish. I love the job.'

'I know and you're darned efficient. Good, you're pinking up nicely. You were as white as a sheet for a while there.'

She was disappointed. 'Pinking up nicely? I hope you weren't afraid that I would fade away on the job, Hamish.' She thought he had cared enough for her to want her company.

He said nothing but looked at her while the waiter put a plate in front of her. 'No,' he said when they were alone again. 'I wasn't thinking like that at all. I was thinking how pretty you are and how that sweater somehow makes your eyes even greener, and I was also thinking that I really ought to see more of you.'

She smiled at him. Such words, balm to her bruised spirit. 'We're almost joined at the hip as it is.'

'That's the irreplaceable Ms Winter. I was thinking how nice it is to be sitting in a bar with Sophie.'

'Me too.'

She was not surprised when he kissed her goodnight at her door at one o'clock in the morning. 'See you tomorrow,' he whispered against her hair.

'See you tomorrow.'

The fire was still on in the living room and the room was beautifully cosy; she almost wished that she had invited him in but caution had prevailed – too far, too fast. Then she saw the winking little light that told her that someone had called and immediately her pleasure turned sour as the memory of her mother's call pushed her lovely evening with Hamish out of her mind. She decided to leave it till the morning and turned off the fire and got ready for bed but wherever she was it seemed that that little red light kept winking at her. She tried to ignore it and got into bed but although she could no longer see it, she was aware of it. 'Damn it all. Don't spoil my evening, Mum.'

She hurried into the living room and pressed the button.

'Hi, Sophie; it's Harry. I'm going to be in York at Easter and if you're not busy, I thought you might enjoy the weekend; old university chums, but nice. You'll like them. I'll try again tomorrow. *Ciao*.' Harry who was an authority on medieval manuscripts. Harry who had bought a fragment of a manuscript that could have disappeared from the Castello de Nardis.

'*Ciao*, yourself, Harry. Yes, I'll come to York.'

The next day, it was as if there had never been those moments of intimacy in the bistro but when Sophie got back – again well after seven – to her flat, there was a florist's delivery outside her door. The out-of-season roses were from Hamish and Sophie was still putting them in water when her phone rang. It was Harry and, holding Hamish's flowers, Sophie agreed to meet him in York. She knew that Hamish was already fully engaged for the Easter weekend and, should he ask, it would do him no harm to realise that there were other people anxious to utilise Ms Winter's time. She made up her mind quickly and spoke before she lost her nerve. 'Harry, may I ask you something?'

'Of course.'

'It's about the Battista manuscript.' She could not yet tell him that she had been branded a thief by her husband's family, not until they knew each other better.

'Dad's treasure.' She could hear him chuckling. 'All his working life he wanted to own a medieval manuscript and I bought him that one to enjoy but he looks at it only once or twice a year. He's afraid that light and air will ruin it.'

'And will they?'

'Possibly, but why the interest?'

The truth? No. 'I've heard of ancient manuscripts and I wondered how easy or how difficult they are to obtain.'

'There are dealers; manuscripts, old books, they do come on the legal market now and again. That one I bought probably fifteen years ago from a reputable dealer in Venice. That's why I paid so much for it; there is a black market, I suppose you would call it. I'm asked to authenticate things people have found in very shady circumstances; sometimes they're genuine and, unfortunately, sometimes they have been reported as stolen.'

'What happens if you come across a stolen manuscript or a book, say, or even a painting?'

'I report it to the authorities.'

'That's what I thought.' Fifteen years ago. His father had not been sure. 'How would the dealer get the manuscript, Harry?'

'The owner has to sell. I don't think anyone sells a treasure unless they have no other choice. Sophie, this isn't simple interest.'

'No, no it isn't.' She had gone too far to back out now. 'You see I thought my mother-in-law reported a Battista manuscript as stolen.'

'And you thought Father's might be it?'

'No, of course not.'

'I have the receipt somewhere and I'll look it out for you.'

She was unbelievably embarrassed. 'Harry, I'm sorry. Not for a second do I think . . . oh, God, this is so difficult.'

He laughed and his voice that had gone quite cold and stern was warm again. 'Sophie, dear. It's happened before and will happen again. A family gets into financial difficulties. The owner sells his assets legally but for any one of many good reasons he doesn't tell the family. Did you ever see a film called *I Remember Mama*?'

'No.'

'Shame, it's a real weepy; I love it. This woman brought up a huge family during the American depression. She always told her children she had a bank account. She didn't but it made them feel secure.'

She thought for a minute, trying to work out what he was actually saying. 'I see; someone might sell a treasure and not tell his family so as not to worry them?'

'Exactly. After the war, during the war, family heirlooms were stolen, sold on the black market, and sold legally. It's difficult to tell which one is which unless you have a bill of sale from a recognised dealer. That answer your question?'

'Yes, thank you, Harry. Food for thought.'

'See you in York. I'll try to find my receipt.'

He hung up before she could say, 'Don't do that.'

She was humming happily when the telephone rang again and it was her father from Italy. 'More vandalism, I'm afraid, Sophie, and I thought you should know right away. I've talked to the police and filled in a zillion forms.'

'It wasn't an accident?'

'Not unless the storms were strong enough to take the filter system out of a locked cupboard and I have to say I'm unhappy with Ernesto's attitude. We've paid that firm regularly to maintain the pool and in the middle of winter he swears he's too busy to come up to assess the damage. I drove to his office and it was closed – I mean really closed, shutters up, not out to lunch shut.'

Sophie kept looking at the vase of roses. 'What are you going to do?'

'Come home probably. The wheels of justice grind more slowly in Italy than almost anywhere else; no point in hanging around by myself.'

She already knew the answer but she had to ask. 'Dad, is there any damage to other properties in the area?'

'Nothing winter storms didn't cause. Hang in there, sweetheart. It's got nothing to do with you. Who knows, maybe I didn't tip enough last summer. I'll talk to you soon.'

Because of the unexplained vandalism and the severe winter Kathryn and Archie decided to go out before Easter to get the house ready. Kathryn telephoned. 'It's much too cold for me but I'll stay indoors close to the fire and enjoy the mountains from the windows. There's the work on the filter system to be done and the fence on the hill down to the river will need propping up again. Can't you come, even for Easter weekend?'

Sophie tucked her feet up under her. This was going to be a marathon and she might as well be comfortable. 'Mum, I'm going to York for the Easter weekend. I'm meeting Harry Forsythe there.'

Immediately Kathryn's aura of expected doom disappeared and wedding bells began to ring in her head. 'My son-in-law the pianist' was about to be replaced by 'my son-in-law the professor'.

'How wonderful. What is he doing there or is it rude to ask?'

'Don't be coy, Mum; it doesn't suit you. He's staying with an old college friend at the university. I will be at a hotel in town. We shall have dinner with about twenty other people and possibly we'll go to the races. Great fun.'

Sophie could almost read her mother's thoughts. Part of her was thrilled that her daughter was seeing a personable and respectable man and part of her wanted her wayward child in the bosom of the family for the holiday.

'Mum, you do realise that Harry is twelve years older than I am and he has never been married.

'High time he did. High time for you too, Sophie. All right, all right, I know what you're trying to say so subtly. He's older than Rafael but it doesn't matter so much when a woman is in her thirties and you can't afford to wait much longer if you want to have a home and a family.'

Best to say nothing.

Her mother waited and then said impatiently. 'York is quite a way from Edinburgh.'

Sophie took pity on her. 'Mum, I like Harry enough to want to go to York to spend some time in his company. That's all there is to it.'

'It's a start. But I wish you were coming here. The weather should be perfect; it will be too cold to swim in the Tavernelle but we should have the pool fixed and heated.'

'I don't get holidays like Ann and George.' Had her mother allowed her to continue Sophie might have told her that she planned to stay in Edinburgh because her boss had hinted that he might get theatre tickets. No, that would sound so sad: Cinderella staying at home by the fire waiting for the prince. As always, though, Kathryn remained focused on herself.

'Have a lovely time with everyone, Mum,' Sophie managed when her mother stopped for breath.

Eventually Kathryn let her go.

Her next telephone conversation was with Carlo and since he very rarely telephoned, she was delighted to hear from him. 'How lovely to hear from you, Carlo. Apart from Christmas the last time you telephoned was to say Tonio was on his way. Am I to assume . . . ?'

'A new baby? No, *cara*. I'm afraid I am really calling . . . This is difficult.'

She felt herself grow cold. Rafael? Something had happened to Rafael. 'Tell me, Carlo, what's wrong?'

'It's *la contessa*; she has had a few health scares recently. She thinks maybe you two should talk.'

If she had listed a million reasons for Carlo to telephone, this might just have been the last. 'Carlo di Angelo, if it was anyone else I'd say too much chianti. Unless, Carlo, someone ripped out the pool filter at Villa Minerva. Is that why the countess wants to talk to me? Does she know who did it?'

He sighed and she realised that it was very late for him. 'I don't think so, *cara*, and I'm sorry if you have suffered from some vandalism. The countess is in Rome; it is unlikely that she would know anything . . .'

'Insignificant. Is that the word, *amico*?'

'Anything, Sophie. I meant anything at all about the valley.'

'I have no intention of speaking to her, Carlo. Should she wish to speak to me, she can pick up a telephone – all by herself. Goodnight, *amico mio*.'

George had taken his laptop to Tuscany and the messages from the twins kept coming. 'We wish you were here. Everybody talks about Aunty Zoë's baby all the time. We went to see a castle yesterday and when we came home there were flags and lights all over the *castello*. Granddad says the contessa had a birthday but we think it's because Rafael got engaged. Stella told us. Granny never has birthday parties now she's old. Can we come next mid-term and see Edinburgh Castle?'

It had to happen. She was relieved in a way. An engagement. She was surprised really that he had not married again. He needed a wife, at least he needed a woman and although he found them and enjoyed them – if what the papers said was true – Rafael had always been quite moral and, although he wore his Catholicism lightly, he would prefer the married state.

She was really pleased that she was going off to York. Part of her had thought, Hold it a little, but no, the more she thought about it the more enthusiastic she became. She took the smart little dinner dress – good for any occasion in any company – out of her suitcase and replaced it with a dainty Fortuny-style pleated dress in shades of olive, buff and aqua that she had picked up in Lerici one summer and had never worn. In the little shop it had seemed to mould itself to her and yet had moved effortlessly when she walked. Oh, yes, that and a ridiculous pair of high-heeled sandals were just right for a dinner in an academic setting.

In York she took a taxi to her hotel to find a message from Harry. He gave his friend's telephone number and added that he would pick her up next morning to go sightseeing. They would have lunch at the racetrack and after the races they would return to their various lodgings to dress for dinner.

'My mother would approve. Room service and then an early night.'

Harry was waiting in the foyer when she left the dining room next morning. Her heart lifted at the sight of him. He looked almost as he had looked the first time she had seen him in Lunigiana, tall, dishevelled, a little anxious that he was in the way.

'Harry, how lovely to see you,' she said and she meant it. 'It's been such a long time.'

They kissed easily, like Italians.

'It's been far too long and I'm sorry to be so early; I can wait if there are things you would rather do.'

She smiled up at him. 'Sightseeing in this wonderful old city with you sounds just right. Let me get walking shoes and a coat.'

'Wait, something you have to see first.' He reached into the breast pocket of his dilapidated tweed jacket and took out a folded piece of notepaper. '*Voilà*. One receipt, legal and above board. It took me ages to find it. With work I'm amazingly organised. Everything else, letters, bills, receipts – you've seen the flat – I'm a mess.'

With unsteady hands she took the paper. It looked as if it had never been opened since it had been folded up and handed to the buyer in the first place. The letter heading was of an established books dealer in Venice. The date was long before her marriage. She felt exhilarated and totally destroyed at the same time and it must have shown in her face.

'Sophie, are you all right?'

She smiled. 'Of course, Harry.' She handed back the receipt. 'Clears everything up nicely. Thank you. I'm so sorry you felt you had to go to so much trouble.'

'No trouble. A good clean out every ten years or so is quite exhilarating.'

They visited the minister and the Shambles. Harry knew York well and took her unerringly in and out of tiny streets so that here she saw houses that were no higher than she was herself and where plague victims had lived and been cared for by the priests at the wonderful old church they reached by diving up a secluded alley.

'Don't they want people to find this place?' Sophie asked as they walked across the grass to reach the church. 'Don't know why but I try to visit the local church first when I go somewhere new.'

'This one is a gem,' said Harry, opening the ancient wooden doors.

'My goodness, look at that,' breathed Sophie. She stood for a while accustoming her eyes to the dark and allowing the atmosphere to enfold her. She remembered a Spanish boy who had toured with her when they were students at St Andrews. The most practical of young men, he received no messages that were not sent in a stamped envelope. At the Clava stones near Culloden he had turned to her and said, '*Aquí, hay fantasmas.*' Here there are ghosts. And that was what Sophie felt in this little church. But like the ancient ghosts among the Clava stones, these phantoms were holy ones. Never had she been in a church like this one. A gate closed every pew and over the hundreds of years of use, the floor had subsided in the middle of the church and the pews had leaned forward towards one another. The doors in the middle pews billowed out so that all the seats looked as if they were part of a great wooden ship.

'Look at the altar; I think it's among the earliest in the entire country and it's made of copper.'

Sophie wondered with him, touching the stone walls, running her hand along the tops of the magnificent old stalls, thinking of all the people through the ages who had come into the church as she was doing. Did they all say prayers? She found herself whispering, 'Let Rafael be happy,' and then, ashamed of herself, added, 'God bless my family,' and walked back to the doors. Just inside the door was the plaque that is seen in many many old churches, asking for contributions to help the relentless decay of the fabric. This church had stood in that spot for hundreds of years, ministering to the rich, the poor, the well, the sick, and now it was the church that was in need of ministry. Sophie copied down the address. She would certainly make a donation.

'How awful if this church falls into such a state that it's no longer used.'

'Have you visited the little country churches in Tuscany? They are in the same state. Governments, wealthy benefactors, give to St Paul's in London or to St Mark's in Venice, but who looks after the old churches with the falling congregations? Keeping this place going is a labour of love.' He looked at his watch. 'Have you seen enough? We're late.'

They hurried out, found the car that Harry had rented and drove to the racetrack.

'You drive like an Italian,' said Sophie.

'I'll take that as a compliment.'

They laughed and Harry took her hand as they hurried to the meeting place. His friends, who were almost stereotypically academic, were waiting in the bar. A burly greying man, Harry's age, and his attractive wife, and another much older but very scholarly looking man. Harry introduced everyone. 'We were all at Cambridge together. Now John and Trish are here, and Tim is at Sheffield.'

'Which was your university, Sophie?' asked Trish Hampton. 'Harry didn't know. It wasn't an Italian one, was it?'

'No. St Andrews, but I confess up front that I never graduated.'

'But Harry says you have some marvellous international job, some kind of administration. How do you get a job like that with no qualifications?'

The questioning was not rude, but friendly. These were academics who wanted to know where, and if, they were going wrong.

'I'm fairly fluent in Italian and German, and have a passable working knowledge of French. I travelled with my former husband who is an Italian. His job his . . . profession almost requires him to be multilingual and I learned mainly by living where the languages were spoken.'

'The only way to learn a language,' said John. 'Do you know, Sophie, I spend every winter trying to learn German and I never get any further. Very good on paper but when I have to speak . . .' He threw up his hands in mock horror. 'There must be a knack to it.'

A great deal of the rest of lunch-time conversation was anecdotal as each one revealed appalling blunders made at one time or another; Sophie enjoyed every minute. What nice people they were. Harry was modest about his ability in Italian and Sophie remembered that Zoë had said he had an appalling accent but he obviously spoke Italian well enough to lecture in it and John, who said his German was atrocious, was an authority on Goethe and Brecht.

'Oh, yes, my dear, I can read it, but speak it . . .' Again the hands in horror.

They went to the races and won and lost small sums all afternoon. Sophie knew nothing about horses and bet on names that appealed. She won more than anyone and promised to buy the first round of drinks at dinner. It was a delightful day and the dinner at the university was just as enjoyable. She had insisted on taking a taxi and so saw Harry's look of delight as her shapely legs in their Italian shoes slid neatly out of the car. The dress, not Armani, not Dior, was a great success.

'My goodness, you look good enough to eat,' he said as he took her hands and kissed her, not Italian style but quickly and gently on the lips. 'Was that forward of me but, my goodness, how lovely you are.'

'Thank you,' she said demurely and walked on prepared to demolish the rest of the dons.

After dinner they all went to Trish and John's cosy apartment. 'I'll ring for a taxi from here.'

'Wouldn't hear of it. I shall be seeing your parents next week. What would they think if I put their daughter in a taxi.'

She saw the sense in that and she relaxed. Harry was going

to want to kiss her again, and properly this time. She was going to let him; in fact, she was looking forward to the experience.

He stopped several yards from the brightly lit front of her hotel and she turned towards him. 'Sophie.'

'Your friends are very nice, Harry.'

'Yes, they are.'

'I particularly liked that they did not ask me about . . . Rafael. Do they know?'

'That you were married to him? No. That was a long time ago.'

'Indeed it was.'

'Time to move on.'

'Good heavens, Harry. Have you been talking to my little sister? I moved on, as you say, five years ago.'

'Great,' he said and bent to kiss her.

Sophie had meant to respond but was angry to find that part of her seemed to be looking on, over her shoulder, analysing her feelings. To show herself how angry she was, she responded to Harry with more feeling than he had expected. Only when she felt one of his hands on her breast did Sophie pull herself together. 'No,' she said quite curtly and pulled herself away.

What a gentleman he was. 'Forgive me, I went too far.'

'No, Harry, I did. I like you and it was a very nice day but I'm not ready to go any further yet. You had better drive up to the hotel.'

He did and this time when he stopped he got out of the car and came round to open her door. 'May I see you again? I could come to Edinburgh.'

'Yes, Harry, that would be very nice.'

'And if you're coming to Tuscany?'

Tuscany. She would never return to Tuscany. She had said that before but this time she meant it. 'Give me a ring, Harry, any time you're coming to the UK or send an e-mail. I have a wonderful correspondence with the twins. Sensible adult conversation would be nice for a change.'

She kissed him very lightly on the lips and hurried into the hotel. She did not look back.

★

The next day she woke late and decided to walk once more around the lovely city. She discovered yet another ancient timbered pub and sat so long over lunch that she almost missed her train. As usual there was a message on her answering service: her brother-in-law George. 'Sophie, please phone us as soon as you get home; no matter what time. I'm afraid there's been an accident.'

To whom? Who had had an accident? Her mother? Her father? It had to be one of them. If it was Ann or the twins, Kathryn would have rung her or if she had been too hysterical Dad would have. By the time she had worked this out Sophie had reached the number.

'*Pronto.*'

She recognised the voice. Stella. Who or what was Stella: maid, cook, baby-sitter, family friend? 'Stella, it's Sophie, what's happened?' She spoke in Italian and a fountain of rapid Italian dialect spouted back at her and she listened as best she could. The dialect was a better option than Stella's English, limited, and, in hysterics, lost completely.

Sophie managed to get her to stop and to start again because she could not be right. She must have forgotten a lot of idiomatic Italian because it sounded as if Stella was saying that *il signor* was dead. It couldn't be.

'*Morte, morte, morte.*'

Il Signor? Dad? Oh, God, no.

Stella was now sobbing uncontrollably and Sophie let her cry while her mind raced. What to do? Where to go?

'Stella, be quiet,' she said loudly in her firmest most idiomatic Italian and, shocked, Stella obeyed. 'I'm coming, Stella. As soon as I can. I'm coming.'

14

'*Signorina, I have to tell you . . .*'

'*You have murdered my brother. I know. I saw it. I saw it.*'

'*Gabriella, I did everything I could.*'

'*As you did everything you could to have my father returned. Good-day, General.*'

She had gone in to the village a young girl. Portofino had said he had seen Ludo, bruised and bleeding, being taken into the town. She had followed and Portofino had held her against her will while Ludo and the others had been shot. She had heard the soldier, 'Dear God, no; he is only a child,' and then the general had tried to speak to her, to justify himself, in her father's study with Ludo's blood still staining the square.

She had walked home followed by the whimpering Portofino and her childhood was behind her. She was a woman who did not remember that her father had believed that there was good and bad in all men. Her father was probably dead because he would not join the Germans and, because of some inept Englishman, her brother was dead.

Hatred festered in her soul.

He was not expected, of course, and *la contessa* had gone to Rome where, occasionally, she would stay at the *palazzo* that Beatrice had brought to the family; they knew he had a series of concerts in Rome but he had called with his usual courtesy to give them some notice. The *Castello* was always ready for the family, but he knew that special preparations would be made for him because he was so much loved. To give him credit he would have been quite happy to find a hotel room or to stay with his friend, *il dottore*, but they would have found out that he was there and would have been hurt, as they would have been hurt if they had not been allowed to scurry around preparing his rooms and food fit for him to eat.

'He never notices what he eats,' muttered old Cesare, but Portofino knew Master Raffaele's delicate appetite.

'Genius is different from other men, Cesare; it has to be tempted, and when he is tense his stomach ties itself in knots.'

'Why should he be tense? Spring is coming; the valleys are full of wild orchids.'

'As it will soon be full of bloody foreigners.' Portofino moved away from the table to spit in hatred of everyone not Italian – except her, of course, *cara* Sophie. He loved Sophie, unlike some he could mention.

'He has not told *la contessa* that he is coming.'

'Even the most loving of sons likes to be away from Mamma's shadow.'

'What about that pool then, Portofino? Is that why the maestro is coming?'

Portofino looked round although he knew that they were alone, two very old men, in the castle where they had lived all of their adult lives. 'Guard your tongue, Cesare. Vandals, nothing more. It is the fault of the English; they come bringing all their bad habits with them and our children learn.'

Cesare moved across the room and took a cup and saucer from a sideboard. He poured a cup of strong, black coffee and loaded the little cup with sugar before he shuffled in his slippers back to the table where Portofino was tearing great handfuls of fresh herbs into a bowl. 'And do they also teach our workmen, our *artigiani*, to lie to their customers, to tell them they are busy when obviously they are not?'

'*Sì, d'accordo.*'

'It is, perhaps, like the war. Some of us were so polite to our German allies and yet, how do you explain, nothing worked?'

'*Ecco la fica.*' The cook made the age-old gesture of derision and then shrugged. 'There were, however, some decent German soldiers,' he admitted. They looked at each other, remembering, but quickly Portofino went on, 'As there were some decent English.'

'Like the English pilot who dropped his bomb right on *la contessa*'s family home?'

'He was a soldier doing his duty. *La contessa* appreciates that, Cesare. This hate should all be gone like the snow melts away from the Alps.'

'More garlic, *amico*. Snow returns every winter and in some hidden places it is never really gone.'

Sophie could not believe that it would be impossible for her to get to Italy that night. The last plane was gone – from Edinburgh, from Glasgow. The last train too was already trundling its way south to London. There was nothing she could do. She would have to wait for the dawn. She tried to reach her mother but the telephone rang and rang in the obviously empty house. She was almost hysterical with fear, desperately attempting to keep her emotions under control, trying not to think of her father, but how could she not? She tried the house again but still nothing. Giovanni, dare she ring him at the restaurant? No, unfair to disturb him at his busy time and why would he know anything? Stephanie; she would swallow her pride and ring Stephanie. The answering service told her that the signor and signora would be happy to ring her back when they returned from Rome and suggested that if she really needed to speak to someone, Signor and Signora Winter would be happy to talk to her. Oh, that they were happy. Would any of them ever be happy again? Hospitals. She cursed herself for her stupidity. He would have been taken to hospital. Which one? She wasted time and tears ringing three hospitals before she found one that had Signor Winter in its emergency room. She rang her parents once more and when the answering service finally cut in left a message that she would be there as soon as she could get the first plane out of Edinburgh. She looked at her watch. Two o'clock in the morning. She could not ring Stella at home.

Unable to sleep, Sophie wandered through her flat. How she loved it. She was happy here, and, more importantly, at peace. It was her bolt-hole, the shell, the carapace into which she had withdrawn in those long painful months after the divorce. She stood in the front room with its tall windows that looked up towards the castle and down towards the palace and Arthur's Seat; she saw her massive stone fireplace and the huge Mexican candlesticks she had bought a few years ago in a shop in the Grassmarket, deep in the Old Town under the shadow of the castle. She filled her mind and heart with the view of the old city as she tried to push images of her father lying crumpled on a hospital bed. No, he would be lying . . . she could not bear it. Her heart called out to her father and she turned and looked at her little dining area with its round table and four old chairs picked up for a song in the same little shop.

Was he dead? Had he suffered? She would not think. Mother? No, she would not think.

Her mind's eye saw another flat, another dining room, a splendid apartment with floor-to-ceiling French windows that let light in all day long. Its wall coverings were pale lemon hand-painted linen panels, each depicting a musical instrument, and applied like wallpaper. The painted swags at the top of each panel echoed the magnificent curlicues of the eighteenth-century candlelit mirror above the fireplace and the blue itself was echoed in the silk that covered the twelve chairs. Solid silver candlesticks marched down the table between the silver place settings and the delicate but ornate Venetian glass. Where were those treasures now? Did Rafael use them since she had refused to take anything that she had not bought herself, or were they hidden away in boxes in an attic somewhere?

She did not go into her bedroom; she wanted no reminder of bedrooms she had shared with Rafael. This one he had never seen but sometimes it seemed as if he were very much there, an unwanted intruder. As she, it appeared, had also been. Sophie sighed. How young and trusting she had been.

Useless to say, 'Rafael, I don't think your mother likes me very much.'

He would not accept it. 'Don't be silly, Sophie. You are my wife.'

But . . .

She said nothing. That's why she doesn't like me, was what she wanted to say and perhaps she should have said it, forced it all out. Perhaps she should have been brave enough to compel Rafael to see what he did not want to see. His mother was perfection, in beauty, in accomplishment. He always spoke of how she had sacrificed herself for her sons.

'She was so beautiful, Sophie. Many men wanted to marry her but she preferred to stay alone so that she could devote herself to us and to the estate. The *castello* and our estates were bombed in the war, you know, and my father's family lost everything. Mamma's family was much grander than ours, blood of the Dukes of Savoia, Mamma used to say, and for them the last war was even harder than for the de Nardises. She doesn't talk about it but her father died and her brother. She did not blight our lives with tragedy; she put it all behind her.'

Very sad, thought the young Sophie who harboured a belief that a strong-minded husband might not have allowed the countess to do exactly what she wanted. That was another thought that came to Sophie's mind as she sat at the huge banqueting table and tried to find a niche for herself.

'Raffaele's little bride' sounded so condescending somehow.

Mamma, why don't you show Sophie how to order supplies?

She doesn't need to worry her pretty little head with housewifery. Do you, my dear? She will never have to do it here anyway, darling. Better that Sophie keep you happy. How well your language studies are progressing, Sophie. We must have a little party, Raffaele, before your winter tour.

The little party had involved hundreds of guests and an army of caterers and by the time the third course was being served

Raffaele's young wife had a blinding headache. Tenderly Rafael had helped her from the table.

Oh, the murmurs, *diletta*; they hope you are with child.

But she was not although both she and Rafael hoped very much to be parents.

But I would miss you so, Sophie.

Miss her. Why should he miss her? She looked at him in astonishment. But I'll still travel with you. Babies travel easily.

Mamma would never allow it – unless, of course, we have a little girl. A de Nardis heir would have to be brought up here.

I won't have a girl to suit your mother and my sons will go where I go.

Mamma would prefer a boy.

Was he teasing her? A boy like you to spoil.

Certamente. Of course.

With hindsight she could ask herself why she was never brave enough to fight with him. For four years she travelled with him everywhere. In his New York apartment a couple, hired, long before Rafael's marriage, by the contessa, ruled their lives with unbelievable efficiency. They were polite to Sophie and deferred to her but still did things the way they had always been done and Sophie decided to wait a little, to learn a little more, to become more assured, before she dealt with them. Because everywhere the one thing that mattered above everything was Raffaele's music. The longer she lived with him, the more Sophie realised his genius. She would sit in a rehearsal studio watching him, totally absorbed in his music as he practised and practised. In an auditorium she would sit where she could see his face, seeing it show love, anguish, understanding. Only in the dark of their bedroom did she feel important, more important than anyone or anything because her brilliant, demanding husband needed her love.

'I am a vampire, *carissima*, and I feed on you. I adore you, every single little inch of you, every little curl, and I cannot live without you. Love me, Sophie, love me.'

How long into the marriage did he learn that he could indeed live without her? She was his first wife but she had always known that he had loved other women before her.

I never went to bed with a woman just for sex, Sophie. They meant something to me but no one but you has ever got inside my head.

Unhappy pictures but better than the ones that waited to intrude. *Il signor . . . morte.*

Sophie waited for the moment when she could fly back to Tuscany, to her family; nothing else was of any importance. She made tea, chamomile with honey, and sat hardly tasting it, her mind full of grief and fear, and waited for the dawn.

She flew to Pisa and hired a car. This time there was no lost luggage, no delays. In less than an hour after landing she was at the hospital.

'Oh, Goddess of Wisdom, tell me what to say.'

George was in the waiting room. 'Thank God you're here, Sophie; it's dreadful. They don't think he'll make it.'

Make it? 'Oh, thank God.'

He looked shocked. 'What?'

'I thought he was dead. Stella . . . What happened? Where is he? May I see him?'

'Kathryn and Ann are with him. The staff won't let us all into intensive care.'

'Thank God you were here for the spring break, George. Mum would have fallen apart.' Sophie sat down and tried to breathe as Rafael had taught her and it worked. She could speak. 'I couldn't get anything coherent out of Stella.'

'It was a heart attack. Things have been pretty nasty around here; people they've known for ever pretending they don't see them, anonymous letters telling them to get out of Tuscany, your father getting angrier and angrier . . . it was the awful nature of it, Sophie,' George tried to explain. 'Rumours, incidents in the night, no enemy he could confront. He's been getting really upset, so unlike himself and then yesterday the fence he had propped up after the winter storms – it was broken, pulled up. He saw it when he went for bread and he was almost hysterical and went down to look at it and he came scrabbling up the hill from the river. We thought he was just a bit out of breath, out of condition, I don't know and then he keeled over.' He went over to the water cooler in the corner and fetched a cup of water. 'Here, Sophie, I'll get you some coffee in a sec.'

Sophie felt herself getting colder and colder. This nightmare could not be happening. She looked up at George who looked away, unable or unwilling to meet her eyes. 'Zoë?'

'Ann persuaded Kathryn not to ring her. Better to know something definite.'

She nodded her acceptance. *Calma, calma.* 'Everything will be fine,' she whispered. 'It has to be.'

The door opened and Ann was there; she had aged terribly. How could she get so old so quickly? 'Sophie, at last. We had almost given up. You'd better go in and see if you can persuade Mum to leave him; he's stable, and the nursing staff want us to go home to sleep. We'll wait for a few minutes and then we'll go.We've been up all night.'

The unspoken 'while you were obviously having a good night's sleep' hung between them but Sophie had hurried out of the room. She would not explain the paucity of flights. Ann too had been up all night; she had a right to be bad-tempered.

Archie was lying in a narrow hospital bed. He was connected to several machines that continuously sent messages that only the medical staff could understand. Kathryn, looking shrunken, her face pallid, was sitting by his side, holding his hand, careful not to disturb the needle inserted into a vein. She said nothing and did not look up.

'Mum, I got here as quickly as I could.'

'He nearly died.' Her voice was flat, emotionless. 'He loved you best, Sophie: he always has and look what you've done to him.'

She was not looking at her daughter who felt a pain in her heart as if she had been stabbed. Sophie bit back the tears. 'I'll go and talk to the doctor.' Still her mother kept her eyes on her husband's face. Sophie bent over and kissed her father's white, almost grey face. 'I'm here, Daddy; I'm here,' she whispered.

Archie had survived the night. The family were to go home and sleep and eat and then they could return to sit by his side; he would remain in intensive care for some time. Kathryn begged to stay but the doctor and her daughters were adamant. 'You need to rest. When he wakes he'll want to see you.'

Kathryn neither spoke to nor looked at Sophie. 'Very well,' Kathryn looked round. 'Where are the boys, Ann?' Another worry to add to the score.

Sophie heard Ann blow her nose loudly. 'It's all right, Mum, Stella took them home with her for the night and then Giovanni picked them up.' She looked at Sophie 'Stella's daughter has a new baby. Stella's up to her eyes too. They must be such a nuisance in a busy restaurant; besides, they're terribly upset. Will you drive over and get them and bring them home? George and I would really appreciate that.'

Sophie was registering nothing. Adrenalin, she supposed, had kept her going but now, after seeing her father lying there and experiencing her mother's hostility, she wanted to lie down somewhere and cry. 'Sorry. Ann, I just . . . What are you asking me to do?'

'We've had nothing to eat since yesterday – sounds sordid talking about food, but Mum must eat and rest. I asked you go get the boys.'

'Of course.'

'I'll get the twins, Ann.'

'Don't be silly, George; you have to drive Mum home. Sophie has her own car.'

'Sophie . . .'

'Ann's right, George. We have to think of Mum.'

George looked at his wife. 'Sophie's exhausted too. It must have been a nightmare trying to get a flight in the middle of the night.'

Sophie smiled at him gratefully. 'I'm fine, George. I dozed on the plane. I'd like to stay with Dad for a few minutes and then I'll get Peter and Danny; I'll enjoy that. Please.'

Sophie returned to the intensive care unit. Archie looked just the same. She sat down beside him. 'I'll find out who is causing the trouble, Dad. I promise. Paolo will help; he would be really angry if he knew there was a campaign against the family. I don't know who it is that hates me so much – if it is me; I haven't even been here since July. There must be another reason and I'll find out. So you get well. Don't die, Dad. I'm going to Giovanni's to get the twins; they'll be upset and so you have to get well and you just have to come home soon. You hate hospitals, remember. You were always absolutely awful to nurses if one of us got hurt. Do you remember? We used to cringe in embarrassment and didn't understand that it was because you were so afraid for us. Now we're afraid for you but this is a wonderful hospital and the staff are very well qualified so behave yourself when you wake up.' She leaned over and kissed the top of his head. 'I'll see you later. I'll bring the paper and we can do a crossword.'

She spoke to the nurse on duty and then left the ward. The family was gone and she drove out of the car park and for once was unaware of Italy around her. In that automatic state she drove to Giovanni's restaurant where the boys threw themselves into her arms. She hugged them, murmuring reassuring words as she looked across them at Giovanni.

'*Carissima.*'

'*Amico.* I've come to take them off your hands.'

'What? They're my best helpers,' he said, but she could see that he was relieved. 'When did you arrive, *Cara*?'

'A few hours ago. Seems for ever.'

'Come on, you sit down, you kids too, and we'll have some *panini*. You gotta eat, Sophie.'

'I know but you're busy.'

'I gotta eat too. Boys, you go choose the fillings and we will have a little wine. Sophie, for the digest.'

Happy that their aunt was there and that they had something constructive to do, the twins went into the kitchen.

'You hear the Italian they're learning? Giuseppe's a bad boy, teaching them to swear.'

'You're a good friend, Giovanni.'

'Eh.' He made the gesture, uttered the sound that all Italian males seem to do so well. Its monosyllable covered everything. 'I know Archie a long time; a good guy, no. What's happening, *bella*?'

She filled him in while the boys returned with sandwiches and Giovanni poured some wine. No one had much appetite and the boys were quiet and brooding. Sophie tried to draw them out and now and again she thought that one or the other was going to say something important but they held back.

She commented on their Italian on the way back to the villa and even tried to make them try their new-found knowledge on her.

'We speak Italian with Giuseppe and Giovanni and sometimes Stella because they're Italian. You're English. You speak English. Stella reads her paper sometimes, *La Nazione*. She read us a bit about Rafael once.'

'It's good to practise.' She tried to make them laugh. 'Once when I was married to Rafael and I was learning Italian he told me a hoary old story. You see there's a very famous hall in New York and it's called the Carnegie Hall. Rafael played there. He was so excited; every time he played there he was as excited as if it was the first time.'

She had their attention and for the moment they were not thinking of the horror that had blighted their Easter holiday.

'Why?'

'Because you have to be really super-good to be invited to play there. Well, his story was that one day a man who was lost stopped a violinist in the street and asked, 'Excuse me, sir. Can you tell me how to get to Carnegie Hall?' She could see their pale little faces in the mirror. They were listening carefully. 'Do you know what the musician said?'

They shook their heads.

' "Practise, practise, practise." '

Nothing. No response and then Danny began to laugh. Peter was still puzzled. 'What's funny?'

'The man thought he would say, turn left at that street and go down, you know, directions, to get to the place, but he said – practise.'

His twin still looked confused. 'That's not funny.'

'Practise playing the bloody violin till you're good enough to get there, stupid.' Danny burst into tears and Peter started to pummel him. Fighting on the back seat was probably better than crying.

Sophie decided to ignore the fighting and the language. 'Boys, when Grampa gets out of the hospital he won't want to see his grandsons black and blue.'

'But he's dying. Everyone says he's dying.'

Sophie pulled over to the side, turned off the engine, and turned round. 'No, he's not,' she said and she prayed that she was correct. Stable means he's not going to die, right? 'He is very, very ill but the doctor said he's going to get better. Now cheer up and don't let your mother or poor Granny see such miserable faces.'

Ann was lying down when they got back to the villa. George was dozing in a chair. Kathryn, who should have been in bed, was sitting on the terrace listening to the river. 'Look, Sophie, do you see? Dad got into a frightful state because the fence was down but look at it; it's perfectly all right. Why did he get into such a state about nothing?'

It was obvious to Sophie that work had been done on the fence within the last few hours if not minutes but this was not the time to say anything. 'Maybe you should lie down too, Mum. I'll keep an eye on the boys till George wakes up; they can help me make . . .' She looked at her watch. 'What, late lunch, early dinner?'

'Dinner? How can you think of food, Sophie?'

Sophie looked at her in disbelief. I can't cope with this.

'What a good idea,' George intervened. 'Off you go, Kathryn. I don't suppose Sophie was able to sleep last night wondering what was happening. Here, Sophie, I think a brandy and then you have a nap here on the settee. I'll take the boys down to the river.'

Sophie looked at him gratefully and was glad to do as she was told. The last thing she heard was George's voice as he went to pour her drink. 'It's just got to get better, Sophie. Believe me.'

15

Tuscany 1942

By 1942 it appeared that the defeat of Italy was likely. The merchant fleet had been destroyed and so there were was a desperate shortage of food and coal. Rationing was introduced. Allied air-raids accelerated.

Portofino left the cellar first and tried to persuade his mistress to stay where she was until he had checked the house.

For a young girl Gabriella was unnaturally calm. 'This house? Nothing fell near this house, Portofino, but the town . . . The bombers were over the town.'

She began to walk towards the heavy clouds of smoke and he could only follow her. He was in tears, begging her to return to the safety of their shelter and the two maids still hiding there, but, despite the darkness and the state of the road, Gabriella walked faster. Fire fighters, rescue services, all impeded her journey but unerringly she hurried through the side streets, streets that she had never explored before. Portofino followed. For her he would do anything. He did not wonder if she knew that he would protect her with his life. For him it was enough that he did. Their journey took hours for dawn was breaking through the acrid smoke, but at last they were at the villa.

For some time Gabriella said nothing. She merely stared at the burning building that had been her home. A bomb had fallen directly on the house and another in the gardens.

'Were all the Germans killed?' She caught the sleeve of a scurrying man.

'What Germans? No one was killed in that house, signorina; lately it was an administration building, offices; no one lived there.'

They had not even told her they were leaving.

'They should have been there, Portofino, and they should all have been killed, all of them.'

'Signorina.'

She was looking up at the lightening sky. She heard voices, first her father's. 'The general is a decent man.' Next she heard the voice of the young German soldier who had admired her in the square. 'No; he is only a child.' But they were drowned by the sounds of bombs falling.

For the first and last time in his life, Portofino touched her. 'Signorina, come away. Come, please.'

She smiled at him and he saw that her eyes were wet with unshed tears. 'There is nothing left, Portofino. When my father comes home he will find nothing.'

'He will find you, signorina.' But, of course, he never did return.

'Who mended the fence, Sophie?'

Fence mending. What an odd turn of phrase. Was that what they themselves were doing, mending fences? Her father had been so close to death and so everything else seemed insignificant. It would rise again and grow and grow like mould on a damp wall, ugly, stifling.

Sophie and Ann were on their way back from the hospital where they had left their mother with Archie who was now out of the intensive care area. Almost instinctively they had realised that not yet could they cope with returning to their parents' villa and so they had driven up into the hills, parked the car on the side of the dusty road and gone for a walk. How good to feel the warm sun, to smell dust and olives, and to breathe freely.

Sophie felt woefully inadequate to help her father. She had tried to contact Paolo, *il conte*, but so far none of her messages had been answered. Perhaps the mountains would clear her head and help her think. They had stopped on the path that wound in and out of the overgrown tangle that had once been a flourishing vineyard. Without the sound of their footsteps on the pebbles, and Ann's tortured breathing, there was absolute silence. On the hill above them the empty eyes of the red-roofed village stared down and made no comment. Sophie noticed that an olive tree was growing right out of the window of one of the houses and just then Ann spoke.

'Who mended the fence?' So she had noticed, had known.

They walked on again, further into the grove, the dust from the *strada bianca*, the little road made of white pebbles, coating their feet in their strappy sandals. Sophie bent down and picked up a little stone. It was worn smooth by the passage of countless feet, hooves and carts. Had it once been part of that glorious white mountain at Carrara? Was it thrown here to Lunigiana by some primeval volcanic eruption? She threw the stone as hard as she could towards the distant mountains and it fell, miles short, in the middle of the vine and blackberry jungle.

'I don't know, Ann,' she said at last and her tone was weary. 'I had only one conversation with Dad; he tried to dismiss any trouble.'

'Oh, he would for his precious Sophie. It's been awful. As soon as he's well enough to travel I want us all out of this evil place.'

Sophie looked at the beauty spread out before them and further to the snow glinting in the sunshine on the tops of the mountains; or was that the marble mountain shining in the distance? 'Evil? The place isn't evil. Someone doesn't like us.'

'You. They hate you. You and your divorce caused all the trouble. Dad has lived and worked here for years, used local tradesmen, supported local businesses. No one hates him. Whatever you did—'

'Dear God, Ann, you, above everyone, know I did nothing.'

'Stephanie lives here all year; she says the rumours about you being a thief have started again. They say one thief, probably a family of thieves.'

'Don't overreact, Ann. We have to think rationally about who could have stolen the valuables from the *castello* and sold them; that's the hard part, I think, selling on priceless artefacts.'

'The count hasn't bothered to answer your phone calls; he's not taking messages. He has access to the castle; he could have sold everything.'

'They belong to him. He doesn't have to ask permission to sell them. Besides, their father built up the estate again after the war. Paolo is a rich man.'

'This way he gets insurance too.'

'No, never. Paolo was my friend.'

'Then it's Rafael's mother.'

Sophie looked at her and laughed. 'What a preposterous idea. She was nearly killed saving them during the war. And it wasn't Paolo or Rafael, and it certainly wasn't me.'

'Maybe they didn't go missing at all?'

Sophie stood as if transfixed. Not stolen at all. No, that was too bizarre and, besides, the crucifix had been found in their flat – and had she not herself seen a fragment of the manuscript on old Mr Forsythe's dining room table? 'Let's go back; we're both over-tired.'

'There's going to be a *denunzia*, you know that, don't you?' Ann's voice was rising.

'A *denunzia*?' Sophie could scarcely believe what she was hearing. Yes, Ann was overwrought but surely she had not heard that someone was prepared to go to the local authorities and say that they knew that Sophie Winter, once Sophie de Nardis, had stolen Italian treasures. She knew that she had to keep calm or they would both be hysterical. 'That's outrageous. And don't talk like that in front of Dad; we have to be very calm.'

Ann rounded on her. 'Don't tell me to be calm. Any minute now the police are going to knock at the door saying that you have been accused of theft. The disgrace, the humiliation. My sons. I can't bear it.'

'You won't have to bear it,' said Sophie, who could feel terror icily invading her mind and body.

'It'll kill Dad.'

'Enough.' Sophie was surprised at the strength of the anger and frustration that had wiped out the fear. 'Stop thinking about yourself for a moment and—'

'Me, me think of myself? You're the selfish one, even ruining my wedding.'

Whatever she had expected her sister to say, it was not that. Her wedding. Sophie could barely remember it.

'You did it deliberately, just to annoy me, marrying Rafael within a few weeks of my wedding. Mum and Dad hardly had a minute to spare on my simple little ceremony with all the international fussing they had to do over yours.'

'I had tried to get married the summer before, Ann,' Sophie tried to point out. She did not add that the contessa had taken over the wedding so that there was nothing for her parents to do but be there. Rafael was touring America. His phone calls said, 'Leave it to Paolo and my mother, *mio tesoro*. They'll handle everything. We just need to be there. You will be there, *carissima*? You won't change your mind at the last minute and fly away from me like a sprite?'

His seductive disembodied voice sent shivers of anticipation and fear through her. The primary feeling was of love and longing, longing for fusion, to be together, to be one, Signor e Signora Raffaele de Nardis. How right that sounded.

'I miss you, Rafael. I want to be with you.'

'Soon, Sophie, and then we will never be apart. Listen, I am playing Mussorgsky for you at the end of every recital: tonight the "Ballet of the Unhatched Chicks." My message, *diletta*.'

Ann had been speaking, yelling really, her eyes wide, her face red with anger and dislike. Sophie registered the last part. 'You haven't changed. You always were selfish and self-centred.' She turned and began to run back down the white road towards where they had left the car.

Sophie looked after her fleeing figure and heard the stones squealing in resentment as she ran. Don't slip, Ann, and don't have a heart attack, running in this heat. Even in April the midday sun was hot. When it was obvious that Ann was neither going to stop nor return she walked on towards the village. She will have cooled off by the time I get back to the car, she thought. But she was wrong. A spray of small white stones and a skid mark showed her that her sister had driven off angrily, leaving her to walk back to the villa. She looked down at her red sandals, great for an afternoon's shopping in Florence but not really fashioned for a hike. She shrugged and began to walk. Surely George would come for her if Ann reached Villa Minerva without her, but no doubt Ann had already recovered her lost temper and was sitting somewhere beside the road, admiring the blue flowers whose name they always meant to learn and which grew wild all over the hillsides.

She walked on and stopped when a small stone worked its way under her bare foot and stayed happily pressing into the soft skin of her arch. She hopped over to the grass and sat down to take off the shoe and dislodge the annoying little pebble. How so small a stone could cause so much pain. For a while she sat on the sweet early summer grass and looked around her. In a few weeks the grass would be hard and dry but now it felt soft and cool through her light dress. On the other side of the road was another abandoned house or was it? The shutters, all in need of extensive repair but fairly recently painted green, were closed, but that could mean that the inhabitants were enjoying the siesta.

Mad dogs and Englishmen.

The garden was overgrown, brambles and roses gone to briar intermingling and threatening to choke the vines and the olives. What had Rafael said? 'Olives grow near water.' Or was that figs? 'Where there is water you will find figs?' Was that it? It was all such a long time ago. Behind her stretched the valley. Beyond the valley the hills with their villages clinging to their sides like suckling babies. How did they ever build them in the first place? A good shake and they would fall off – so it seemed – but these villages had survived everything that man and nature had flung at them.

Peace wrapped itself around her as she sat. There was no sound at all. Mingled perfumes hung in the air, woodsmoke, the smell of the season which itself is made up of so many other scents, broom and gorse and olive and lemon and even dung and dust, all mixed together to make the scent of Tuscany in April, Sophie sighed and got to her feet. She had loved it once. It was not evil and neither were the people. One, just one, disliked her, but who and why?

She began to walk down the road with its terrifying blind corners and perpendicular drops and she wished she had brought a hat. A car engine began to disturb the quiet, the low ululating sound of a magnificent machine. A dog barked somewhere across the valley and the sound of the car grew louder and nearer. A flash of silver and blue, like the wing of a kingfisher and then it was round the corner and Sophie heard it screech to a stop. She hurried forward. Someone had been killed, no, she had heard no screams, but why then had the driver stamped so severely on his brake pedal? An old lady perhaps, tilling her dry plot of land, had stepped into its path?

'Oh, god, no.' The last person in the world she expected to see, Rafael, was standing beside the car. He always did drive too quickly, perhaps convinced that Saint Cecilia had an in with Saint Christopher. She had time to compose herself, to remind herself that this was only someone she had known a very long time ago. '*Ciao*, Rafael.'

'Where is your car?' he asked angrily as he strode across the grass to meet her. 'No sane person would be out here walking at this time of the day.'

What could she say? My sister got cross and left me. 'How are you, Rafael? I'm surprised to see you in Italy: I thought you went to South America after Rome.' Damn. Now he would know that she was aware of his schedule.

He ignored her remarks. 'Where is your car?'

'I was with Ann; we had . . . a disagreement.'

'Come, *cara*, let me drive you home.'

She got into the low sports car and he slid in beside her. She tried not to be aware of his masculinity but the interior of the car had such little space that the scent of his hard male body, his shampoo, his soap, his shaving lotion had impregnated the leather. Had she found this car abandoned on a lonely road somewhere in the Andes Mountains and slipped inside it would have called out Rafael. She tried to relax. It is perfectly natural to be aware of the scent of someone with whom you have lived intimately for almost five years. This does not say that you still care but merely that your senses are in perfect working order. Congratulate yourself.

'I'm glad you have changed your mind about Tuscany.'

She sensed that he was glancing at her but she said nothing; she could not. Her throat felt as though it were stuffed with an old woollen blanket.

'Are you pleased that I am not in South America, Sophie? I cancelled a recital,' he said into the silence and she heard the regret in his voice. He had always hated disappointing the music lovers who came to hear him.

For a second she thought that he had come for Archie but he could not know, not so quickly. He must already have been on his way. 'Is there a problem at home?'

'My mother fainted and fell when they were in Rome. She says the fault was hers; she stood up too quickly. She did not even tell us that she was unwell. It's nothing serious. I fly out tonight. And you? Perhaps you succumbed once more to the magic of Tuscany?'

'My father had a massive heart attack. He's in hospital, in Pisa.' Could she say more, tell him that his mother had asked to see her? No, what was the point?

He stopped the car but, thankfully, not so fiercely as he had done before. 'But this is terrible. I did not know.'

She hung her head, not a familiar action, but it made her hair fall forward to hide her face. She did not want him to see her face.

'Sophie, tell me.'

'Nothing to tell, Rafael. He had a heart attack and is recovering.'

He was quiet for a few moments, thinking, reasoning. 'I will send wine, Brunello, to build him up.'

'Thank you.'

He hit his hand once very hard on the steering wheel. 'Sophie, tell me what is happening. Paolo called me to talk but then

Mamma was ill and we did not finish. There is trouble here in the valley, no, it involves you or your family?'

Paolo was not ignoring her. Oh, joy; he did not know of her calls. 'Paolo is here?'

'Naturally. He brought our mother back. Why do you ask? Sophie, tell me.'

'It's too late, Rafael.'

'You have tried to speak with Paolo? Why? He has ignored his office. I too. Tell me. Surely you can speak more freely to me than to Paolo.

She looked at him and her eyes blazed with anger.

'Sophie, *cara*—'

'I'm not your *cara*. Take me home, Rafael, or let me out and I'll walk.'

He started the car and drove quickly to the villa. 'I will tell Paolo that you wish to talk with him. You will be here?'

'I'm going into the hospital at seven. Don't.' Sophie put her hand on his right arm as he made to leave the car to let her out. 'I can manage and you are expected at the *castello*. I'm glad your mother is better.'

She opened the door and slid out but he was there in front of her blocking her way to the house. 'Sophie.'

'I heard about your engagement, Rafael. I'm glad, I really am, and I'll tell Daddy about the wine. Goodbye.'

He stood aside to let her pass and she was aware of him standing there in the sun staring after her, but why he should look so stunned she did not know.

Ann was ironing in the kitchen and she did not look up as her sister entered.

'I managed to get a lift, Ann. Rather childish of you to run off,' said Sophie, reaching behind her sister to take some bottled water from the refrigerator.

'A lift? You are so good at that. Another Italian playboy, I suppose.'

'No, sister dear, the same one.' Clutching the bottle of water, Sophie walked to the terrace. Their father was ill and his dream of retirement in the Tuscan sun was turning into a nightmare, but she and Ann were like bitter enemies sniping at each other instead of sisters united. She looked down at the river. She could see the sturdy figure of George trying to make sure the twins did not fall into the raging torrent. How different the little river was today from the sparkling stream along which the little yellow ducks had bobbed and whirled such a short time ago. He looked up and waved. Soon she saw the three of them coming back up. They could not play in that icy water for too long.

'I'll take Ann in this afternoon if you'll keep an eye on the boys, Sophie. We had hoped Stella would be able to help out more.'

'First things first, George. She loves Dad but she can't be in two places at once.'

'You're right. Everything fine with you and Ann? Sudden illness draws people together, doesn't it?'

She nodded and he went inside. She could hear him soothing and cajoling his wife and his children. George would grow into another Archie, going through life avoiding issues and, who knows, perhaps that was the best way. Rafael never avoided anything – or did he? Of course he did. No discussion of Mamma was allowed.

I don't care. I don't care what Rafael did, does, will do.

The telephone rang and it was Paolo. 'Sophie, I was very sorry to hear of your father's illness.'

She thanked him and commiserated about his own mother's illness. How civilised we are.

'Sophie, Raffaele tells me that you have been ringing my office. I told them not to disturb me; I'm sorry. Please tell me how I can help you?'

'I don't know where to begin.'

For a moment he sounded like his brother. 'The beginning, perhaps.'

'Paolo, first, before I continue I have to know . . . I have to know. Paolo, I stole nothing from your home.'

'This is over years ago, Sophie. I have not even thought of it.'

'But do you believe me?'

'If you say so.'

That was hardly encouraging. Resentment and frustration welled up. 'How can I talk to you about this *denunzia* if you believe I'm a thief?' Sophie began but it was not Paolo who answered.

'Sophie, we are coming down to see you. Paolo will drive me to the airport. You will not run away or hide, not this time, *cara*.'

If she went to the hospital, instead of Ann, Rafael would be in the air before she came home. She need not see him. 'I won't run away.'

'Who was that you were talking to?' Ann came in from the kitchen. She looked stormy but determined to be civil and so she did not wait for an answer. 'Sophie, will you baby-sit this afternoon while we visit the hospital? George said you wouldn't mind taking the twins down to Lerici.'

Sophie smiled and was not quite surprised to hear herself saying, 'Of course, Ann. We'll find something to do.' She prayed that Rafael and his brother would not get there before her sister left for the hospital and her prayers were answered. It was nearly half an hour after Ann and George had left before a car that surely belonged to Paolo slid to a halt at the top of the hill.

'Wow,' yelled one of the twins. 'A Mercedes. Who do we know that has a Merc, Aunty?'

'Hello, Sophie, hello, boys.' Two men had got out of the car and were walking down the hill. They were tall and slender and it was obvious that they were related. Paolo had changed much more than Rafael in the past few years. His forehead was slightly wrinkled and although his hair was still dark, silver sweeps covered each ear, making him even more distinguished. The twins were looking from one adult face to the next and then at each other. 'You're the princes,' they said and Rafael laughed.

'No, but may I introduce my brother, Count di Nardis. I am . . . Rafael,' he said if he were not sure how to introduce himself. As always he was immaculately if casually dressed; Sophie did not want to look at Rafael.

'Then you're our uncle,' said Danny. 'Does that mean we can

see your castle? We're doing a project,' he added, since he had been brought up to believe that no decent adult would refuse to help with schoolwork.

'Boys, will you play on the terrace for a while?'

They looked mutinous and Rafael looked ill at ease. The count was a father and had no problems. 'Things are a little difficult at the moment, boys, but in the summer – if your parents allow.'

'Promise.'

Sophie flushed. 'Boys,' she began despairingly and Paolo smiled.

'Promise,' he said and solemnly crossed his heart.

Sophie led the way into the house. She did not offer them anything.

'Your father?'

'He is much better. And your mother?'

'She too is feeling well. Sophie, I know and Raffaele knows too of the trouble. The days are gone when Il Conte de Nardis ordered this or that but I still have some influence; so too does Mother. I do not know why this is happening, Sophie, but there will be no formal *denunzia* because I would have to make it.' He smiled grimly. 'I will not and, from the bottom of my heart, I regret if any of this . . . unpleasantness has caused your father to be ill.' He looked at her across the table and at his younger brother sitting as Sophie had once seen him sit, quiet and still as if carved from stone. Neither Sophie nor Rafael said anything and the count leaned across the table and took Sophie's cold hands in his. 'Sophie, when . . . when you and Raffaele decided to divorce I was told of the thefts from the *castello*. I believe my mother that these treasures were there but I myself never saw them; they were part of our maternal grandfather's inheritance and *la contessa* has agreed that, when she is well, the archivist will take me through her family records. Raffaele too will have to know these things because I have no son and he should know. I want no dark clouds over my daughters' heads.'

At that Rafael looked startled. '*Basta così*, enough, Paolo,' but the count smiled and went on.

'Bad things happened in these hills – centuries ago, as recently as the last war, but I think this is the way all over the world, not just here. Memories of evil seem to live much longer than memories of goodness. Why this should be so I do not know. I think the tortured reasoning behind what is happening, possibly what happened to you, *cara*, wears scars we cannot see. In the car Raffaele has some Brunello from our own vineyards for your *papà*.' He looked questioningly at his brother and Rafael got up and went out. 'Will you trust me, Sophie?'

She nodded and slipped her hands away.

'My brother would not appreciate it if I were to try to fight his battles, but you may trust him too. He regrets much.'

'*Santo cielo*.' Obviously Rafael heard as he returned carrying the case of wine that he took into the kitchen with age-old familiarity. 'I must go. Paolo, the boys wish to come to the end of the road in your car. This is permitted, Sophie?'

She nodded and went before them out on to the terrace where the twins were lying pretending exhaustion in two chairs. They recovered as soon as Paolo told them that they could go a short distance with him. Sophie walked up the pathway between the two men; she did not know what to feel, what to say. They made it easy. 'I will be in touch, Sophie,' said Paolo and kissed her on both cheeks. Rafael did not touch her.

She held out her hand and he took it. '*Ciao, bella,*' he said and bent his head.

She felt his lips, soft as silk. The effect was like a jolt of pleasurable electricity. '*Ciao, bello,*' she whispered to his back and stood there on the verge until the car disappeared.

————◆————

16

'The child has more than talent, Contessa.'

'Genius?' She thought so but then she was a mother.

He shrugged. 'Who knows? He is beyond my poor talents. Vienna is the place, or London maybe.'

'Never London.' She had gone once to London with Mario and had not seen the beauty Mario saw but had seen in every English face the prisoners of war whom Ludovico had led to safety at the cost of his own life. Her anger had frightened her.

'Vienna?' It was not German but still. 'Very well, if he must leave Italy.'

Money. She could not take for Raffaele what should be used to rebuild Paolo's estates. Had she not promised Mario that she would carry out his plans for reconstruction? But Raffaele? He was a genius and genius needs its own rules. But she could not take from Paolo.

The twins came back and seemed their old selves; it was as if, at least for a few minutes, they had forgotten the sorrow and worry of their family. 'It's a fab car but Paolo says Rafael has a fabber one. Rafael didn't talk but he'll take us one day. D'you remember Dr di Angelo's car at the wedding? That was absolutely the fabbest ever car but we think Rafael's is better but he didn't tell us. Is it fabber?'

Sophie had caught one word in ten. Listening to the twins was like standing by the side of the road as wild horses galloped past. One had to concentrate to catch the right one. 'What does fabber mean: faster, prettier? I don't know, boys. Dr di Angelo always had faster cars.'

'It's his secret vice, *diletta*, his fast cars which he drives like an old man, so carefully round all the twists and turns.'

'Thank goodness one Italian has some road sense.'

'Will we start dinner for Granny coming back?'

They did not hear her, for they were rushing out being fab cars. She wondered if there was some way that they could be bribed to keep her visitors a secret. An hour or so later when she had some *sugo* simmering beautifully she heard them again, voices raised, telling their parents, their grandmother.

'Take out an ad, boys,' she groaned but tried to smile as she went to greet the family.

Her mother looked directly at her for almost the first time since she had arrived. 'Sophie, dear. He was sitting up for a little while. He's talking about coming home.' She hugged her daughter, hard, too hard, as if she were trying to squeeze away the memory of her rejection.

'Gosh, Granny, you'll squeeze all her air out.'

Thank God for the children; everyone laughed.

'How far did my sons travel with Rafael and his brother?' Ann's voice was hard.

'To the corner, no further. I stood and watched them drive away and I stayed and watched them walk back; they were perfectly safe.'

'The road is so dangerous. Why were they here?'

'A drink, everyone?' George had been opening chilled white wine from the refrigerator. 'Come on, everyone, a toast to Archie's health. Are you driving, Sophie? There's some carrot juice open.'

'Carrot juice. Ugh.' The boys expressed their feelings.

My feelings exactly, thought Sophie, but she gamely drank her juice that was not nearly so bad as she had expected.

The telephone rang and everyone looked at it but no one made any move to answer it.

'Oh, dear,' said Kathryn finally as she hurried across the floor. 'I just know it's Judith.' She picked up the receiver. '*Pronto*.' Change of voice. 'Judith, how lovely.' She put up her hand as if to tidy her already perfectly neat hair. 'I know, dear, and I did mean to ring but we've been every second with Archie. He's fine, dear, fine. Of course you must come out. No, no, there will be heaps of room. Sophie's going.' She looked across at Sophie who nodded vigorously. 'Zoë'? Yes, I told her and Jim says she's fine, blooming like a rose, getting cold there now. No, I won't go. Maude will. Yes, it should be her own mother. No, dear, thank you. My place is here. But we'll talk later, Judith. Yes, let me know the time of your plane and' – she looked across at dependable George who nodded – 'George will pick you up.' She was smiling as she hung up but the animation disappeared and her face and voice were cold again. 'Now, Sophie, why were Rafael and his brother here? Neither one of them has been here since the divorce and so I ask, why now?'

Sophie moved to a comfortable chair near the empty fireplace and looked at the huge arrangement of lifelike sunflowers that hid the gaping mouth of the chimney piece. 'I rang Paolo to ask if he knew anything about the . . . incidents.'

'Incidents. I hate that word.' Kathryn, who had come in so happy, was working herself up into a state, just what Sophie had hoped to avoid. 'A murder is an incident, a vandal pulling up roses – that's an unfortunate incident. There surely is a difference. Now tell me what he had to say.'

Ann fussed over her mother, getting her to sit down, put her feet up on a pouffe. 'Drink your wine, Mum; there's a whole case on the table. Where on earth did that come from? George, keep an eye on the boys, dear.'

If George resented being dismissed he gave no sign and went out on to the terrace. They heard one of the boys shouting, 'We're counting lizards,' and Sophie waited until everything was quiet again and her mother and her sister were sitting looking at her. 'At the moment Paolo has no idea who started this nonsense but he feels it is organised. His mother is unwell too at the moment – that's why he's here, and Rafael – but as soon as she's up to it, they're going to try to get to the bottom of the trouble and stop it once and for all.' That was not exactly what Paolo had said but surely it was what he meant. Should she say more? 'He says there are buried resentments in the valley, one or two families, perhaps.'

'Rubbish. What buried resentment could anyone have about you or us?'

'That's the point; we are, or, all right, I am, merely a focal point for resentment against foreigners.'

'Foreigners?' Ann's voice was scathing. 'Surely you mean Germans?'

Sophie stood up, her conversation and her carrot juice both finished. 'No, Ann. Some Italians actually harbour grudges against the British. I'm going to the hospital. Don't save anything for me. I'll grab something there.'

The young German saw her as she crossed the square. A child, just a child, but she was the most exquisitely beautiful human being he had ever seen. She was walking towards him and since he too was very young, his romantic mind compared her to the heroines of all the great Germanic myths. Her carriage was straighter than any princess, her waist more slender, and never had long black hair shone so like silk. Aware of his solid grey presence there on the steps of the church, she looked up and her dark blue eyes noted him with an indifference that pierced his soul and then she continued to look past him to the door of the church.

'Buon giorno', he tried politely but she merely nodded her head in dismissal before disappearing into the quiet darkness of the old building.

Where was he now? Dead like all the others, like Ludovico whom he had tried to save? To her dying day – was that today? – she would hear his voice. 'No; he's only a child.'

Her father was lying down when she arrived but the nurse propped him up on pillows.

'*Hai fatto bene*; that's better,' she said briskly, like competent nurses all over the world. 'Just for a few minutes.'

'*D'accordo.*' Sophie smiled and sat down. 'Hello, Dad. They tell me you'll be out in no time.'

He squeezed her hand. 'I want to go home, Sophie.'

Her smile was even brighter and more false. 'Rafael brought you some Brunello; have you tasted it? Yummy wine to build you up.' She looked at his face trying to gauge his strength from his eyes. 'The count is looking into the problems you've been having. It will stop now, Dad. He's a decent man and much respected.'

'That's how I would have described myself a few months ago.'

'Oh, Dad.' She must not cry. 'Of course you're respected here. Please, please don't get upset again. Paolo thinks it all goes back to the war but he'll find out and he will stop it.'

'The war. How strange. The doctor says I can go home and I'd feel better if I could talk to my own doctor; this one's good but he doesn't think in English.' He sagged back on the pillows and his eyes were dull again and he looked old. 'I've decided to sell the house. I want to get away from Italy and your unhappiness. The shabby way that family treated you.'

Had she not explained? Had she not said, 'I do not want Rafael's money?' Was that one more thing that had preyed on his mind? 'Dad, listen. This distress – it's for nothing. Every gift Rafael ever gave me is in storage. The London house is in my name – I just don't want it. If the contessa thought he was marrying a gold-digger, I've proved her wrong and that gives me some satisfaction.'

He struggled to sit upright. 'Sophie, what are you saying?'

She cursed under her breath. Never once in the years she had been married had she even hinted that she was unhappy. 'I didn't mean to let that out,' especially to a sick man, she added under her breath. 'It's fatigue talking, Dad. Forget it. I'm fine. If I want or need anything I only have to ask.' She stopped talking but her mind refused to stop working. I won't ask because what I wanted is gone. When I am back in my lovely little flat and doing my busy little job I will be able to pretend again that I no longer love Rafael de Nardis.

She looked again at her father. When had he grown old? His hands, old hands, so thin, the veins standing out against the fragile skin, moved restlessly on the starched sheet and she reached for them, soothing, calming. 'Not good enough. My God, Sophie, what made you so secretive? Why did you never tell us anything, speak to us about your marriage? Rafael's mother thought my daughter was after her son's money?'

Sophie thought sadly that she seemed suddenly taller and stronger than her father. Perhaps illness made him appear shrunken. She leaned forward and kissed him. 'No, she thought I was in love with de Nardis, the pianist. Leave it, please, you'll make yourself ill again.' She tried and failed to make him laugh, even smile. 'And then what would Ann say? Listen calmly. No girl would have been good enough for her precious son. Mothers are like that – with sons at least.'

'You gave up your settlement just to score over his mother?'

Sophie sat back in her seat. Was that what she had done? No, it was much more complicated than point scoring. 'My marriage was over a long time ago and I do not want to talk about it. I didn't five years ago and I don't now. Not my style, Dad. You must remember that.'

He reached for her hand now and held it tightly. 'We wanted to help.'

'You did,' she said, smiling as brightly as she could. 'I knew you were there and that was enough. Please, Dad, don't scrape the scabs off old wounds. Getting absolutely perfectly healthy is your priority. Rafael is engaged to marry Miss Raisa and I am happy for him, I really am. Were I ill I can't think of a nicer place to recuperate than here but if you're determined, then we'll just have to get you home and then you'll sit looking at rain running down your windows and you'll change your mind about your dream house. Would you like me to look into a flight for you as soon as the doctor says you can go?'

At once he was animated. She pushed him back down on the pillows. 'If you can't behave yourself they'll keep you here with beautiful Italian nurses for ever and you wouldn't want that now, would you?'

He smiled. 'You're my medicine, *bella*, but don't tell your mum till it's arranged. That woman loves to worry.'

*

Her mother was still awake when she got back to the villa even though Sophie had deliberately stopped to eat at one of the wonderful petrol stations that line the autostradas in Italy; she had lingered long over a salad, water and two coffees, defiantly incorrect ones. Kathryn stood quivering with anger, her frilly pink dressing-gown rippling round her, and stared at her daughter out of eyes that were sparkling with unshed tears. So would Ann look in twenty years' time. 'How dare you, Sophie, how dare you interfere. You stay out of our lives for years and then you come back and organise everyone and don't even bother to consult.'

Sophie was totally bewildered. Interfere? Organise? 'I have no idea what you're talking about.' She tried to be calm and not to let her hurt show. Her father had never before been really ill and she knew that the strain of the seriousness of this attack would affect her mother for a long time. 'I've been at the hospital. Sit down, here, and finish your tea.'

Kathryn slammed the cup she was holding so hard on to the marble tabletop that it broke and the remains of her drink spread itself among the fragments of pottery and over the tabletop. She stood looking at it, surprised by her own violence, and Sophie, trembling, went for a cloth.

'Leave it alone. It's a cheap cup.'

'It might stain the marble.'

Sophie wiped the table methodically, rinsed the cloth in the sink and wrung it out. She took a mug from the cupboard above the sink and then reached for a second one. This looked like being a long night. 'We'll sit down, and you can tell me what on earth I'm supposed to have done.'

'Why did Rafael offer his plane?'

Sophie was very busy pouring exactly the correct amount of tea into each mug and she started and tea slopped over the side into the sink. 'Good heavens. Is that what this is all about? I didn't know he had. We said nothing about planes this afternoon. I take it you mean to take Dad home.'

'Some German fellow rang and said Mr de Nardis would send

his plane back and that it was at our disposal. I told him we were going nowhere and when we did decide to return to England we could afford to pay for ourselves, thank you very much.'

Kathryn was now sobbing in despair and Sophie moved to her with that mingled affection and understanding that was her uppermost feeling in dealing with her mother these days. 'He was just being kind.' This was not the time to say that her father did want to go back to England as soon as he could, and that to travel in a luxuriously appointed private plane would be wonderful. Their village was so far from the London airports. Rafael's pilot would obtain permission to fly direct to a smaller airport closer to them.

'Why, why on earth should Rafael de Nardis be kind?'

Sophie looked at her mother; a moment ago she had seen a resemblance to Ann. Fluffy, and insubstantial like her pink dressing-gown, but her mother was slight, as she and Zoë were, while Ann was built on sturdier lines. 'Generosity, I suppose. He didn't stop caring because he fell out of love with me, Mum; that's why he played at Zoë's wedding. Divorce is funny, isn't it? Two people are very deeply involved but then there are all the other relationships. Did you stop caring about Rafael as soon as we were divorced?'

Kathryn sipped her tea, perhaps hoping that its warmth would give her strength. 'I was interested only in my daughter,' she said almost belligerently. 'Did the countess stop loving you?'

'She never loved me in the first place. Rafael, on the other hand, is almost a religion with her, just short of idolatry, I would suppose.'

'But the other son?'

'Paolo. She loves him. He is her son, her first-born.'

'What a shame you never had children. None of this rubbish would have happened; I just know it.'

Basta: enough.

Sophie stood up and almost pulled her mother to her feet. 'Bed, Mum, you're overtired and you know how difficult it is to cope with everything when you're too tired. Dad was looking so much better and he'll notice if you're not yourself and then he'll worry.'

Kathryn saw the sense in that argument and together they walked to their rooms and Kathryn kissed her daughter at her door. 'Goodnight, Sophie.'

Soon the house was still and dark and Sophie lay and listened to the river and to the distant thunder in the mountains. King Arthur and the Knights of the Round Table playing bowls, her father had told her when she was small and frightened. It was he, surely, who felt small and frightened now, alone in his hospital bed, but he would get well. She thought of Rafael somewhere above the Atlantic. He would be sound asleep, his mind untroubled. He had cancelled a recital; he must have had good reason to believe that his mother was really ill. Would he have cancelled for me if he had known? She preferred not to think about that. She would remember instead his kindness. First the wedding and now his plane at her father's disposal.

That afternoon he had looked exactly as he had looked that day all those years ago on the wall at Lerici: tall, slender, slightly over-long black hair ruffled by the wind; today the shirt was silver grey, the slacks dark blue. He should look older as she did. There ought to be a thread or two of silver among the black. Perhaps he helped it stay dark. At the thought of Rafael, who accepted his physical appearance as an inherited arrangement of classical features, dyeing his hair, Sophie laughed. It's sex. I wanted to jump on him or have him jump on me. Animal magnetism, that's all. Not love. Not after all these years and just as well since he's engaged to Ileana. Not that it would matter if he were not engaged. I'm over Rafael.

Her hand seemed to burn where he had kissed it. Oh, Rafael, the healer, heal me. I do not want to still love you, still go weak with desire every time I see you.

Next day, much against her will, Kathryn told Archie of Rafael's offer and, to her surprise, her husband was delighted.

'I've always wanted to fly in a private plane. Sophie, pet, are you going to stay and fly back with me?'

But Sophie left that day. Archie was getting better and her job was waiting.

Back in Edinburgh she was immediately caught up in her work and she tried to put all other worries out of her mind and after a few days she stopped rushing to the telephone, sure that this time it would be Paolo with all the answers.

Hamish was espousing the cause of asylum seekers and was involved in trying to find a site where they could be housed while their claims were being investigated. Several areas were pin-pointed, abandoned airfields being among the favourites. All Sophie's admiration for her employer surged to the surface again.

'We must find a place that is close enough to shops and schools. It will have to be on a good transport network and it mustn't be any uglier than it absolutely has to be.'

'Any uglier? What do you mean, Hamish?'

Hamish put the cap on his pen; he always used a fountain pen. 'If we find or build a state-of-the-art facility with lovely views, good communication links, etcetera, etcetera, every tenant of every inner-city development is going to scream "preferential treatment". What we need to find is a presently unused site, no damp, no rot, sound walls, floors; we can't stick these poor people in a hole that's worse than the one they've just escaped from.'

'Assuming that all of them have escaped from somewhere?'

'Do you want to choose, Sophie? Do you want to look at fright-ened faces and say, "This one's a shyster, this one's heard too much good about the NHS, the benefits system, free schools." Will I go on?'

Sophie went to her desk, his sincere voice still ringing in her ears. He was such a decent man. His constituents were so lucky to have him. She wished somehow that everyone could see how genuine he was, could see, in spite of the prevalence of articles about crooked slimy politicians, that there were men and women too who put their fellow man first. She was proud to be his assis-tant. Believing in Hamish and her work made staying in the office well after hours all that week acceptable, if not pleasurable. If she did fume a little when she heard that she had indeed missed a call from Paolo she was able to take assurance from the tone of his message. The archivist was engaged in making some sense of family records. The almost total destruction of one wing of the *castello* in 1943 had put paid to some of the de Nardis family records, and his mother's family archives had simply disappeared during the war.

'It has been very difficult for my mother to talk of these things, Sophie; I do not know if you were aware that her father, our grandfather, was sent to a labour camp in 1942 because he refused to collaborate with the Germans even though we were, by that time, allies. He died there just before the end of the conflict in Europe. His home, my mother's childhood home, was commandeered and then, unfortunately, totally destroyed when Aulla was hit in an allied air-raid. You see how it is almost impossible to find what was where and when. We rely on my mother's memory that is excellent. I wish indeed that some of her memories were not so vivid.

'As to the whispering and the unforgivable vandalism of your lovely property, I have not found the instigator but I think you will find that it stops. I will call again later.'

Sophie sat with some iced water and played his message over and over again. She found herself pitying the countess; how awful it must have been to lose one's home and father in such appalling circumstances. She remembered too that in the years she and Rafael were together *la contessa* had never said one word in disparagement of the English, or the Germans for that matter, and surely she had reason to mistrust both.

Sophie began to make herself some supper and while she chopped she found that she was looking at her mother-in-law with kinder eyes. She said I was too young, lacking experience. She never said, 'And she's English, Raffaele.' But someone must have been thinking that. Who else is there who was with Rafael's mother from her childhood? All of them. Marisa, Cesare, Portofino. Sophie could not imagine any one of these elderly people in the role of Machiavellian manipulator. Rafael read

Machiavelli. But then he also read Boccaccio's *Il Decamerone*, and Franco Sacchetti's *Il Trecentonovelle*. He spent hours in concert halls reading.

'This you must try, *tesoro*,' he would say with the excitement he usually used only for music. 'Sacchetti, fourteenth, fifteenth century: such unpretentious short stories. I will find for you a good translation and one day you will enjoy them in the original.'

She did not.

Rafael studied Machiavelli and his cunning. Sophie sliced a carrot so fiercely that she was in great danger of adding part of her fingers to her salad. Your brain is fried, Sophie. Rafael didn't steal his mother's things; if he wanted a divorce all he needed to say was, Sophie, I don't love you any more.

But he had never said that.

17

'*Marisa. I want you to do something for me, a very delicate task.*'
'Certamente, *Contessa.*'

They went to the east wing with its uncarpeted floors, its vast empty rooms where once priceless paintings had hung. They opened the boxes that Portofino had carried there so many years before, before the marriage of the young Mario, before even the love had flowered between the young people.

'*This will do,*' *she had said, removing a jeweller's box that contained her mother's emeralds, a wedding gift from her husband. She kissed the box. '*Take them to Rome, Marisa, and get me a good price, but . . . discretion.*'*

'Davvero, *I will be discreet.*'

Sophie had been so involved with work that she had been remiss about keeping in touch with her parents and so she decided to ring them first thing in the morning before she went to work. With time difference she knew she would not catch her mother asleep. She had scarcely pressed the button when a voice spoke to her in Italian.

'Wow, that was quick, you answered before I'd even dialled. Dad? Is that you?'

'It's Carlo, Sophie. You answered before I heard it ring.'

As she recognised the voice, fear snatched at her heartstrings and pulled hard.

'Sophie, are you still there? I am so sorry to call so early but it is *la contessa.*'

Relief, oh, sweetest of sensations. 'Carlo, I'm sorry. What did you say about the *contessa*?'

'She wants to see you.'

She could not believe what she was hearing. 'Carlo, we have had this conversation.'

'She is ill, *cara*: it's her heart, and she wants to see you.'

'No.'

'Just think, please, instead of rushing, rushing as you used to do. You said you had changed.'

'I have, oh, I have and I have learned a few things that make me a little more accepting of *la contessa*, but, Carlo, I find it hard to understand why she would want to see me. And why now? Her sons knew I was in Tuscany – and she was ill then, for Rafael was there. Am I supposed to drop everything now and rush back to see my former mother-in-law? If she is ill again I'm sorry, but it is nothing to do with me. My own father is my priority.'

'That is as it should be, Sophie, but as to Raffaele's mother, she says there are things you have to talk about, to straighten out.'

It couldn't be. Yet another act of vandalism and within weeks Rafael's mother sends me a message. Why? Because she suspects who is causing it or is it even more important? Sophie's heart began to beat with excitement. 'Oh, Carlo, does she know who took her treasures? Does she know who's at the bottom of all our troubles?' She stopped for a second, lining up her thoughts; the rumours and the accusations in the last year of her short marriage: 'Your wife has been seeing another man while you were on tour, Raffaele,' 'Your wife has been . . .' No, the countess would not call to tell her anything. But the rumours and the vandalism this year had to be connected. 'Whoever is responsible nearly killed my father.'

'I'm sorry your father was so ill, Sophie, but at this moment I am thinking only of my friend and his mother. I don't know why she needs to see you now but I am sure it is very important, to you as well as to her. She gave me no reason.'

'Have you told Rafael? Is he rushing back again, cancelling concerts? Perhaps she merely wants to prove that she's more important than the Edinburgh Festival. She's very manipulative.'

He winced at the anger in her voice. 'A solipsist? A little, maybe. I know her only as the mother of Raffaele, Sophie, and she has never tried to get between him and his career. She refuses to allow her own doctors to call him but I am not her doctor. I have spoken to both Paolo and Raffaele; he is now in Australia but will get home as quickly as he can. Listen to me. As I have told no one of your medical history I have never before shared what little I know of hers. She asked me not to tell her sons when she had an attack just after Christmas. She told them high blood pressure and it was, but there are complications. This time, since I am bound by no oath, I telephoned them.'

'I am sorry if Contessa de Nardis is seriously ill, Carlo, but she is nothing to me and I am nothing to her. If she has found out who is doing this terrible thing to my family she should tell my father.'

'Your parents are flying home today on Raffaele's plane.'

'What? Oh, Carlo, how wonderful. I was about to ring them when you telephoned. When you see Rafael you can give him my thanks, my sympathy and also my congratulations on his engagement. Goodbye, *amico*.'

'Engagement? Sophie?'

'I'm going to be late for work and you too. I'm sorry, Carlo, I'm sorry, but I will never return to Tuscany and therefore I will not see Rafael's mother. My father's well and I find I don't really care about anything else now. Paolo will explain everything to us, I'm sure. *Ciao, amico, ciao.*'

He said goodbye and for a second she felt regret. She hoped he was not hurt by her refusal. Carlo was dear to her and she would never willingly hurt him. Thank goodness her office was just across the road; she would still be there before Hamish and then she would lose herself in work and try not to think of anything else until she could rush back at lunch time to phone her parents. 'Your parents are flying home today.' Rafael had sent his plane. But it would be in Europe when he needed it in Australia. Rafael, I'm sorry.

She tried to dismiss the countess from her thoughts but Carlo's voice kept echoing in her head as she frantically looked through her wardrobe, seeing nothing that remotely attracted her. She eventually settled on a short grey dress with a cheery scarlet jacket. Then she rejected the red jacket and took out a dark blue blazer. Severity and competence was what she was looking for today.

The countess had asked for her. *Five years after the divorce she asks to see me. Why?*

'Really, Sophie, do you learn nothing in these English girls' schools?'

'When you can grace the table as the wife of Raffaele de Nardis should, Sophie, then you may sit at the head. Until then, I will be my son's hostess. You must cultivate some conversation. You embarrass Raffaele.'

'Do I embarrass you, Rafael?'

'Embarrass me? You fill me with delight.'

'Your mother . . .'

'You are married to me. Poor Mamma, she has only memories. Come here, forget Mamma, and love me.'

The snatches of conversations, humiliations, embarrassments went round and round in her head. She remembered her early year at the *castello* when she did not have enough Italian or French to join in the multilingual conversations. Even when the conversation was in English she found she knew so little of the subtler points of music and art and politics that she still could not participate. Was there anyone alive who really understood Italian politics? And Italians all talked at once anyway. Did anyone listen? She had been sure that her mother-in-law led the conversations to show up her weaknesses. Carlo was her lifeline, for Rafael said she was exaggerating, that he saw nothing, that conversations were always about music and art and: 'All you need to say is that you appreciate de Nardis.' And he would sweep her into his arms and love away all her doubts until the next time they were in his mother's company when they would resurface more strongly than ever from having lain dormant, like weeds after the winter.

Sometimes she would rage that Rafael was as self-centred as his mother but he would look at her in unfeigned surprise. His attention was not really on himself, he said, or he would be with her all day, making love. When he was working he was totally caught up in his music.

'Can you comprehend, Sophie, the genius, it is . . . oh, what the Americans say so well, mind-blowing. De Nardis is only the conduit, the interpreter; the awe is reserved for the masters: Bach, Beethoven, Rachmaninov, Liszt. You understand that I must work.'

She did of course. She loved to sit listening to him, even when he went over and over the same piece, the same phrase. Best of all was to sit in his music room in their apartment in Rome, the two of them alone, or were they accompanied everywhere by the spirits of musical geniuses? Sophie grew to love them too, Chopin first, then Beethoven, and latterly Rafael's favourite Russian composers.

'I practise so hard because I hope that at every concert, every recital, there will be young people who might suddenly under- stand that they too are part of this great *real* music; it's not for some old fuddy-duddy but for everyone.'

'Why don't you play in a football field then and really reach people?'

'Prove to me that these events reach new people. I don't believe it. They are for making money and it is obscene to put making money ahead of making music. Music is art and lately the world is going insane. To really appreciate music it is necessary to be in a concert hall. The vitality, the exuberance, you can't capture on a recording. I want low prices everywhere so the young people in jeans and anoraks can come. If my fee makes the ticket too expensive for some sixteen-year-old then it's wrong. I love the Edinburgh Festival and the Promenade concerts because they are for the people who love the sound I make, who say yes, that's what Beethoven wanted or Prokofiev or Chopin, or your beloved Mussorgsky with his *simple* tunes!' How excited he was when his devoted disciple sat on the floor and watched him as he walked up and down, gesturing and pontificating at the same time, or stopping to play a chord or, better still, a melody. 'There must be huge state aid for the arts. I know governments have to think about education and health and unemployment but it's short-sighted to cut the arts budget because the arts are medicine. They are cheaper than psychiatrists and medicines and, of course, much cheaper than alcohol and drugs.'

She knew he played in hospitals and homes, concerts he did not allow to be publicised. He waged his own personal war against the misuse of alcohol and had no tolerance at all for drug misuse.

'Never take the pills, *diletta*. If you have the headache, lie down for a few minutes. If you have the stress listen to Mozart while you are resting. I, Dottore Raffaele tell you. Lie down with Mozart if you cannot lie down with me who is the best doctor of them all for you.'

They did not eat, they did not drink because he forgot when he was working and she had learned to suit her appetites to his rhythms. He would play and play until he was exhausted and exulted and then they would make love.

'We will make a baby, Sophie, the greatest artwork of all.'

No, she did not want to think of that. She would think of him eating. He would sit at the kitchen table in his bathrobe, his hair standing up round his head as if he were surprised. 'See what a healthy appetite I have. All my appetites are healthy.'

'Look where you're going, stupid cow.'

The angry voice startled her and she shouted sorry and waved an apology to the taxi driver who had screeched to a halt inches from her. The Royal Mile was always busy and Sophie should have learned to keep her mind strictly on crossing it safely.

'Are you all right, hen?'

Sophie looked at the people crossing with her, some concerned, some indifferent. Her heart was pounding and her stomach felt very dicey but mainly she felt really stupid. 'Sorry, I wasn't looking. He got as big a fright as I did. Sorry.'

She hurried on and reached the safety and anonymity of the

office block where she stood for a second getting her breath back before getting into the lift and being whisked up to Hamish's offices.

'What happened to you, Sophie? You're as white as a sheet.'

'I'm fine, Margaret, just been dodging traffic on the street.'

'They drive like idiots at this corner.'

'Is the coffee on? Be an angel, and it wasn't the traffic; it was me. I just walked right out in front of a taxi. Teach me to wool-gather.'

'Everything all right?'

Sophie's spirits that had been low began to surge higher again as she forgot Rafael and remembered that her father was home. 'Couldn't be better. My father's on his way home.'

Hamish was standing at the door of his office and, as usual, his hair was badly in need of a first-class stylist. She looked at him in exasperation, mentally transposing Rafael's longer hair that seemed to stay tidy no matter how windblown. 'You need a good haircut, Hamish,' she said and walked into her office, closing the door behind her. She was humming as she unlocked her computer and punched the button on the answering service to hear the messages that had come in during the night. She had office hours; her telephone did not.

Sophie went in later to see that he had all the papers he would need. She handed him a file and, surely by accident, he touched her fingers as he reached for it and he held on to the papers and her fingers far longer than he needed. 'Tell you what, Sophie, if I get a decent haircut will you have dinner with me this evening?'

'I sent my plane back to pick up Sophie's parents; now I cannot leave until tomorrow morning.'

'*Calma*, Raffaele. I think you do not need to return so quickly. Mamma is quite recovered. She wanted to stay awake to speak to you herself but I would not allow that. Dottore Moretti says, in a few days he will allow me to take her to Rome.'

'You are sure, Paolo? I should be there with you, with her. Besides, she hates Rome in the summer; it's too hot.'

Paolo stretched out on the day bed in his brother's music room where he had gone to make the telephone call to Australia. Their mother was well; she did not want her son to disappoint the audiences. 'I must confess that I was surprised that she capitulated so easily, but she will not be walking about in the city, only resting on a shaded terrace. She will recover quickly knowing that your recitals are well received. Now tell me, Sophie's father, he has recovered?'

'He seems to have.'

'You are very concerned for the family of your former wife, Raffaele.'

'It is nothing.' Paolo could almost see his brother shrug his shoulders. 'But I feel some responsibility for the stress he has suffered. Are you any nearer finding out who did these stupid destructive things?'

'Let me say only that I have never seen so many highly intelligent people suddenly become bovine.'

'A conspiracy?'

'Keep your drama for the concert hall, *little* brother. I have asked several reputable antique experts to try to trace the missing items that I myself can identify. In the meantime the archivists are working on the estates of both families but that will take time. When Mother is much stronger I will ask her to give me any date of which she is absolutely sure.'

'*Grazie tanto*, Paolo, now go to bed, *old* man.'

It was good, thought Paolo, to hear him laugh.

Sophie went back to her flat during the lunch break. She opened a carton of cottage cheese, got a spoon, washed an apple and tried to phone her parents. The Italian number had been disconnected and there was no answer at their Surrey home. On their way. Wonderful. She finished her lunch, changed the dark jacket for the rather jaunty red one and went back to her office, making absolutely sure to watch lights and traffic as she crossed the road.

Hamish was out of the office building all afternoon but the jacket was not totally wasted; the security officer admired it. Any

admiration is balm to the troubled mind. Her spirits stayed high
all afternoon and she left promptly so as to have time for a long
chat with her mother before she went out again.

'Hello, dear, how did you know we were here?'

'Carlo phoned to tell me,' she said quickly, and since she
preferred not to go into depth over that conversation she hurried
on. 'How's Dad? Was the flight all right?'

'I have to say it was wonderful; the crew were so attentive. The
steward wanted your father to lie down but he was too excited.
"I'm going to enjoy this," he said, "and I can't do it lying down."
They had the most delicious lunch for us; I've never had food like
that on a plane and then there was a car waiting at the airstrip to
drive us right to the door.'

'Good. And when is Dad seeing his own doctor?'

'Tomorrow. He's standing here now, can't you hear him
breathing, your father, not his doctor?'

'Very funny.' Her father's voice was a joy to hear. 'A glass of
prosecco at lunch and your mother's the life and soul of the party.
I suppose the *castello*'s the place to send my thank-you letter?'

'That'll be fine. How are you?'

'Never better. Rafael's people couldn't do enough for us.'

'Dad, I mean *how* are you?'

'I am fine. Steph is going to keep an eye on the place and your
Aunt Judith is staying for a while and then Ann et al. during the
school hols. Our Italian neighbours were all wonderful when I
was in the hospital; Charles and Stephanie drove your mother
everywhere but the phone never stopped ringing with offers, and
the food, fresh trout, figs, peaches left at the door – amazing. I
should get sick more often.'

She winced. 'Don't even joke about it. Paolo was going to
speak to his mother about all the stolen things but she hasn't been
very well either and so he hasn't really found out anything. No
more problems?'

'It's as if it had never happened. The pool man has time; the
joiner has time, the gardeners have time. Do you know what was
the worst thing, Sophie? When I went out first to look at the

damage, I went to La Dolce Vita for dinner. They said every table was reserved. I have been eating there for over fifteen years and they didn't want me. I have never felt so awful in my entire life.'

Her poor parents. No wonder her mother was so angry with her, with Italy, with life. 'It's all over; everything will be fine from now on. Your love affair with Tuscany can go on.' That was the right note to strike. 'Dad, I have to go; Hamish is taking me out . . . yes, Hamish, and no, it's not business, it's a date date. Go to bed early. *Ciao.*'

'*Ciao, bella.*'

She had barely changed when the doorbell went and she ran down all the winding stairs to let Hamish in. He was carrying what Kathryn would have called a corsage, the first one Sophie had ever received and she was moved. It was an old-fashioned touch and she realised that Hamish himself was a little old-fashioned; perhaps that was one of the many things she liked about him.

'Isn't there some thingie that buzzes to let guests in?' he asked as he followed her back up the stairs, stopping at every landing to see the views from the little balconies. 'Two minutes from the office and I had no idea this place was here.'

'It would probably be far too expensive to install and this way only guests can get in; safer.'

He waited, refusing a drink, while she finished her make-up and from the look in his eyes her effort was worth while.

'You look good enough to eat, Miss Winter.'

'It's the gardenia,' she joked. 'I like the new image,' she said and it was true. There was little even the most talented hairdresser could do with the short back and sides that Hamish affected, but what could be done had been done, and the tuft was gone. 'Wait till your constituents see the new you.'

He blushed. 'It's only a haircut, Sophie, and he complained that there was nothing left to work with.' He had made a reservation at a French restaurant on Rose Street and of course had no idea that his date was particularly grateful for his choice. 'I thought you might have had enough spaghetti for a while.

Personally I love Italian food but even Italians need a change now and again.'

Sophie smiled. She could not, at that point, think of a single Italian she knew who would cook anything else. They talked about her father, his recovery, plans for summer holidays, almost anything except work and Sophie really relaxed and enjoyed the evening. She was touched by the fact that he had taken her lightly thrown remark so to heart and the scent of the gardenia on her jacket lapel did not make her compare it with flowers sent by . . . anyone else. It was Hamish who brought up her ex-husband. She had forgotten that he knew; the information was somewhere on her application forms but her former life had never been an issue.

'Your family spends a lot of time in Italy, Sophie. Do you ever run into your ex?' He flushed. 'Sorry, none of my business but I was thinking about him and what he was like when I made the reservation.'

'Italy is a big country, Hamish, and as to what he was like, well, never once did he send me a flower to pin on my lapel.' Both facts were true even though they did not answer Hamish's questions.

'Rafael, you're mad; what am I supposed to do with all these flowers?'

'You don't like flowers?'

'They are beautiful.'

'Not nearly so beautiful as you, *diletta*.'

They found a taxi as soon as they reached Princes Street and when they arrived at her flat Hamish insisted on walking up to the top floor. 'This climbing must be what keeps you so fit, Sophie. Perhaps you'd come hill walking with me some Saturday?'

'I'd love to,' she said as she inserted her key in the last lock. She turned to say goodnight and found herself being thoroughly kissed. Surprised, for a second she did nothing, but then she relaxed. Very nice.

'I'd love to come in.'

'Not a good idea,' she began but got no further.

'Necking at the door is for teenagers,' murmured Hamish a few pleasant minutes later.

'And for people who have to go to work in the morning.'

'We could go together.'

Not yet. She knew she was not ready, not yet. 'Hamish.'

He let her go. 'You are absolutely stunning, Sophie Winter. See you tomorrow. I'll be good and make sure the bottom door is closed behind me.'

She waited until she heard it close before she went in. She had an idea that a rather silly smile was on her face and it was not down to the wine or not only the wine. Hamish Sterling, DC. Decent character or DHB, decent human being.

'You have had a glass too many, Sophie Winter.'

18

Zoë's baby was obligingly on time but, like many babies, he waited until his parents had gone to sleep before announcing his imminent arrival. His proud and exhausted father rang the family to bring the good news and Sophie heard of it from her delighted parents.

'I can't tell you how much I wanted to be there, Sophie, but Maude is Jim's mother so that's almost as good and I just could not leave your father.'

She heard her father's voice disclaiming in the background and then he took the receiver. 'I'm insisting she goes as soon as possible, *bella*. Be quite glad to have some peace and quiet.'

'Really, Mum's going now? How exciting.'

'You know your mother; the doctors couldn't possibly have known exactly how to treat Zoë, and as for Maude, what do mothers of boys know?'

'Possibly a lot more about baby boys than mothers of girls,' she suggested and enjoyed his laughter. 'You're not well enough to go?'

'I'm fine. Frankly, a baby is a baby and I can wait but your mum really needs to get her hands on him. They haven't told us his name yet. Will you wait to see him next year?'

A newborn baby, her godchild. 'I'm with you. I'll wait.'

'We'll keep our feelings to ourselves then, shall we?' He stopped and again she could hear him talking to her mother in the background. The radio or television was also on and so she couldn't decipher what each one was saying. 'Mum wants me to tell you that I'll stay with Ann while she's away, give me a chance to get the twins started on rugby. If I had my druthers I'd stay here but they'd only fuss.'

He was either much better or doing a really good job of faking it. No, he was fine; his humour was too unforced. She would relax.

A few days later her mother rang again. 'It's about the house, Sophie. Judith's having a lovely time and Ann and George will go out for a month, but the house will be empty most of the summer if you feel like a visit on your own. If you don't want it we may get a tenant in. Your dad's worried about his garden and we don't want him to start worrying again.'

At least he had stopped talking about putting Villa Minerva on the market. 'Carlo and Josefina are coming to the Edinburgh Festival; I promised I'd be here.'

'You must do what you think best, of course.' Friends before family. She would think it and brood but she would not say it. 'Rafael is playing, I take it.'

'He's in the programme but the countess hasn't been very well either this year. Harry will be here for a week; he loves the festival, and I've promised to go to Inverlachar with Hamish for a few days.' Should she say anything? It was still too early although most people in the office now saw them, mistakenly, as a couple. 'We love hill walking and besides, there's an empty air station right in the middle of his constituency and the Executive is suggesting it as a possible site for housing asylum seekers. It's in a beautiful part of the country, not too far from several large towns, hospitals and school districts, and it still has an excellent rural bus service. We were laughing over dinner the other night. It's Brigadoon, I told him, or Camelot and no one has noticed until now.'

'You do get so enthusiastic about everything, Sophie.'

'Mum, how could I possibly work at something I didn't believe in wholeheartedly?'

'Well, I worry. You've always been the same, so fired up. Do you remember your Girl Guide leader or whatever? You thought she was wonderful and then when she ran off with her boss and all the takings from his wife's shop your heart broke.'

Was that true? Somewhere a dim and distant memory stirred. Exaggeration, that's my mum. 'Mum, I was a child.'

'Are you grown up yet?'

What could you say to that? Sophie got back to the easy subject of grandson number three and at last was able to hang up.

Harry e-mailed to say he had decided against the festival in favour of the Proms. That way I can see Dad. How about coming down, Sophie, possibly for the last night. I really love all that oompapa.

'If you can get tickets, I'd love to go – or is it easier for me to try from this end?'

'The Internet is king. Watch this space.'

Hamish loved the Festival Fringe even more than Harry but where Harry liked plays Hamish was into what Sophie thought of as alternative music because she recognised none of it; it was unbelievably noisy and she could make no sense of it at all. He had taken her twice to a nightclub where he was obviously very welcome and Sophie had been delighted to see him join in. But later, when she was sitting up in her lovely bed in her little eyrie with a cup of steaming herb tea and two aspirins, she reflected that never once had Rafael's music given her a headache. If Hamish talked about fringe tickets she would gently decline; she would encourage him to go but she could suggest that he have supper with her first.

Paolo telephoned from Rome. After a few minutes of polite chat about their respective parents he got to the point. 'Sophie, I have spent several hours with the archivist here in the *palazzo* and we are beginning to make some sense. Mother has a handwritten list of the items she was able to remove from her family home before it was requisitioned but, *d'accordo*, it is in Tuscany and we are in Rome. Some things we may not be able to read any more because of age; we are speaking about sixty-year-old paper that was folded but we will try. When my parents married, Mother brought her . . . dowry, I suppose one would say, but because they reminded her of too many sad things, she did not look at them for years. Apart from the crucifix that was in the London house – she thought that was delicate, 'the London house', not 'in your dressing-table' – there was a silver tankard that Raffaele remembers. He says he put beer in it when he was sixteen and Cesare was furious.'

She interrupted him. 'Is Rafael there, Paolo. I want to thank him for sending the plane; it was so kind.'

'No, he is still on tour.'

'But Carlo—'

'I know, my dear, but I rang him when Mother recovered; she was adamant that he remain in Australia.'

'So he will come to the festival?'

'There is no reason why he should not. Now, the thefts, Sophie.'

Again she interrupted. 'Paolo, do you know why *la contessa* wants to see me?'

'I was unaware that she does. She has never spoken to me. How do you know this, Sophie, if I may ask?'

'Carlo rang me.'

'Then undoubtedly she has asked for you; she is very fond of Carlo. Do you wish to speak with her now? She is on the terrace.'

Speak to *la contessa*? No, there was no need, and if she had changed her mind about wanting to see her beloved son, then possibly she would have reconsidered speaking to his former wife. Episode closed. 'I'm sorry, Paolo, there is nothing for us to say to each other. I'm sorry I interrupted.'

'If you change your mind . . . For now I will continue. There was also a carriage clock decorated with Sèvres porcelain panels and another with enamelled Limoges on the sides; the Vezzi teapot – that was probably extremely valuable since there are so few Vezzi pieces in existence; three very old betrothal dishes painted by Nicola da Urbino around the beginning of the sixteenth century, one with the name Gabriella on it – probably why my great-grandfather bought it. There were many small things that she cannot recall, brooches and earrings and some glassware but also the Battista manuscript which was, Mother thinks, in rather poor condition when she looked at it perhaps six or seven years ago. I will contact you again when I see the list and have spoken with Raffaele. We think it would be good to trace these objects on the international market, we will find, perhaps, who bought them, if they have not completely disappeared, and then, who knows, who sold them. Are you happy for us to do that, Sophie?'

He was telling her that he still was not sure of her honesty and that hurt. 'Of course, Paolo. I wish it had been done five years ago.' She tried to make her voice as assured and honest as she could. Politicians were coached to make their voices sincere when they were not. But she was sincere.

'I believe so too does Raffaele. It will be good to put everything correct now. I will keep in touch. *Ciao.*'

'*Ciao.*'

They were a nice family, the de Nardis family; Rafael sending his plane for her father just because he had once been his father-in-law, Paolo trying to make order out of chaos created by a world war, *La contessa* telling her son she was not ill when her doctor, who should surely know better, said she was.

It was too late to ring her parents to say that the count was cataloguing his family archives. How wonderful to be able to tell them something concrete. The Battista manuscript, for instance, that the countess thought Sophie had stolen . . . what if it was, in fact, the one owned by old Mr Forsythe, and bought legally by Harry in Venice several years before *la contessa* thought it had gone missing? Nothing made sense.

She had such a pleasant evening with Hamish; still she had not invited him in when he had come back with her very late. She was not quite ready to take that step, almost but not quite. She had slept with no one except Rafael. For her it meant commitment, and was a step she would not take lightly. She had experimented a little with Harry who was attractive and interesting; they had a great deal in common but he lit no sparks in her. Hamish lit sparks and why she did not know; was it because he was so unlike Rafael? Was she deliberately seeking a relationship that would not constantly remind her or be compared?

She was the only person in the world, she had thought complacently, who really knew Rafael. She was the only person with whom he laughed. With everyone else, perhaps with the exception of Carlo, he was serious, but with Sophie and Carlo and later too with Josefina he would laugh and be frivolous.

You make me human, my darling Sophie: stay with me, keep me sane.

Oh, God, she had not wanted to remember that but the mind . . . she began to laugh and she laughed hysterically until she was crying and then she laughed again and cried until her stomach hurt. She had found herself saying, the mind has a mind of its own. She sat at the window looking out on to the comparatively quiet Royal Mile but instead of seeing late-night customers from the many bars hurrying or in some cases staggering home she saw Rafael and his mother, Ann and her own mother, the faces swirled together like the colours of spilled oil in a puddle, beautiful but horrible at the same time. She closed the windows, not against 'noxious night air' but against the noise, and went to bed. There she lay courting sleep but it refused to be wooed. 'If I had asked Hamish to come in . . .'

She refused to think about 'what if' any longer and instead decided to be thankful for the morning and a day's work. She did not deliberately avoid being in her office but she seemed to find that, most of the day, her work took her outside the office building. Hamish was waiting for her when she returned.

'Hello.'

She smiled at him and his smile warmed her.

'Lovely evening, wasn't it?'

'Absolutely.'

He moved very close to her. 'If you're free, Sophie, we could go to Inverlachar this weekend, see the airstrip, perhaps meet a few constituents. If I ring my mother this evening, she could arrange a wee party; we could spend some time at the site, go for a long walk in the hills, and then we could hear what the locals really feel about the project before it comes up officially.'

'Sounds lovely.' She opened his door and stepped out into the main office. 'You haven't forgotten the meeting?'

'On my way there now.'

He wanted to kiss her; she could feel it but caution intruded. She had never been one for kissing in public. 'I'll see you in the morning then.' She closed the door.

'Was that for our benefit?' Margaret was sitting at her desk.

'I don't know what you mean.'

'We're all delighted, Sophie. He needs a wife. When he took off in his office time to have a haircut we saw the future and we like it.'

'Margaret, Mr Sterling is on his way to a meeting.'

'I know, but later, will he be climbing up stairs to the princess in the tower?'

'You're verging on being offensive.'

Margaret got up and came round the desk. 'Oh, Sophie, no offence. Everyone likes you and those of us who've been working for him for years have despaired of fixing him up. We never thought of you, Miss Cool, until he started gazing after you with big spaniel eyes. Go for it; don't let his being in the public eye hold you back. You'd make a great political wife.'

Sophie decided not to be annoyed. They meant well. 'We're friends, that's all.'

Never deny anything, *diletta*. Just smile and say nothing.

She smiled and hoped it was not too late to say nothing.

'I think you should send Raffaele for a year to America.'

'America; surely there is no school in that place to equal Venice, or Rome, or Vienna.'

'The Juilliard is good.' He mentioned teachers known to her from their European reputations. *'Besides, Contessa, it is a very democratic place and will be good for Raffaele in many ways. We do not want him to be insular.'*

'This will need careful thought.'

★

'Signora, why not tell Master Raffaele that there is no money for New York? He is a good boy and will understand. Besides, he is a genius; he does not need more teaching.'

But she had brought up her children to be unaware of the sacrifices made. Nothing should worry them. Paolo would leave Oxford if she told him there was no money to send his brother to New York.

'Do you remember before the war, Marisa, how lovely life was? I don't think I was ever angry.'

She pictured herself; white dresses with ribbons that matched those in her long black hair. She was laughing as she ran through gardens that were always full of flowers.

'Il conte *never asked about my boxes, Marisa, and I need only one or two treasures to remind me – and even those I would sell, easily, gladly, if it would help my sons.' Slowly she lifted a package wrapped in delicate silk from its resting place. 'The Battista manuscript. Take it to Venice. The right scholars are there to evaluate it, but, Marisa . . . discretion.'*

Gabriella sat, propped up by lace-edged pillows, and looked slowly around the bedroom to which she had come as a bride, where both of her sons had been born, and where Mario had died. It was, she decided complacently, a fit setting for La Contessa de Nardis. She could see herself reflected in a gilded Venetian mirror that hung above the Italian ebony cabinet with its secret drawers, one of which contained the paper that she would have to give to Paolo. The Nevers faience ware on the eighteenth-century console table in the west window was on the list and could be crossed off by her son, for it had never moved from that table since the day she unpacked it herself and put it there. She had never known her mother but her father had assured her that her mother had treasured it, a wedding gift from her own mother to the new Contessa Brancaccio-Vallefredda. The chairs were eighteenth century, a gracious period, and so too was the enormous chest of drawers that stood against the painted wall opposite the marble fireplace. It was a shame, perhaps, to hide the painting;

how bright it would be if the chest were ever removed from this room – as it might be, one day; Beatrice preferred light, delicate furniture and would keep all the chairs but she would hate the chest. It should be hers, of course, for the chairs and the chest belonged to this house, this family.

Marisa removed the tray, tutting as she saw how little her mistress had eaten.

'Today I breakfasted on memories, Marisa.'

'No protein,' sniffed the maid as she carried the tray over to the door. 'Signor Paolo is coming to see you. You look tired. Shall I tell him later?'

She waved her hand in annoyed dismissal. Paolo had to see the list. What did it matter now anyway? 'Tell him to come.'

'*Mi figlio*. How very distinguished you look this morning.' He kissed her and sat down on a chair by her bed.

'*Grazie*. And you, Mamma, are you as well as you look?'

'We both know the answer, Paolo, but I am content. To see Raffaele happy – that would be good and perhaps, who knows, maybe . . .' She stopped talking and reached under her mound of pillows. 'The key. This usually stays in that dish over there' – she pointed to the faience ware – 'and is to the top drawer of the cabinet. The list I made is in there. To find it is like peeling an artichoke; with this key you open, then one drawer comes out and another and at last I will show you the secret drawer, very useful for you, or maybe Beatrice.'

'We have no secrets from each other.' He smiled.

'We all have secrets, *caro*. Now go and begin to peel.'

He followed her instructions and eventually the cleverly concealed drawer slid open. 'They were great craftsmen in those days, no? Take out the paper, Paolo, but be careful.'

The count saw that there was indeed a faded, folded paper in the cavity. It had been folded many times but there was something more, something even worse that would make deciphering it difficult. He looked at it for some time with his back to his mother, held it up to his nose, and then, his face pale, he turned. 'It's blood, Mamma.'

She was lying back against the pillows and was as white as they were. 'Yes, blood, the life-blood of Ludovico Brancaccio-Vallefredda, my brother and your uncle. He was sixteen when he was killed, murdered by the Germans because he had helped the British. I took it out of his breast pocket, still warm, and I carried it everywhere for years. Your papà showed me the drawer and told me to keep it there. "You must forgive, Gabriella. Every nation commits sin in war." Poor Mario; he was so like my father. He believed that too, and what happened to him, Paolo? Dead in a camp in Poland.'

'Mamma . . .'

'It's all so long ago. Take the paper. You will see that the German general who commandeered our home was generous; he allowed us to take many things. Just as well, no, since a British bomb destroyed everything that was left.'

The count looked at her amazed at the tone of her voice. 'Mamma?'

'Yes, Paolo, I hate. I have covered it well. I never wanted you to know about it, about the feeling of impotence. We were allies of Germany and so we gave up our home, the villa where I was born, where my mother died, and we lived in a small house outside the village. Such indignities my father bore with such fortitude but I, Paolo, I seethed with anger. Your father said I was like a volcano, calm on the surface and bubbling away underneath. Take the paper and show it.'

Paolo carefully unfolded the paper. After almost sixty years, even without the heartbreaking bloodstain, it was difficult to make out some of the words. 'They're so faint.'

'I know,' she said simply. 'There was no ink and so I used a pencil. I never thought how important this paper would be. I kept it only because of the blood. Go now, Paolo, and read what you can. I will rest and then later, after lunch perhaps, I will be able to help you. Portofino too, he should remember; he helped me pack.'

19

Sophie looked at the suitcase lying empty on her bed. She was going away for the weekend with Hamish Sterling. There had been many times before when they had been out of Edinburgh together but those times had been strictly business. This was not. They would not be staying in a hotel but at his family home. The visit could be classed as work related, she argued with herself; there would be the inspection of the airfield, the constituency meeting, the party for supporters, but there was also the invitation to join him hill walking. That was not a party outing; it was two people, Hamish and Sophie, the same Hamish and Sophie who went out to dinner together, who went to art shows together, who went to dreadful concerts together, and who kissed each other goodnight after each of these outings. Would Hamish be content to kiss her goodnight outside a door in his own house? And what in the name of heaven did she want?

She did some rapid thinking about suitable clothes, packed her suitcase with speed and efficiency, and telephoned her mother. 'Hi, how's everything?'

'Your dad gets stronger every day. Why are you ringing so early, dear?'

'Because I'm off up to the Highlands with Hamish; we're leaving straight from the office and I worried that I might be too busy to let you know. You have my mobile number if you should need to ring.'

'Well, it's always lovely to speak to you, Sophie. What are you doing in the Highlands?'

'You know, constituency business; Hamish is inspecting a

disused airfield that has been suggested as a hostel for asylum seekers; before that there's a coffee morning thing in the village where he'll listen to the views of all the people in the area and in the evening party workers and supporters are invited to his house for drinks.'

'Where are you staying? There should be some lovely hotels in the Highlands.'

'There are, but his mother has asked me to stay at their home.'

There was silence for a moment and then Sophie heard her mother, obviously with her hand over the speaker, talking to her father. She came back. 'That's nice. Sophie, you have been seeing him quite often lately.'

'I like him, Mum. Is that what you want to know? He's a decent man of high ideals. He has a lousy taste in music but apart from that I can't think of anything negative at all.'

'Good gracious and he's a politician. I'd grab him, dear.'

There was no point in saying that not all politicians were corrupt; her mother moved through life making sweeping statements for which she usually had no sound factual basis; at the drop of a hat she would declaim on anything and everything. Her children had long ago accepted this as one of 'Mum's little foibles' and paid no attention.

'A month or two ago you were telling me to grab Harry.'

'What happened to him? We really like him.'

Sophie had absolutely no intention of discussing her love life with her mother and so, even though she had initiated the conversation, she backed off. 'I like him too, Mum, but enough of me and my love life. How is everyone?'

They chatted for a few more minutes about family matters and then Sophie managed, her conscience clear, to hang up. She was reflecting as she walked across the cobbled High Street towards her office building, pulling her little suitcase on wheels, that each of the clichés she and her mother had recited could have, in fact probably did have, basis in fact. She refused to look for an example.

By the time she reached her own office and booted up her

machine there was an e-mail from her mother. 'What about tonight?'

She laughed. Had she really expected the supreme list maker of the western world not to notice that Friday evening had not been discussed? 'Travel, Mum, travel,' she muttered as she opened the rest of her mail.

As it happened they were late leaving the office, and getting out of Edinburgh is never easy in the rush hour. Hamish rang his mother at nine to tell her they were still at least an hour away from Inverlachar.

'She says it's poached salmon, so no problems.' Sophie said nothing. He looked stunned. 'You hate salmon?'

Sophie turned from the window. 'Sorry, Hamish. I was looking at the view. Unbelievable scenery.'

'Wait till you see it from the top of a Monro; that's a hill over three thousand feet.' She smiled. 'Sorry, you knew that. It's the most beautiful place in the world, as far as I'm concerned. Where's your favourite place, Sophie, and do you like salmon because I'll have to ring my mother again if you don't?'

'I love salmon. I hope Mrs Sterling isn't waiting for us' – oh, heavens, how many ways could that statement be taken – 'before she eats, I mean.'

'She's a great snacker; she'll have had a sherry and a wee something. Skinny as a stick; don't know how she does it.'

'It's easy; it's how much of a wee something that counts.'

They were silent for several miles of narrow winding roads where they saw not another vehicle. 'And your favourite place?'

Tuscany. The Usher Hall. Her eyrie.

'The river below my parents' home in Tuscany. There's a huge flat rock that somehow got thrown there a million years ago and the river rushes past and trees and ferns bend over to shelter it and exquisite little rock plants grow in tiny fissures so that sometimes there's a splash of bright yellow on the rock like lemon curd or bright red like drops of blood and there's heat from the sun and the sound of the river . . .'

'Sounds idyllic . . . especially for someone in love.'

'Heavens no,' she lied. 'My nephews whoop like dervishes as they jump from the rock into the pool. Wouldn't do at all for a romantic interlude.'

She stood poised on the edge of the rock and was so aware of him behind her. She could smell the wet ferns that hung above her and hear the drop, drop, drop of the water that seeped through the cliff from the ground above.

'Sophie.' His voice was soft and gentle. 'You cannot go any further, *carissima*, or you will fall in.'

She turned and she was in his arms. Home, safe, where she had wanted to be since the first moment, since the beach at Lerici, since the shoe shop in Florence.

He held her, not as if to save her from the fall behind her, but more as if he would never, for any reason, let her go again. 'I love you, Sophie Winter,' he said and kissed her, very gently at first and then, as she responded and his passion rose, his kiss was more intense, searching, demanding. 'I love you, Sophie.' She could say nothing; she knew only that if he let her go she would fall into the water because her legs no longer seemed to belong to her, and this time she kissed him and he laughed and scooped her up into his arms and whirled around on the rock with her to a tune that was playing in his head. He stopped, out of breath, and put her down but still he did not let her go. 'In Beunos Aires I would suddenly see your face, Sophie, do you remember, so nervous when the dust marked my slacks. In Lucerne – there you would be looking up at me so hurt because you thought I had forgotten you when we met in Florence. Your eyes haunted me, Sophie, *mi diletta*, those lovely eyes that saw Raffaele, the man. I looked for you every time I was in Edinburgh, every time I came home to Tuscany. Marry me, Sophie, marry me, for I am nothing without you.'

Too painful, too painful.

'Look, there's the first signpost. Inverlachar. Do you know, Hamish, until I saw that sign I was beginning to believe it didn't exist?'

Mrs Sterling was in her drawing room waiting for them. She was so like Hamish that Sophie could have picked her out from any number of women, but where Hamish was, to be brutally honest, slightly overweight and rather . . . dishevelled, she was pencil slim and perfectly groomed. Her tweed suit could have been made any time in the past twenty years, and possibly was, but it was perfectly cut and, given that fashions in traditional tweeds don't change too much, she would no doubt be wearing it for the next twenty.

'I've got a wee fire on; it gets a bit chilly in the evenings,' she said as she welcomed Sophie to the drawing room. It was a mellow room, old furniture, old carpets, old curtains. Like its mistress it too had changed little in the last twenty years.

Sophie sat down gratefully beside the fire. 'What a lovely room.'

Mrs Sterling smiled complacently. 'Do you know, once or twice Hamish has said we need a new this or that but my mother chose the furniture for this room and I think she had perfect taste.'

'It's lovely,' said Sophie again.

Hamish had brought glasses of cream sherry over from a small octagonal table near the door. 'Before dinner ritual.'

Sophie wondered if she dared tell them that she absolutely loathed cream sherry and decided that she did not. There would be, after all, only two dinners, and she was perfectly sure that that equalled two glasses. She could bear two glasses.

'We're not centrally heated, Miss Winter, but you'll find an electric fire in your room should you feel the need.'

'How kind,' said Sophie, manfully downing the sherry, as a gong sounded from just outside the room. 'And it's Sophie, please.'

'That's Marjorie; she loves a chance to belt that thing. Wait till you hear her tomorrow night,' said Hamish. 'Mother, will you show Sophie where to wash her hands and I'll go and open a nice bottle of wine.'

The dining room was a rather gloomy room, almost, thought

Sophie, as if some film set had been trying to establish a mood. Set two. Victorian Highland home.

'Marjorie again, Miss Winter. It's far too big for three people and I have a hard job to stop her laying this great table just for me. She loves it when Hamish comes home, doesn't she, dear?'

'Just tell her firmly, Mum.'

'Easy for him to say. Marjorie's even older than I am; should have retired years ago, but where would she go?'

Marjorie herself came in carrying an enormous soup tureen. Three cups of what had been hot broth swirled around in the depths. Sophie struggled with cold soup and then poached salmon and lukewarm boiled potatoes. Neither Hamish nor his mother seemed to notice. The wine was nice. Thankfully hot coffee was served in the drawing room beside the fire and they chatted about Hamish and his career through two cups each. And then, 'Hamish tells me you're a divorced woman, Miss Winter.'

Heavens, thought Sophie, she thinks I'm a painted harlot after her son. How can he be so nice with such a ghastly mother? 'Yes, Mrs Sterling.' She would say no more.

'There's never been a divorce in my family.'

'Nor mine actually,' said Sophie, who had deferred once to a dominating woman and would not defer again.

Hamish almost jumped to his feet. 'Sophie, we have an early meeting. Time to call it a day; I mean, let me show you to your room. I'll come back down and lock up, Mother.'

'My mother's—' he began as they walked side by side up the wide staircase.

'Very nice,' she interrupted.

He smiled gratefully. 'A bit rigid. It's her upbringing. She takes her time getting to know a person.'

'Do we ever get to know a person really, Hamish? Sometimes we have to give them the benefit of the doubt.' She was thinking, not of him nor his mother, but of Rafael and his mother who was so unlike Mrs Sterling but so very like her too. 'Don't worry. She loves you very much and wants what's best for you. Mothers are like that.'

'I'm surprised that she mentioned . . . divorce.'

'It's not a dirty word, Hamish, just an unpleasant one. Goodnight.'

She laughed at her worries about whether or not she should welcome an advance. What a conceited woman I am, she decided. She was sure that Hamish was prepared to advance; he hinted often enough. She looked fearfully at the door. Would he perhaps wait until the mother dragon was asleep or, like all good dragons, did she sleep with one eye open? The picture of the very tidy Mrs Sterling sleeping with one eye untidily open kept her happy until she was in bed. She hoped she might win a Brownie point for not using the electric fire and, in trying to conjure up ways to get the fact that she had steeled herself not to waste electricity into her conversation, she fell asleep.

Marjorie brought her tea in bed.

'Gracious, Marjorie, you shouldn't be waiting on me. I haven't had tea in bed since . . . You're very naughty to carry that tray all the way up here.'

'Och, lassie, it's nice to have a pretty wee thing in the house. It's not a bother. There, isn't that a nice view,' she said, throwing open the heavy curtains to show the hills of Inverlachar in all their purple and green glory. 'Hamish says you've lived in foreign parts; you'll not have seen a view like thon.'

The Alpi Apuani, their snow-covered crowns brilliant in the sun. 'It is absolutely lovely, Marjorie,' she said and she meant it and since the old lady seemed in no hurry to go, 'May I ask how old you are?' She could have been sixty; she could have been eighty so wrinkled and grey was she.

'Would you believe seventy-three?' She laughed at the look of astonishment on Sophie's face. 'Well past the pension, lass. I like it here and Mrs Sterling is good to keep me. I've quite a bit put by but I'll give it to Hamish the day he weds.' She looked coquettishly at Sophie as if to see if this was seen as an inducement. 'Old age is natural, lass, but old age with not a soul that belongs to you or cares for you is not.' She pushed open one of the sash windows and cold air blasted in from the hills.

'The tea was lovely,' said Sophie, hastily getting out of bed. 'It was nice to talk to you, Marjorie.'

But Marjorie had found a listener and was loath to let it escape. 'Mrs Sterling has wanted a nice smart wee lassie in a pinny for years but she keeps me because she knows I have nowhere in the world to go. I couldn't go to a home. Mind you, if I get that Oldtimers disease, I won't care, will I, and I can certainly afford it, if Hamish doesn't marry. He's a good lad, should have a wife and children around his feet; maybe a woman with a past would be good for him.'

Good lord, was she a woman with a past? 'I shall try to find one for him, Marjorie, and now I must get ready for the meeting.'

The old lady took the hint and Sophie dressed. Mrs Sterling would fight tooth and nail to keep her beloved son from the clutches of a fallen woman while Marjorie was all for it. Would any new Mrs Sterling look forward to living with a housekeeper who not only couldn't cook but who was approaching eighty at a rapid rate of knots? Where was the almost innocent weekend she had imagined?

She went down to breakfast and found Hamish and his mother already in the huge dining room. 'Marjorie's taken a fancy to you, Sophie. Visitors she doesn't like have breakfast in the parlour.'

'Better to be disliked in the winter, Miss . . . I was going to say Miss Winter but it sounds strange, in the winter, Miss Winter.'

'Yes, it does, doesn't it, and my mother hates snow.' That remark made no sense at all to the Sterlings but they ignored it.

'I didn't realise that divorced women took their maiden name back. Have some coffee. Isn't it rather dishonest?'

'Thank you, yes.' She held out her cup and waited while Mrs Sterling filled it. 'Only if the divorcée was trying to hide her former married state, I would say.'

'Mother . . .'

Mrs Sterling looked at her son in some surprise. 'Have I said something wrong? Was I offensive? I didn't mean to be – if I was.

We see so few people up here, especially since Hamish moved to Edinburgh. I'm direct and maybe that's not right in this day and age.'

Not direct enough. Sophie buttered some toast. Cold bacon and eggs did not fill her with enthusiasm; She wondered how Hamish could bear it. He surely did not eat cold food in his flat and never, as far as she could remember, had he ever ordered anything cold in a restaurant. Home to him must mean cold food. Poor Hamish. Or was that only when this ugly, pretentious room was being used?

They got through the weekend. The visit to the airfield almost made her forget the less than warm welcome from Hamish's mother. Once again Hamish was the dynamic, forceful man she admired and respected. 'Just look, Sophie, plenty of space, plenty of accommodation. Needs some work to bring it into the twenty-first century – showers as a priority.'

'I'd hate to live here.'

'I know and so would I. But think; you are escaping from oppression; you come here. The mountains above you are not hiding men with rifles—'

'The barbed-wire fence is hardly welcoming and the colour, Hamish.'

'You're talking cosmetics, Sophie. A lick of paint, a few tubs of flowers. There are good schools in the area, at least two under the threat of closure since their rolls are falling. Buses came here for RAF personnel; they can come again, not every five minutes or even every hour on the hour; it's not London or Edinburgh. The village shops are bound to be delighted to have more customers; almost every local drives to the nearest big town to a supermarket.'

'Because they're cheaper and have a greater selection.'

He stopped walking and gesticulating and turned to her. 'I thought you liked the idea.'

She laughed. 'I love to see you marshalling your arguments. No, I'm in favour as long as that non-existent bus will come and take people to the big town too.'

They spent most of the morning assessing the airfield, and after lunch with Hamish's campaign manager they were able to drive up into the hills to do some walking. It was a lovely late summer day and Sophie enjoyed the wonderful feeling of freedom that she always experienced away from cities. The air was clear and still warm enough so that she could discard her sweater. They walked steadily upwards for over an hour, talking easily of the morning, the people they had met, and the potential of the airfield. At last they stopped for a rest. Sophie sat on the warm surface of a rock and Hamish lolled on a heather-covered knoll beside her. A few sheep were scattered all over the hills and a buzzard circled lazily in the sky above them, its wings almost black against the blue of the sky. The heather was past its days of glory but there was still some purple there, tiny brilliantly yellow flowers, and creamy whites. Hamish had brought a Thermos of cold water that they drank thirstily and then they ate apples and threw the cores down, secure in the belief that some small foraging creature would eat them. Sophie leaned back against her rock to feel the warmth of the sun on her face and then the sun was blocked out and Hamish was kissing her.

'I'm sorry about last night, Sophie,' he said at last. 'It was such a ghastly evening, an awful meal, and my mother so prickly. I honestly don't know what got into her.'

Sophie did. She was just like *la contessa* but without her social grace. 'Are meals always cold?'

'No, only when Marjorie insists on pulling out all the stops to impress people. It's miles from the kitchen.'

'I like Marjorie.'

If he noticed that she said nothing about his mother he made no comment. 'Wonderful, isn't she. Absolutely determined to keep going.'

'What will happen when she finally admits that it's too much for her?'

'Mum will keep her; they've been together a long time.'

He still had her hands and Sophie edged away from him slightly. 'Hadn't we better be getting back?'

'Yes.' He picked up the small rucksack in which he had had the apples and the Thermos. 'I was actually apologising for the whole evening. Knowing you were sleeping just along the corridor drove me mad. I'm awfully fond of you, Sophie, but I couldn't, so close to my mother.'

Santo cielo. 'Hamish, I like you very much, and that could grow, and I really respect you as a politician, but surely you weren't expecting that I would fall into your arms.' She shut up because, being honest with herself, she had to admit that she too had considered a romantic interlude. 'It's way too early for that. We have been dating for a few months now.'

'And surely we should be further along than a chaste kiss at the door?'

She looked at his dejected face. Was he right? Was she mistaking respect and admiration for the stirrings of love? 'I don't know, Hamish. I've never been part of the dating scene. I met my husband when I was sixteen; we married when I was twenty-one.'

'You must have . . .'

'Actually no, we hadn't. I was very young, Rafael was on tour most of the time, and he was aware that he was older and more experienced. He was . . . patient.'

Oh, my Sophie, I so much want to be your husband.

'I won't rush you. Maybe tonight, after the party, we could go into the hotel in the village for a romantic dinner?'

'With hot food?'

'Absolutely.'

They walked on quite happily together but later when Sophie was steaming in the huge deep bath she found herself remembering her feelings when she saw Rafael or heard his voice or listened to a record or read a letter. Her whole body had been on fire; every nerve ending longing for his touch. Stupid woman, she castigated herself. That was first love. An emotional state caused by inexperience. Of course, it's not going to be like that the second time or the third.

She remembered that she had enjoyed the walk back down the hill and knew that she was looking forward to dinner in the hotel with an anticipation that was not wholly on account of the promise of hot food. She felt herself to be at a different stage, maturity, where surely there was no breathless anticipation, no sighing, no being unable to sleep or eat.

She did not manage to convince herself.

As it happened Mrs Sterling accompanied them to the hotel and later all three walked upstairs together.

'Pleasant dreams,' she said as she waited till Sophie was inside.

Sophie tried not to laugh aloud. She could see Mrs Sterling guarding her virtue – or was it her son's – outside the door all night. She was sure that Hamish would not come and was glad; it felt sordid somehow.

She looked at herself in the badly marked dressing-table mirror and wondered if she was looking at the face of a woman with a past and wondered what Rafael would say about the Sterlings? *Santo cielo.* She could almost hear his voice using his favourite expletive that was pretty innocuous as swear words go. 'Dear God,' she said to the wavering face in the pock-marked glass, 'I am tired, for I see yet another error in judgement.'

She hurried into bed. Errors in judgement. She was renowned for making them. Error upon error upon error. She was no longer thinking of Hamish and his over-protective mother. She was thinking again of Rafael.

He had had the right to know that she was pregnant but in danger of losing the baby. She should have told him that her body had decided to play a cruel trick on her when he was listening to lies and unsubstantiated rumours. Battista manuscript . . . Vezzi teapot . . . jewelled crucifix. But she had believed that it was no time to say, 'At last, if all goes well in the next few weeks, we will have our baby.'

They should have been together but he had gone to South America alone. 'I think we need some space, Sophie. I can't cope with all this.'

She understood his need for space; she liked being on her own too. On tours it was easy to be together twenty-four hours a day so sometimes she stayed at the hotel, waiting. She had always waited because he came back needing her. But this was the first time he had gone away without her. He had left her in their lovely house in London because his mother had told him his wife was a thief and her sister . . . what had her sister told him?

She had taken to wandering around the city, not eating properly, hardly sleeping. There were some pills in her bag; Carlo had given her medication for slight depression but she had stopped taking the pills when she found out that, at last, she was pregnant. It wasn't the right time to tell him, when he was angry, when he was so distant, when he was so confused, because of all the poison seeping into his brain from his own mother's mouth. Because of what Ann told him.

Sophie punched the pillow. Did she tell him that I was taking pills?

Rafael would equate pills with drugs and he hated drugs of any kind. Now in this chilly bed with its cold linen sheets Sophie realised that her husband should have asked her straight out about the pills. She should have told him that they had been legally prescribed, nothing sinister, nothing untoward. But he had heard nothing but his mother's accusations.

The nightmare stifled her but it wasn't a nightmare because she was wide awake, sitting up in this cold bed in this cold house. She could not think clearly. Two beautiful faces flashed before her eyes, the contessa's so judgemental, and Rafael's distant and sad, so sad. She remembered or dreamed that she had been sitting on a park bench when she had felt the warm blood begin to flow down her legs. She had called out, 'Dear God, no. Rafael. I want Rafael.' She had no idea who had summoned an ambulance or taken her to the hospital. She had forgotten to find out.

'Sophie Winter. My name is Sophie Winter.'

Rafael was playing Debussy, the fiendishly difficult études, his mother's favourites. Sophie did not want him to hear of the miscarriage from a journalist. Even in extremity she protected him and did not think to ask whether he wanted or needed protection. Error, error. 'No relatives here,' she had insisted. 'My home is in New York. Husband? No, no husband, no family.'

Sophie Winter had lost her baby and had been ill for some time and Rafael had telephoned the house constantly for two weeks and then had stopped calling. Sophie had telephoned Carlo.

'My God, Sophie, where have you been? Your parents say they have no idea where you are. Raffaele is going out of his mind. He is on the point of alerting Interpol.'

'Where is he?'

'Buenos Aires.'

He does not care enough to cancel so that he can look for me. 'I lost the baby, Carlo. There is no need for Rafael to know.'

'Of course there is. Ring him right away, Sophie, or I will.'

'You can't, Carlo. I do not give you permission. It's over, *amico*, over.'

She went to Scotland just because she had been to university there and had loved the country and nothing reminded her of Italy. Her depression was even worse but she sought no medical attention and Carlo, the only person in the world who knew almost everything, had been powerless to intervene. She remembered the disgust on Rafael's handsome face at their London meeting to discuss their divorce. He mistook depression and physical illness for drug abuse and Sophie was too dispirited to tell him the truth.

She had not wanted to talk to him anyway, having decided that she did not want a husband who was sorry for her or who did not really want her. She blamed him for believing whatever anyone told him and could not forgive him for that, as she could not forgive her sister, Ann, for trying to cause trouble. She remembered the last thing Rafael said to her.

'The London house is in your name, Sophie, and I will make a reasonable settlement. Anything you want from the *castello* that is mine you may have, anything from New York too.'

She had refused to take anything at all, had gone back to the house only to remove such clothes as she would wear, had never accepted the settlement. She had rented a small flat, found a job using, for the last time, her married name and its connections, and started rebuilding her life. She had fought her way through the depression. It had been hard but she asked for no pity.

She got up and went to look out of the window. The view outside was lovely. Surface beauty can hide such ugliness.

20

The last week in August was set to enter the history books as the most ghastly week of the year so far. She had almost said the ghastliest week ever but no, it did not come close to that. She had returned to Edinburgh with Hamish, both of them so embarrassed and disillusioned that they hardly knew how to talk to each other.

'We'll let things slide for a while, Hamish, don't you think?'

'Absolutely.' He tried to laugh. 'I still think you're terrific, Sophie, but every time I even reach my hand out, I seem to see my mother. A few days to clear the fresh air of Inverlachar from our lungs . . .'

'That's best.'

He did not climb the spiral stair. Sophie did and found that her weekend had left her exhausted. She undressed, fell into bed and was asleep before she had turned off the light. She had not noticed the little blinking light – usually the first thing she saw as she walked in and there were two messages.

'Hi, Sophie. I have Last Night of the Proms tickets. Will you stay in Surrey or would you like to use Dad's guest room? He'll be in the flat.'

Kind, considerate, lovely Harry.

'Sophie. Mother is well again and so I will come to Edinburgh. Valentina will send you a ticket – Tuesday evening, the Usher Hall. Please come. Paolo has found more. *Ciao.* No, wait, Carlo says sorry. Next year for sure. Katia and Tonio have the chicken poxes.'

Poor little things. She sincerely hoped the *chicken poxes* would not be too itchy. She had no time to phone Harry and decided to e-mail him from the office. Rafael she would ignore. The ticket would come and she would decide.

She had already decided, but she refused to buy a new dress and only went to her hairdresser because a radical overhaul was due. He played Prokofiev, Schumann and Liszt, and his encores were by Beethoven: 'Variations on "God save the King" '. It had once been a private joke, like the Mussorgsky, but both he played because he loved them. There was a reception for him after the concert and she managed to stay in the background so that he could not introduce her to anyone. There were definitely one or two people there whom she did not want to know of her association with a world-famous concert pianist. Behind the potted plants she was able to eat quite heartily and so refused his offer of supper.

He insisted on walking upstairs with her. The bottom door was slightly ajar. 'I do not like this open door, Sophie; so easy to enter.'

She shrugged. 'It should be closed at this time, Rafael, but probably one of my neighbours is expecting company after a late-night show. It's the festival; everything is different.'

He said nothing but his expressive face told what he thought of apartment buildings that were accessible to anyone at any time.

'Listen, Rafael, there's a party on this floor; they're expecting latecomers.' They climbed on. 'Is the music still in your head, Rafael?'

'Of course,' he answered seriously. 'I lingered too long in the suspension at the end of the second movement; I shall work on that.'

'It was sublime.'

'You always were my favourite critic.'

She had turned to smile at him but she said nothing because she had a dreadful feeling, a premonition. They were on the top floor and she just knew that something was wrong. She had a strange uneasy feeling and moved closer to him. What was wrong? She could see nothing that she did not expect to see.

'Good heavens, who moved my little table? And look, they have knocked over the plant; poor thing, its roots are exposed.' Was she talking because she did not want to admit what her eyes and her senses were telling her? The tall plant table that usually stood against the wall between the two flats was now standing right in the middle of the little lobby and the plant that usually stood bravely reaching for what light was available was now lying on its side, the soil spilled out on to the floor. She fussed, picking the plant up, scooping the spilled soil back.

'Sophie.' Rafael's gentle voice made her focus on the fact that the door of her lovely little flat was ajar, having been jemmied open with some considerable force.

'Rafael.' Instinctively she turned to him.

'Wait. I will push open the door and you will look in but no more, just look in. Do you understand, Sophie?'

'Of course. I'm not stupid. Someone has broken in to my flat.' Anger was replacing shock. 'Damn it.'

He pushed the door until it stood quite wide and they could see into the flat. None of the lights was on but the streetlights lit up the area quite clearly. A chair stood in the middle of the floor and a soup tureen balanced drunkenly on the settee.

'You wait here, Sophie. He may be in your bedroom.' He shook off her restraining hand and advanced into the apartment. Sophie followed him and pointed out her tiny bedroom and the bathroom.

'No one is here, Rafael. He had to leave the way he entered.' She reached for the tureen.

'Don't touch that. There may be fingerprints. I take it you don't keep it on the settee, *cara*.'

'Someone has been in my home.'

He put his arms around her and she leaned against him. 'Sophie, we will call the police. You have a number, and they will say, I think, to look and see what is stolen. But first we will telephone and then you will have some brandy.'

'No, I won't. They've pinched it. Drinks were in that cupboard. Oh, Rafael, why did they have to break it? The door was open.' She had made no move to leave the shelter of his arms and it was he who pulled away and Sophie remembered that he was her ex-husband and a famous concert pianist and no doubt his staff were waiting at his hotel. 'The number for the police is on the telephone.'

He looked at her but said nothing as he dialled. He reported the break-in and, as he had supposed, was told to look round to see if anything obvious was missing. 'They will be here as soon as they can come, *cara*. In the meantime, can you say what is missing, without to touch anything?'

'Just look at my bedroom. They have emptied everything on to the bed, and look at the mess. Why do they have to make such a mess?'

He let her talk and he returned to the kitchen. 'I have put on your coffee pot, Sophie.'

'What about fingerprints?'

'I don't suppose they took time to make coffee. Come, sit down, you are trembling.'

'It's my home, Rafael, my own special place and someone has been in here raking through my clothes, throwing my books on the ground because they were of no interest to them. I'm so angry.'

'Anger is good. Can you see if anything is not here?'

She looked at him standing there in her tiny bedroom, his height somehow making it look even smaller than it was and she remembered her bedroom in the *castello* where the closet for her clothes was larger than this room. 'I suppose you think this is very small.'

'I was thinking how very pretty it must be when it is not burgled. May I look from the window?'

She squeezed herself against the bed as he passed. 'Fantastic, the whole of Edinburgh is there,' he said as he stood for a few minutes looking out at her favourite view. 'Come, the coffee will be ready.'

He poured coffee and they sat warily on the settee with the tureen like an unwanted guest between them. Sophie started to laugh. 'My chaperone,' she said and laughed harder until he saw that she was close to hysteria.

He took her cup and put it down and then pulled her up and he held her until her laughter turned to sobs and there they stood silent until a voice from the doorway spoke. 'Evening, sir, madam, is this where the trouble was?'

Two policemen stood in the hall. 'The lock on that ground floor door always open, is it, sir?'

'No, I closed it.'

'Open now, sir. What seems to be the trouble?'

What seems to be the trouble? Are they given a script? What does it look like? 'Someone has forced the door of my apartment.'

'Can you tell me when you were last in the flat?' The policeman addressed Rafael and that made Sophie even angrier.

'It's my flat, and I left to go to a concert just before seven.'

One officer asked questions and wrote the answers down in his notebook. 'Is anything missing, miss?'

'I don't think so, apart from a few bottles that were in that little cupboard. Brandy, gin, I think, and some kind of liqueur.'

'Anything here that wasn't here?'

She looked at him in surprise. 'Housebreakers don't put things in houses, do they?'

'You'd be surprised at what housebreakers sometimes do, miss. I take it that chair doesn't usually sit there?' he asked, pointing to the wooden chair that stood in the middle of the floor.

'No, it's at the table. I suppose he put it there to get things down from the top of the cupboard and look, he's broken it. I loved that chair.'

'That coffee smells good.'

'Would you like a cup? Does smell good, doesn't it? Is it all right to open the cupboard?'

'No problem, miss; there won't be prints on that surface. The tureen now, lovely set on each side.'

Sophie looked and saw that the dust on top of the antique tureen had been disturbed. 'Pays not to be a great housekeeper. Can I put the chair back? It looks so untidy.'

'Better wait till the fingerprint people get here. Might not be until tomorrow some time and you'll need to get a joiner to mend those locks. Good coffee, thank you. What about the flat next door, miss?'

'I never see the tenant. I've heard noises occasionally but I think whoever lives there works abroad or just rents it out sometimes. I don't know. There's no one there now as far as I can tell.'

'What about the bedroom, officer?'

'Tidying it up, you mean, sir. Difficult. Is there somewhere else you can sleep tonight, miss?'

'The settee folds down.'

'You can't stay here, Sophie. You must come with me to my hotel.'

'And leave my home with its door open?' Her voice rose as if the hysteria was not far from the surface.

'We should have your name too, sir, and a telephone number.'

'But it's nothing to do with him.'

'We'll be discreet, miss,' said the policeman and Rafael laughed.

'Raffaele de Nardis, officer, and I can give you a telephone number but I am leaving Scotland tomorrow morning.'

'Think we can take it for granted you're not the perpetrator, sir. We don't say things like, "Can you account for your movements?" in incidents like this, sir, not to the victims.'

Sophie was smiling. 'He has a few thousand witnesses to his whereabouts, officer.' She stopped. 'Good heavens, how did they find that cupboard? When it's closed it looks just like a piece of the wall. What were they looking for?'

'Very clever bit of design,' said the policeman as he examined the kitchen units. 'Probably not hard to find, miss, wasn't designed to be hidden, just not to stand out, if you know what I mean. Just holds household cleaners, does it? We can't tell you what to do, miss, about leaving the flat till the fingerprint boys get here.'

'I'll stay with her. My plane is not until eleven and by then they should have come, no?'

'I would think so, sir, and soon as they've been you can get a joiner in to get the door fixed and that one downstairs too. We'll go now and talk to anyone who's awake – party going on down-stairs – and tomorrow we'll see the rest of the building. Someone might have heard or seen something. Difficult area this, especially during the festival, all those pavement sellers and all, but you never know. Goodnight, miss, goodnight, sir. Thank you for the coffee.'

They put on their hats and left and Sophie stood with Rafael in the middle of the floor. They looked at each other. 'You can't stay, Rafael. You must be exhausted and I'll be fine.'

'I will stay. First I will make some calls and I would like more of my excellent coffee as drunk by the city of Edinburgh police department.' He put his arms around her and they stood again silent, motionless. 'Come, *cara*, some coffee please while I call Oliver.'

Sophie went to pour more coffee but every nerve ending in her body was on alert. Not only was she in a state of shock from the break-in but every feeling, emotion was intensified by Rafael's proximity: Rafael who, according to Stella, was engaged to Ileana. The beat of his heart as he had held her, the scent of his aftershave, the feel of his arms about her, everything was telling her that she had been without him too long. He could not stay in her flat; he could not. She heard his voice as she had heard it so often before; she heard him reassure Oliver about her well-being, that he could wait to shave until the morning, that he could change on the plane.

'What are you thinking, *cara*, staring so hard into that little cup?' He was behind her. She could lean back and she would be against his body. She willed herself to stay close to the table. 'Come.' He took the cup from her and as his hand touched hers she started. 'Everything will be all right, Sophie; they will find your housebreaker and we will put new locks on the doors. We will have to make enough keys for downstairs, I suppose, for every flat. You have to ask permission, a community decision?'

He was so calm that she too became calmer. 'There is a tenants association; we'll have a meeting, I suppose, if the police recommend new locks for downstairs. I was thinking that Italian is a musical language,' she answered his first question.

'*Davvero*. That is true. Shall I move very carefully your tureen? You must have large parties to need a tureen so big.'

She smiled but said nothing and he carried the tureen over to the table. He would not have needed the chair to reach it.

'There is a bed in this? How very clever. Now you have room for guests.'

'That was the idea.' She would not look at him as he pulled the bed out but, instead, opened the door of the cupboard with her elbow and extracted a duvet and some pillows.

'Go, Sophie. I will watch this so interesting city from the windows; there are many soldiers out here. Shall I call that a princess in a tower needs help?' He did not turn but stayed looking out as the performers and audience from the night's performance of the military tattoo marched, strolled, or hurried down the street.

Sophie rescued a nightgown from the heaps of clothing on the floor of her bedroom and hurried with it into the tiny bathroom. A few minutes later she was ready. It was a post-Rafael nightie and more modest, she thought, than the ones she used to wear but still she stood, her hand on the door handle willing herself to go out. Would he see nervousness and fear in her eyes or naked desire? What would he do? Where would he sleep? With the settee opened there was no chair in the tiny apartment big enough for a man of his size. Had she deliberately bought furniture on a smaller scale for this flat so as not to remember, compare? Don't be stupid. You bought what you could afford: end of story. 'A princess in a tower.' I had forgotten. I did not buy this flat because it reminded me of Tuscany.

He had turned all the lights off and the flat was lit only by the streetlights. He was still standing by the window. 'Go to bed, Sophie, and try to sleep.'

'You can't stand there all night,' she said in as normal a voice as she could muster.

'I won't.'

She lay down and pulled up the duvet but every sense was alert as she heard him move around. He was in the bathroom for several minutes. Poor Rafael; like me he hates to go to bed without cleaning his teeth. But he's not going to bed. Where is he going? What is he doing? Who broke into my home? Why? She could hear him at the door.

'I have put my coat against the door to keep out the draughts. No one will come, *cara*. You are safe.'

'Rafael.'

'I will lie here on the cover. Sleep, Sophie. You are safe with me.'

She tried to relax, to be calm, as she felt his weight beside her on a bed for the first time in almost six years. What was he thinking? Of his music? Of course, music comes first, that hesitation only an expert would have heard.

Eventually she fell asleep and Rafael lay beside her, looking at the way the lamplight shone on her hair and he wanted her as much or more than he ever had, but she was too vulnerable, shocked, dismayed by the violation of her home. She moaned a little and he touched her shoulder gently and she sighed and lay still, comforted. A break-in where nothing was taken. What had that policeman said? Something about the burglar leaving something instead of taking something? Was that possible? Did the tentacles of the monster in Tuscany that hated Sophie stretch so far? Now, I am imagining things. Sophie says nothing is taken and nothing is here that should not be here but would she tell me if there was something? There is nothing here that I have ever seen before; she has kept none of the gifts I gave her, not a spoon nor a cup nor a painting. She has scraped me from her life. Oh, Sophie, *diletta*, forgive me for making you hate me so.

Sophie woke in the morning and remembered everything. She sat up quickly, feeling alone, abandoned. He was gone. 'Rafael.'

'I'm here, making coffee. How is it that you have excellent coffee, a satisfactory machine and yet you say my coffee is better?'

She shrugged. 'Coffee, pianos. Some people are naturals.'

He smiled. 'Go quickly and dress. Maybe these fingerprinting men will come soon.'

She looked at the clock. 'Gosh, only seven. I felt as if I had slept for hours. I can ring my office when I'm dressed. You can see it from the window, Rafael, my office, across the road and down at the corner. We're on the third floor. There are bagels in the freezer, top drawer of the fridge. Put them in the toaster.' She hated retrieving the clothes from the floor, thinking of them being tossed down by some unfriendly hand. She contented herself with giving everything a good shake and when she was ready she returned to the main room to find Rafael again at the window but this time with a mug of coffee.

'I would never tire of looking out of this window, Sophie.'

She joined him. 'Look, there's a light on in the office building.' She was in the middle of the phone call when the policemen arrived.

They looked like bankers, not policemen; at least so Sophie thought, but they knew their job. 'Nice little cabinet,' said one as he dusted the broken door of the blue cupboard. 'Locked, was it?'

'No.'

'Wasteful,' he said and went on dusting. 'These surfaces are difficult, but there is a good thumb on the glass there and the tureen is a goldmine. They didn't lift the lid; wonder why?'

'The antique dealer who sold it told me they're quite collectable, not valuable: everybody's granny has one.'

'Glad you've still got it then, miss. That coffee smells good.'

Rafael smiled. 'Would you gentlemen like some coffee?'

'That's very nice of you, sir; two sugars for me, and three for Spence here. We'll do the door; nasty mess they made of it. You had a Yale and this original lock?'

'Yes.'

'Took some force, a crowbar or something. Hard to walk around Edinburgh in the middle of the festival with a crowbar. Was there anything in the hall that could have been used?'

He was moving into the hall as he spoke and Sophie and Rafael went with him. 'Anyone next door?'

'I don't think so.'

'We'll check. This door? Another flat, is it?'

'No. Oh golly, it's open; that's next door's basement, as it were, and it's always locked, as far as I can remember.'

'The lock's been forced too.' They looked inside. There were pots of paint, a sorry-for-its-condition ladder against the wall, some left-over wallpaper and a box of tools containing a large heavy chisel. 'Lovely, we'll take this in. Struck it lucky – the burglars, Miss Winter – unless they knew it was there.'

They went back into Sophie's flat and the policemen went into the bedroom.

'Is Oliver sending a car for you, Rafael?'

'No, I'll leave for the airport from here. Oliver will bring my shaving things and a change of clothes. You will permit?'

'Of course, but you mustn't miss your flight.'

'It can't leave without me,' he said matter-of-factly.

'Oh, dash,' began Sophie, who had heard voices in the stairwell and Rafael looked at her in surprise. 'Hamish, what on earth are you doing here?'

Hamish Sterling hurried across the room and took her in his arms. He looked at Rafael. 'I came as soon as I got in, Sophie. This is terrible. You poor girl. Thank God you weren't here; did they steal much?' His eyes never left the unshaven face of Raffaele de Nardis.

'Hamish, how nice of you to come.' She looked from one man to the other. Rafael's face was inscrutable, Hamish looked as though he might just be ready to fight. 'Rafael, this is Hamish Sterling, my boss; Hamish, Raffaele de Nardis. He, we, he was with me when I discovered that I had been broken into. He very kindly—'

'You do not have to explain me, *cara*, or yourself.' Rafael held out his hand. 'How do you do, Mr Sterling. I am delighted that you care enough about your staff to visit in times of crisis.' He looked towards the door as fresh voices were heard. 'That will be my driver with my change of clothes. Sophie, coffee for your guests; I have made a fresh pot. She makes dreadful coffee, Mr Sterling, but possibly you know that.'

Sophie ignored him and his so uncharacteristic behaviour. 'Oliver, how very nice to see you again. Hamish, this is Oliver Sachs, Rafael's manager. Hamish is a member of the Scottish Parliament, Oliver. Shall I pour coffee? I'm afraid I have nothing suitable to eat.'

She poured coffee, listening to Hamish and Oliver making polite conversation. She was aware of the policemen working steadily on, and of Raffaele de Nardis singing in the shower. She would not think of him but she was forced to look at him when he emerged from her bathroom, freshly showered and shaved, in a tailor-made designer suit. She looked at Hamish, dear Hamish with his new haircut, and the elegant Oliver, and decided that her boss looked like an untidy bundle of hay beside two streamlined bales. She was convinced that he would not thank her for the comparison.

'Does anyone know a good joiner?' she asked into the weighty silence and Hamish came into his own.

'I'll arrange that, Sophie,' he said, standing up. 'Gentlemen, a pleasure to meet you both. Sophie, don't worry about coming in today. I'll pop in at lunch time, bring you a sandwich.'

Game, set, and match to Hamish.

The policemen had gone, their work completed; Rafael and Oliver left, she hoped in time for Rafael to leave Scotland at his allotted time. The worried Oliver had said, 'Maestro, if we miss the slot, it may be hours before you can leave.'

'Will you go to your work when this joiner has mended your door, Sophie?'

'I couldn't bear to come home to this mess so I shall stay here and clean up.'

'Call me to let me know that everything is all right.'

'Rafael, of course it will be fine.'

'Have you told your parents?'

The thought had never occurred to her but she remembered that the countess had always expected to be told everything her sons were doing. 'They don't need to know. They can't do anything.'

He looked worried, even ill at ease. 'A parent wants to know.'

She kissed his cheek. 'That's not a good reason for worrying them. I'll be fine, Rafael. Goodbye, thank you. Oliver.' She held out her hand to Oliver who bowed over it before picking up Rafael's small case and still Rafael stood, like an alien being, in her wrecked apartment.

'I shall think of you in your tower, Sophie.'

'Not like this, I hope; it's usually very tidy, and quite elegant.' She wanted him to go and she wanted him to stay.

'Call me? Please, just to tell me about the criminals.'

'I'll call. You didn't tell me about Paolo.'

'Nothing; we'll talk later.' He bent his head and kissed her very gently on her mouth and she closed her eyes and so did not see him turn and hurry down the spiral staircase. She stayed for a few moments until she knew that she was absolutely alone and then she turned and looked out of the window. Rafael was hurrying across the pavement to a sleek black car that stood with its rear door open. He stopped as he reached the car and looked up and she raised her hand and then let it fall to her side. He got into the limousine and it pulled out into the traffic.

He had made one last pot of coffee but she decided to tidy the living room now that the police were finished with her furniture. She was perfectly happy as she washed all the cups her various visitors had used and straightened the chairs. The joiner had taken her lovely little blue cupboard and the broken chair away to mend in his shop and so, in no time at all, she was ready to tackle the more unpleasant chore of her bedroom. First she put back all the emptied drawers and returned the books to her little bookshelf.

What had they been looking for inside the pages? No one uses banknotes as bookmarks or do they? Wills are frequently in books in detective novels. My burglar was an avid reader. Should I tell that nice policeman that? When will they tell me if they have a match of fingerprints?

She heard the bell that alerted her that someone was downstairs. It was Hamish with the sandwiches. She decided not to tell him that Rafael had made the coffee, even when he told her how good it was.

'You've got the place shipshape again, Sophie.'

'I have to wash down the furniture and cupboards and my clothes are still all over the bed and the floor but it shouldn't take much longer. This is very sweet of you, Hamish, a lovely sandwich.'

'I want to do a lot more for you, Sophie. I have to say I felt awkward finding another man here, especially your ex-husband. I'm not asking you to explain.'

'Just as well because I wouldn't.' He flushed a little and looked down at his sandwich and she took pity on him. 'Hamish, I was married to him for five years. We are trying to be civil to each other. Occasionally he plays at the Usher Hall and sends me a ticket. He's Italian and he's courteous; like you, he walks me to my door. We discovered the break-in together and I am, very frankly, delighted that he was here.'

'Of course, of course, I'm pleased too, must have been quite terrifying. What do the police think? Will they catch them? Have you discovered anything missing yet, apart from your brandy?'

'There's nothing missing in here. Possibly they meant to take the tureen' – she looked across at it where it now sat on the floor – 'or they thought it was better than it is. I shall tidy my bedroom later and inventory there. The police will get back to me if and when they find out anything. I'll wash the tureen when I'm washing down the furniture.'

He took that as a hint that he should get back to work. 'Everyone sends good wishes. I wish I was free this evening but I have a sub-committee meeting, but you have my mobile. I'll keep it on and you ring me at any time.'

She walked with him to the door. 'Thank you, Hamish,' she said and responded to his kiss more heartily than she meant to because she was angry with herself for feeling stifled by his concern. 'Make sure you close the bottom door behind you.'

She did not watch him cross the road and so did not see him stop at the edge of the pavement to look up. She was already in her bedroom hanging up clothes that had been pulled from their hangers. She worked until she had a pile of clothes, especially underwear, that she would wash before wearing, and everything else back in its allotted place. She had forgotten the soup tureen. It was still on the floor between the table and the tall cupboard.

Why didn't I ask Rafael to put it back up?

Unlike her burglar she was not so heavy that she would break the seat of her remaining antique chair. She brought the chair over to the cupboard, picked up the tureen, looked at its dusty finger marked top, and took it to the sink where she washed it. Only then did she climb on the chair to lift the old dish to its original place. I know I should dust up here while I'm at it but I have dusted enough for anyone today, she said to herself as she tried to arrange the dish in its place. Something was preventing it from sitting in the exact spot. Her mind full of angry thoughts – don't tell me he's broken the top of the cupboard too – she got down, put the tureen on the table and climbed back up with a duster.

The top was not broken or damaged in any way. Sitting in the spot where the tureen had been originally was a small porcelain teapot with the globular body typical of the first Venetian factory, Vezzi, founded in the early eighteenth century. Sophie reached for it but her hands were trembling and she did not dare touch it. She stumbled down from her chair and almost fell on to her newly tidied settee. The Vezzi teapot; so rare that it was impossible even to hazard a guess as to its value. It had disappeared from the castello over five years ago and yesterday – dear God, was it only yesterday? – someone had put it in her apartment. The policeman had been right.

'You'd be surprised at what housebreakers sometimes do.'

21

Twenty-one journalists from all over the world attended his first press conference at the Lucerne Festival. He listened to and answered questions in Italian, German, French and English. Many of the journalists were light-hearted, others extremely intense. Sometimes he needed an interpreter; sometimes the journalist did. He was used to it. So were they.

'It is better if I can be in one place for a time; I hate flying in and flying out. For me, it is tiring. Jet-lag exists. I prefer to stay a few days before the concert. On the day I must be there at least three hours before.'

'Morning recitals, too, Maestro?'

'Of course, and that means being in the recital hall at maybe seven o'clock in the morning.' He smiled a beautiful blue-eyed smile, disarmingly, engagingly, so that she would not believe what he was about to say although it was perfectly true. 'I fuss, you see. I need to explore the acoustics, the dimensions; I evaluate my experience or inexperience of the venue. The piano has to be just so and the stool in exactly the right place, not too close, not too far, and the correct height for my long legs and arms. Everything has to be in perfect balance. I practise for three hours maybe four and maybe I change the dynamics, the tempi.'

'Your favourite piano?'

'My particular favourite is a Steinway in my family home in Italy but liking is subjective, is it not? To play in a concert hall? There are many.'

'Composer?'

'It depends on whether I am in the audience or on the platform.

J.S. Bach if I am listening. He is incredible; there is no difference that I can hear between his secular and his religious music. All is filled with the glory of God. Take "My Only Desire is to Marry . . ." ' He was silent for a second as if perhaps he played the piece in his head. 'Stupendous, no? Beethoven, of course. I stayed away from Beethoven as a performer for a long time because I was afraid that I was too inexperienced in performance and in life to really understand him. His music is metaphysical, transcendental. I hope I would please him. Mozart was a most pragmatic composer but his music sings; I enjoy to play Mozart. The great Schnabel said that Mozart's sonatas are unique in that they are too easy for the children and much too difficult for the artists. This is true, no?'

They laughed and he knew that more than a few understood, not just the words but the meaning.

'You are exploring the Russians, Maestro.'

'Absolutely. They are very exciting, yes. Prokofiev, Rachmaninov.'

'And Mussorgsky, Mr de Nardis? You end usually with Mussorgsky.'

Wide-open, blue-eyed charm again. 'Do I? No. Beethoven variations, surely, Chopin, Liszt?'

'I have had the pleasure of hearing you play thirty-two times, Mr de Nardis, and in twenty-one of those concerts you finished with Mussorgsky.'

'Thirty-two times? I hope you get the complimentary ticket.' Much laughter. 'The whole body plays the piano, not just the fingers. Perhaps my head tells my hands to play Mussorgsky, maybe it is my heart, or, who knows, maybe the conductor is Russian.'

Everyone laughed and he stood up, signalling that the inter-view was over.

Oliver was waiting and Valentina with his list of appointments. 'An Italian station wants a little interview before the concert tonight, Maestro, and Swiss television are taping for a later broadcast. They would like an extended interview after you have played. They'll give you time for a shower. The Japanese media would be grateful if they could record an interview after tomorrow's afternoon recital.'

'*D'accordo*. Send all these flowers to a hospital, Valentina.'

'They're being picked up at five, Maestro. The masseur is waiting in the lobby. Would you like coffee first?'

'No, send him up but give me a few minutes to check in with my brother.'

He used the hotel phone to contact his brother. '*Paolo, ciao! Come stai? E Mamma?*'

'We're fine. Good as new. How was the concert?'

'It didn't break my heart enough. Mozart 24; I allowed my mind to wander.' He thought of shoulder-length fair hair on a pillow, shining in the light from a streetlamp, and dismissed it with an iron effort of will. 'Paolo, have you found out anything?'

'Yes and no. At last I have the paper where Mamma and our uncle Ludovico wrote the list but it is impossible to see with certainty what is not there: it is sixty years old, Raffaele, and is folded and folded. One thing is troubling me. A fragment of a Battista manuscript came up for auction in Venice several years ago. The title seems to be the same as the one Mamma says was stolen but it was bought before you were even married so it is a puzzle.'

'She mistook the manuscript, Paolo, or the date.'

'*Certamente*. There is an expert on Battista's work at the university in Florence. I will ask him to meet me when we return to the *castello*.'

'Good, keep me posted. I must go. I need a massage.'

'Lucky you. I hope she's beautiful.'

'*She* is a *he* who weighs two hundred pounds and I have kept him waiting nearly thirty minutes already. I am in Switzerland for the rest of the festival and then – I'm crazy – but I have promised to go to Toulouse and after, Stockholm, and then October to New York and then . . . never mind. *Ciao*.'

'*Ciao*, Raffaele.'

★

Sophie's first coherent thought after her discovery was to contact Rafael. Rejecting that, she reverted to little girl and wanted to ring her father. That was out too. The police? She ought to ring them and say, 'They did put something in my house. Can you believe the burglar made me a present of a piece of Vezzi porcelain? Would the police know that at the last count there were fewer than two hundred verified pieces of Vezzi porcelain in the entire world? Possibly not. When the constable had said, 'You'd be surprised at what housebreakers sometimes do,' she was quite sure gifting their victim a nice little pot that would fetch, easily, twenty or even thirty thousand pounds at auction was not what he had in mind.

Paolo. She could ring Paolo and beg him to believe her. 'Paolo, I've just been burgled and, guess what?' I wouldn't believe me. She looked at her watch and decided.

'*Pronto.*'

'Valentina, *sono* Sophie. Is Raffaele available?'

The maestro was having a massage. That left shoulder was giving trouble again. She had promised to squeeze in one more American journalist for a five-minute interview and then they were going to dinner. He had not eaten since breakfast. *La signora* knew what he was like when he was performing.

La signora knew very well and she knew about that left shoulder. Pianists, conductors; they are always in need of a massage, and Sophie had become accomplished at easing his neck, his shoulders, when no masseur was available. 'Tell him it's not important; tomorrow maybe.'

She hung up and sat looking up at the priceless treasure on her cupboard. How had Rafael missed it? He was tall enough to see the top, but who looks up at the tops of tall cupboards? Should she take it down? She stood up and then sat down again. No, her fingerprints were not on it and neither would they be. The phone rang and it was Rafael; she tried not to think of how he would look, fresh from his massage.

'*Cara?*'

'*Ciao*, Rafael. You shouldn't have bothered. What about the American journalist?'

'She was expected at an earlier press conference. Who knows, perhaps she wants to sell, "My five minutes alone with Raffaele de Nardis"? If so, she will wait for a few minutes. The police have found someone?'

'No, at least no one has contacted me yet.' She was quiet again, wondering what to say now that he was there, listening.

'What is it? You can tell me.'

'Rafael, do you remember . . . of course you do . . . the day your mother . . . when she was so upset? She mentioned a teapot, a teapot that I swear to you I had never seen, never mind stolen.'

'I was not listening to words, *tesoro*, grief, weeping, those I heard. What teapot?'

'A priceless antique one that was stolen from the *castello* is on top of the tall cupboard in my living room.' He too was silent. 'Rafael, do you understand me? The tureen was taken down and the teapot put in its place. That's why the burglar left the tureen; he didn't want it or need it. He knew I'd put it back and so I'd see the teapot.'

'This is crazy. You can't know it's the same one.'

He believes I have never seen it before. Suddenly there was a note of joy. 'Thank you for that – but it has to be. Someone must hate me very much, Rafael.' She was sobbing and she tried hard to stifle her tears. 'Why? What have I done to be hated so much?'

'It's not the same pot,' he said quickly. 'The last owner left it – you just didn't see it before?'

'Raffaele de Nardis, you cannot tell me that a burglar would break the door of my apartment down and steal nothing – if the pot was there he would have taken it. You know what I mean – it wasn't there. I do dust once in a while you know. The police were right. The house was broken into to put something in, not to take something out.'

'Sophie, *calma*. Are you sitting down?'

'Of course I am. Why?'

'Because you are very upset and I am very far away. *Calma.* Breathe, Sophie.'

Mornings on the floor watching him. 'I'm fine.'

'Have you telephoned that so nice policeman?'

'No, not yet. I should have, I know but I . . .'

'Please don't tell the police, not yet, and leave the pot. Maybe it is this Vezzi teapot, maybe it is not, but don't touch it.'

'I thought of that too.'

'Good girl. Sophie, I have two more concerts and then I will return. By this time Paolo should know about this teapot and everything else. *O che diamine!* What in the name of all the angels is special about a pot for tea?'

'I looked it up. Vezzi is the earliest of the Venetian factories and there are only a few hundred pieces still in existence. It's a very small pot, white with a kind of red flowery pattern on it. The handle is as tall as the pot and it's pure white.'

'Sounds dreadful.' He tried to make her laugh.

'It is without doubt the ugliest thing I have ever seen in my life,' she said as she looked up at the exquisitely beautiful little pot. 'I don't care what it's worth.'

'Will you live with it for another week?'

She nodded her head and, as if he could see her, he added, 'And you will tell no one, not the police, not this nice Hamish who walks into your apartment without knocking.'

'The door was open.'

'I must go, *cara.* Call me at any time.'

She felt better. She should tell the police but she would not and so she sent up a small prayer that they would not contact her. Rafael would not cancel his concerts but he would come to her as soon as he was free of his obligations. What if . . . No, Sophie. Life is full of what if and, instead of wallowing in self-pity, get on with your life.

She believed that he would come and she waited for a message. The Lucerne Festival was over; yes, she knew he was due to play in France but he would come to her first; she knew it.

Valentina called her from Toulouse. 'Signora, *la contessa* is ill. The maestro has been summoned. He will contact you from the *castello. Mi dispiace, signora.*'

Why on earth should Valentina apologise? And what should she say? I'm sorry that the countess is ill? Was that merely a worn platitude? 'I'm sorry that *la signora* is ill. Thank you for calling.'

He did call next morning. 'Sophie, I'm sorry.'

'I know. How is *la contessa*?'

'She has rallied, thanks be to all the angels and saints.'

'And a good doctor, Rafael.' She was angry with herself as soon as she had spoken but he laughed.

'Upbringing, *diletta*.'

'Rafael, I am not your *diletta*. I am your former wife who has found a Vezzi teapot on top of her cupboard. It did not get there by itself.'

Was he translating what he wanted to say in his head that he took so long to answer? Sometimes she believed he could think in English, at other times she was not so sure. 'I think, Sophie, I would like very much to have the right to call you my delight again. Last week, lying there with you on that funny bed, I did not sleep, not at all. I thought and thought of our meeting and our marriage and of all that went wrong. If I could go back, Sophie . . .'

To go back to those days of innocence, to finding unbelievable, sometimes almost unbearable delight in each other. Everyone said that, didn't they? If I could just go back, do it all again. I would . . . What would I change? Nothing, because those experiences, all of them, the pain and the pleasure, made me what I am, the good, the bad. 'Oh, Rafael, we can't go back; we would just do it all over.'

'No, I was selfish, arrogant. I assumed, Sophie; it is an arrogance. Still I assume that my plane will be on time; that my hotel room will be perfect, that my clothes will be ready, but most of all I assume that the people I love know that I love them. I give them lavish gifts, I send gardens of flowers when they are unwell, I set them aside when I am working because I assume that they understand that the most important thing for me is to see if I can show the world that this music is better than I have ever made it sound. I assume they will be there, waiting for me, when I am ready, and until you, *preziosa ed unica*, they always waited.'

'I waited, Rafael.'

'Until that summer.'

What was he saying? 'Rafael, what are you talking about?'

'Your sister, she told me about the man you were seeing.'

'Ann told you I was seeing another man?'

'No, *cara*. I have reason to doubt Ann's words; it was Zoë.'

'Zoë? How could you, Rafael; she was a baby.'

'She was exactly the same age as you were when we met and she loves you. Why should she lie?'

Zoë knew Sophie had not been unfaithful. What had she been thinking of? What was it she had said at her own wedding? Damn, I can't think rationally now. She was not ready to talk to him about all that. It was too painful and she needed to see his face. 'Rafael, I have never been unfaithful and Zoë knows that. I will not talk about it now; it's too complicated to talk about by telephone. Right now I have to discuss this teapot.'

'Sophie, come to me, here, in Toulouse.'

'I can't.' An instinctive reaction.

'You are working in the weekend? You can come. I play on Friday night, Grieg perhaps, one of your favourites that you can hum.'

'Very funny.'

'It is a great concerto; you have superb taste. Come, Sophie.' How tempting and seductive the voice was. 'We need to talk. Come in time for the concert; it's the Piano aux Jacobins Festival in the cloisters of Les Jacobins Monastery in Toulouse, so beautiful, so much atmosphere. Then we can drive somewhere, find a little village where we can be just Sophie and Rafael, where we can talk – about this blasted teapot and what Zoë said and . . . other things, maybe. Cards, all of them, pretty and ugly, all on the table, discussed and then, I pray, destroyed for ever.'

The teapot sat serenely on top of the cupboard. Sophie looked at it while she thought. It was supposed to have been stolen by her during her marriage and yet someone had entered her flat – had they known that Rafael might be there to find it? – and put it there just a few weeks ago. Till she knew who hated her so much she could not move on. 'If I can get a flight,' she began grudgingly.

He laughed. 'Sophie, I will send the plane or arrange a ticket. Let Oliver earn his salary.'

'Poor Oliver, he's overworked as it is.'

'You will come?'

'Not your plane, Rafael.'

'*Davvero*. Whatever you wish.'

'Will Ileana be there?'

'Ileana? Why on earth should she be in Toulouse? It's for pianists, Sophie.'

She wished she could see him. Were his eyes wide open, so blue, so innocent? It made no difference.

'I have to go, *cara*. Paolo is on the other line.'

She did not remember until next morning that she had not worked out what Zoë had been trying to achieve or that he said he had reason to distrust Ann.

Oliver met her plane in Toulouse. 'The maestro is rehearsing, signora,' he said and she wondered how many times he had greeted her at airports around the world with the same words. 'I will take you straight to the hotel.'

'Did Raffaele book a room for me, Oliver?'

'No, signora, it was not possible – the festival. He suggests that you use his suite to freshen up. Valentina has made room reservations for the weekend at a small hotel a few miles north.'

Sophie relaxed. In a few minutes they were at the hotel and, as in the old days, she and her luggage were whisked upstairs.

'I will be outside to drive you to the monastery, signora. Seven?'

'I'll be ready.'

She looked around the luxurious room. It could have been a

hotel room anywhere and there was absolutely nothing lying around to show that Rafael was living there: no scarf was thrown on a chair, no letters or sheets of music scattered on the table, no photographs.

'Why should I need photographs, Sophie? I remember everyone I love.'

'It's so impersonal, Rafael.'

'*Diletta*' – he had stared at her in astonishment – 'it's a place to shave.'

'But you spend so much time in hotel rooms.'

'When you're with me, I have everything I need; when you're not, it's where I sleep.'

She would not go into his bedroom and made a guess as to which of the doors led to the bathroom. She was right first time but evidence of Rafael's presence was everywhere. His dark blue silk dressing-gown hung on the door; his toothbrush was by the sink. She laughed at the toilet bag, so unlike Rafael. This one had cartoon characters on it. 'It has to be a gift from his nieces or Carlo's daughter.' She would not touch it. She heard the telephone ringing and went into the sitting room to answer it, hoping that she would not be met by a flood of rapid French.

'Sophie, how was your flight?'

'On time.' Could he hear her heart racing?

'Did they put fresh towels for you in the bathroom, and bath things?'

'Yes, Rafael, thank you.'

'You understand they are busy because of the festival. The omelettes are delicious, something light, unless you prefer to eat well and then sit watching me.' He was beginning to sound desperate.

'An omelette sounds perfect.' She knew that her voice was flat and emotionless but she could not inject any warmth into it. Why was she so unaccountably nervous? 'I'll see you after the recital. What are you playing?'

'Mozart a sonata, Chopin, the Polonaise-Fantasie, maybe a little Debussy as an encore. Enjoy the omelette.'

She put the receiver down and sat on the chair beside the table, her knees feeling a little woolly. What am I doing here? I should have forced him to come to Edinburgh, to my ground. What on earth can we say about the teapot in Toulouse? Teapot in Toulouse. If he were a composer he might write a fantasy, like Chopin. Hysteria was near the surface. She was behaving like an idiot. Heavens, I'm behaving like Aunt Judith. That appalling realisation sobered her. Nothing is going to happen that I do not want to happen. We are here to discuss the robberies. She picked up the telephone and ordered an omelette, bread and coffee. There, that was perfectly straightforward.

Trying to avoid looking at anything that belonged to Rafael while she was in the bath was difficult and so she finished with her eyes closed. What an idiot you are. She heard the waiter arrive and realised that she had not unpacked her robe. The choice was a towel or Rafael's dressing-gown. She wrapped it around herself and hurried to open the door.

'Eat it while it's hot, madame. *Bon appétit.*'

Silly to waste time changing. Good food deserves respect. She sat curled up in a large armchair and ate her *omelette aux fines herbes*, the soft, cool silk gentle on her shoulders, and tried to ignore the faint scent of masculine cologne that hovered around her.

What to wear for a recital in a church? Decisions. A short-skirted suit, brown, with black silk cuffs and collar on the close-fitting jacket and black court shoes. Beatrice: 'Always court shoes, Sophie, medium heel and always black or perhaps brown; Sergio Rossi if possible.'

She had had this pair for seven years and they were as perfect as the day she had bought them in Milan. Rafael could not possibly remember that he had paid for them.

What a venue. Soaring walls, incredible stained-glass windows, plaster saints, great altars, smaller side altars with blue candles, with red, with white; huge arrangements of beautiful hot-house flowers, and simple vases side by side. Over everything the smell of incense. It was as packed as any concert hall and the voices that rose in an excited babble with the smoke from the candles were the same voices that could be heard in London, New York, Vienna, Rome: American accents, German, English, Australian, Italian, Japanese, but they did not overwhelm the French, justifiably proud of their festival and their monastery. Sophie was glad that her jacket had long sleeves; ancient churches are always cold.

Rafael did not play in tie and tails. He was wearing a white cotton polo-necked sweater and a dark blue velvet jacket; as usual there was no flower in his lapel. 'It isn't a wedding!' He had worn a flower at Zoë's wedding.

Sophie smiled at her memory of her first de Nardis recital and surrendered herself to the music. 'Listen to the Chopin, Sophie; it is full of different colours and is more fantasy than polonaise. Listen to the middle section, the most exquisite duet between the left and the right hands; you are the right, shy, and I am the expressive left.'

The programme was as he had said on the telephone and he played some Debussy as an encore. After all, was he not in France? She did not have to wait while he hosted the usual visits from friends, admirers, reporters; no getting together for drinks, a little supper.

'I am free until Sunday afternoon, Sophie,' he said as he kissed her dispassionately. 'It is called family business.'

They drove north on the motorway to the ancient town of Cahors. 'I promise myself a visit every time I am in France but . . .' and an Italian shrug. Then on to Labastide-Murat and from there, north-east. 'There is a small village called Saint-Céré and a small hotel on the banks of the river. More importantly there is a superb chef who has agreed to wait for me. Are you hungry, Sophie, because we are in his hands? Impossible to dictate when I am keeping him from his bed.'

'Rafael, I have to discuss the teapot.'

'Keep it, *cara*. It is yours.'

'That's not good enough, and, besides, I really do not want it.'

'We are still trying to discover everything. Believe me, as yet,

Paolo and I, we do not know how it came to be in your apartment, and we do not know when it disappeared from Il Castello de Nardis. My mother has been too ill to discuss this; she has given Paolo the list of treasures that she thinks are missing. Oh, Sophie, it is a long, sad story that goes back to the war. Can you believe the hatreds that affect all our lives?'

'What I believe is that you are unwilling to face the truth.'

He said nothing for several miles. 'There is as yet no proof,' he said finally. 'If I am given proof, and Paolo too, we will face it, Sophie, whatever it is, and we will try to make reparation.'

'I want that thing out of my home.' Thus she dismissed a priceless work of the potter's art.

'*D'accordo*. Have it packed and sent to Paolo in Rome.'

He said no more and Sophie sat sensing France but unable to see much except occasionally and incongruously a cardboard cut-out that showed that just here on this road someone had been killed. It did not make Rafael slow down; nowhere that she could see were there any shrines to the Madonna.

The hotel was small and picturesque and definitely not where one would expect to encounter a world-famous pianist. The owner met them as if it were eleven in the morning instead of at night.

'We will eat as soon as it is ready, monsieur.'

'The chef thought a salad of duck breast to start, monsieur, madame, and then a steak, perhaps some cheese of the region, and then for dessert—'

'We will do well to reach the cheese, monsieur. Some wine, Sophie?'

She nodded.

Rafael handed the wine list back to their host. 'Select for us, *s'il vous plaît*, a white and then a red.'

They were alone in the dining room and the lights were very low. The salad seemed to melt in the mouth so perfect was it and then the steaks arrived with their exquisite vegetables, flat mushrooms stuffed with a purée of spinach, tiny potatoes each the exact size and shape as its brothers. A basket of rolls was placed on the table with the salad and the smell of just-made bread was irresistible.

'No pudding and no cheese,' sighed Sophie when their plates were cleared away.

'Cheese for one, 'said Rafael. 'Coffee, Sophie?' He looked from the waiter to Sophie as he asked the question and saw her try to stifle a yawn. 'Oh, *cara*, you are exhausted. *Mi dispiace.*' He turned again to the waiter. 'The meal was superb and please thank the chef. I think, perhaps, for tonight, nothing more. My wife is too tired.'

What the owner of the hotel thought as he led his late-comers up to separate bedrooms he did not say and nothing could be read on his face.

'Goodnight, Sophie. We can be late tomorrow and we will go for a long walk and we will talk.'

He bent to kiss her, but it was more a polite salutation than a kiss.

'Goodnight, Rafael.'

The door was closed. How different this room was from Rafael's suite at the hotel in Toulouse but the water was hot and the bed was wide and comfortable. Sophie was asleep in minutes and woke hours later with the sun streaming in, since she had been too tired to pull the curtains. For a moment she could not remember where she was. Saint-Céré, wherever that is. I shall look it up on a map.

The bedside radio read eight o'clock. She jumped out of bed and hurried into the shower and when she came out Rafael was peering through the window.

'Good, you're awake. It's a nice morning,' he said, studiously ignoring her déshabillée. 'Breakfast in five minutes and wear walking shoes.' He was gone.

Walking shoes. The best she could do was a pair of comfortable flat shoes. I should have remembered Rafael and exercise.

The French country dining room was almost a scene of devastation. A family group, mother, father, three children and the grandparents sat at one table finishing one last cup of hot chocolate. There were two or three tables of single men, salesmen probably or possibly hunters – and three other tables lay in a state of disarray.

Rafael stood up as she sat down. 'We have chosen a good hotel. The family have been coming here for years and so too a group who have just left. I have ordered coffee for you; the chef makes his own croissants and it is suggested you do not put butter on them.'

But Sophie had spied a basket of home-made rolls on their own spotlessly clean blue cloth. 'I shall have these with butter and jam.'

'Good, then we will walk to La Cascade and you will not get fat.'

'What's La Cascade?' she asked as she poured her coffee.

'A famous waterfall. We will take a picnic because it is five miles or more. The owner knows who I am but,' he said with a smile, 'he guards my identity with his life. I have promised to sign his recordings. How did you sleep?'

'I lay down and then I woke up.'

They laughed. 'Finish your breakfast while I get our picnic. You have a raincoat?'

'No, but it won't rain.'

'I hope you're right.'

There was a car park near the beginning of the walk. Sophie sat down on a rock. 'Rafael, we need to talk.'

'*Certo*, and we need exercise. Come, Sophie, we can do both.'

'Not one step.'

She expected him to insist but he sat down beside her and she edged away. 'Rafael, do you believe that I stole anything from your mother's house?'

'No, and never have I believed.'

'Then why, Rafael, why didn't you say something, why didn't you fight for me?'

He sat with his hands on his knees and his head down but he was not thinking himself into whatever concerto he was to play, whatever mood he needed to convey. 'The simple answer is that I do not know. I escaped, Sophie, into my head. I could see your face so full of horror but I could hear Zoë saying you were seeing someone and Ann and Judith talking about drugs, and then my mother. I thought my mother was the most beautiful, perfect person in the world and she is, Sophie, she is.' He looked at her and this time his face was a face of anguish, his eyes filled with tears. 'I did not want to believe anything and you said nothing, not one word in your defence. You turned and ran away . . . and then the Medici cross was found in your dressing-table.'

Agitation made her stand up and begin to walk back and forth across the almost empty car park. 'A Medici cross – me; you know I loathe such jewellery, Rafael. It would have been the last thing I would steal, if I were going to steal. You, of all people, should know that I would never, in any circumstances, wear such a thing.'

He said nothing but still sat, his hands now between his knees.

'It's not for wearing, is that it?'

'It is for wearing, yes.'

'But the thief would not steal it to wear it?'

He nodded sadly. 'I believed only for a moment, Sophie, but you had gone; you ran from the *castello* and I thought you were with your parents but you were not there and you were not in London but you did go there and the cross was there and for more than a year I did not know where you were. Your parents at first could not say and then would not say where you went when you left the London house. I was wrong, Sophie.' He stood up and approached her. 'Will I get on my knees to beg for forgiveness?'

'You would look very foolish.'

'I would still do it.'

'Rafael, you are still avoiding the issue. Who hated me enough to want to ruin our marriage? Who started a whispering campaign about me? Who actually did steal these treasures?'

'I do not know.'

'Or you do know and will not accept it. This is evil, Rafael, and that is what you cannot admit.'

He looked away as if he could not bear to look at her eyes. 'It cannot be, Sophie, perhaps a servant.'

'Who? Cesare? Marisa who worships you and would do nothing that she thought would hurt you? Portofino, my friend, who welcomed me?'

'Portofino has been with my mother since she was fourteen years old, Sophie. He would die for her.'

'No, it can't be him. I trusted him.'

Tentatively he reached out and took her hands. 'And I trust . . . everyone else. I swear to you that Paolo and I are going to find out the truth; it is the only way forward for everyone.'

She let him hold her hands but she did not respond. 'Rafael, are you sure these items were stolen? You see I have seen the Battista manuscript; I have held it, part of it, in my hands.'

'The professor. I knew that I knew the name. Paolo contacted a Professor Forsythe and it is the same professor—'

'Who taught Zoë and Jim.'

'He showed you the manuscript? When?'

'Last Christmas.'

'But it's not possible. We did not know where . . . No, *mi dispiace*, you tell me, please.'

'I met him in London. His father showed me his treasure, a piece of a Battista manuscript that Harry, the professor, bought years and years ago, Rafael, before we were married.'

'*Santo cielo*. Please, may we walk? It is too much. A terrible mistake. Paolo too has spoken to this professor who has the sales documents in England.'

He turned and walked off, almost ran, to the path and was soon out of sight and Sophie followed at a more reasonable pace. He would wait – eventually. He would walk and walk, trying to outdistance the terrible thoughts that were running through his brain, demanding that he face them squarely, and then he would wait. She walked on and on, going higher and higher up into the trees. Below her a small stream ran and gurgled over rocks, washing roots of trees and flowers and ferns clean of soil. Branches bent down to her face and she smiled at how much more difficult it must have been for Rafael to walk this way. At some parts the path was so narrow and so steep that she had to scramble on all fours and once or twice she was forced to hang on to a root or a rock and wondered if help would come if she called. Rafael was probably too far away even to hear her. She felt completely alone but at the same time her heart was lighter than it had been for some time. Was this scramble along the rocky path a metaphor for her struggle to reach happiness?

She struggled on and eventually came to an easier part of the walk and there shining through the trees was La Cascade, the waterfall. How very beautiful it was with the weak sun filtering through the leaves that were already changing into their autumn colours and glinting on the water. She followed the path of the fall up, up, up, until she was forced to close her eyes against the dazzle and when she opened them again, Rafael was there walking back towards her.

'Forgive me, *carissima*, for everything.'

She held up her face for his kiss, no polite Italian salute but one that seemed to be saying, promising, everything that she wanted it to say and promise.

They walked hand in hand to where he had left the little rucksack that Tomas, the hotel owner, had loaned him to carry their lunch: fresh bread thickly buttered, sausage, cheese, plums that were already dripping with juice, wine and coffee.

'To sober me up for the drive back,' said Rafael.

'The walk back down will do that.'

By unspoken mutual assent they said no more about their problems but spoke about the festival, the hotel, the lovely place where they had found themselves, and about the immediate future and, at first, because of the canopy of trees, they did not feel the rain. Only when a large drop fell right into Sophie's cup did they realise that the rain that had threatened had in fact come and they quickly threw the little they had not eaten back into the bag, emptied the remaining wine and put the top tightly on the Thermos flask.

Rafael reached for her hand and pulled her up beside him and despite the rain that was now falling quite heavily they kissed again, their bodies almost welded together, and then he drew away and laughed. 'Maybe we should stay in the rain, *tesoro*. We will have to stay in this little hotel where no one will find us.'

'The world would find you,' she said, but her comment did not spoil their mood. It was only the truth that they both accepted. Hand in hand they slipped and slithered back down to the car park but this time when Sophie was unsteady two strong arms reached for her, steadied her, and held her just a little too long. They said nothing as Rafael drove through the torrential downpour, hesitating only once at a junction, accompanied by the low, distant grumblings of thunder. They reached the hotel and ran for the outside stair that would take them to their rooms without dripping all over the tiled floors. Outside her door Sophie turned to discuss a time for dinner, to say thank you for a pleasant day. What did it matter? He bent his head again to kiss her eyes, her nose, her ears and at last her mouth.

Who said, we had better open the door, but the door was opened and they went inside. The door closed behind them and they stood looking into each other's eyes. Sophie pushed away the note of caution that tried to remind her of how much suffering she had gone through, that he was engaged to someone else. She held out her arms to him. No crashing chords, no sublime sweeping of hidden strings; the beat of their hearts, their gentle murmurings, their sighs as they rediscovered each other, these were the only sounds. They fell asleep together in a tangle of damp, abandoned clothing and woke later to discover each other all over again.

'Sophie, don't speak; just listen. I will go to Stockholm tomorrow because I cannot cancel more. Then I will return to Italy and face the truth, all of it. Will you trust me this time?'

She kissed his throat.

'Good, and now I must creep like a thief in the night to my

room to shower and change. I said dinner at eight; can you be ready?'

She watched him pull on his damp clothes and then when he left her room she lay back on the place where he had been and relished the memories of the afternoon. She loved him; she had never stopped loving him, and she had told him so, over and over. Had he said he loved her? She could not remember if she had heard the words but what did it matter? He had promised. Everything would be all right.

22

'The Leeds Competition, Contessa. He should be heard there. Herr Höffgen thinks he could win.'

'The Sèvres tea service, Marisa. Go to Milan, but . . .'
'Discretione.'

Sophie did not enjoy the drive back to Toulouse. They were determinedly gay; everything would be better now, all would be explained. This was not the end but the beginning. His responsibilities would take him to Sweden and hers to Edinburgh but, eventually, everything would work out. She would trust him; she had not trusted him enough before. For the moment she would say nothing about Ileana; she would leave him to deal with his personal entanglements. Entanglements? 'I can't believe it. I forgot Harry.'

He glanced at her quickly and then turned his attention to the road. 'Crazy French drivers.'

'Perhaps they are all Italian.'

'They're British. Who is Harry?'

She reminded him and added that she had accepted an invitation to the Last Night of the Proms and had completely and utterly forgotten. 'I can't believe I was so rude. Do you see how you affect me, Rafael?'

He took his hand off the steering wheel briefly to squeeze her knee. 'Poor Professor Forsythe, and we need to keep him happy, *diletta*.' His face grew serious again. 'Paolo wants to discuss the Battista manuscript with him.' He proffered his mobile telephone. 'This works everywhere.'

She shook her head. That would be just too insulting. 'I'll ring him from home.'

'And you will tell him that you are unavailable for even the most wonderful concert?'

'Am I, Rafael?'

He did not answer immediately. 'Sophie, that is for you to decide. We have the dead branches to cut off, no, and then the tree will grow again.'

'More strongly than ever?'

'So the gardeners say.' They drove through Cahors. 'I must visit here.'

'You said that on the way north.'

'See how much I meant it. We will go together.'

She was a girl again, deliriously in love with him; the past was just that. Her plane was ready for boarding when they reached the airport. He took her hand and ran with her to the departures gate. 'I will telephone.'

'Me too.'

He kissed her and pushed her through the gate. She showed her ticket and her passport but when she turned he was gone.

Harry was in Florence and was not pleased. Sophie decided just to accept blame for appalling rudeness rather than trying to excuse herself by talking about the burglary and then the discovery of the Vezzi teapot.

'We could have had something going, Sophie, something serious, worthwhile. If you ever get over your husband, let me know.'

'I'm sorry,' she whispered.

'Not nearly so sorry as I am.' Even in distress, his grammar was perfect.

'I'm sorry,' she said again. 'I do like you, Harry, and I thought it would work.'

'Until the great Raffaele snapped his fingers.'

'It wasn't like that.' She was almost blustering. 'It wasn't,' she added quietly. 'Forgive me, Harry.'

'Goodbye,' he said curtly and hung up.

Well, you deserved that one, Sophie, but I wasn't leading him on, or was I?

'The great Raffaele snapped his fingers.'

It wasn't like that.

She telephoned her father and her mother, who had been in Australia, answered. 'Mum, when did you get back?'

'On Friday: we've called twice. Your father says he didn't know you were going away. You have been away?'

This was not the time to say that she had seen, was seeing Rafael. 'I went to France with a friend, Mum. Tell me all about the baby. What's his name?'

Kathryn made a cooing sound. 'He is absolutely beautiful and finally has a definite name. James Alexander, Alex for short.'

'Lovely. And Zoë?'

'She's in great form. Who were you in France with? Harry?'

Might as well tell her and get it over with. 'I'm afraid I'm not seeing Harry any more, Mum.'

Her mother was angry and so forgot to ask the name of Sophie's companion. 'High time you sorted yourself out or you'll end up like Judith.'

Kisses in the rain by the waterfall. She let memory soothe her for a moment. 'I'm fine, Mum, really.'

Kathryn thought for a moment. 'But you're still seeing the MSP, what's his name, Hamish?'

'We work in the same office.'

'That's not what I meant. You were going off for the weekend with him.'

'His mother doesn't like me; she thinks I'm a fallen woman.'

That was true, anyway.

'A fallen woman, you mean a . . . one of them? Archie, do you hear what Sophie has just told me?'

Sophie hardly knew whether to laugh or cry as she listened to the conversation between her parents but at last her mother got back on the line. 'Your father thinks she should be ashamed of herself. It doesn't really matter though, dear, what parents think; marriage is between a man and a woman. Families don't matter.'

They most assuredly do. 'Mum, I only phoned to say hello. I must get off to bed now. I'll talk to Dad tomorrow.' She put the receiver down and looked up at the Vezzi teapot. Was that one of the branches that had to be cut off before she could sort anything? She remembered that Rafael had said to wrap it up. If only Simon were still here; he would know how to wrap a work of art. Dash it all. I do not need anyone to show me how to wrap a teapot.What a stupid thing to say even to myself. She climbed on a chair and took the beautiful little pot down and then she found a box that was big enough; she looked wildly around for wrapping material but all she had was tissues. She jammed as many as she had in and around the teapot, closed the box and put it inside the cupboard, on the floor, well away from anything that might knock it over. Then she put the soup tureen in its place. She would never part with that tureen.

She lay awake for a while, hoping that Rafael would call but eventually fell asleep and in the morning she was too busy getting ready for work to think about him, or to allow herself to think about him. He could banish her; she could banish him. She made tea; she would not think of breakfasts of coffee and freshly baked bread.

It was raining; such unfriendly rain, almost sleet. She stood at the junction waiting to cross. Not one but two double-decker buses amused themselves by throwing ice-cold water over her legs. A desire to scream in vexation was quashed by the expression of alarm on the face of the old lady waiting patiently beside her.

'You'll get pneumonia,' offered Margaret cheerfully as she dripped into the offices.

'Your concern is appreciated.'

Margaret laughed. 'Take your shoes off and I'll get you a nice cup of tea.'

Sophie did as she was bid and stood beside a radiator in an attempt to dry the front of her skirt. How miserable everyone looked in the street below. They scurried along trying to avoid puddles, tidal waves from buses, and death by umbrella. Sunny France. Huh. It rains in Tuscany too. The sun does shine in Edinburgh. Think of summer lunches in Princes Street Gardens, lying on the grass, tree branches filtering the sun and images of the castle at the same time.

'How was sunny France?'

'Rainy.'

'You brought it back with you then, thanks very much.'

'If anyone needs me I'll be in my office.' She closed the door behind her and sat down at her desk. Several e-mails that required answers. Two telephone calls to make. Real life; at least it would stop her wondering every minute if Rafael would call. It did not.

'Mamma, do you want to tell me anything about the list?'

The countess lay back against her pillows. 'Has Raffaele seen it?'

'No, not yet.'

'I tried so hard, Paolo.'

'You have been wonderful, Mamma. I see how you rebuilt the estates; I know how much we owe you.'

She pushed herself up. 'No, you owe me nothing. A mother brings her children into the world; they do not ask to be born.'

Gently he pushed her back against the pillows. 'Mamma, rest.'

'I will have time to rest, Paolo, all the time I need. I have been thinking and there are things of which I am not proud. Sophie? I did not give her a chance.'

'Of course you did; you were gentle and supportive.'

'I was patronising, and deep down, this hatred that was not her fault and which I scorn in others. The region of Massa was in the front line in the war, Paolo. We Italians got it from both sides.' Her voice grew stronger. 'I did not want him to marry an English girl, Paolo.'

The count was surprised. 'You hid it well, Mamma, don't worry. If it's true, she never knew. I did not.'

She laughed weakly. 'Darling Paolo, you never see ill in others, especially those you love. Raffaele worried sometimes but I hid it from him too and, of course, he did not want to believe. Shall I blame it on the war? It was such a bad time.' She closed her eyes again and he sat back in his chair hoping that she had gone to sleep but she was gathering strength. 'You are like your grandfather, Paolo, my father; he too was unable to see evil in anyone. He trusted and thought that if he did what he believed to be right, then all would be well. And they took his home and sent him to a camp. They let him die there,' she almost shouted and, her strength gone, lay back.

He soothed the hair from her unlined brow. How beautiful she was, his mother. 'Rest, Mamma, it's all over. Raffaele has seen Sophie. She told me that you wanted to see her. Raffaele will ask her to come. Rest now and gather strength and when she comes you can say whatever it is you feel you have to say.'

Behind him Marisa moved quietly to close the curtains on the tall windows; he had completely forgotten that she was there. He shook his head. 'She likes to see the mountains in the morning.'

The old lady sat down again and they waited together. 'She'll recover again, Marisa.'

'She's waiting for him.'

'Her doctors say she is a little stronger.'

'The girl should have come when she asked her. It's on her mind, worrying away at her.'

And it was suddenly all clear to him. 'You know it all.'

'*Macché*. Of course not, but yes, I helped her. "Marisa, his teachers say he should go to Vienna." "Marisa, the Sèvres, but discretion." Nothing that belonged to the de Nardis estate, nothing that was yours by right.'

Tears started to his eyes and he fought them unavailingly. 'She could not believe I would deny my brother.'

'Signore, she knows you love him; we all do. He accepts it without thinking and that's our fault. I told her once that he was a good boy and the lack of ready cash could be explained to him but she would have none of it. Your paternal grandfather suggested they bring some treasures here while the German general was billeted in the house. They were for her brother, for after the war, but he died because he helped the English. And then the RAF destroyed their home; her father's beautiful gardens, everything. Can you wonder that she hates them? Later Mario, your papà, struggled to rebuild his estates and he worked hard but it took such a long time. Years of struggle of putting every lira back, doing without, restoring the *castello* but without money to refurnish the rooms.

'*Basta.*' Enough. The voice was faint but still authoritative and Marisa almost jumped from her chair to go to the head of the bed. A fine sweat had beaded on the contessa's white skin and gently she wiped it away with a soft cloth.

'*Calma, Mamma.* Gather your strength so that you can talk to Raffaele. He is coming.'

He bent down to listen. 'And her? She is coming?'

'I'll call her. *Dormi, Mamma. Dormi.*'

He caught Sophie at home at lunch time. She had hurried through a break in the wall of rain in order to change her skirt that seemed to be shrinking as it dried.

'Sophie, it's Paolo. I am ringing to ask if you could come out here for a few days.'

'Why? Has Rafael spoken to you?'

'If you mean about asking you to come, no. He is in Sweden. I had hoped that he would be allowed to finish one tour this year without having to rush home in the middle but I regret very much to say that our mother is failing.'

'I am sorry, Paolo.' What else could she say?

'She has asked for you again, Sophie; she says there are things she wishes to discuss. And Raffaele; she wants him now.'

Poor Paolo, the first-born, the son who did everything he was told, the right career, the right wife, the right number of children, and in this day and age he could be forgiven that they were girls, and still his goodness was not enough. He would be there as he had always been there while the gilded butterfly that was his younger brother flitted from Rome to London, from London to New York, here, there and everywhere, amazing those who heard him with his skills and his personal beauty.

'I can't come to Tuscany, Paolo. I don't wish to be hard but I have a job.' He did not insult her by offering to pay her fare and she went on. 'She has asked for me before and I thought she had discovered something, something that would prove I was not a thief.'

He hesitated. 'There are . . . issues. Sophie, this is very difficult but I think, perhaps my mother . . .' He stopped.

Sophie took pity on him. She could hear the despair in his voice, despair because he believed that his mother was dying and, possibly more difficult to tolerate, he was beginning to see that she was not the perfect creature he had always believed her to be. She was suddenly absolutely exhausted, as if she had been struggling in frustration for a long, long time. 'Paolo, tell your mother that I forgive her.' And she realised that she was speaking the truth. She did forgive the contessa for all the little slights and disparaging remarks. She had been too young, too insecure and had not trusted Rafael enough. Had we loved each other enough she could not have destroyed us, she thought, but she did not say it. 'I forgive her, Paolo,' she said again and added in her mind, I forgive her for trying, and succeeding, to sabotage my marriage.

Margaret met her in the corridor as she returned to the office. 'I'm off out for a smoke, Sophie. I've left some letters on your desk for you to sign.'

Sophie thanked the secretary and continued on into her office. I like it here. I like my boss, my work and my colleagues. If it doesn't work out I will be perfectly happy to remain here until I retire. Liar, said a little voice. If it had been Rafael on the phone instead of his brother you would have been on the first plane.

She worked steadily all afternoon and left the office just before seven. Edinburgh's famous east wind was blowing and so she pulled a multicoloured Nanook hat from the pocket of her duffle coat and rammed it down to anchor her fly-away hair as she walked. She loved Edinburgh at that time on an early autumn evening. Twilight softened edges and softened grime into a pale blue-grey and, since the rain had stopped and the air was fresh and clear, she walked up the Royal Mile past Lady Stair's Close and on up to the esplanade of the castle. She stood at the wall and looked out over the city and then she turned, as she always did, to look up at the weathered mass of the castle. Her heart never failed to lift at the sight of it. Its bulk and power did not threaten but seemed instead to look down benignly on the city that had grown up around it. It had not always looked down kindly on Edinburgh but had closed its gates and stood out often through the centuries against oppression of one sort or another. She had not stood against aggression and now the aggressor, the countess, was gravely ill, and Rafael would go to her. That was right and natural. 'He'll be too involved to ring me. He'll be too occupied with family matters especially if . . .' She could not bring herself to say, 'especially if his mother dies'.

She decided to continue her walk. Long walks were good for thinking through issues. She walked until she was tired. This is the world's most beautiful city, she told herself. When she had been married to Rafael she had said exactly the same about Paris, Rome, Vienna, San Francisco. Sophie smiled. How long was the list of the world's most beautiful cities? She had never walked hand in hand with Rafael through the streets of Edinburgh. He had played here, almost always in the Usher Hall, but there had been time only to practise, to play, before leaving for the next city.

Next time, my Sophie, next time.

But there had never been a next time and still she found Edinburgh beautiful. 'I love it here,' she said out loud.

'Thanks for sharing that,' said a young man as he passed her and she blushed furiously. Was she turning into a lonely old woman who spoke to herself in the streets?

Good heavens, I'll talk to myself if I want to, but she looked round carefully before saying defiantly, 'I love it here.'

She went home and as always she looked first at the telephone. The little red light was pulsing. She ignored it while she picked up and sorted through her mail. A letter, with photographs, from

Zoë. She would read that after she had listened to the answering service.

'Hello, Sophie, It's Aunt Judith. I need to be in Edinburgh on business next week – three days. Hotels are either full or exorbitant. Can you find a corner for an aged relative? Ring me back; there's an angel.'

Her heart, that had been singing, groaned. Judith? Of all people in the world, why Judith? The apartment was too small. She looked at her watch. Be there, be there, she prayed as she dialled his mobile.

'*Pronto.*' It was Valentina, his secretary, who made no concessions to country.

Sophie could almost see her shrugging. '*So let them learn Italian.*' In the background she could hear music, a Chopin mazurka. *Rare and luminous as the most priceless porcelain.* Which critic had said that?

'*Ciao, Valentina, sono* Sophie.'

'*Ciao.* What do you think? Can you hear it? Chopin, for release next year. Great, No?'

'Yes. Is he there?' It sounded so live.

'No, he was in Sweden; I thought you knew that. He's on his way to the castle, signora. He should be there this evening; perhaps he has arrived.'

'I won't bother him then. I'm sorry, Valentina.' She said goodbye and hung up.

She went to the radio and switched it on. Voices, she needed voices, to clear her mind of Chopin and the senseless telephone call. She was startled when the telephone rang again.

She picked up the receiver, her heart beating wildly; she would promise him anything. 'Sophie, dear. I hoped you might have had the courtesy to ring back when you got in from work.' The voice was plaintive, heavy with gently borne ill usage.

She sat down with the receiver in her hand. 'I have just got in.'

'Dear, I rang twice in the last ten minutes and you were engaged.'

She was tired, she was hungry, and she was ready to howl. She did not need Judith. 'I got your message and would have called some time this evening.'

'Will you pick me up at the station on Wednesday? My train gets in at two.'

Amazing. Not even a 'may I stay?'

'I'm sorry, Judith, but I just don't have room in this tiny apartment.'

'But Ann says you asked if you could take the boys.'

Judith? Was she yet another of the branches to be cut off? 'Aunt Judith, this is a tiny apartment,' she began. Think, Sophie, think. 'If it's only a few days, of course you can come. I have an important meeting on Wednesday afternoon. There's a taxi stand at the station.'

'Can't you slip out for half an hour or so? Your lovely MSP will let you go and Scotland surely won't grind to a halt while you pick up an elderly relative?'

'Elderly? Coming it a bit too strong and I don't use the car during the week if I can avoid it. Public transport is the best bet in Edinburgh.' She did not ask why Judith was coming. She would be told in minute detail soon enough.

'I've just had a wonderful idea, Sophie dear. I'll take a cab to your office; I'd love to meet your boss.'

Before Sophie could say another word Judith had said goodbye and hung up. Sophie thought for a moment and had almost decided to cook something when the telephone rang again. Rafael?

'Hello, darling. How nice of you to put Judith up. She just rang us and said you'd offered to have her while she's at the Antiques Fair. I worry so about Judith. What on earth will she do when we're gone?'

'For goodness sake, Mum, she'll find another neck to drink from. Why on earth are you concerned about her? And what's all the nonsense about *when we're gone*? Where were you planning to go?'

'Darling, don't get hard. Dad and I were just saying that it will be good for you and Judith to talk, get it all out in the open, just the two of you there. It's easier sometimes.'

Was it worth telling her mother not to be so hypocritical? 'Mum, I really have to eat.'

'Dad's standing here – can't you say a word?'

'Hello, Dad.'

'Thanks for having Judith, Sophie. I know she's difficult but she means well.'

'I'm almost looking forward to regular hours, Dad.'

'Thanks, pet.'

I am going to demand that she tell me everything she told Rafael. Does that make me the biggest hypocrite of all?

23

---◄►◆►---

'It was too horrible, but the war . . . I cannot speak of it. We were ruined, penniless but for a few small treasures, and I hid them for Ludovico. Later Mario, your papa, struggled to rebuild his estates and there was no money, nothing for anything else. But I knew, I knew you were a genius and that I had to do everything in my power to help you.' She could not speak, her memories too awful. She shook her head to shake away the horrors of the war and once again looked directly at her younger son, compelling him to look at her eyes. 'I took my brother's inheritance – Mario had no interest in my treasures; they were Ludo's, and Ludo was dead – and I used it to get you the finest piano, to let you go to Vienna, and to the Juilliard, to pay for the world's finest teachers. I could not take from Mario's estate; you understand, carissimo, that was, by right, Paolo's.' She looked at him and, for a moment, wavered. This was right; it had to be right. It was all for the best. 'And the few things left, my brother's treasures to give to the nephew he never saw, your wife has been stealing.'

'Paolo.' The voice was very low but il conte heard it where he sat looking out of the window at his estate. He saw landscaped gardens where rubble had been, miles of flourishing vineyards.

'Come si sta bene qui! How nice it is here, Mamma. I remember what it was like when Raffaele and I used to play in the gardens, no pathways, broken statuary, fountains that did not work. Would you like me to take you into the garden? It is such a beautiful day.'

She took his hand. 'Caro Paolo, no. I can see it in my head. So many beautiful pictures in my head. Is Raffaele coming?'

'Fra poco, soon, Mamma.'

She lay still for a time as he stroked her thin hand. 'Paolo, the Battista manuscript. I sold it many years ago. You will tell Raffaele if . . . he is late?'

He could not tell her that Raffaele already knew. 'Don't fret, Mamma. It was yours to sell,' he said gently.

'Three times I have tried to tell her . . . Sophie.'

He smoothed her hair and rearranged her lace-edged sheets. 'Would you like me to ring her now?'

'When you do someone a great harm, you deserve to see the hate in their eyes, Paolo.'

'Mamma, I talked to her; I asked her to come. She does not hate; if there is anything to forgive, you are forgiven. Listen, I am going to put on some music. Do you remember this?'

She sighed.

'His first sampler, Mamma. Remember how proud we were. Rachmaninov, Liszt, Chopin, and your favourite, Debussy.'

She closed her eyes and sighed and he thought she had fallen asleep again. 'I thought I was right. I believed she was not good for Raffaele but she made him human, didn't she?'

He bent his head but said nothing.

'So she will not come and give me absolution.' Contessa de Nardis lay in the great bed and waited for Death. She knew he was coming and she welcomed him, if he would just wait till Raffaele arrived. No use to see now that her hatred of an entire nation had been totally irrational, that it had been like a cancer growing and choking the beauty that had been Gabriella Brancaccio-Vallefredda. She managed to speak to her lawyers that morning. How stupid to wait so long to try to make amends. How futile to be in the midst of negotiations with Death before she admitted her errors. No use now to say I merely tried to do my best. I thought I knew better. The others were here; she could see them vaguely as if a gauze curtain was in front of her eyes and she could hear them, Paolo, weeping. She tried to summon the strength to tell him that she was sorry because she had never loved him as much as he deserved or wanted to be loved but her usual iron will refused to obey her commands and she could only look hazily at her weeping son, helpless to comfort him. Raffaele had been her favourite and God would punish her for that injustice. Her will, however, would show Paolo that she had cared.

I had to devote myself to him, Paolo; without me he would not be the pianist he has become. I gave my son to the world, Paolo, did I not? I did not keep him, my treasure, to gloat over. I forced him out into the world. But her, I did not want her to have him, or maybe . . .

Come, Gabriella, Death is hovering; don't lie now. You did not want her to have him because he chose her above you. A simple little girl who knew nothing, nothing of what it takes to be the greatest pianist in the world. Had she been worthy, had she been fit . . . oh . . . She sighed and her son saw her chest rise and fall.

'He's coming, Mamma, please don't die. He'll be so unhappy.'

Oh, Paolo, even at a time like this you care for your little brother. You know he loves you too, please know, Paolo.

I am lying even now. The angel of death, there he is, great black wings, wait, wait, let me live long enough to ask my son to forgive me. If she had come when I first asked, Raffaele. Had she come then I could have tried. She has forgiven me, Raffaele. I wanted to ask her to fight for you. I wanted to tell her that you are unhappy without her, that not even your music is enough. I wanted her to take you back and make you human again. Forgive me, my son. I am sorry, Raffaele, sorry. The angel swooped and caught her as she fell.

Their voices echoed in the great chamber as did their shoes on the restored terracotta floor. Paolo moved on to a silk Kashgar carpet and immediately stepped off again, his mother's voice in his head. 'That carpet is to look at and appreciate, Paolo, not to stand on.' He smiled at his memory.

'I must see the paper, Paolo.'

'This is not the time.'

'Paolo, we are alone, and there is so much that has to be done.'

He stopped, aware of his mother lying in state in the chapel.

'Even at a time like this. The family will begin to arrive tomorrow, the lawyers; there will be no more time for us to be alone.' He was leaning against the back of an enormous white sofa. 'Come and sit down, Paolo, you are going to wear out those rugs.' He waited until the count, almost reluctantly, moved back into the sitting area of the east drawing room. 'I need to know.'

'Some of the words are impossible to read but I managed to make a new list, with a great deal of help from Portofino. He helped Mamma pack her treasures.'

'Portofino?' For a moment Raffaele allowed himself to be diverted. 'Why was he not in the military?'

'He's from Turin and was injured in the bombing there. Later, when he was old enough, he was still unfit for military service.'

'I have lived with him all my life and knew nothing of this. How did he get to Il Castello dei Nardis?' I am as reluctant as my brother to discuss this but it must be talked about, even though it causes pain. It has caused too much already.

'His parents were killed and his aunt who lived in Monti took him in. Our grandfather hired him to look after Mamma, and he has done that ever since.'

'How much we take for granted.'

'Most parents try to protect their children from sorrow, Raffaele. The archivist and I have had long talks with him; what stories he has to tell, of Mamma as a young girl, of our uncle Ludovico, of our grandfather. She was the most beautiful creature in the world, he says, and brave as a lion. I suppose we can now hazard a guess as to why he has never married?'

'You're crazy. Portofino and Mamma.' Raffaele moved to the cushions while he thought of the man who had been with his mother longer than her father, her brother, her husband and her sons. Such selfless devotion. 'What would he not do for her?'

'He worships her. She takes it for granted.' He hesitated. 'Took it for granted.'

Paolo looked at his brother and smiled and Raffaele laughed ruefully. 'You are telling me that we all take people for granted, their devotion, their loyalty.'

'Yes. We must not love our mother less, Raffaele, but sometimes I wish I had never seen the list.'

It could not be avoided. 'Tell me. How many items on the list were stolen while I was married to Sophie?'

'I want to say none but if I do it tells me that what I have been thinking for some time is true and, oh, Raffaele, I do not want it to be true.'

'Show me the list.'

'It was in our uncle's breast pocket when he was shot and is therefore almost indecipherable. Poor Mother. Be assured that originally there were eighteen or twenty items of value packed by Mamma, her brother and Portofino and taken to the small house in which they lived when their own home was commandeered by the German general who was assigned to this area. He seems, by the way, to have been a decent man, very conscious of the feelings of the villagers. Our paternal grandfather, at some point, offered sanctuary to our mother, Ludovico, and what they had managed to salvage. Mother accepted a hiding place for the family treasures. She lived alone with such servants as she had until news came in 1944 that her father had died in Poland. Then she went to relatives in Rome and that's where she met Papà properly.'

'I know how our parents met, Paolo. The treasures? You will remember that my wife was accused of stealing them.'

'I know, Raffaele.' The count stood up and paced around the floor again as if he wanted to go to the door and leave, abandoning this whole unfortunate business, but it would not stay in the room; it would not settle up there in the great dark beams of the ceiling with the toy soldier that he had thrown on to a beam one day long ago and that his father had ordered should stay there for ever. 'Four heating systems and still this room is cold. Tomorrow we must make sure that there are fires lit in all the fireplaces.' Raffaele sat, hands on his knees, waiting, and at last the count went on. 'At least ten are unaccounted for; that is, they are not in the boxes stored in the empty wing. A blue Sèvres tea service is now in Paris. The owners bought it in London seven

years ago from someone who had bought it in Milan. We have
been unable to contact the original buyer who is in the United
States on business. By the greatest of good fortune, you
remember, I was directed to this Professor Harry Forsythe, an
acknowledged expert on medieval manuscripts.'

'Yes, I know him. Sophie and I talked; he is a family friend. But
there is a greater coincidence. He actually owns a Battista
manuscript.'

'The Battista manuscript, Paolo; I sold it . . .' Can I tell him? I
do not wish to break his heart.

'*Porca miseria*. How did he get it?'

'He bought it, Paolo, at least a fraction of it, quite legally from
a dealer in Venice about twelve or thirteen years ago. The receipts
are in his London home. He gave the manuscript to his father as
a Christmas gift.'

Raffaele was now on his feet pacing: the sharp clatter of his
shoes on the terracotta and then the more muffled sound on the
ancient carpets accompanied his wild thoughts. He turned to his
brother who was also standing, as if defensively, beside the main
fireplace. 'The Battista manuscript, Paolo, bought more than ten
years ago. You know what this means?'

'*Sì*. Neither Sophie nor any member of her family could
possibly have stolen it.'

Her alarm woke her quite early and she groped for it and shut it
off. It went on ringing and she realised, through the fog of sleep,
that it was the telephone. She was wide awake. So many night-
mares recently. Something else had gone wrong. Who was it this
time? She picked up the receiver and croaked into it.

Relief, oh, sweetest of sensations. 'Rafael. At last: I was sound
asleep. What did you say?'

She could imagine him there in the early hours. Clean, controlled, no doubt he was still as immaculate and handsome at
three a.m. as he was at three p.m. No, sometimes he was not
immaculate or controlled and she smiled. Kisses under the trees,
in the rain.

'I'm sorry, Sophie, but I couldn't wait to call you, to tell you that my mother has died.'

What did she feel? Shock? Sorrow? She had waited for him to call, waited for him to say he relived every moment of their time in Saint-Céré, that he had spoken to Ileana – cut off one of his branches. She had told Carlo that the countess was solipsistic. Who was thinking only of herself now?

'Rafael, I'm so sorry.' And she was; she was sorry for him because she loved him and he was a son mourning a beloved mother and she did not know how best to help him deal with it. 'I'm sorry,' she said again. 'I wish . . .' But what did she wish? That she had gone when Carlo and Paolo had said the countess wished to speak to her? She did not need to justify herself. Why should she have gone to the dying countess? She was no longer her daughter-in-law. They meant nothing to each other. A trip to Italy was ridiculous. She would not be made to feel guilty. The contessa had only had to pick up the telephone.

'Tomorrow all the family will come from all over the world and she will be buried on Thursday.' His voice was calm and controlled. 'There is so much to discuss, Sophie, but for now I have to say that you are mentioned in her will. You should be here to hear the will read. *Mi dispiace*, Sophie; it's an imposition, I know, but . . . everyone would be happy if you could come.'

She could not believe it. *Mentioned in her will.* That usually meant that something pleasant, and possibly expected, was about to happen. But she hated me, resented me. Why would she leave me something? Unless it's something horrid. No, don't be paranoid, Sophie. 'Your mother has left something to me, Rafael?'

'Yes.'

'And that's why you want me to come, to see what it is?' She could not ask about the proof of her innocence, not now. The countess had won again. 'I don't want it, whatever it is. I told you five years ago that I wanted nothing. I see no reason to change my mind. I'm sorry that your mother is dead because she is your mother but it is nothing to me, Rafael.' Against her will she found herself trying to justify her attitude. 'She never tried to make me love her.'

He sighed. 'She never tried to make anyone love her, *cara*. If you won't come for me, come for Paolo. He wants everything *corretto* and he has asked so little.'

'That's not fair.'

'Life isn't, Sophie. It's not a fairy story for children where the princess finds the prince and they are happy ever after. You have to work for happiness. I want you to come, me, Raffaele, your husband.'

'You are not my husband.'

'You can say this, after Saint-Céré? In the eyes of God, I am.'

How dare he? Five years and he has the audacity to say, *In the eyes of God, I am.* Had he once showed that he thought of himself as her husband still? Yes, oh, yes. Saint-Céré. She began to cry. What should she say? How could she explain? I am so frightened, Rafael, terrified that I will say the wrong thing. I waited for you to call me, to say everything was wonderful, that you had begun to cut off all the ugly branches. She said none of these things. 'I am sorry that *la contessa* is dead but I cannot come to hear a will read.' She hung up.

She sat on the sofa where she and Rafael had sat on the night of the burglary and looked at her telephone but if she was willing it to ring, it did not. She gave no thought to the unexpected legacy. What could the countess give her that she would want when Rafael had showered her with costly gifts that she happily left behind: a gold diamond-encrusted watch from Chopard, Manolo Blahnik shoes, Roberto Cavalli dresses, the New Year emeralds by Roberto Cohn. *Jewels as precious as my Sophie . . .*

Rafael, why do you want me to come to Italy?

Next morning the rituals of brushing her teeth and drinking her milky coffee did nothing to bolster her spirits. 'I would need an acre of cucumber under those eyes to lessen the bags,' she muttered as she scowled into her mirror. 'You look your age this morning, Sophie.' Thoroughly depressed by that judgement, she crammed a fur hat over her hair and tied her coat savagely around her middle. Today Hamish was going to tell the assembled parliament that he agreed with the proposal to turn the disused airfield in his constituency into a safe haven for asylum seekers. It was a wonderful and generous idea and maybe, just maybe, she had helped him decide.

She did not see Hamish until the afternoon session; all morning he had had meetings and she too had been very busy. She had no real reason to go to the debating chamber to hear his speech but she found an excuse and went; it would be so wonderful to hear him showing the world how a real politician behaves – the common good before self.

He was beginning to look as if he was used to his new haircut and it appeared to Sophie as if it might just have been tidied up. He looked calm, reassuring, responsible. She sat back calmly to listen to him speak.

'And, therefore, I say that after much discussion with representatives of all interested parties, after weeks of consideration and debate on every aspect of this issue, I have decided that I cannot, in all conscience, be in favour of utilising the disused airfield at Inverlachar. It is, as has been pointed out eloquently on a number of occasions, a healthy and spacious area – as well as being, if I may boast a little, in the most beautiful part of our country – but it has also been pointed out that the necessary infrastructure is just not there, and will not be for the foreseeable future.' He abandoned his prepared notes and looked up, not at his fellow politicians but at the newsmen and other constituents in the public galleries. 'It is simply too far away from a big town. These people need, deserve, easy access to hospitals, schools, sports facilities, churches, theatres; in fact, all the amenities we expect for ourselves.'

Sophie looked down at him but he was studiously avoiding her. He knew she was staring; could he not feel her astonished gaze boring into him? He had reneged. When it came to it he was no better than anyone else. He was saying no to the providing of a centre for asylum seekers because one or two powerful constituents had made it clear that the project was to be filed under Nimby, not in my back yard.

What a fool I am. I thought he was perfect, that he would go out of his way to do what he believed to be right. He lied to me; he has been lying for some time. Inverlachar is perfect for asylum seekers. The base is there. It has amenities; the school bus could easily divert a few miles and so could the town bus. She still had work to do and so she tried to avoid even looking at him as she listened half-heartedly to the rest of the debate. It was over, not just the debate but her belief in Hamish, her assurance, her conviction that he was prepared to take a stand, and, no matter the consequences, do what he thought was right. He was no better than anyone else and probably no worse. Perhaps the fault lay in Sophie Winter who imbued the people she . . . yes, loved with what she considered perfections and who was then disappointed when they failed to live up to her expectations.

'I'll ask him,' she said as she hurried across the cobbled street against a chill wind. 'Perhaps there really are telling arguments; perhaps it's just not we want to do all we can for genuine asylum seekers but – not near our own homes.

Hamish did not return to the office although she waited until after seven. There were no appointments on his calendar.

It was early morning before she actually managed to sleep that night. Her mind was too busy with all the things that had assaulted it recently; the main one was the countess's death and her conversation with Rafael. She wondered if she had not been receptive enough. He had promised to find out the truth of the thefts and the whispering campaign and he would. It was tragic that his mother had died, not only for the family but for her; she was sure that it meant that some truths would never be asserted. She would trust Rafael; he loved her. He did love her. Saint-Céré had proved that. Therefore she would go on from there. But she could not simply abandon all the work she had done recently. She would challenge Hamish and she would challenge Judith and then, when Rafael contacted her again, and he would after the funeral, she would have a clear mind. How could she ever have thought she might love Hamish? Easily. He was a very nice human being and she had enjoyed being with him. Harry too. But it was not the same as the overwhelming power of the feelings that Rafael raised in her. I should have gone when he asked me even though I want nothing from the countess's estate. I don't have to accept it but I could have been there. She would think no more about Rafael. If she were going to fight with Hamish, she would need to have all her wits about her.

They did not fight – at first. He was too much the consummate politician. 'Sophie, it's just not the right time. You understand.'

'No, I don't. We sat over a bottle of good wine only a few days ago and we were both very excited about this. What happened between then and now? Who spoke more loudly? What turned the crusader for human justice into just another politician taking care of his back?'

He was furious, but he was more experienced than she was and had more to lose. 'People worry about crime; we have to respect their fears.'

'We don't have to encourage them in irrational worry.'

'There is one policeman to cover how many miles?'

'Who says there will be an increase in crime? Are you saying asylum seekers will commit crime?'

He looked weary. 'Of course not, Sophie, but it is a fact of life: the more people who live in a community, the more likelihood there is of an increase in crime. Young men with nothing to do get into trouble.'

'Then give them something to do.'

'In the back of beyond? What do you suggest, for God's sake? The best brains on two committees are fresh out of ideas.'

'You could have talked them into it, Hamish. You said this was perfect. Your word – perfect.'

'Wiser heads showed me the imperfections.'

'I suppose none of these wiser heads owns property in or near Inverlachar.'

'I resent that.'

'Why didn't you tell me you have changed your position?'

'You're merely an aide, not a member of the Scottish Parliament.'

'I see.' She stood up. 'Would it have been different if I had slept with you?'

He blushed scarlet. 'That's offensive.'

'No more offensive than a member of parliament who puts his chances of re-election before what's right. You didn't just decide this, Hamish. You've known for weeks, weeks in which you knew that this asylum issue is very important to me, weeks in which we . . .' She got no further.

'You've said quite enough.'

She picked up her coat. 'You are so right. I almost made a complete fool of myself over you, Hamish Sterling. You see, I thought you were a perfect politician. Maybe you are. I suppose it all depends on the definition of perfect, doesn't it? I'll send for my things.'

She walked out, taking care not to slam the door behind her. She did not stop at her office but went downstairs and out into dreich Edinburgh weather that echoed her spirits. Grey, grey, grey and driving rain that stung her face with its bitterness. It wanted to hurt and she cowered from it and ran to the safety of her eyrie.

As she got inside her beautiful little apartment and looked at the rough stone fireplace and at the minute kitchen where Rafael had conjured up perfect coffee, she thought only of how on earth she was going to be able to make the payments.

24

To my daughter-in-law Sophie Winter de Nardis I leave the chest in my bedroom because she understands its value.

'How extraordinary.' The comment had been surprised out of Beatrice.

'*And the contents thereof.*'

Raffaele sat, his hands resting lightly on his knees, his eyes on the hands of his mother's lawyer. His brother knew that he was listening and remembering every word. Count de Nardis knew too that Raffaele would not hold Beatrice's remark against her. In fact he thought he had detected the faintest suggestion of a smile on his younger brother's rather austere if handsome face.

Portofino and Marisa were sobbing quietly. They were distraught and so could not hear their legacies read aloud. It scarcely mattered. They had known for years what their mistress had decided to leave them. Like the grandchildren, they were crying because they were unhappy, and because they were already lonely for their lifelong companion. Portofino would stay on in the *castello*; he would die there. It was his wish. Marisa would go to live with her cousin in Rome. She was too old, too set in her ways to work for any other woman, but in Rome she would see Beatrice and her daughters. She would enjoy telling Contessa Beatrice about her maid's shortcomings and sometimes she would be allowed to show that she still knew best. She would never give the young contessa her proper title. She never had and saw no reason to change.

The great chest was the only surprise.

Oh, Mamma, if only . . . began Raffaele and then he disciplined his mind to stop.

The lawyer's dry, dull tones went on and on. Beatrice looked up at her husband as he stood beside her chair and he rested his hand on her shoulder. Sons, one daughter-in-law, nieces, cousins, friends, servants, everyone mentioned in the long legal document was there, except Carlo who had received his personal legacy some months before, Paolo's daughters whom their parents had decreed 'too young' and Sophie Winter de Nardis who had refused to attend.

At last the distressing day was over. Cesare had arranged rooms and Portofino had provided superb meals with their customary efficiency. Portofino knew the count would insist on a younger man some day but not today and no one would ever take his place here.

The elderly aunts and cousins had been persuaded to retire and the brothers sat late into the night.

'Must you leave tomorrow, Raffaele?'

Raffaele nodded. He knew it was not really a question. Paolo knew his brother's schedule, the demands on his time. He knew too that concerts and recitals had been cancelled and had some idea of how much the pianist hated to do this. 'New York and Sydney have given me new dates. I wish they were not quite so far apart and then I have two months in South America.'

'Sophie?'

'What do I tell her, brother? I think I will go to her first. I have to see her face when I talk to her.'

The count remembered his mother's words. 'You deserve to see the hate in their eyes . . .'

'You will come home for Christmas? Beatrice thinks that it will be good to be very different this year. We thought we would stay in Rome until the 26th and then, what do you say to skiing somewhere, Austria perhaps?'

'I will come to Rome.'

'While Portofino is able to do some cooking, Raffaele, I'll keep the *castello* open. It will always be here for you.'

'I know.' He stood up and poured his brother some brandy. 'We will have to think seriously about Portofino. I would take him

with me but he's too old to fly around the world.' His voice broke
for a moment. 'He's older than Mamma.' He stood as if unsure
of what to do. 'Has Aunt Rosaria gone to bed?'

The count read his mind and laughed. 'If she hears you play
she might come creeping down in her nightie. Come on.' He put
his glass down and stood up beside his brother. 'May I sit and
listen or do you want to be alone?'

'I don't want to be alone.'

Lights had been left on in all the corridors and they walked
along to the music room. They were a long way from the guest
rooms and Raffaele had no intention of playing thunderous
chords. 'I'm ashamed of myself, Paolo, but only a very little. Poor
old Rosaria.'

'It was the wrong time to ask you to play.'

'She's very old and she is aware that she is even older than
Mamma. I should have played for her but my nerves were too
raw. What did Mother leave her?'

'The emeralds,' said Paolo and laughed, and his brother
laughed too.

'Oh, God, and she will wear them constantly, with everything.'

'You hadn't expected them to be left to Sophie?'

'No. She dislikes such large stones. She would never wear
them.'

'I think Mamma hoped Rosaria would sell them – for an
income, you know.'

Raffaele sat down at the piano and looked idly at the keys.
'Poor Mamma. You, brother mine, are stuck with Aunt Rosaria
and her emeralds.'

'I know and my darling Beatrice reminds me that she too has
indigent relatives.' He struck a pose by the piano. 'I see the future
and it is full of bad-tempered, frightened old ladies.'

Raffaele smiled but already his mind was focusing on his
music. He ran his fingers lightly over the keys. 'I'll play just for
you, big brother, a private recital. What would you like?'

'Chopin. A polonaise perhaps.'

Immediately Raffaele began to play the 'Polonaise Brillante' and his brother sat listening and watched the pianist's face. He finished playing the polonaise. 'Schubert,' he said and began to play again.

'What do you think about when you play, Raffaele?'

'Nothing.' He played on. 'The music, my technique. Tonight Mother . . . and Sophie.'

'You love her still?'

Raffaele said nothing. His hands continued to control the piano but where was his mind?

Thirty minutes later Paolo started and looked guiltily at the door. Beatrice put her finger to her lips and walked quietly across the floor to sit beside her husband. Paolo smiled and taking off his dinner jacket slipped it round her silk-clad shoulders.

'*Mi dispiace, cara,*' said Raffaele. 'For you, a variation on a minuet, and then, bed.'

'Mozart?' she asked but he was already playing and Beatrice listened intently and smiled as the flying fingers caressed the keys.

'Come, Paolo,' he said when he was finished. 'Do you remember Mamma's fiftieth birthday?' He moved over on the piano stool and gestured to his brother. 'We played together for her, Beatrice.'

Paolo moved over to the right of his brother. 'I'll play but only if you will play it properly for Beatrice when we're finished. Do the left hand, Raffaele, and most of the really fast bits.' He turned to his wife, as she sat with her feet tucked up under her to keep them warm. 'These are variations in D major, darling, of a Mozart minuet. I'll play one with you,' he promised his brother, 'but don't tell my daughters how bad I am.'

For fifteen more minutes they sat playing, and Beatrice sat wrapped in her husband's jacket and watched them.

'Now you, Raffaele.'

'I didn't promise, *cara*. Time for bed. I have kept your husband up too long.'

'I thought about not coming down and then I decided I too would like to hear you play.'

He bowed his head in acquiescence. 'Variation 1. One minute and two seconds and then goodnight, my best beloveds.'

They walked back to the family wing together but late next morning when the family gathered for breakfast Portofino announced that Il Signor Raffaele had left before dawn.

The girls were upset. 'Zio Raffaele didn't say goodbye.'

'He'll telephone, Gabi.'

'He could have said goodbye. Where has he gone?'

Paolo and Beatrice looked at each another. 'Edinburgh, I think,' said Paolo. 'He is playing a date he missed.'

'Papà, is he going to see his wife?'

'I don't know, *cara*, but it really is not our concern. Now, have you packed everything you want? We will not return here before the summer.'

'We want him to marry Ileana. She's gorgeous, isn't she, Mamma? Zia Rosaria says Nonna left Sophie her chest of drawers. She's furious.'

'I will arrange for the cars, *cara*,' said the count, thus leaving his wife to deal with their daughters.

'Come along, girls.'

'Mamma, we're not babies,' complained Mari'Angela. 'Why did Nonna leave that woman the family chest?'

'And its contents,' said Gabi. 'What's in it? Can we look?'

'Absolutely not. I forbid it.' She turned and walked out of the room and her daughters hurried after her like ducklings after a duck.

'Mamma?' The girls stopped, two slender dark-haired girls in identical white dresses. Apart from the brown eyes either could have been taken for the young Gabriella Brancaccio-Vallefredda.

'Yes.'

'We refuse to move another step. Why did Zio Raffaele leave without saying goodbye? Did he fight with Papà?'

'Don't be silly. Last night when you two were asleep as all good little girls should be Zio Raffaele and Papà played the piano together and they talked and Zio played just for Papà whom he loves very, very much.'

'More than he loves Ileana?'

'Do you remember Sophie?'

'Gabi shook her head. 'No,' said Mari'Angela.

'We did not see her very often because of their lifestyle but we, Papà and I, we liked her very much. She is never to be spoken of as *that woman*. She worshipped your uncle.' Suddenly she seemed to remember that she was talking to quite young girls. 'What we all want is that your uncle is happy. Whatever is right for him, whoever . . . we will accept and welcome.'

'Well, we want Ileana. She's fun.'

Raffaele had not even undressed after he had bid his brother and sister-in-law goodnight. He had sat, still in his dinner jacket, looking out over the valley. Somewhere down there was Villa Minerva and, further away, the beach at Lerici where he had first met Sophie. He groaned almost with pain as he remembered her innocence, her embarrassment when she realised that the red dust from the road had transferred itself from her pale legs to the pristine white of his slacks. His fingers touched the spot and his senses remembered. *Stodgy food.* She had thought she was too fat and she had been plump with the roundness of a young girl. He remembered her face the day he had told her he wanted some time to himself. Her eyes were dull, those eyes that used to sparkle with mischief, with love of life, with love of him.

What did I do to you, my best beloved? What did I not see?

Because she understands its value.

Both he and Paolo knew what the great chest meant. It had been made for some ancestor hundreds of years before and, until Sophie, had always been given to the eldest daughter or to the wife of the oldest son. Paolo's baby clothes were lovingly stored in it and Raffaele's and even their own father's.

Because she understands its value.

Beatrice had no interest in the chest or in its contents. She would, perhaps, wish to have Paolo's baby clothes or, knowing *la contessa*, those had already been removed and stored somewhere else.

Raffaele sighed, stood up and stretched. His overnight case was on the chest at the foot of the bed and he pushed some shirts and underclothes into it. His manager, as always would make sure that he had the proper clothes for his recital. Then he changed from his evening clothes to the suit he had been wearing when he arrived for the funeral. Everything else could stay until he returned – whenever he returned. He looked at his watch, picked up his mobile telephone and made some calls to New York. Then he called Linate airport and a few minutes later he was letting himself out of the castle.

He did not look back but concentrated on the wonder of Tuscany wakening for the day. As always the sight filled his heart with joy. *I am going to see her. I will beg for forgiveness. Everything will come out. The truth of what happened six years ago. It was my mother, my beautiful, wonderful mother. I won't ask about the drugs or the other man. Her sister and that aunt: grasping, avaricious, frustrated women.* He could scarcely bear to remember Ann's attempt to comfort him after she had told him that yes, little Zoë was right, Sophie had been slipping out to meet someone. He had rebuffed Ann's advance, more contemptuously than perhaps she deserved, but he would never tell that to Sophie and it would be Ann's punishment, to wonder if her sister knew. Zoë? She had been so uncharacteristically coy, almost as if . . . He took his hand from the steering wheel and slammed it against his knee. '*Idioto, idioto!* She hoped to make me jealous. Silly little Zoë and my sweet Sophie. All the faults were mine, *diletta*. I did not consider you or your needs. Forgive me for all my sins of neglect and obtuseness. I thought love was enough, Sophie.'

No, I cannot allow myself to think of Sophie or I will not be able to drive.

Instead, in his head he played Mozart's Concerto Number 17 and laughed as he thought how wonderful it sounded. He made no mistakes; his pace was perfect, his touch assured and the orchestra was superb.

His plane did not pass Sophie's as they flew in different directions across Europe and it was some time before he knew that she had travelled to meet him. When he found out he was exultant and played his recital in Sydney as he had not played for a long time. He had to see her. He could not talk to her on the telephone. She would not be afraid if she could see his eyes, if he could see hers. She would know that she need not be afraid, that she need never be afraid again. He looked at airline schedules. Damn and blast. Whatever he did, a recital or a recording or a meeting would have to be cancelled, postponed. Raffaele de Nardis struggled like a man in love for the first time, a man who doubted that he was loved as much as he loved. 'I don't care; love me a little, Sophie. Forgive me for all my sins of neglect and obtuseness.'

Sophie had spent so much of her energy in thinking: about Rafael and his sorrow, about Hamish and what she saw as his treachery, that she was late with her weekly call to her parents. They rang her.

'Hello, Dad. No, no, I'm fine. It's just that . . . Rafael rang me to tell me that *la contessa* has died.'

She heard him gasp. 'No, sweetheart, I'm so sorry. How is he?'

'As you would expect. But it seems she has left me something in her will and he wanted me to go out there now, last night, when he rang, to hear the will read.'

She could hear him talking excitedly to her mother and then Kathryn spoke to her. 'Sophie, how exciting. What is it? Did Rafael say? How absolutely wonderful of her.'

Sophie held on to her temper. Don't get annoyed. Sophie, she told herself. Your mother is not a grasping, avaricious woman. She is merely excited for one of her offspring. She tried to speak gently. 'Mum, try to understand that I have told Rafael I do not want this legacy. I have never—'

Her mother interrupted. 'What did she leave you?'

'I don't know.'

'And you just turned it down. I despair of you, Sophie. Didn't Rafael tell you?'

'The will hadn't been read; some time today or tomorrow, I suppose. As far as I know Rafael knows no more than I do.'

'Of course he knows.'

'Mum, have you made a will? I don't know what's in it. Why should Rafael know what's in his mother's will?' That was when she knew her decision had already been made, even before she dialled her mother's number. 'Mum, listen; Judith wants to come to stay with me next week. I won't be here; she'll have to find somewhere else.'

'Oh, darling, you don't mean that; you're upset, naturally. Poor Judith can't afford hotels. She can house-sit for you.'

Easier as always to give in.

'Where will you leave your keys, dear, at your office?'

I have no office. Too soon to tell her. She did not want to listen to her mother wail over that. 'No, the man in the shop downstairs. Goodbye, Mum.'

Her next call was to Carlo and she reached the answering service. She swore softly, hoping, too late, that the dratted machine had not picked up her profanity.

'What a naughty word,' was what Carlo said when he telephoned just before noon. 'I was sure you had forgotten all those picturesque words. What can I do for you, *cara*?'

'Rafael telephoned . . . about *la contessa*.' She waited but he said nothing. 'Was I wrong, Carlo?'

She heard him sigh. 'Wrong to do what? Not to come here when she was dying, not to come to hear the will being read, not to fight for your marriage? *Cara*, if you are still in love with Raffaele it would have been wise to have come to Italy.'

'Why did she leave me a gift?'

'I have no idea. Perhaps the legacy itself will tell you.' This time she said nothing and he laughed a little. '*Va bene*. A few years ago you would have asked if it was a poisoned cup.'

'I've grown up.'

'The will was read this morning but I do not know the contents because I did not go to hear it read. Paolo will, no doubt, save your legacy should you change your mind. I must go, *cara*, but my advice is not to wait too long to decide what you want. Death affects us all, I believe, and makes us aware of our own mortality.

Maybe Raffaele is thinking that he should settle down soon. He is forty-two, Sophie, and time is passing for both of you. If you come to Tuscany, please come and see us. Antonio is pulling himself up on the bronze elephant in the foyer; such sacrilege to so abuse a work of art – but soon he will launch himself across the floor. Share our joy and laughter with us, *cara*.'

'*If you still love Raffaele.*

If you still love Raffaele.

In the eyes of God.

In the eyes of God.

She arrived in Amerigo Vespucci airport near Florence late the following evening and hired a car. It was an easy drive but she did whisper a few incantations to the Madonna as she headed up into the hills where the home of Il Conte de Nardis dominated the area. Feuding and feudalism had grown hand in hand in the almost constant warfare that was part of the history of medieval Italy and the castle had been built for safety and not beauty. It looked to be a great impregnable square with towers on each corner from where soldiers of old could see in every direction. The portcullis of yesteryear had been replaced by ornately carved iron gates and these slid open as Sophie said her name, allowing her, in effect, to breach the walls and drive into the inner court-yard. Portofino was weeping when she slid to a halt beside the main stairs. He was in black and the colour emphasised the fact that he was an old, old man. Of course, he was in mourning for his beloved contessa. 'Signora,' he whispered. 'Signora, wel-come. Welcome home.'

'How are you, Portofino? I'm sorry about the countess.'

He shrugged, as Carlo did, as Rafael did. It meant everything, and nothing. 'Come, come, *signora. Si accomodi*.' He gestured to the stairs behind him and Sophie looked up at the great bronze doors.

'Signor Raffaele, Portofino. I want to see Signor Raffaele.'

The old man stopped. 'Let me make you some coffee, signora. Il Signor Raffaele is not here. He left last night.'

Stupid Sophie, stupid. She tried to smile. 'And the count?'

'The family returned to Rome this morning, signora. Only a few staff are here, not Cesare or Marisa, just the useless old like me. Coffee, signora?'

She was going to cry. She had to get away. No time to soothe Portofino, no time to make clucking comforting sounds. Of course Rafael had gone. She turned and almost stumbled back to the car. It did not start so smoothly this time but jerked its way down to the gates which opened wide for her to go. To her distraught mind they seemed to be wider than she had ever seen them, as if they were colluding with everything that had ever objected to her being here. Leave, leave, we do not want you here. She drove down the mountain and when the tears threatened her ability to see at all, she pulled over and sat staring across the magnificent valley and seeing nothing. She cried so much that she began to retch and had to stumble out of the car to throw up at the side of the road. When she opened her eyes she felt such a rush of terror that her knees almost gave way. She had pulled the car to a halt on the very edge of a precipice.

'Calm, calm, Sophie. Put it into reverse. It's not a problem if you very gently, very carefully, go into reverse.' The relief as the car slid backwards on to the road and, for once in Tuscany, there were no bicycles, no scooters, no beaten-up old cars coming down the mountain for her to crash into. '*Grazie, Madonna, mille grazie.* I will light candles.' She blew her nose and started to drive, automatically, to Giovanni's restaurant.

It was, as always, busy, but he stopped for a moment to envelop her in a warm hug. 'Of course you can stay. There is some food in the kitchen, *carissima*. Here is a key. I see you tomorrow – some time.'

Dear Giovanni. No questions, just a welcome. She had thought she was too tired to be hungry but when she let herself into his apartment she discovered that she was not so tired after all. She opened a window and looked out. Italy the seductress, expressive, exaggerated, irrepressible, called to her. A bat flew unerringly past her face and, startled, she stepped back. 'Thank you, little bat,' she said. 'For a moment there, I was going to get all soppy.' She heard the low murmur of voices from the seats under the gnarled olive trees and she looked out again. There they were, two old men in open-necked shirts, wiry grey hair showing where the top button might be, two old women with their black-clad arms folded across their massive chests. Were they there the last time she was in Italy? Any night in the last hundred years probably. Every now and again the women unfolded their arms long enough to drink from their mugs and the old men drank their beer and sucked on their pipes and they talked and talked and laughed, and usually all four at once. They were as much a part of Italy as the de Nardis fortress or the Uffizi Gallery and one was not Italy without the other.

Sophie closed the window and took her case into the guest room, showered, dressed in her nightclothes, and went into the kitchen. She could smell cheese and salami and she sat sipping wine and nibbling lovely things while she tried to decide what to do. Call his mobile. Tell him I've changed my mind. Say, I would like to see what *la contessa* wanted me to have. I want to know what was in her mind. That's not true. I don't care about the legacy. I want my husband back. She stood up abruptly, put the food she had not eaten into the refrigerator and covered the wine flagon with its clever little bead-bordered net and went to bed.

When did Giovanni sleep? There he was in the kitchen when she stumbled out of bed. The coffee was ready and the bread sat, warm from the oven, on the wooden breadboard. 'You wanna talk?'

'I don't know where he is.'

He gestured to the telephone. 'So call him.'

'I think I'll go home. I've blown it again, Giovanni. I can't explain it well enough in Italian. Gamble, Giovanni, I gambled and lost.'

'You have to decide if you picked the wrong horse, *principessa*. I don't hear no fat lady singing.'

'They say that about opera, *amico*.'

'No, honeybun, they say it about life.'

He insisted on driving her to the airport and she allowed him. After all, what did it matter now? She sat in the airport for hours waiting for space on a plane but she was pleased that, because of the restaurant, Giovanni had to leave her. It was obvious that he felt that he was abandoning her. '*Amico*. I'm fine. I need some time to think, to be alone. Go back to the restaurant and I'll call you from Edinburgh.'

At last he left and at last there was space available. Was it only twenty-four hours ago that she had arrived in Italy so full of hope?

She shared a taxi into Edinburgh with two salesmen and insisted on paying her share of the fare. Her head was splitting when she arrived at her own front door and the little red winking light from her answering machine beckoned to her across the hall.

'*Salve*, Sophie. I am in Edinburgh. I want to see you. Please call me. I can be here only one night and then I must be in New York, then Sydney. *Te amo*, Sophie.'

He was gone.

25

Messages from secretaries; messages through secretaries; messages on answer machines. Probably they do make life easier. At least Sophie knew that Rafael had wanted to see her.

'*Te amo.*' I love you; surely the most beautiful words in any language. She listened to them again and again and then at last it was so late in the evening that she knew he would be awake in New York. She got his answering service but decided to be positive; he was there and would ring her back.

His voice cut across her message. 'Sophie, I'm here; I was taking a shower. Where are you? I tried, Sophie. As soon as I could I went to you.'

'I was in Tuscany; I changed my mind.'

'*Diletta, te amo.* Do you hear what I am saying?'

'Yes and I love you too. Rafael, I want to see whatever your mother left for me; I want to try to understand.'

'Sophie, it is hard to say everything that has to be said and it will take a long time. Will you hang up and let me call back.'

'No, you have to speak now.'

'Sophie, *mio tesoro*, I am without clothes. Two minutes.'

'*D'accordo.*'

They disconnected. Her heart and her mind were full. She was more nervous than when she and Rafael had first met. Then she had been unsophisticated, naïve; she smiled at the world and it had always smiled back. Today she felt as unworldly as she had ever been. From the moment she had heard his disembodied voice every nerve ending in her body had been on fire. I want him back. She wanted him more than she had desired him in those early days but she was no longer a young girl dazed by love. Tired from her hours of abortive travelling, she sat waiting and she felt again the pain of her miscarriage, the desolation, the aridity, the overwhelming sense of failure. She was afraid, afraid that one ill-considered word would shatter the fragility of whatever existed between them. Help me, guide me, but she did not know to whom she spoke: Minerva, goddess of wisdom?

Two minutes. She thought about families. Perhaps we take our families too much for granted; treat family members with less patience, less consideration than we do our friends or our work colleagues. Now there were no work colleagues, but had she snapped at them the way she snapped at Ann or at Judith? No, she was unfailingly polite.

Rafael had always been unbelievably patient and courteous with others. It's the only way my crazy world works, *diletta*. I'm mad as hell but what good to make everyone around miserable?

He had never snapped at his mother either. Did that mean he was never *mad as hell* with the contessa? She did not know. She had not really known her husband well. I was afraid of him, afraid that he would look at me one day and realise that he had never loved me after all. And why was I afraid? Because I never really believed I was good enough to be his wife. I believed what his mother taught me, that I was too young, too unpolished, too inferior.

If only I could go back. No, I can't go back and if I could I'd probably do the same stupid things. But I'm older and wiser and *la contessa* wanted to see me when she was dying. Why? Could a proud woman like Gabriella de Nardis ever admit that she was wrong? Was she going to ask my forgiveness? I have to see what she wanted me to have. I don't need to take it but I have to understand. He says he loves me. Love? It can't be simply turned off like a light when you leave a room but it has to be nurtured.

She snatched the phone when it rang, ready to slam it back on its cradle if is was anyone else.

'Sophie. I have some dreadful things to tell you. I wish you were here. Can you come to New York? They are giving a reception for me in the Grand Promenade at the Avery Fisher Hall. So many people. Will they even notice if I slip away?'

'Of course they will. Rafael, tell me the bad things.'

'My mother wanted to look at you when she told you, *cara*. She wanted to tell you that she knew you had stolen nothing.'

She knew, she knew, and she had told Rafael. Wonderful. But who had stolen them and blamed her? Who hated her so much? 'I'm so glad, *caro*. I knew she didn't want us to marry but at least she knew before she died that . . .' Oh, no. How stupid, how obtuse.

'Sophie?' His voice was hesitant, quiet.

'They never were stolen, were they, Rafael?'

'No.'

'And the vandalism? That too?'

She could scarcely hear his whisper. '*Sì*, that too.'

The pain of the miscarriage was nothing when compared with the pain of hatred. Sophie bent double on her chair.

'Sophie?'

'I can't bear it,' she cried and put down the receiver.

He called several times that night but she refused to answer the phone. Her mother rang and so too did Judith. Judith? She had to entertain Judith. Imagine being grateful for Judith. When she was able to speak without crying she rang Rafael's business number and left a message that he would understand with his secretary. 'I need space.'

The days with Aunt Judith were not so bad as she had feared they might be. At dinner on the first evening Sophie heard a tale that the family had listened to in one variation or another for as long as she could remember. 'I'm trying to set up a new business; small antiques, things I can get in my car. Stephanie is buying in; she haunts the markets in Italy, you know. Again we will deal only in small objects.'

'I hope it's successful.'

'You don't seem yourself, Sophie. Archie says you went to Italy.'

'Yes, I went to meet Rafael but I missed him.'

Judith assumed the 'someone has died and therefore I must look solemn' expression. 'How is poor Rafael taking the loss? Archie told me about the countess.' Judith managed to sound as if she and Rafael were well known to one another and, as far as Sophie could remember, they had met only a few times. 'He was always so close to his mother.'

'Rafael is forty-two years old, Judith. How do you expect him to behave? He's sad, especially that he didn't get back in time. Paolo was there.'

'Kathryn says she left you something in her will. Jewellery, I hope, Sophie. She had some stunning jewels.'

'Mother had no right to tell you anything but since you ask, yes it appears that I have been left something. But it doesn't matter, Judith. I have decided to refuse it.' She looked at her aunt and saw jealousy, anger and eventually avarice struggle across her face.

'Sophie, think. You have to use your assets.'

'What did you say to Rafael five years ago? It's no use pretending that you don't know what I'm talking about. Zoë told him I was seeing another man; Ann told him I was taking drugs and you . . .'

'How do you know? Zoë was being silly, trying to make him jealous; she didn't realise how serious everything was.'

'But you did, Judith, you and Ann. You knew exactly how serious it was.'

Judith drained her wine glass. 'I just wanted him to like me.'

This was surreal; she mastered a desire to scream, to hit out. 'So you told him lies about his wife?'

'They weren't lies. I wanted him to see that at least one of the family knew how to behave. Ann had thrown herself at him once: how unbelievably embarrassing. I was trying to help.'

'Help? What did you tell him?' The message about Ann was disregarded as soon as heard.

'I can't remember.' Judith started to cry. 'You don't know what it's like to be poor, to have no future, to know you're seen as a burden. I just wanted Rafael to like me.'

Sophie stood over her aunt. 'What did you tell him?' The old lady cringed away, and, feeling angry with herself, Sophie went back to fuss at the coffee pot.

'Only what Ann said, that a man rang you, that you spoke on the phone late at night, furtively, that you went off for the day without saying where you were going, that you were taking pills of some kind.'

'And you have the audacity to ask me to open my home to you.'

'It was all true.'

'It's all in the way it's told, isn't it?'

Judith put down her fork and leaned across the table. 'Desperation does funny things. One day you'll be like me, Sophie, in your sixties, no husband, no children, no income. Your father is my nearest relative and he's ten years older than I am. What on earth will happen to me when I'm old? I don't want to be a burden to you girls; that's why I keep trying to get a business off the ground. That's why I tried to make a friend of Rafael; he was family and he's rich.'

Old Marjorie, carrying trays upstairs at seventy-three. 'Old age is natural. Old age with no one is not natural.' Marjorie laying tables in huge cold rooms that Mrs Sterling did not want used. Judith scrabbling around trying to start a business. 'Judith, please.'

'You can't believe you'll be old, Sophie, but you will – sooner than you think – and who will want you? Ann? You can hardly bear to be in the same room. But none of that matters any more, does it? Sophie, I'll sell it for you. Stephanie will pick it up.'

For a moment Sophie had no idea what Judith was talking about and when realisation dawned, she was coldly furious. She stood up. 'I can't stop you and Stephanie Wilcox talking about me but I won't have you in my home repeating it back to me.'

She stalked furiously out of the room and, in the middle of the hall, started to laugh. She had been about to sweep grandly into her room but since Judith was sleeping there she had no room to stalk to and no door to slam. Poor lonely old Judith frightened for her old age. Not for a second did Sophie believe her aunt had any real concern for her. But the thought of Stephanie Wilcox going to the *castello* and carting off whatever little thing the contessa had wanted her former daughter-in-law to own made her physically sick. She went into her bedroom and took her raincoat out of the tiny closet. 'I'm going for a walk,' she said in the general direction of the kitchen.

Outside, she stopped herself from her first impulse to breathe deeply. On some evenings Edinburgh's air seemed to hang heavy with the smell of fermenting hops. Just one more thing she had always meant to find out about.

Rafael's mother hated me. There, she had said it. It was out. It wasn't just that she thought I was not the right wife for her son. Dear God, I cannot begin to conceive of the force of her hatred. She must have had my flat broken into to put that teapot there. Maybe she told her burglar to leave it where the tall Raffaele de Nardis would be bound to see it. And my father? Her hatred nearly killed my father. Anger swelled up in her so that she felt in herself the urge to hurt, to deface, to kill. *Calma, calma.* If I submit to this anger then I am as bad as she was.

Breathe, cara.

I'm breathing, Rafael.

She walked on and on and she went over her conversation with Judith. Her anger swelled again. She told my husband lies and now she asks me for bed and board – I cannot understand her arrogance. Why isn't she running away into a hole to hide? Because she's afraid. She is growing older and no one, except possibly my father, loves her.

'You'll be old one day, Sophie.'

I know, I know, and I do not want to be alone. I want to be with Rafael. Maybe he wants me too but we have to come to terms with what his mother did. Is it harder for Rafael to admit that she could be so evil or for me who was the subject of the hatred? Oh, Contessa, I never considered you, not for a moment.

She walked until she was sure that Judith would have gone to bed. Stupid to walk alone in a city's streets at night. She looked around and the city that a few days before she had found so beautiful was now dark and threatening. The trees and shop doorways held menace. It's the same city. She tried not to run but her nerve had gone and she beat world records in her mad dash back to her flat.

Judith was sitting in the living room. She had changed into her nightclothes. She had also been crying. 'I'm sorry about every-thing, Sophie. There's so little time left for me. I know your grandfather left me some money and it should have lasted but it hasn't: one thing and another, stupid investments, one or two men, the wrong ones, of course. You and your sisters didn't think I'd had my chances, did you? I wasn't born sixty years old.' She looked up from her teacup. 'I have a pension of forty-two pounds every week. Your blouse cost more than that.'

I want this woman out of my house. I want never to have to see her again. 'Let's start all over again, Judith. We'll say I over-reacted. Now, shall we finish that bottle of wine?'

On Monday, when some boxes arrived from the Antiques Fair, Sophie smiled fairly grimly and had them shipped to Judith. Small price to pay for future peace. She doubted very much that her aunt would ring her again in the near future.

Her mother rang often, of course. Kathryn was glad that Ann had married dear sensible George. She wondered if things would have been different if they had never allowed Zoë to attend the university in Pisa. In fact, if she had not encouraged Dad to buy a house in Italy none of the misfortunes to befall the family would have occurred at all.

Rafael was not a misfortune but Sophie said nothing and she did not tell her mother that she had lost her job and that life was in more turmoil than it had ever been. It was obvious that Judith had said nothing at all about her few days in Edinburgh.

Rafael tried to ring her every day from wherever he was but a telephone conversation is not the same as face to face.

'I need to see you, Sophie. I need to see your face, your eyes, when I tell you how sorry I am. I need to beg your forgiveness for everything, my sins, my mother's.'

Was what his mother had done unforgivable? Sophie had said, 'I forgive her,' but when she had said it she had had no true idea of the depth of the contessa's deviousness.

He told her the nature of her legacy and she hung up, speechless. The bride's chest, that magnificent old chest that had pride of place in the contessa's bedroom. Why? Why? Sophie knew the history of the chest and to give it to a divorced wife of a younger son was not part of its history.

He called again. 'Meet me, Sophie. Let me speak to you.'

'There is too much hate, too many lies.'

'No, *tesoro*, was. It is in the past and I say we can learn from the past.'

She sighed. She wanted him to be right. He must be right. 'I will come to Tuscany, Rafael, to talk.'

She arranged to stay with Giovanni; Giovanni would tell no one that she was there.

December in Tuscany is mild. In the mountains there is snow and sometimes a cold wind blows down on to the valleys below. Sophie sat at her bedroom window in the flat above Giovanni's restaurant and looked out. The same old people sat under the tree. They looked exactly as they had looked in the summer except that the old woman was wearing a coat over her shapeless dress. Sophie thought of the morning and wondered what she would say. All those years ago, on the night before her first real date with Rafael, she had felt exactly the same but that night she had not cried herself to sleep.

Because Giovanni was at work in the restaurant she took a taxi to the castle gates where Rafael had promised to meet her. She wanted to speak to no one else.

He was there, standing in the open gateway, a black sweater thrown around his shoulders. His face, that had been so tired and strained, relaxed as she stepped out of the taxi. 'Sophie, *cara*.'

Better to get it over with.

'I'm refusing the bequest.'

'You hate her still, so much.' It was a statement and his voice was unbearably sad.

Sophie was quiet for a few minutes and he waited, still, composed. 'I find I don't hate her at all, Rafael. I did for a long time and hate is such a corrosive emotion – it eats the hater. I was too young when I fell in love with you, I didn't understand love. I was so sure that she would always be first with you – she was so elegant, so intellectual, so urbane and she was your mother. I didn't fight because I thought the war was already lost. I knew that when you compared us . . .' She looked at him but still he stood, alert, listening, waiting. 'When you compared us, all my weaknesses would show so glaringly.'

'But I never compared you, *cara*. You were my wife, my heart, my love, and my solace. La Contessa de Nardis was my mother. I loved her, Sophie. I worshipped you.'

'You never told me,' she said childishly.

And then he moved. As if the conductor had nodded or he had heard the note from the orchestra that told him it was his time, his turn. He pulled her round savagely to face him. His fingers were like vices on her shoulders and she winced but he did not relax his hold and they stood in the gateway, neither in the castle grounds nor outside. 'I thought I told you every moment of the day and night. Did I never say the words, "Sophie, I worship you." Surely I did.'

'I needed reassurance, Rafael. Your life was so full of other people. Every one with demands on you, on your time. I was not jealous of music, your real love.'

'Music is very rarely a consolation in an empty bed.'

She blushed a little. 'In bed I knew we were all right, in the beginning anyway.'

'Until you began to have this fanatical desire for a child.'

Stung, she retaliated. 'But you wanted a child; your mother wanted a child.'

'Don't be silly.'

'Of course, of course, Mamma, the perfect, must never be criticised.'

He released her then and she stumbled.

'She is . . . was my mother.'

'I criticise mine constantly,' she said and turned as if to walk out of the gates and down the long winding road to the town.

He reached out and pulled her gently so that she was forced to turn back 'Look at me, Sophie, please.' She looked up into his eyes and then down again but he spoke.

'We knew, Paolo and I, that our mother wasn't perfect. Together we could say "She's driving me crazy," but not to others, not in public.'

'I was part of your public?'

'You are deliberately making this difficult for me. If I loved my mother too much to realise that she was making problems for you, I regret it, Sophie. And never, for a single second, did I think that she could conduct this campaign of hatred against you. I have tried and tried to understand, tried to make excuses, listened to all the stories, from Paolo and Portofino and even Marisa, but my mind can't assimilate this.'

'I knew she disliked me from the first moment, Rafael, and she did nothing to help me learn quickly.'

'You're wrong. Constantly she said, "I will help little Sophie." '

Little Sophie. 'Look at me. I am five feet seven inches tall! Couldn't you see that that was so bloody condescending?'

'When did you learn to swear?'

She almost laughed. He looked quite shocked. 'I'm not a child, Rafael. I am . . . I was your wife. She patronised me and you never even noticed.'

They were silent for a time as if each were afraid to speak, afraid to say too much or too little. Rafael spoke first. 'There is room at Villa Minerva?'

She looked at him, genuinely puzzled. 'I don't understand.'

'For the chest. In the hallway, perhaps. It's a magnificent piece of furniture and . . .'

'Should be with a de Nardis bride; that's what your mother

always said. And I still say I don't want it. I promised only to look. There are obligations attached to that chest, Rafael.' She stole a glance at him, to see if she could read anything in that beautifully sculpted face. 'Beatrice.'

He laughed. 'Beatrice thinks it a monstrosity. Had it been left to her or to the girls she would have put it somewhere, certainly not in her bedroom. The contents are yours also. Perhaps there is something there that will explain my mother's thinking. She said she was giving it to you because you would understand what it meant.'

'Once again *la contessa* shows she is much cleverer than I am.'

He stepped backwards towards the castle entrance and held out his hand. 'Will you come to see it? And to see Portofino – he loves you very much.'

Admission weakens. 'I . . . love him too.'

She did not take the proffered hand but merely walked beside him to the steps. He stood back to let her walk in to the *castello* and she stood a moment in the dim chill of the huge front hall. Ancestral portraits looked down on her from the armament-heavy walls. This was a castle that had been ready at all times to repel invaders.

'Everything is as it was, Sophie. Will we go upstairs to see the chest, or would you like coffee? You will see Portofino, won't you?'

'Later, perhaps.'

They went up the great staircase and, to Sophie, seemed to walk for miles through echoing corridors to the contessa's bedroom. Everything was as it had always been. Not a speck of dust lay anywhere and fresh flowers bloomed in a vase on a table. Fresh flowers in December. 'Portofino?' she asked.

'*Ben intenso.* Of course,' he said shortly. The great chest with its five deep drawers stood against the wall between two windows. 'There it is. It is yours to do with as you want. Shall we look inside?' He did not wait for her to answer and indeed her tongue seemed to be incapable of moving. He pulled open the top drawer, took out a large oblong packet wrapped in black paper. 'Oh, I know these,' he said in surprise. 'Her grandmother's table-cloths; they're exquisite, Sophie. Such fragile lace.' He opened one out. 'This was on the table when I made my First Communion. How nice of Mamma to give it to you.' He was taking out other packets and putting them on a table, offering them to Sophie but she stood and looked and absorbed the atmosphere of the room where she had spent very little, if any, time. Rafael closed the top drawer and bent down to the deep bottom drawer and then he stood up straight and tall. In his hand was a tiny dress. He laughed. 'Look, they are my baby clothes.' He held the wisp of lace up against his chest. 'Wasn't I sweet?'

How could he joke? It was unbearable. 'Stop. I want nothing.' She turned and ran from the room along the corridor lined with portraits of disapproving de Nardis wives who would never run no matter who or what was pursuing them. Her footsteps echoed in the vast emptiness and so too did her sobs. Then she heard his footsteps behind her and she tried to run faster.

'Sophie, don't, *cara*.' He caught her at the end of a corridor when she had to stop to open a heavy door. He turned her round and held her against him. 'Don't cry. I thought you would laugh; it would have made you laugh before.'

She knew she should fight, push him away, but she was tired and it felt so right leaning against him, feeling his heart beat, smelling him.

'I'm surprised she left you my dresses – unless . . . Sophie, look at me.'

'No,' she mumbled into his sweater.

'You don't have to take your legacy. No one can make you do anything you don't want to do. But you must see what Mamma was doing when she left you the bride's chest. Once she thought you the wrong wife for me but this shows that she had changed her mind; she had learned that I am no good without you, Sophie.'

Oh, what beautiful words. If they were true . . . 'Don't be silly; you are more and more famous, more and more sought after, lionised.'

'And insufferable.'

She laughed croakily. Humility did not suit him. 'You were never that.'

They stood almost jammed against the great oak door. 'It's too oppressive here. Can we drive maybe, have some lunch?' He looked down at her and she turned her head away, so tense was his gaze. 'No woman has ever excited me the way you do, Sophie. Is that love or lust?'

'It doesn't matter now, does it?'

'But it does. I don't mean excite in the merely physical sense. God knows I have tried hard enough to make my body forget you.' He touched her cheek gently with his fingers. 'It won't, Sophie, and you are still in my mind and my heart.'

She flinched away from him and immediately he opened the door and she went through into the long gallery with its windows looking out over the valleys.

'Don't run away, Sophie. Look, I will stay here by the window while you walk away; and if you choose to go, then I will accept your decision. I'm asking you only to have lunch with me, to talk more, a little late . . .'

'Years late.'

'Carlo said you had changed.'

'What did you expect – someone still overawed by Raffaele de Nardis?'

'One of the many things I loved about you was that you were never awed by Raffaele de Nardis.'

She remembered how she had felt listening to him play, watching the others in the concert hall, listening to the rapturous applause for this man who was her husband. 'We didn't know each other at all, did we?' she said.

He turned away so that she could not see his face but his whole attitude was one of dejection. 'How self-absorbed I must be, Sophie. I thought I made you happy. Just being in the same room with you made me delirious with pleasure, knowing that you were somewhere in a concert hall changed the very atmosphere for me. And all the time I was deluding myself.' He turned and smiled and he was, once more, the world-famous pianist. 'You are at the villa; let me drive you.'

This is my last chance, the last chance to win what is right for me, for Rafael. Say you still love me, Rafael say it again, just those simple words. I am in his heart. Does that mean he loves me as a husband should love his wife? 'You could take me to lunch; we have to eat.'

For a moment he stood undecided. Had she dealt him too severe a body blow? In these early days when they had been so deliriously, magically in love had she thought of him as de Nardis the pianist or as Rafael, the man, her man? Or were the man, the husband, the lover and the pianist all fused together into one beautiful one? She sighed. How long ago it all seemed and who was that girl, that man?

The sigh seemed to jerk him out of his inertia. 'I'll drive you home.'

She had lost. She should have clung to him, accepted whatever it was that he was offering. '*D'accordo*. Fine. I'm staying with Giovanni.'

He followed her out of the gallery, along another corridor to a part of the *castello* that boasted an ancient elevator. Facing the doors was the stunning Caravaggio, the vision of flame and light that was the angel, Raffaele. As a bride Sophie had spent hours absorbing the masterpiece; Raffaele, the angel, was nothing like Raffaele, the pianist, but at the same time there was a dynamism, a fire, a breathtaking sensuality that was shared by both Raffaeles, for this was no amorphous, androgynous creature but a man. Sophie shook her head lightly as she passed the angel and walked into the elevator. Inside she and Rafael were less than a yard apart and yet Sophie felt that they had never been further away from each other. If there was a way to avoid driving with him now she would do it but better, better by far, to say no more, to get into his car and get out as quickly as possible.

The low, dark blue machine was quite restrained in comparison with the cars he had owned when they were together but she made no remark and sat quietly on his right while he drove expertly down the winding road from the castle towards the town. She did not register when, instead of taking the turn-off that would direct them towards Licciana Nardi and then on to Comano he headed for Aulla and it was only when they neared the town that she took notice.

'Rafael?'

Even driving a sports car, he managed to shrug. 'I have to eat; I prefer to eat with you than alone in the *castello*. Remember how you loved the coast? We could drive for a while, if you are in no particular hurry. Maybe we stop in La Spezia or Lerici or Fiascherino?'

'I haven't been to Fiascherino since . . . in years.' Sophie lay back and tried to give herself up to enjoying the drive and the incredible scenery. In some places the road seemed to be carved out of the very edge of the cliff; above were overhanging cliffs where, in the spring and early summer, wild flowers rioted, desperately trying to encroach on the crumbling bare rock; below lapped the turquoise-blue waters of the Gulf of Spezia. She sighed again, relaxing into the soft leather of the seat.

'That's a happy sigh, *cara*. What are you thinking about?'

'Italy; its incredible beauty.'

'I keep pictures in my head when I am away. The view when you come down the hill of Lerici and there below is the gulf and the colour is like no other colour anywhere.'

'Do you still stop dead up there to look?'

He laughed. 'I was a very arrogant driver; these days I look behind me before I stop. The bougainvillaea still spills all over the walls of the villas up there; the purple against the stark white is . . . painful almost. Do you understand?'

She was quiet, remembering the first recital she had attended after their marriage. He played the Chopin Nocturne in E Flat as an encore. Next day in the reviews Sophie read about her husband's *unique fluidity and technical mastery, his perfect technique*. Are those words synonyms for the pain experienced when something is so beautiful that the human spirit feels it is unable to bear it? she had asked herself. It was a question she was to ask often in the years of their marriage. 'I understand,' she said.

He pulled on to the side of the road and stopped. 'Can we walk a little?'

She got out and looked around. On one side was the sea and on the other the soaring cliffs. 'It's lovely,' she said. 'Sometimes winter is the best time for the beach.'

'Fiascherino is just a few miles. Give me those silly shoes. Try not to get your tights wet.'

'I didn't dress to go for a walk on the beach.'

He smiled and held her steady while she slipped off the high-heeled shoes. 'Italian?'

'*Davvero.*'

It was unusually mild. They began to walk just outside the waterline and for some time neither spoke. They were completely alone on the beach. Not a red-striped chair nor a multicoloured parasol anywhere. The sand was quite flat and damp, either from the departing tide or the recent rainfall, and the sun was determined not to shine, but it was not cold although she was glad of her lightweight woollen coat. The sea was calm and whispered as it lapped at the edge of the sand. Sophie looked down as she walked and saw that only seabirds had passed this way recently, perhaps looking for the edible creatures that dug little tunnels in the sand. A bird screeched nearby and, startled, she looked up at the face of the huge cliff where several seabirds nested. Their nests and a solitary beach house clung impossibly to the inhospitable rock face. Ahead of them they saw a child throwing sticks for his dog and the excited cries of the boy and the barks of the dog disturbed the companionable silence.

'Why have you never married again, Sophie?'

'I could ask you the same.'

'I was too busy. No, don't pull your hand away, that's not true. I never wanted to remarry.'

'But you are engaged to Ileana.'

He stopped in the sand and turned to look at her. 'To Ileana? Where did you get an idea like that?'

How stupid, 'The twins told me,' would sound, 'Stella,' she mumbled. 'She said something about an engagement.'

'To accompany her in a recital in Prague, to make a recording.' He laughed and then was serious again. 'I never wanted to divorce. No matter what my mother or Ann or Judith said – when I was sane I didn't believe it.'

At the mention of Judith she had tensed but she relaxed again. It no longer mattered what Judith had said, Judith who had been so thrilled that she was to marry Rafael, Judith who had hoped that Rafael and his family, his connections, would be 'useful'. Judith had confessed and would be forgiven.

He was still talking. 'Little Zoë, she said you were meeting another man, when I was away that time in Paris and you wouldn't come with me. I prefer not to speak about Ann, but she told me about the pills and I was angry because you know how much I hate the misuse of drugs. But it worried me because . . . let us just say I am never at ease with Ann and I thought, maybe she seeks to make trouble, and so I asked Judith, the sister of your father.'

Ann? 'Ann had thrown herself at him.' Poor Ann. And he does not want to tell. Oh, Rafael, how often I misjudge you.

There was one last thing that he had to be told: the final issue. 'Carlo,' she said harshly. 'The only man I ever saw on my own was Carlo. We were snapping at each other all the time and I could see a divorce – it was like a crack in that cliff opening wider and wider and I didn't know how to stop falling in and then . . .' Suddenly she was furiously angry. Why protect him? In his gilded cage he felt nothing anyway. 'I found that I was pregnant, Rafael, but everything was going wrong. I had had a problem conceiving, remember? I didn't want to tell you. And then, at last . . . and even at a few weeks, I was bleeding, and so much sickness. I was terrified that I would lose the baby and terrified that you might worry, that you might be distressed. I would have done anything to save you pain, Rafael. Carlo wanted me to tell you but I thought, he mustn't stay with me if he doesn't love me, and in the end it didn't matter because . . . because I lost the baby. The pills weren't tranquillisers then, and I hated you for even thinking that they were.'

He stood as if stunned. How much had he taken in? 'Carlo?' The word sounded as if it had been choked out of him.

'The only person in the world it seemed I could trust.'

'Oh, *carissima*, you could have trusted me.'

She was calmer than he and she looked straight into his eyes for the first time. 'I didn't believe that. Everything I did that summer was wrong; things took on gigantic significance. Remember when we entertained Sir Matthew?'

He ignored Sir Matthew. His face was drawn and strained and his blue eyes were suspiciously bright. He came forward as if to touch her and then stepped back and looked at the silly shoes held in his strong hands. 'Sophie, what are you saying? I never thought . . . it never occurred . . . A baby? We were having a baby, we two, that summer, that ghastly summer?'

'Yes. Carlo had dinner with us in Milan, remember, and you were angry with me about something. I don't remember, something, nothing, and I felt faint. You said, "*It's nothing, Carlo. Silly girl doesn't want to go to the castello.*" Have you any idea how much I loathed being referred to as "a silly girl"? Your mother did it all the time in that sweet, condescending way that you absolutely refused to see. You were called to the telephone, someone who had been trying to catch you for months. We went outside, Carlo and I, and he was so sweet and gentle and I cried and told him everything and he said, "You should see your own doctor but I will do the examination if you really can't wait. *Cara mia*, it sounds to me as if your miracle has happened."'

'Why didn't you tell me? Sophie, I had a right to know. Why?'

She turned away and walked quickly along the sand and he walked with her and then took her hand again and stopped her. 'No running away, Sophie. Everything out.'

'I didn't want to tell you until I knew for sure. I made an appointment to see a colleague of Carlo's in Milan; that's who I saw when you were in Paris, an obstetrician. I told no one because I wanted you to know first. Only Carlo has ever known.'

He closed his eyes to ward off the pain her confession had delivered. 'Was it my fault, that you lost the baby?'

She sighed. 'No, it wasn't your fault; it was just one of those things. "It happens, you'll have a healthy baby next year." That's what the consultant said but *next year* I didn't have a husband.'

'And you told no one; all that suffering and you told no one?'

'Carlo knew and I thought it best to go away and lick my wounds by myself and then the divorce papers came . . .'

'Because I thought you wanted it.'

'Like I wanted Sir Matthew for lunch.' But she smiled at him as she spoke.

He smiled back and put his free hand tentatively on her cheek and she did not flinch or move away.

'It wasn't funny, Rafael. It is now, maybe, but when it's the first luncheon your mother-in-law suggests that you co-ordinate and the world-famous conductor who is your guest of honour is Jewish and vegetarian and you serve nothing he can eat . . .'

'He loved the fruit salad.'

'That's not at all amusing, Rafael. I was devastated, and you knew about all his fads and fancies and didn't tell me.'

'I assumed,' he said and threw up his hands. '*Per favore*, Sophie, *scusi tanto*, I never thought. Food just appears; I never think about it.'

She had never seen him like this, almost babbling, so insecure, almost frightened. She wanted to hold him, to tell him it was all right, but if she did it would be the wrong time; there was still so much to say. 'Do you know what my father said when we had our first ever meal in a restaurant in Italy? He said, some people eat to live, some live to eat, and then there are Italians. But you fit in to none of those categories. Only music is a passion with you.'

'And you, Sophie.' He gripped her arms and looked at her, forcing her to look at him. 'From that first moment in Lerici when an innocent little sprite who didn't care that I was de Nardis snapped my head off for offering her an ice cream. You were so good for me, Sophie, so right. I knew it almost from that moment. Ah, *mia diletta*, your beautiful face when you saw the dust on my slacks. I wanted to hold you in my arms right there and tell you nothing would scare you again, that nothing you could ever do would make me change my mind.'

She pulled away from him. 'I wish I could have believed that.'

'Is it too late?'

She looked at her watch. 'It is for lunch.'

'We're in Italy, remember, where food is a passion. They'll feed us in Fiascherino.'

She was exhausted. It is harder to deal with emotions than with anything else. She needed to curl up in a little ball somewhere. 'Maybe you should just take me home.'

'Please.'

'Too much, Rafael.' She shook her head and turned away from him again in an effort to keep control. 'I wanted to see you to explain about the will and then I wanted to just go away from Italy and everything that reminds me of you.' She started to cry but tried to hold back the tears. 'Then you picked up the baby dress and you laughed and I remembered that our baby never lived and I just can't bear any more.

'Oh, please don't,' she whispered as she felt his arms on her shoulders. 'Please, it's too much.'

'Come, I'll take you home. Let me help you with these silly little shoes.' He bent down and lifted each foot in turn. 'You should take off your tights; your feet are damp,' he said as he dusted off the sand with his handkerchief and eased her feet into her shoes.

Wordlessly she walked back up to the road.

'Careful, *cara*,' he called as a sputtering old van backfired as it raced past them.

'Italian drivers,' she said and stood quietly to let him open the car door for her.

They said nothing as he drove. 'Minerva,' he said at last, 'I think I'll make her an offering today.'

'There is a well at the little house where I stayed for the wedding.'

He looked at her and laughed. 'Must we have well water? All right; direct me.'

They were silent as they drove to the old farmhouse and just as quiet as they crossed the empty dusty courtyard to the well that stood filling the trough below it with water. Rafael put his hand in the water where the boys had bathed their little feet. '*Santo cielo*, that's cold. All right, what shall we offer the goddess?'

She shook her head.

'Give me your hand.'

She had no time to think of how his touch inflamed her, for he plunged their joined hands deep into the icy water and she gasped with shock. 'Give us wisdom to learn, Goddess,' he said and she feared that he was mocking her but his face was in deadly earnest.

26

He dried her hands on his already over-used handkerchief but he did not let go and instead pulled her into his arms. 'Come back with me now, Sophie, please.'

How she wanted to do just that but instinct told her that it was too soon. She reached up to kiss him and as their kisses grew in intensity her resolution wavered but, perhaps sensing this, Rafael pulled back.

'I love you, *mio tesoro*, and I will prove it to you for the rest of my life,' he said. 'Come, I will drive you to Giovanni's and then I will go. I have some gardening to do.'

Later that evening Giovanni drove her to the airport and for an hour, although she had no way of knowing, she was no more than a few yards from Rafael as he sat in the executive lounge waiting for clearance. He had been so businesslike when they parted, shaking hands with Giovanni, refusing the offer of a glass of wine, anything. But within an hour he had telephoned her and it was of that call that she thought as she sat waiting for her plane. Outside a bitter wind was blowing down from the Alps, driving ice-cold rain before it, but inside she could hear only his voice, murmuring of love and passion and death and life and regret, of forgiving and forgetting.

'I will tie up the loose ends, *tesoro*, and then I will come for you.'

Every inch of her body tingled as she listened. Now she too would tie up loose ends.

From Edinburgh she rang her parents. They were shocked to hear of the countess's perfidy.

'It never occurred to me, Sophie; Rafael's mother.'

'Mum, this has to go no further. Rafael insisted that I tell you because he feels guilty about Dad's heart attack. Paolo will see you both to apologise personally when you return to Tuscany.'

'Rafael's not to blame himself for my illness,' said her father, who had been listening on an extension.

'He blames himself for a lot, Dad, but we were both to blame for our marriage break-up. Forgiving has been fairly simple; it's forgetting that's hard.'

'What do you want to tell Judith . . . and Ann?'

'Nothing. Rafael says I won't have forgiven Ann properly until I tell her but I just can't speak to her yet.' She could hear Christmas carols in the background and almost laughed as the volume increased. 'Mum, nothing subtle about you, is there? I made a mistake earlier; I'm not ready to forgive Ann yet. Now, do I have your promises? This ugliness has to disappear, to be forgotten.'

'We won't tell anyone, sweetheart. I'll vouch for your mum. Sophie, what comes now?'

She wanted to shout, Rafael is coming for me, but she would tell no one, not even this dear man whom she loved so much. 'I wait, Dad.' And mend and heal, she added to herself, as Rafael has to do and it is so much harder for him.

She hung up and went to the window that looked out over the Royal Mile. All the lights were on in the office windows; she could even see people she knew and had worked with walking back and forth. Little artificial Christmas trees were on several desks. She thought she saw Hamish as a youngish man with a lick of hair sticking up at the back hurried across the road to the committee rooms. She had liked and admired Hamish but there was an overwhelming release in the knowledge that she regretted nothing, missed nothing. Perhaps someone else would encourage him to return to a good hair stylist but to her, it did not matter.

She felt totally different from the woman who had worked for Hamish and from the stammering, wounded woman who had run all those long years ago from Rafael. 'Rafael, my angel, heal me.' Now she added, 'And I will heal you.'

Rafael sent her a tape by special delivery. 'What do you hear, *mia diletta*, when you hear me play?'

It was, of course, the complete *Pictures at an Exhibition*, and she sat in the light from the streetlamps and Christmas lights and listened.

One day he sent two antique dining chairs, beautiful but solid. 'May I sit at your table when I come, *mio tesoro*?'

She laughed and cried. Could she ever really love her nest again? It had been violated but Rafael had kept her safe there.

She looked up at the top of the cupboard and instead of her soup tureen she pictured the Vezzi teapot. The contessa's influence was here. But wherever Rafael was, the countess would be. She was his mother, he had loved her, and Sophie would have to accept that. Time, all healing needs time, and peace. She made no plans, did no Christmas shopping, wrote no cards. She waited. He would come and she would be ready. She sat at her bedroom window looking not down on the bustling Royal Mile with its noisy hordes of Christmas shoppers but out over the soaring roofs of Edinburgh towards the sea.

27

She heard the doorbell as it pulled her unwillingly from sleep. Then the telephone rang. She stumbled to the hall phone and groped for a light switch, still so asleep that she could not remember where they were. In the light she looked at her watch. Five o'clock in the morning.

'Yes?'

'Sophie.'

Fatigue vanished and adrenalin raced through her body.

'Rafael.'

'I have come.'

'I'm not dressed.'

'I'll wait. Dress warmly; it's snowing.'

She showered quickly and dressed. Snow? Boots? Boots?

She retrieved a long brown coat from the depths of the tall cupboard in her living room, and a pair of rubber-soled brown boots. Elegance was needed here and falling flat on her back in the snow would hardly be conducive to achieving the desired effect.

It was pitch dark outside but by the hazy glow of a security lamp she could see Rafael standing in the doorway of Lady Stair's House. He was in black except for a red cashmere scarf draped around the neck of the long coat; his head was bare and as Sophie carefully crossed the courtyard she saw snowflakes settle like little stars on his dark hair. Even had she obeyed her instinctive urge to catch one it would have been impossible; each fell, rested for an instant, and melted.

'Come,' he said without smiling, and tucked her brown woollen-covered arm into his cashmere one. 'We will go down.'

They walked down the steps of Writers' Close, steps illuminated only by feeble light from the streetlamps that fought not only the darkness but also the snow. She relaxed; he was holding her; she would not fall. He said nothing and Sophie gave herself up to the once familiar feeling of closeness as he matched her stride, his long legs effortlessly pacing with hers. She laughed; he was a musician after all; beat came easily. They turned left and walked down the Mound to Princes Street. Falling snow blurred the great forms of the two art galleries, their railings making them appear like something out of an old Russian novel.

'We always meant to walk here, Sophie. Why was there never time?'

She did not answer, for he knew it; there was never time. They waited for the lights at the corner and crossed Princes Street, which looked better in the snow, its sometime gaudiness softened and muted by the quietly drifting whiteness. She directed him to the right; even at a moment like this she wanted him to see her adopted city at its best and therefore they had to walk past Jenner's Department Store.

He spoke. 'This is lovely; we are in London, New York? Christmas is such a good time, Sophie. We were always happy at Christmas.'

They stood and looked in the glittering windows with their beautifully dressed mannequins and discreet decorations.

'I remember your first Christmas in New York.'

'Me too.'

'You were like a child. Do you remember Tiffany's windows, with the bears?'

She smiled. 'Mamma Bear had a beautiful new diamond ring and the baby bear played with a doll.' For a moment she let herself feel the memory of that time. 'Come on, we'll walk down to the New Town.' She shivered but not with cold.

'You're cold. How thoughtless I am to drag you out into the snow without even breakfast. There is somewhere we can have coffee?'

'Your hotel; my flat. Come on,' she added quickly. 'I always wanted you to see the New Town.'

They walked on down past Queen Street Gardens and on to Heriot Row. She wanted the walk to end and she wanted it to go on for ever. 'I love this area. See the beautiful Georgian buildings on one side and then the gardens on the other; restful, isn't it? I like trees all year round.' She stopped for a moment to look at the trees that stood gaunt and black against the grey white of the snow. Was she babbling? 'Rather sad, aren't they, but you should see the New Town in the summer when all the window boxes are full of geraniums and petunias and even roses.'

He stopped and gently kicked at the snow until he uncovered one of the cobblestones with which this part of the city is paved. 'Sometimes the absence of colour is very beautiful. Today all is soft unfocused grey, except your eyes, Sophie, and your cheeks pink with cold. You should have a white fur coat and you would look like a princess in a Nordic fairy tale.'

She remembered a floor-length mink coat. 'No one wears fur any more, Rafael; it's politically incorrect.'

He stopped and took her in his arms. 'Is it also politically in-correct for me to say that I have been a fool, Sophie, to throw away what meant more to me than anything else in the world?'

She looked up at him into the intensity of his blue eyes. 'You didn't throw it away.'

'Don't make excuses for me. Always, always people make excuses. Raffaele needs quiet; Raffaele needs this, that and the other thing. It has been so hard to accept that my mother was not as I saw her, to accept that she could be deliberately cruel, that she could lie . . . my mother.'

'She did what she thought was right.'

His face, like the park opposite, was bleak. He turned away from her. 'Now you make excuses for her.'

She touched his back with her gloved hands and then she pulled off one fur mitt and reached up to touch his neck and he leaned back against her fingers. 'She was sorry. Each one of us has to say sorry: my sister who lied to you deliberately, my aunt, Marisa, you Rafael, and I.'

He turned at that and caught her hand in his gloved ones. 'You, no, *diletta*, not you.'

'Of course me, Rafael. I didn't trust you enough, or our love enough. "For my daughter-in-law Sophie de Nardis, because she will understand." Your mother was a remarkable woman and that is how I will remember her.'

He pulled her to him and she closed her eyes and stayed there against his snow-wet coat, smelling a mixture of cashmere and shaving lotion and she smiled. Only the lotion was constant.

'You have to go to work?'

She pulled away and looked into his face. 'No.'

'You have cut off all your branches?'

'Yes. Except my flat.'

He laughed and she thought that never had she heard a lovelier sound; she would always associate it with Edinburgh in the early morning, lamplight filtering through snow, and weak winter rays struggling through cloud. 'I love your little tower. Keep it. Sometimes, maybe, I can hide there?'

She smiled, her eyes filled with love.

'I am starving, *tesoro*. Who knows what I will do if I have no food? You will return to the hotel with me?'

'For breakfast?'

'*D'accordo*,' he said – of course – but he was smiling and she tucked her hand back into his arm as they retraced their steps to Princes Street.

He never ate in hotel dining rooms but he walked unerringly to this one and if the *maître d'hôtel* was surprised to see him he recovered and showed them to a table. 'Coffee, and then we'll think.' The head waiter bowed and withdrew and almost before they had time to settle themselves a waiter was back with a silver pot. 'I'll pour,' said Rafael as he picked up the coffee pot. 'These are ridiculous,' he said. 'The handles get too hot.'

'Watch your hands.'

'Why, *diletta*? My delicate hands are very tough.' He poured the coffee. 'Let's eat everything on the menu.' He held up the menu and the waiter hurried back. 'Two breakfasts with everything.'

'Sir?' the flustered waiter muttered.

'British breakfast,' said Sophie. 'And orange juice.'

'And hot, hot toast with melting butter.'

He waited until the man was gone. 'Maybe I would like cold oysters with my bacon and eggs.'

'Not on the same plate.'

'See how I need you, Sophie.' He put down his coffee cup and reached for her free hand. 'Sophie, can you learn to trust me? I told you I would come and here I am. Will you marry me again, now, today?'

Very deliberately she returned her own almost empty cup to its lovely pale green saucer – such a pretty green like the unfurling leaves of a beech tree in the spring. She put her hand over his and felt the bones of his hand; in her head she heard Mussorgsky, Beethoven. She heard her voice and his and his mother's and dear Giovanni's. 'Why?' she asked simply.

He looked at her for a moment and then put his free hand on top of her small pale hand. 'I am so used to asking music to speak for me. When you hear me play Mussorgsky, Sophie, what do you hear? Certain notes in a certain order at a certain speed? Or do you hear my voice?'

'I would like to hear your voice.'

'*Mio tesoro, te amo.* I love you. I have loved you for a long, long time. I have never stopped loving you. As I signed the divorce papers, knowledge of my love for you rose in my throat and almost choked me, Sophie, and I thought, *santo cielo*, what a fool I am.'

She sighed. '*Te amo, Raffaele.* How I tried to stop . . .'

A waiter, trying to look as if he could not possibly have heard any of their intimate conversation, was standing at her side. 'Breakfast with everything,' he said, putting an overly laden plate in front of her.

'*Santo cielo*,' said Rafael again, but this time he was looking at his own plate which seemed to have even more of everything on it.

'I seem to lose my appetite when I see such a full plate.'

'I lose mine when Sophie says she loves me.' He released her hand. 'See, take your fork, for I must touch you, hold you. Say it again, Sophie. Say, I love you, Rafael.'

'I love you, Rafael.'

'I wish I had a big bag, or better still, a big dog to eat all this food. I do not want to eat, *cara*; I want to look at you, to love you.' He looked around the beautiful dining room, at the few other early birds who in turn looked at him strangely.

'They think I'm a crazy man.'

'They see Raffaele de Nardis holding hands with his ex-wife and trying to eat an obscenely large breakfast with one hand. They will go home to Salzburg, Austria and Dayton, Ohio and Melbourne, Australia and they will tell all their friends that you eat like a horse and yet you stay so thin.'

'And will they rush out for piano lessons? The new diet.' He was quiet, the laughter dying out of his eyes and his voice. 'Sophie, I want to take you upstairs.'

Her captured hand trembled in his and he raised it to his lips and kissed her fingers, one after the other.

She would go. Nothing would stop her. 'You have chopped off all the unwanted branches, Rafael?'

'*Sì, d'avverro*. I saw Ileana in New York.'

A waiter was hovering, looking distressed; there was everything that anyone of any nationality could possibly want and these two were leaving their food to congeal on the plates. 'Is anything wrong, sir, madam?'

Sophie looked at Rafael and smiled, a smile that said, 'We have the rest of our lives.'

'No, it's wonderful.' He picked up his fork. 'You too, Sophie.'

'Ileana?'

'She hopes you will take me back; she says she has always known that part of me was always with someone else.' He poured more coffee. 'This is not so good as the coffee I made in your so charming apartment.'

'We can go there after breakfast,' she said demurely and began to eat.

'I had promised Paolo that I would go to Rome for Christmas Day. He will be devastated unless I have a very good reason for breaking my solemn promise.'

'A good reason?' asked Sophie, reaching for his hand.

'Marriage is good,' said Rafael and read the answer in the pressure of Sophie's hand and the smile in her eyes.

'Can I get you something else, sir?' Their worried waiter was back.

Rafael smiled, and he was looking at Sophie. 'No, thank you. I have everything I could ever want right here.'